Warp and Weft

by

Merryn Fergusson

The Conrad Press

Warp and Weft by Merryn Fergusson

Published by The Conrad Press in the United Kingdom 2023

Tel: +44(0)1227 472 874
www.theconradpress.com
info@theconradpress.com

ISBN 978-1-915494-97-9

Copyright ©Merryn Fergusson 2023

All rights reserved.

Typesetting and Cover Design by: Levellers

The Conrad Press logo was designed by Maria Priestley.

Printed and bound in Great Britain by Clays Ltd, Elcograf S.p.A.

This book is dedicated to

Sam
Lucy
Leah
Zoe
Maia
Mara
Fyn

With my love

Warp and Weft

Warp: those threads of a fabric running lengthwise throughout the piece.

Weft: those threads carried by the weaver transversely across the warp

Book One

Antique White

1899-1907

Chapter One

The Hefford family took possession of the house in Granby Street in the centre of Leicester in the English Midlands on Michaelmas Quarter Day, Friday September 29, 1899.

It was a considerable comfort to Reginald Hefford, a mill owner, that the decisions he had made over the years, combined with a favourable economic climate, enabled him to prosper despite the encumbrance of a household of women. His wife, Eleanor, had been nothing if not dutiful and had produced seven daughters, their only son dying after just a few days. They would be moving in the best circles of society and the prospect of good marriages for his daughters cheered him.

Reginald was a fit, sturdy man of a little under fifty years old, who had worked his way from the weaving rooms of the family business until he had taken over the management from his father. He was aware that his wife would adapt less well to their new position in the town, but he felt sure that she would understand his objectives. Eleanor was unsophisticated but had supported him throughout their early years of hard graft and now that their youngest child was no longer in the nursery, Reginald hoped that she would enjoy the little luxuries of life and the new acquaintances that they would make.

Over the first weeks the household settled into a routine. Reginald could give more time to domestic matters now that he was able to leave later for his office. Eleanor was adapting to her new role of managing a larger household, and the servants were familiar with their duties. When Reginald suggested that they host a dinner party, Eleanor was less flustered than she would have been ordinarily. The house lent itself to entertaining and it would be an opportunity to use the new china dinner service and crystal glassware that her husband had persuaded her to purchase.

Eleanor was a few years younger than Reginald, but had not weathered as well. She met every situation with a degree of trepidation, particularly regarding the upbringing of her daughters, and this drain on her constitution had deprived her of much of her looks. She was thin in an age when a matronly figure denoted a more leisurely lifestyle. Reginald, however, was pleased that since their eldest daughter Flo willingly shared the supervision of her sisters, Eleanor was gaining some confidence.

His wife was, like him, eager for their older daughters to marry but assumed that, for the foreseeable future, there would always be one daughter to take on the role that Flo now provided.

Eleanor was seated in the morning room and the house was quiet while the older girls went about their tasks and the younger ones were at school. Reginald entered the room and stood behind his wife. It had always been the case, when he and Eleanor were alone, that there was an ease of communication between them.

'Who do you suggest we invite to our dinner party?' Eleanor asked.

'We'll restrict ourselves to a small party,' Reginald answered, 'no more than eight. How about the Brindsley-Smiths and their son?'

Reginald was referring to his new co-director, although it was Reginald who was new. Brindsley-Smith senior had been owner of a large mill for many years and was already a partner with Peter Whitehorn, the director and owner of a prestigious Fashion House. Joining industry with fashion was a new concept, and adding Reginald's successful mill to the existing partnership strengthened their position within the competing companies.

Eleanor hesitated, 'Would they want to be invited?' The Brindsley-Smiths were almost landed gentry and had educated their son accordingly.

'I see no reason why not, besides Mrs Brindsley-Smith could introduce you to some of the ladies in town.'

This was not such an incentive for Eleanor that she was persuaded, however she smiled indulgently. 'I suspect that a son of a suitable age has influenced your choice.' Eleanor stated. She then said with slight defiance. 'We'll invite Flo's lad, Thomas.'

Reginald paused for only a second, 'Yes, my dear, Flo will want us to invite him. We should also include the Vicar and his wife, it's what you do, I'm sure. We have, after all, attended his church.'

Eleanor wrote their names, copying them from the parish magazine that had been pressed into their hands the previous Sunday by an enthusiastic sidesman. Reginald continued, 'And the Devenicks. Their son will be company for young Brindsley-Smith.'

Mr Devenick was the lawyer who had brokered the purchase of their new house. Their son Mitchell Devenick had been entrusted with many of the details, had showed Reginald and Eleanor around the house and drawn up the bill of sale. Mitchell Devenick seemed a presentable young man, and could be a suitable prospective husband for one of the girls.

While Reginald knocked his pipe against the fireplace and filled it with tobacco, Eleanor sketched out a seating plan. 'We'll need Bett if we are to seat everyone correctly,' she said as she leaned back and handed him the table layout. 'What do you think?'

Reginald studied the plan. He accepted that Thomas should sit next to Flo, despite his aspirations for her. He was pleased that Bett, who although eighteen appeared younger because her frequent spells of ill-health often precluded her from family gatherings, would also be seated beside Thomas. Eleanor had placed the two young men, Mitchell and Brindsley-Smith, on either side of Lil, his second daughter. Lil was more than capable, and he would enjoy watching her engaging with two such different personalities.

'Excellent. That will make a very happy party. Now for a date.' Eleanor opened her diary and between them they decided that a fortnight was reasonable notice for their guests, and would give them ample time to prepare.

On the evening of the party, although the three girls had not intended it, their delayed arrival to the drawing room created a favourable impact. There was an almost audible intake of breath and there was no mistaking the effect that they created. Flo, composed and conventionally pretty, Lil, statuesque beside her and Bett holding back so that, like a dark gem, she was the last of the three to be noticed.

Reginald stepped forward, well satisfied. 'My daughters, Florence, Lillian and Elizabeth.' As they were the only young women present, there was no risk of the girls being over-shadowed or under-dressed. Their mother looked well in a mauve satin skirt with an elaborately ruched silk blouse to match and was unlikely to be worried if she was outsmarted by Mrs Brindsley-Smith, Mrs Devenick or the Vicar's wife, provided that her daughters made a good impression.

Reginald approved of the young men, designating them silently as 'Lil's suitors'. Brindsley-Smith was handsome, there was no denying it. He was tall, well-proportioned, with his dark hair brushed in a controlled quiff. However there was a lack of definition in his features that was mildly disconcerting. His expensive education led him to favour an extravagant use of words, and he had a tendency to deliver his pronouncements with a slight elongation of selected vowels. Mitchell Devenick, on the other hand, had unruly sandy coloured hair, a ready smile, and was already conversing animatedly using expressive gestures, much as Reginald had noticed when he had first shown them around the house. Mitchell's enthusiasm for his work had already warmed him to Reginald, the more so because his father was fast becoming a much-needed friend in an environment where he was hoping to make his mark.

The room fell silent, and to relieve the girls of the awkwardness of being offered a drink, Reginald lifted his sherry glass, finished the contents and placed it on a tray. He then suggested to his wife that she lead their guests into the dining room.

'Handsome daughters you have, Mr Hefford,' said Mrs Brindsley-Smith. She was gratified that he had taken her arm and placed her on his right at the table. She felt, as the wife of the owner of one of Leicester's largest mills, that he recognised her position. Since this had been acknowledged she could be expansive and generous, and could not expect the timid Vicar's wife to open a conversation.

'You have not been long in Leicester. I understand that for many years you were in some northern town.'

'We were in Shepshed,'

'You'll have a lot to learn, we do things differently here. I should know since I've lived here all my life. You can ask me for my opinion whenever you need advice.'

Reginald, reassured that his wife had risen to the occasion and was managing to entertain the guests at her end of the table, turned his attention to his august neighbour.

'We were so pleased that you were able to accept our invitation.'

'Delighted to be able to do so, and to meet your pretty daughters. They are a credit to you,' Mrs Brindsley-Smith observed.

'They are indeed,' Reginald said, warming to his companion.

'I have no daughters, you know, and my daughter-in-law died a few months ago.'

'I had no idea, Mrs Brindsley-Smith. What a sadness. So no female companionship?'

'Well, not quite. There is the little girl, my son's daughter, who stays with us meantime.'

'How delightful for you,' gushed the vicar's wife, who was anxious to join in the conversation, 'and how old is she?'

'Just three years. Yes, we do find her entrancing. We have found a very good nursemaid for her.'

For some reason this appeared to deflate the Vicar's wife and render her speechless. Sensitive to her predicament, Reginald enquired about her own family only to discover that she was childless. He turned to the guest on her left. 'And you, Mr Devenick?'

'I have three daughters. Mitchell is surrounded by sisters, but we are lucky to have Michael at the end who is twelve and has recently gone away to school.'

At the other end of the table the Vicar and Mr Brindsley-Smith were sparring. The highly intelligent parson was ready to score points over, as he saw it, a mill owner who produced hosiery for women.

Eleanor, oblivious, fussed over the hors d'oeuvre and worried whether her guests were enjoying themselves while watching for the moment when the plates should be cleared. She had ordered a beef dish to please the men and for Reginald's sake it was important that she made a good impression. She was concerned that the vegetables might be overcooked or the gravy cold, but her cook did not let her down and everything was as she would have wished. She had kept the menu simple so as to minimise mistakes. Perhaps at a later date she might be more adventurous. She took a moment to see if the younger guests were enjoying the evening.

Thomas appeared to be at ease and was not in any way overawed by the company. Eleanor reminded herself that Thomas had as little experience as Flo in town ways, but she should not have been surprised that, in his habitually assured manner, he took this occasion in his stride. Flo was endeavouring to do the same, and Eleanor had to admit that her daughter was rising well to the challenge and appeared to be having a lively discussion with Mr Devenick.

Lil was fielding attention from his son, Mitchell, and young Brindsley-Smith, who were seated on either side of her, and realising that they had nothing in common with each other felt obliged to take a lead.

'Do either of you play sports?'

Having started them on a topic on which both had

strong views, Lil had to mediate between Brindsley-Smith, who considered that fox hunting, shooting and fishing were the only sports commensurate with a gentleman's life-style, and Mitchell, who played Rugby football in the winter and cricket in the summer and who had a poor opinion of blood sports.

'What about winter sports?' Lil asked. At last the two men agreed and a lively discussion on the relative merits of ice hockey ensued. Lil had nothing to contribute, the terms that they were using being beyond her knowledge, but she silently congratulated herself. The dessert course arrived and Mitchell turned the conversation.

'And how are you enjoying your new home?' He asked Lil.

'You found it for us, I believe. It's a very nice house. My father is delighted with it.'

'And you?'

'Of course.'

Mitchell noticed her ambivalence. 'It was my father who suggested this property, it's him you should thank.' Lil looked across the table but Mr Devenick was speaking to Flo.

Before replying Lil had time to notice that Brindsley-Smith, who out of politeness should have been engaging Mrs Devenick in conversation, was observing Bett with a curiously speculative look.

Meanwhile Mr Brindsley-Smith was saying to her mother, 'A knowledge of French is essential these days, even for girls, wouldn't you say? The commerce between our countries is mutually advantageous.'

'All my daughters speak French fluently,' Eleanor

exaggerated and, in an attempt to include young Brindsley-Smith she continued, 'you'll have learnt French and German would you not, at your private school? It must be invaluable in your line.'

Brindsley-Smith, excluded from the conversation between Lil and Mitchell, paused before he drawled. 'French? Yes. My French is a bit rusty I must confess. Much the same with German.'

He attempted to wrench Lil's attention from her animated discussion with Mitchell, but was thwarted by Reginald, who suggested that the ladies might like to retire to the drawing room.

The men stood and drew back the chairs for the departing ladies, and then regaining their seats, relaxed.

The soft touches that a room acquires over the years were absent from the drawing room. The usual mixture of styles which accumulate over a period of time were not evident as it had been furnished directly from a department store. The ladies separated as they entered. Mrs Brindsley-Smith made her way across to the large armchair by the fire. Eleanor kept Bett beside her while ensuring that her guests were seated.

Mrs Devenick placed herself beside Lil. She liked young people and was intrigued by a girl who had kept her son so absorbed. 'Lillian, isn't it?'

'I'm usually called Lil.'

Mrs Devenick concealed her amusement at Reginald's affectation in introducing them formally. She liked the girl's directness and the trace of Leicestershire accent that elocution lessons had failed to eradicate. 'Do you like it here in Leicester? Does it compare well with where you used to live?'

'Do you know Shepshed?'

'Not well,' Mrs.Devenick answered, 'we have always lived in the centre of town because of my husband's work. You'll enjoy being close to the theatre and concert hall. We have some passable productions, and some that go on to London. We are very fortunate. It must have been quiet in Shepshed. You'll meet many young people now and find that you never have a minute to spare.'

Lil was relieved that she had not had to explain Shepshed because it was impossible to communicate in words the comforting homeliness of their former life. Even with a sympathetic ear, and Mrs Devenick was demonstrably attempting to set Lil at her ease, she would struggle to describe her home.

They had lived on the edge of Charnwood Forest and had unrestricted access to the countryside. They had few visitors and most people were employed making hosiery or gloves or worked in her father's textile mill. She had been happy before they moved, spending days in winter with the younger girls skating on the ponds, and in summer swimming or rowing on the river and going on picnic expeditions. She hoped that the attractions of the town would replace the loss, but Leicester, with its budding wealth and newly constructed municipal buildings, made Lil feel ill educated.

'Flo will go back to live there one day, we expect,' she said, and Mrs Devenick, hearing a wistfulness in her voice, determined that somehow she would rectify Lil's initial impression.

Flo was standing by the window with the vicar's wife

and since Mrs Brindsley-Smith was sitting alone, Eleanor had no option but to cross the room, accompanied by Bett, to join her.

'Sit beside me,' Mrs Brindsley-Smith said, 'now, you are Elizabeth?'

'Yes, I'm Bett.'

'And you are the youngest?'

'Oh no,' answered Bett controlling a giggle, 'I have four sisters younger than me.'

'Four?' Mrs Brindsley-Smith looked at Eleanor and for a moment lost her composure. She turned to Bett and said almost pityingly, 'that must be an awful lot of work for your mother.'

'We all help,' Bett assured, 'I help Maisie, the youngest, in particular, because she's deaf.'

'How extremely distressing. It is such a terrible handicap. Do you enjoy helping with the younger ones?'

'I amuse them by drawing and creating stories.'

'So you are fond of small children?'

Eleanor intervened, 'Bett is wonderful with her sisters. Do you have any family other than your son?'

'No, Mrs Hefford, I only have one son but I do have his small daughter living with me, as I was telling your husband. My daughter-in-law died leaving three year old Sheilagh.'

Neither woman registered the effect on Bett because the door opened and the gentlemen arrived from the dining room. Reginald was saying, 'What else could a man do? With so many women to dress, the natural solution was to amalgamate with a house of fashion.' This was greeted by laughter and then, recollecting himself, he said, 'Eleanor, my dear, have we been an age?'

As the men drifted into the drawing room, Mrs Brindsley-Smith caught her son's eye. 'I've been telling Elizabeth about little Sheilagh.'

Bett looked up as he approached and smiled timidly.

'Elizabeth has younger sisters that she entertains. Perhaps we should make up a party when the theatre next puts on a show for children.'

'Take Sheilagh?' he queried.

'Why not? She rarely sees her Papa. Nanny would look after her.'

His immediate antagonism dissipated, he bent towards Bett, 'Would you enjoy that?'

Bett, who seemed to sense a change in him, appeared confused and addressed his mother.

'My sisters would be extremely happy. We have not had any visits to the theatre.'

Meanwhile Mitchell Devenick had joined Lil and his mother. They were discussing a recent novel by Mrs Humphrey Ward.

'I don't think Marcella would interest you,' Lil observed to Mitchell.

'On the contrary, I read everything. There have been some excellent lectures on English literature recently in the Assembly rooms. I would be happy to accompany you and it might give you the chance to make some new acquaintances.'

Lil thanked him. If she did not make an effort her life would be singularly uneventful and tedious. She noticed a smile of encouragement from Mrs Devenick but could not determine whether this was directed towards her, or whether it was merely approval of her son's good manners.

Flo was beginning to find the uninspiring vicar's wife a conversational challenge and was relieved that a glance towards her father was rewarded with a sweep of his arm in her direction.

'And how am I going to entertain my daughters in their new surroundings? Who can give me advice? I am certain that you, as the wife of our Vicar, will be a fount of all knowledge for the edification of young ladies.'

Reginald did not give her reply his full attention as he was momentarily distracted by the satisfaction of seeing his drawing room filled with pleasant company. He was heartened that his daughters had exceeded all his expectations on this, his first social venture. While exchanging the occasional smile with his wife, he had enjoyed his discussions with the men. Hearing the low hum of conversation in the drawing room he was contented.

Once their guests had departed Reginald placed an arm around Eleanor's waist. 'I must congratulate you, Eleanor. Your efforts have been most appreciated.'

Given the difficulty inherent in meeting new people, the evening had been, if not an uproarious affair, congenial. Reginald hoped that they had acquitted themselves well and trusted that they would be accepted by their neighbours, and reap the reward for their evening's hospitality, in the future.

Chapter Two

'There's the carriage,' Flo linked an arm through her father's while they waited for Horace to open the door.

'I'm sorry I am unable to take you with me today, Flo. Difficult business. I'll explain sometime. Is my scarf in place? Grand. Pass me my umbrella, there's a girl.'

Flo stood on the steps and watched until her father's carriage disappeared at the end of the street, and mildly mystified, walked back into the house. It was a crisp October morning, but one that would warm as the day progressed. The tree-lined street gave some indication of the passing of summer, the leaves were orange and brown and a few had fallen, but apart from the flowers in the window boxes there were no other signs of autumn. She was learning to adjust to urban signals, florists stalls selling chrysanthemums, berries on the shrubs in their garden and the deepening red of the Virginia creeper against the walls of the house. She needed a change from the heavy stone buildings and small expanses of sky that was all that her present environment could provide.

Flo missed the reliable order of the seasons that was so evident in the country. In Shepshed in the well-tended front gardens or in crevices of cracked walls, flowers would change as spring turned to summer, and beyond the rows of terraced houses the newly ploughed earth would become striped with green shoots. As summer moved to autumn the paths in the woods which were parched and firm under their feet became soft with layers of fallen leaves or uneven with shells of beech nuts. Sharp thorns amongst the brambles would catch at their clothes as they gathered blackberries, and hedgerows that were thickly covered with multicoloured berries of bryony, or hazy with the grey mist of old man's beard, would in winter become denuded sticks of wood. She felt their loss and thought that she would not easily reconcile herself to the town, and turned away from the street to enter the house.

In the carriage Reginald sat back in his leather seat with the feeling of contentment that he experienced whenever he headed for the mill. His life revolved around it. Not only was it there that he had proved himself as a young man, but it was an environment where he was among men and women that he understood, whether the lowliest unskilled worker, or a trusted foreman. Delighted as he was with the partnership and the outward endorsement of his success, it was unknown territory and he had yet to find his place. At the mill he knew his workforce and respected them and he hoped that this was mutual.

His carriage took him away from the elegant streets in the centre of the town to the outskirts, where the houses became smaller and the streets narrower but where the activity increased. People crowded the pavements, men carried placards, children ran errands, stalls and shops displayed their produce. The bustle slowed the progress of his carriage and allowed him to absorb it all. It gave him time to mull over the interview that he had ahead of him and he wondered if Flo had guessed the reason that he had left her at home.

The gradient of the road increased and as it neared the mill, which was situated beside the river, it tipped the carriage forward. The driver exerted more control over the horses to negotiate the final bend which opened out into a spacious courtyard surrounded by workshops and warehouses. Reginald's joints were stiff and he stretched out each leg and shifted in his seat before opening the door and stepping down from the carriage.

'Good morning,' he greeted his staff cheerily, aware that his arrival without Flo would elicit some speculation, but not prepared to enlighten them. 'Now where would I find Mr Fletcher?'

'At this time of day he conducts his mid-morning round, probably in the second weaving room, sir.'

The mill sprawled over a considerable area. The tall five-story buildings, which now extended into accommodation, a school, recreation area and a shop, created a community devoted to and providing for hundreds of workers. Reginald had overseen many improvements to conditions at the mill and had encouraged education for adults as well as for children.

He entered the second weaving room instinctively holding his breath, but then he inhaled deeply and with satisfaction as he appreciated the quality of the air. He had been one of the first to comply with the reforms by installing fans into his workrooms, and soon was rewarded with increased production rates due to the better health of his mainly female workers. Inside the room there was a rumble, a rhythm, a clattering, but overall an orderliness that he admired. This undercurrent of sound was what his mill was founded on.

The rows of headscarved women, who barely registered his entry as they concentrated on their looms, were the untiring workforce on which the mill depended. Reginald never thought to question if they enjoyed their work, that would have been beyond his comprehension, work was what you did to survive. It was hard and unrelenting but he had never asked his men to do a job that he had not previously done himself, and he saw no reason to think otherwise for the women. They wanted clothes and food for their children, and they were gaining an education for them too. He could not imagine that they were anything but content with their lot. The notion of working for enjoyment was for those who had the leisure and therefore the income to do so, and he did not place himself in that category. Looking around the room it was fully a minute before Reginald saw Thomas, who was in discussion with one of the women.

Thomas Fletcher was proving a good under-foreman and there had been very little trouble in his workshops. The woman's attention was drifting while he was speaking to her and he appeared momentarily to be irritated, but seeing Reginald, he hastily made his way along the length of the looms. Dressed in his overalls Thomas was a subordinate in the vast operation of the mill, and the evening in Reginald's drawing room seemed as unlikely an occasion as he could imagine.

Reginald was brisk and direct. 'Is the new system working well? The two types of yarn moving easily on the loom?'

'The results are good, despite the cotton thread being larger than the silk,' Thomas answered.

'Excellent. There's an enormous demand for this new fabric we're producing.' The fabric he was referring to was satin. This was a mix of a fine silk warp with a larger cotton weft that produced a sheen that had not been available in such quantities before and which was particularly unusual in plain fabrics.

'It has taken a while to convert all these looms, but widening the gauges has been completed in this workshop and we can work to capacity.'

Reginald indicated that they should walk together out of the workshop and Thomas held the door open as Reginald strode ahead towards the office.

'Come in. I need to talk to you. Sit down.' He paused. 'I expect many changes to come about with the new amalgamation of our businesses and increase in the types of fabric we'll be making. There will be, I hope, interest in our products by fashion houses not only in this country but across the Channel. Before my colleagues start placing their men in key positions or give them promotion, I want to ensure that you are not overlooked. I'm going to make you a foreman. We'll be building new workshops and a good foreman will be needed. If I promote you now, then your position is assured.'

Thomas beamed and made to stand and then sat down again, confused. He shook his head from side to side in small movements and then looked up as Reginald continued.

'I think, as well, this might be an opportune moment for you to offer for my daughter. You and Flo do have an understanding, don't you? I see no reason why you should wait any longer.'

Reginald went round the table to shake Thomas by the hand. 'In your own time, my boy.' And leaving him to contemplate his good fortune, Reginald left the office.

Reginald had watched Thomas and Flo's friendship since they had started attending Sunday school. Every festival at the church had seen their involvement and over the years they had acted in the Christmas play and joined the summer outings that were arranged for the parish children. They had grown closer and neither had ever looked at anyone else. Now that they were older they graduated to helping at church fêtes and would meet at local dances.

This year had seen a change. Flo had been unable to attend the Michaelmas Dance that autumn and no longer did they worship at the same church with opportunities to meet after the service. When Flo came with her father to help at the mill school, her meetings with Thomas had, of necessity, been of shorter duration.

Reginald pondered whether, although he had received his blessing, Thomas' exhilaration at the prospect of marrying Flo might evaporate when he considered whether she would want to return to their village, now that she had the chance of an alternative life in the town. Fortunately there were many other demands on his time and he could not afford to do more than leave it to Thomas and Flo to resolve. He would like Flo to better herself but Thomas was steady and he and Eleanor had started their married life in similar circumstances.

The following week Flo went with her father to the mill and, as was her habit, looked to find Tom during his break in the middle of the day. She hurried towards him.

'Tom,' she said breathlessly, 'it seems so long since I've seen you, and there is so much to tell.'

'About the new developments at the school?' he asked.

Flo had changed over the past months, her dress and shawl were new and more stylish, and her hair was arranged more fashionably.

'No,' she noted his disappointment, 'Tom, I'm sorry. What's the matter? Of course I'm excited about the school but I thought you would want to hear all my news.'

They settled uneasily into their new relationship, Flo content to prattle and Tom sitting on the edge of a desk absorbed by all that she had to relate, until the bell rang for the resumption of work.

'Flo, the Harvest Festival dance. Do you think that your family will come to it this year?'

'The young ones will be insupportable if they're not allowed to, and if Mother doesn't want to accompany them, I will, as I want to come anyway. We'll be there.'

Flo squeezed his hand, wrapped her shawl around her and headed down the corridor towards the schoolroom.

The afternoon post brought an envelope for Lil written in a lavishly cursive hand. Conscious that Bett and her mother were agog with curiosity she opened it with feigned nonchalance. 'There's a Lantern Lecture on the Durbar for the Queen in India next Tuesday night. Mr Devenick has asked if I and one of my sisters would like to accompany him and his friend.'

'Young Mr Devenick? Of course you must go, and Flo can go with you,' agreed her mother. 'How kind of him, and it will give you some amusement.'

Lil expressed indifference. 'The Durbar was years ago, why would there be a lecture on it now?'

'Have you seen the Durbar?' her mother asked. 'I would have liked to see it and I am certain it would interest you.'

Lil barely disguised the fact that domestic life irked her, and she was grateful that Mitchell understood the kind of entertainment that she would appreciate.

Eleanor was launching into plans for a light supper for the party before the lecture, when the maid came into the room to announce that they had a visitor.

'Mrs Brindsley-Smith, shall I show her in?'

Eleanor replied automatically, 'Certainly, yes,' while agitatedly pulling at imaginary wrinkles in her skirt.

'Forgive me for dropping in like this,' began Mrs Brindsley-Smith as she crossed the room to greet Eleanor. 'I was passing and it seemed foolish to send a note when I could just as easily come in person. Elizabeth, how delightful to see you, and you too, Lillian. It is Lillian isn't it?'

Lil knew better than to ask her to call her by her pet

name.

'Please sit down.' Eleanor indicated her own seat. She then sat beside Bett on the settee in an unconscious movement to protect her. 'Would you like some tea?'

'Not for me, Eleanor, and please call me Euphemia, unless you are having some tea yourselves?'

Lil came to her rescue. 'Shall I see if Martha is in the kitchen, Mother?'

'Thank you, dear.' Eleanor relaxed and turned to her guest, 'That's a biting wind outside today.'

'I keep warm enough,' Mrs Brindsley-Smith indicated her ample size, 'and I am well wrapped up.' Eleanor was spared the difficulty of responding. 'I'm really here to ask if Elizabeth and her younger sisters would like to accompany us to a children's evening. I have my small granddaughter to look after and the Albany Players, the local amateur group, are producing a J.M.Barrie play. You know the young reporter who comes to the Assizes?' Instead of turning to Bett she addressed Eleanor. 'We thought we would make up a small party. What do you think?'

While Eleanor and Euphemia were discussing the whereabouts of the theatre and the merits of J.M.Barrie, Martha arrived with a tea-tray.

'Thank you,' said Mrs Brindsley-Smith effusively, 'now, Eleanor, do you know Mrs Leadbetter? Or Mrs Weston? Well I must arrange a rendez-vous so that you can meet some new people. I'm sure that you will soon fit in. Do you do tatting? We have such a good teacher.'

Lil studiously avoided catching her sister's eye, however she noticed that Bett listened to the older ladies uncritically.

'So, Elizabeth, it is to be arranged, the performances start next week and once I have purchased the tickets I will send word.' With that she rose, looked for her coat and Eleanor walked with her to the door.

When Eleanor came back she engaged Lil with a look that temporarily silenced her and spoke directly to Bett.

'Was not that a very nice invitation?'

'Can I go and tell the others?' Bett, her face flushed, smiled happily, and hurried out of the room.

'Mother, what are you doing letting Bett go with that odious woman?' Lil asked. Eleanor held up her hand, but Lil rushed on. 'And do you really want to learn tatting with Miss Stirling?'

'Now Lil,' her mother begged, 'none of that, at least not in front of the others. Just because I would take no pleasure in a sewing circle it does not mean that I am going to deprive Bett of her first social outing, or the younger girls for that matter. I am led to believe that J.M.Barrie's plays are very well regarded.'

When Flo returned from the mill a quiet understanding had been established. She endorsed her mother's encouragement for her sisters' forthcoming theatre invitation and was enthusiastic in her wish to hear the lecture. 'And, Mother, we need to discuss the Harvest Festival.'

'I see no reason why you shouldn't attend the Harvest Festival as usual,' Eleanor acquiesced, 'providing there are no other engagements for us by then. I myself would find that journey not worth the effort, especially the cold homeward carriage ride, but I know that your father would think it his duty to attend and he would be grateful of your company, Flo. You may go too, Lil, if you want and take the others. It is a few weeks away yet,' she ended dismissively.

'Only two weeks, Mother,' Flo protested. 'I won't need a new dress, the one I wore last year will serve its purpose again.'

'I wouldn't hear of it, dear, with the new autumn dresses out already it would be a shame not to take advantage.'

"What about the lecture? Would day dresses be insufficiently formal or should we wear evening dress?'

'What about wearing your velvet jabot, with a wool skirt and your apricot silk blouse to dress it up,' Lil suggested.

'And you could wear your fur over that herring bone tweed skirt. You look pretty in pale green, and we'd better wear our ankle boots. What do you think?'

Once these decisions had been made they began to look forward to the evening.

Mitchell arrived at the house to escort them and proposed that, since the hall was only a few streets away, they could make their way on foot. 'We'll meet Henry at the entrance.'

He called to his friend over the heads of the throng of people endeavouring to press their way through the double doors of the lecture hall. Flo and Lil had an opportunity to appraise Henry as he wound his way towards them. Shorter than Mitchell and slightly portly with his waistcoat and jacket a neat fit, he had a congenial face and beamed broadly.

'If we don't hurry we will be relegated to the back,' Mitchell urged

He placed the sisters together with Henry on one side of Flo while he sat beside Lil.

'So you are the new girls in town.' Henry twisted in his seat to face them. 'How are you finding it?' Before they could answer he continued, 'That's a daft question I know but it is sort of expected. This lecture then, what is your view of the Raj?'

'That's the trouble,' Lil said candidly, 'I know almost nothing about India, and we thought this would be a good chance to learn.' Henry nodded approvingly.

Mitchell said, 'They can become misfits, the fellows that live out there and then try and return. The subcontinent changes them.'

Lil sat back. 'Why is that?'

'It's a difficult climate, a raging heat. They are reliant for native servants for everything and yet they try and create another England. It's not a life that would suit me.'

'Give me London, anytime,' added Henry.

'Why London?' asked Flo.

'Because that's where I'm going. To head office. It's a new challenge and a promotion.' He seemed to be mocking himself. 'Seriously, a change from Leicester will be good for a while.'

'Will it?' said Flo. 'Lil and I wouldn't know.'

'For me, yes, but for you, Leicester will do for the time being.'

The lamps were dimmed and voices lowered. On the

stage the organiser gave an introduction and then there was only the light from the lantern projected on to the wall.

When the lecture ended Lil had forgotten where she was. The strange world that had been depicted through the series of exotic pictures and the lecturer's hypnotic voice had transported her. She was attracted to the idea of travel, to ride on lumbering elephants, to visit temples, mosques and palaces and to capture them on paper with her paints.

'But what about the ordinary people? Why don't we see them?' she mused aloud.

'Now there you have it,' Henry answered, but was prevented from expounding his views because Mitchell indicated that it was time to move on.

'There are refreshments in the small hall, Henry, lead on!'

Later, Henry and Mitchell walked back with the girls to Granby House, and parted on the pavement.

'Great shame I'm having to go to London,' Henry admitted, 'I would have enjoyed meeting up on another occasion. Never mind. Some lucky chap will have my place next time.'

Chapter Three

If the lecture had been a success, the same could not be said of the outing to the theatre. Beatrice, aged fifteen, refused to go. She maintained that she was no longer a child and amateur dramatics bored her.

Then Mrs Brindsley-Smith introduced them to the rest of the party in an unnecessarily loud voice. 'So you are thirteen, Elsie, and you are eleven, Ruth, and that one, Maisie, is nine, is she?'

Bett had received a cold reception when she had to explain Beatrice's absence. Elsie had been mildly reproved during the performance for speaking to Maisie, who needed certain scenes explained, and felt the injustice of her disapproval and Ruth was admonished for not speaking up when spoken to.

At the furthest end of the row from Mrs Brindsley-Smith, Bett sat beside her son. He was charming and attentive both to Bett and to Sheilagh. Sheilagh chattered away during the interval, smoothing over any awkward pauses.

'Au clair de la lune,' Sheilagh sang, her hands on the back of the chair, swinging her head from side to side.

'Mon ami Pierrot,' Bett added with an inviting smile to Sheilagh.

'Do you speak French?' Sheilagh asked.

'Yes, my father has made us all learn.'

Brindsley-Smith looked interested. 'My mother is trying to teach Sheilagh. When we move to Canada she'll probably be fluent faster than me. I should have learnt more at school,' he said without much conviction. Tentatively Bett asked about his move to Canada.

'We're expanding out there, but I won't bother you with the details. Sheilagh, stop jiggling, the curtain is about to go up.'

Bett thought that the evening had been delightful and felt a genuine affection for the motherless little girl. The others were less enthusiastic, but kept their comments and their opinion of Mrs Brindsley-Smith for discussion amongst themselves. They were unwilling to upset their sister, who rarely expressed disapproval of anyone.

Just as nothing would induce Beatrice to go to the theatre, nothing was going to stop her going to the Harvest Festival Dance. Nor was she concerned about flaunting a new dress. She badgered her mother and protested that she was of an age to wear a long skirt until her mother capitulated. All the girls were anxious to see their old friends and to be reunited. Bett, unfortunately, took one of her invalid spells but Eleanor, if she was honest with herself, was relieved that she could nurse her, having regretted her earlier hasty decision not to attend.

Flo kept a motherly eye on her younger sisters, ensuring that they wore their cotton, and not their more sophisticated silk dresses, and was pleased that Lil had followed her example. She could not understand why her mother had allowed Beatrice to make an exhibition of herself but she had had battles with Beatrice in the past and had rarely won. Flo hoped she would realise during the evening that her stance was ill-advised. Beatrice had, unfortunately in her opinion, a mature sensuousness that her older sisters lacked. Flo had watched her emerge from an irresolute child to young girl who enlivened, if she were in the mood to do so, every situation, and tonight Beatrice was charm personified. Even Flo was caught up in her enthusiasm for the evening ahead.

The family travelled in two carriages. Flo supervised the young ones, and Lil and Beatrice accompanied their father. Beatrice had stated that she had no wish to be grouped with 'the children' as she called her younger sisters. Flo felt a quiet glow of expectation as she returned to be amongst her friends, her pupils from the school and the comforting surroundings of her old home. She looked forward to the traditional Harvest Night and living in Leicester had not changed her opinion.

'Father will be leaving around ten o' clock and he will take you home with him,' Flo told the children. It was then that the arranged dances and games which included the children ceased, and the band changed to polkas and waltzes which were the dances of choice for the adults.

'And will Beatrice come with us?' asked Ruth. Ruth was usually to be found in Beatrice's shadow, a restrained foil to her sister's exuberance. Flo could see that she was saddened at the change this outing had given to her status. If Beatrice was no longer considered to be one of the young ones, Ruth would be left isolated with only Elsie and Maisie for company.

'There won't be enough room in the carriage and mother says that she can stay on this year,' Flo explained, but she could feel their resentment and recognised that their small group was diminished. Hurriedly she reminded them of the enjoyment that the evening promised. 'You'll see your old school friends. Maisie, who do you think you will see tonight?'

Maisie could not hear her, due to the noises in the street and the clattering of the carriage. Flo, who was sitting opposite her, repeated the question so that she could lip read. Maisie began to enumerate the friends she would see and soon Ruth and Elsie were chipping in.

The parish hall was teeming with people when the Hefford family arrived. Only a few were sitting and every inch of space between the tables, the stage and the entrance hall was buzzing with jostling parishioners. The Heffords mingled unobtrusively and any shyness on meeting former friends was soon dispelled. The hall had not yet been fitted with electricity. Candles lit the length of the trestle tables and oil lamps burned in wall brackets. The stage had been decorated with plaited straw and bunches of chrysanthemums and various musical instruments were propped up against some chairs. On the piano, candles had been lit and the pianist was organising his sheet music ready for the evening's entertainment.

There was a reduction in the chattering of voices when the Rector walked on to the stage. This was the moment when people found their seats, called to friends to join them, helped the elderly or looked out for newcomers. The Rector greeted the assembled company and said grace, and then steaming bowls of meat and vegetables, carried by perspiring red-faced women, were placed on the tables. Later there were jellies and trifles and finally baskets of oranges and cups of tea.

Once the dessert dishes were cleared the children became restless, and when the tables were folded away they drifted on to the dance-floor and played tag or piggy-in-the-middle, until restrained by their elders. Meanwhile the band gathered on the stage, the elderly found chairs placed along the walls, the men folk made their way to the bar to collect tankards of beer or cider, and the young, the Heffords among them, waited for the music to begin.

The evening started with an ice breaker which had every able bodied parishioner on the floor. The Rector checked that the two circles of people contained equal numbers, and the music struck up. The outer ring walked to the right and the inner to the left, holding hands. When the music stopped there was a burst of conversation as each dancer greeted their new partner. The confusion experienced by a tongue-tied boy or the blushes of a young woman were dissipated as soon as the music resumed.

Reginald watched his children. At times like this he rejoiced in his family of girls. Flo, her fair hair falling luxuriantly down her back and swept off her face with two combs, looked happy to be amongst her friends. Her patterned cotton dress with ruched bodice and full skirt suited her and the delicate flower print was a careful statement between the rustic and the fashionable. While she and Tom kept a careful watch over the younger ones, they had no opportunity to dance together, but Tom often caught Flo's eye and Flo would smile in reply. They were well suited, Reginald told himself.

Lil stood alone. She was one of the tallest in the room, strongly built and slightly forbidding to those who did not know her. She had fewer contemporaries than Flo, because she had chosen to isolate herself and pursue her own path. It was obvious to Reginald that she was making an effort to be sociable and did not as easily blend into the company as did her older sister. Lil's simple plain green dress, which she wore as one might a uniform, only emphasised her difference. She wore her hair in a chignon, giving her the appearance of being older than her twenty years. Few men approached her and she took on her mother's role of ensuring that Maisie was included.

Elsie was a rather podgy thirteen-year-old whose dress, on a body with no contours, was not shown to advantage. Her mouse-coloured hair, naturally wavy and cut to shoulder length, was her most attractive feature. She had small eyes in a round face and she wore a fierce frown as she concentrated on her dance steps, unaware of the comic figure she presented.

Ruth and Maisie were still too young for Reginald to predict how they might develop. Ruth had a pleasant face but was inscrutable and would be seen neither to laugh uproariously nor weep inconsolably, both of which states Maisie resorted to regularly. Ruth moved gracefully where Maisie struggled with coordination.

Reginald nodded in time to the music, happy to see his girls enjoying themselves and he was prepared to join his old cronies when he spotted Beatrice. He had almost forgotten his most unpredictable daughter. He watched as Beatrice held her own small court, surrounded by a group, predominantly of boys. Her new satin dress, the violet blue shimmering in the candlelight, showed off her slim arms below their puffed sleeves, and emphasised her petite figure. Her dark hair moved silkily as she tossed her head to accompany her anecdotes to a rapt audience. It was Beatrice who broke up the group, selecting one of the boys, and encouraging all the rest to follow them on to the dance floor. Reginald had to admit that she was a pleasure to watch but feared that before the year was out she would present them with a handful of problems.

The evening followed the same pattern year on year and the Rector's role was almost unnecessary. Under the arches signalled that it was time for the children to leave.

'Go and find your shawls. Father is ready,' Flo said, gathering up her sisters.

She felt a tap on her shoulder. 'Flo, would you dance the next one with me?' It was Tom.

'Let me see Father into the carriage.'

'I'll come with you. Ruth, let me help you with that shawl. How did you enjoy yourself?'

Ruth's solemn little face beamed up at Tom. 'It was very enjoyable,' she said formally. 'I think Beatrice is having a good time.'

'I'll keep an eye on Beatrice for you. Good night, Sir, good night Elsie.' He stooped slightly so that Maisie could see him. 'Good night, little Maisie.'

As Tom and Flo returned to the dance floor a waltz was already under way and they were soon lost in the medley of bobbing heads and circling feet. The band moved from one tune to another with no intervals to allow for a change of partner. When there was finally a break Tom spied two chairs immediately below the stage. 'Tom, that was just like old times,' Flo said at they sat down, 'I hadn't realised how much I had missed all this.'

'Is that true?' Tom asked, surprising Flo with the intensity of his question. 'Really? Do you?'

'Why, Tom, does it matter whether I do or not?'

'It matters more than you can imagine. Shall we go and cool down outside?'

As they crossed the floor, ignoring the Rector as he called for the next dance and oblivious of the band who picked up their instruments and the fiddler who adjusted a string, a few people watching the young couple gave each other knowing looks.

In the carriage home Lil and Beatrice discussed the evening. Flo did not contribute, but she was prepared for Lil to question her when they were safely in their bedroom.

'What is it, Flo?' asked Lil, 'Is all well between you and Tom?'

Flo moved closer to Lil. 'Very well, thank you. Father has said we can marry.'

Lil put her arm around her sister. 'I am so happy for you, but I shall miss you. How do you know that Father agrees?'

'Because he promoted Tom two weeks ago, and gave him permission.'

'Two weeks, Flo. Two weeks. What has Tom been doing all this time?'

'He wasn't sure that I'd want to. How could he have thought that?'

'I think I understood very well why Tom might have thought that,' Lil answered, 'our circumstances have changed. But, Flo, our first wedding. I do envy you and Tom. You've always known, haven't you?'

Flo looked at Lil steadily. 'You wouldn't be content with a purely domestic existence. I've been a mother practically all my life.

'But now you'll be a wife,' Lil said emphatically. Lil and Flo looked at each other, smiling and happy, glad that their father had not pursued his ambitions for his eldest daughter and sacrificed her happiness.

When the younger girls heard about Flo's engagement they could speak of nothing else. They had known Tom for the greater part of their lives and nothing seemed more natural than that he and Flo should marry. Their sole interest was in their roles as bridesmaids and they pestered their mother with requests for visits to the dressmakers, while she was simultaneously involved in arranging the Banns, setting a date, compiling a guest list and organising the wedding tea. Such was the upheaval to the normal running of the household that the drama that was about to unfold regarding Bett went almost unnoticed.

Lil was helping Reginald to sort some catalogues for distribution amongst her mother's friends. 'Would you ask Bett to come and see me, Lil, without the others knowing'.

Bett knocked timidly.

'Come in, Bett,' her father said gently, 'I don't see you here very often, do I?'

It was an essentially masculine environment; ledgers with their years inscribed along the spines filled shelves on either side of a long window and the air was hazy from her father's pipe. His large leather-covered desk dominated the room. She closed the door and sat in the armchair opposite her father and looked engulfed by it, it was so obviously designed for a more substantial figure than hers.

'Bett, you've had a good spell of health, the less energetic life of the town seems to suit you.'

'I'm very much better than I was, Father,' Bett said eagerly, as her father laid down his pen and nodded in agreement.

'I'm pleased to hear it, but that's not my reason for wanting to talk to you. Young Brindsley-Smith came to see me. The thing is, Bett, he wants to marry you. It seems that you have a way with Sheilagh and he thinks that you'll make a capital little wife.'

Bett sat very still in her chair. 'But he's going to Quebec, Father, he told me so himself. That's why Sheilagh's learning French.'

'You would not be going out at once. He needs to go ahead and settle everything first, but there is the matter of his little girl.'

'What does Mother say?' Bett asked in a small voice. Then she added, 'Sheilagh can't be left can she? Not alone with Mrs Brindsley-Smith. She would be so unhappy.'

'Do you like Brindsley-Smith, Bett. That is what you need to decide.'

'I think I do. Can I go now and speak to Mother?'

With a sigh Reginald watched the weakest of his daughters as she left the room. This was not quite how he had envisaged the future for his offspring. He had hoped that the move to Leicester would produce some eligible young men, and had not imagined how the plight of a young widower might appeal to Bett. Yet, she had not the vitality or strength of character to attract a suitor on her own merits. Reginald thought ruefully of his remaining daughters and anticipated anything but an easy passage as each of them reached a marriageable age. Beatrice was already a handful and if Reginald was honest he knew that he was hardly a match for that headstrong girl. Lil was more measured and could be relied upon to use her good judgement. Fortunately it would be some time before he had to consider the futures of his youngest three daughters, Elsie, Ruth and Maisie, because he now had two weddings to plan for.

Slowly Bett pushed open the door of the drawing room and seeing that her mother was alone, crossed the room and sank onto the rug at her feet. She laid her head on her mother's lap. Eleanor stroked her daughter's hair, smoothing it away from her face, in a rhythmic motion.

'What do I do, Mother?'

Eleanor's hand rested lightly on Bett's head.

'He's respectable and has good manners. You like his little girl.'

'What if I have one of my illness relapses?'

'Little Sheilagh has a nanny and you will have staff to manage the household.'

Bett lifted her head to search her mother's face. 'He's going to Quebec.'

'Why don't you leave the decision for a while? You and I have been asked to Lyons Tea House to meet Mr

Brindsley-Smith tomorrow and it'll give you a chance to know him better.'

She and her mother sat silently. They were often together sewing or discussing the latest catalogues while her sisters skated, or rowed on the river, or went for rambles in the countryside, and this had brought them especially close. Nothing was expected of her at once.

'We won't speak about this to the others at the moment, dear,' Eleanor said as she rose. 'Go and get changed and I'll find an excuse for us both to go out tomorrow afternoon.' Eleanor patted Bett's folded hands, which seemed to be holding her body tightly together, and then gave her a gentle push towards the door.

'Reginald,' Eleanor began as she entered his study, 'are you quite sure about this Brindsley-Smith? Bett is so vulnerable. Do you think he will look after her?'

'I know his type, Eleanor. If his wife causes him no trouble he will give her respectability and a safe home, and we can rely on Bett. We have to face the facts. She is not strong. She needs a secure future. Whatever else he does, his background will ensure that. Besides, she is already taken with the little girl and who knows, our poor daughter may never have children of her own.'

Eleanor was taken aback by Reginald's plain speaking. 'But his age, Reginald!'

'Brindsley-Smith is only twenty-four. That is not old. On balance I think that this is a suitable match for Bett.'

'Nothing is completely settled, is it, Reginald? Bett must decide for herself.' Eleanor was as defiant as she dared.

'I think you'll find Bett understands the situation, and she always aims to please.'

With that Eleanor had to be content. When they left the following afternoon for their engagement with Brindsley-Smith their excuse that Bett needed some winter boots was accepted without question. The November day was drab. There were many empty tables in the tea house, and Eleanor's spirits reflected the somewhat desolate scene. Brindsley-Smith was seated at a table near the window and, guiding Bett with a hand on her elbow, Eleanor quickened her pace and went forward to greet him. He stood up and shook them both by the hand and signalled to the waitress as they took their seats.

The gas lights on the interior walls caused considerable condensation on the windows and shut out the street. The tablecloths were of white damask, as were the napkins, and only the ornate lamps on the tables broke up the austere décor with their sombre yellow light.

As her eyes accustomed themselves, Bett found that the dark timbered furniture and the discreetly patterned wallpaper gave her a feeling of being isolated from the outside world. Mr Brindsley-Smith was good-looking in a groomed, well-practised manner, his eyes looked sleepily from under heavy lids. His movements were slow and studied giving the impression of careful consideration before committing himself, but which in reality had become a habit. Bett imagined how he must be grieving for his first wife and felt sympathy for his plight. She thought about Sheilagh without a mother and felt a surge of affection for the child.

Eleanor started the conversation. 'Why Quebec?'

'We're expanding our business. The senior partner needs someone to explore the opportunities for leather, for shoes and handbags, to add to our range in the haute couture designs of The House of Whitehorn. I'm being asked to do this for them.' It was as if he was rehearsing a prepared speech. 'It is a great opportunity,' he added in his affected drawl.

'What sort of life will it be? Is it anything like Paris? Or is it a pioneer town?

'Quite sophisticated, I believe.' He turned to Bett. 'My mother calls you Elizabeth but I notice that your family calls you Bett. Which do you like?'

'Everyone calls me Bett. I'd like it if you did.'

'Then Bett it is. So, as I was saying, our products have a Parisian influence. You will find these in our most recent catalogues and we will be introducing our products in our department stores here and in Canada. In Quebec we will have access to the fur and animal skin trade.'

'Would you take a ship from Southampton?' Eleanor was more interested in Quebec than in the exports and imports trade.

'Probably the White Star Line from Liverpool, they leave every week or so. They say that sailing on one is like living in a floating hotel.'

Eleanor encouraged the subject to continue, poured out the tea and offered the plate of currant buns and tea cakes. She declined to have one herself and absented herself with the excuse of powdering her nose, so that she could leave the two young people together.

'You are aware, Bett, that I have approached you father?' Brindsley-Smith said and Bett nodded, looked up at him quickly and then played with her knife on the tablecloth.

'Do you think you could like me?'

'Yes,' Bett affirmed at once. 'But why me?'

'Because you are cheerful, charming and caring.' He replied almost too glibly, but Bett smiled, delighted at the unexpected compliment. 'You don't have to answer immediately.'

Neither spoke for a few moments. Bett played with her knife. Eleanor returned to the table and looked from one to the other.

'We could meet again next week if you like,' Brindsley-Smith said.

It was not so easy to slip away unnoticed the following week. Eleanor's lack of explanation was accepted, except for Beatrice who would not be quieted and saw no reason why she should not go out with their mother. Flo stepped in to avoid a scene but agreed with Beatrice later that 'something was up.'

'I'll get it out of her the minute she comes in,' Beatrice asserted.

'Oh no you won't, young monkey,' Flo insisted. 'You'll leave it up to me and then I might tell you if there is anything to hear.'

When they were changing for dinner that night Flo knocked on Bett's door. Bett was sitting at her dressing table, staring into the mirror, still wearing her day clothes. She turned at the sound of the door and seemed relieved to see her oldest sister. 'Flo, will you shut the door?' she asked. 'I want to tell you something. I am going to marry Mr Brindsley-Smith.'

Flo managed to conceal her alarm. 'Bett, is that really what you want?'

'Yes,' answered Bett with studied composure, 'I think I'll do very well. I can manage Sheilagh and she has a nursemaid. Besides I shall not be leaving for ages. We will have the wedding very soon and I will go to Quebec when we are sent for, and that might not be until the springtime.'

Flo put her arms around Bett and laid her cheek against her head. 'I hope you know what you are doing.' She looked at Bett's face in the mirror. It was pale and she could learn nothing of her feelings. 'What about the wedding?'

'He says that we wouldn't want a formal wedding, but we could have the ceremony and a weekend in London before he sails, in the week before Christmas. You know I would hate a great fuss, Flo, and he couldn't leave Sheilagh with me if we were not married.'

Flo hugged Bett to her, unable to find anything to say. Finally she steadied her voice to ask.

'What does Mother say? And Father? Does he know about all this?'

Bett nodded, 'Will you tell the others? I don't think that I can.'

Flo went straight downstairs looking for her parents. She found them in the drawing room. Her parents seemed braced for her onslaught.

'Father,' she began. She was used to challenging her

father.

'Now don't say a word, Flo.' Reginald allowed a moment for the tension to decrease, then he stepped forward and took her hands. 'Your mother and I both agree that this is a good match for Bett. However, it does concern you in a way that I fear that I must bring up immediately.'

Flo fidgeted, frustrated at being interrupted.

'If Bett is to be married before Christmas, you and Tom will have to wait to be married until Easter. I'm sorry about this, but it would not be right.'

Flo could see no reason why she and Tom should have to delay their wedding, but as her concern was for Bett she did not challenge him except to say, 'She's so young, so frail.'

Her mother looked distracted. 'It does mean that Bett will be at your wedding, Flo, which I know you will be anxious about. She is not leaving us for several months and that will enable her to get used to the idea.'

Flo discussed a few of the details with her father. She felt this was essential before facing the barrage of questions which she would encounter when she broke the news to her sisters. 'Well, shall I tell the others, or are you going to?'

They agreed that it would be best if Flo told them immediately, without Bett being present.

'That odious mother,' declared Lil.

'Bett can't be married first,' protested Beatrice.

'But he is so old,' Ruth said quietly.

'Does it mean we will not be bridesmaids?' Maisie asked.

'Yes,' replied Flo, 'but you will be mine.'

' I don't see what all the fuss is about,' said Elsie.

There was barely enough time for all the arrangements to be made before Bett's Wedding was held on the Saturday before Christmas. Eleanor's only act of defiance was to insist on a church wedding for her daughter.

The Brindsley-Smiths had few relatives and at Bett's request only her family and her Father's sister, Helen, were invited to attend. Bett appeared calm. She had shown very little emotion during the previous weeks, and her poise repelled any remarks that her younger sisters might have been prompted to make.

For the ceremony Bett wore a deep blue velvet jacket with a fur collar and a skirt to match with a pillbox hat also in blue. It seemed inappropriate in such an intimate setting to enter the church with a fanfare from the organ. Holding tightly to her father's arm she walked up the aisle with a quiet dignity, and only detached herself from him when she arrived beside her future husband. The service proceeded smoothly, with Bett saying her vows clearly and Brindsley-Smith watching over her solicitously.

Flo wondered if she had fretted unnecessarily. The wedding breakfast was held at a hotel and afterwards the families followed the bridal pair to the railway station. When the conductor blew his whistle Bett and her husband leaned together out of the window and waved. The engine increased its head of steam, carriages bumped and clashed against each other, guards ran along the platform and doors clanged shut. The newly married couple were slowly drawn away from the cheering group of well-wishers.

'My wedding won't be like that,' Beatrice whispered furiously to Ruth as they turned to follow their parents from the platform, 'and I shall have a proper honeymoon.'

Chapter Four

Since the tenets of the church would not allow weddings to take place in Lent, the date of Flo's wedding was set for the Sunday after Easter. Her marriage would be the first significant event in the lives of all of her sisters. To each one of the girls, Flo was the loving figure that their own mother was often too preoccupied to provide. While their mother ran a somewhat chaotic household, Flo responded to each sister with affection and gentle discipline. Flo's influence smoothed the natural frictions that occurred on a daily basis not only with her sisters but with her father. She was the daughter with whom he could relax on returning from the office. Reginald would miss her and a plan had been forming in his mind that would not only further his business, after all he was primarily a business man, but give his daughter some pleasure and enable him to spend just a little more time in her company.

'Flo,' he began, as they sat by the fire in his study, 'how would you like to accompany me to the Paris Exhibition?' He watched her face light up. 'L'exposition universelle,' he said, leaning back in his chair.

'L'exposition universelle.' Flo corrected his French with a gentle smile knowing he was proud of her ability. 'I would like that very much.'

It was the millennium year and the exhibition was due to open in April. It soon became apparent that to keep abreast of the society with which they were mixing, it would be a great disadvantage if at least one member of their family did not attend. Besides, everyone was agog to see this most splendid of extravaganzas. It was rumoured that the whole exhibition, which covered an area of nearly two square miles, was to be powered by electricity, and at night the Palais d'électricité was lit up by more than five thousand light bulbs. The world was being brought to Paris over the next eight months.

Reginald judged that visiting the Paris Exhibition could be good for business. Links with Paris were essential for anyone with aspirations to succeed in the milieu of haute couture. He was energised now that, through his recent partnership, he was entering the competitive world of fashion. If England was the hub of commerce, then the centre for the arts and design was Paris. All that was chic and in vogue emanated from France's capital city. Despite their turbulent history and their championship of the bourgeoisie, the French were still in the forefront of the arts, and Parisian high society set the tone for the rest of Europe.

The senior partner of the House of Whitehorn, under which name the mills of Hefford and those of Brindsley-Smith traded, had suggested to Reginald that he represent them in the opening week. Along with all the other specialist clothing departments, they would be exhibiting their new collection. Reginald had limited knowledge in this area but when he suggested that he took his two eldest daughters, who could wear their newest designs, Peter Whitehorn was quick to appreciate that the girls would certainly do no harm to their firm's reputation.

Five days before they were due to leave, their plans were thrown into disarray. After attending a lecture at the town hall, Mitchell escorted Lil and Bett back to Granby House. When they arrived, Lil was the first to alight from the carriage, and taking Mitchell's proffered hand sprang on to the pavement. As Mitchell turned to help Bett there was a cry from Lil. The temperature had dropped during the evening and the earlier heavy rain had developed a thin film of ice on the flagstones. On one of these Lil had slipped. They turned to see Lil grasping her ankle and struggling to stand. She was unable to walk and only by support from Mitchell and by leaning on the rail could she mount the steps to the house. Horace, alerted by the commotion, opened the front door.

'Would you help me take Lil up to the nursery? Bett, run and call your mother,' Mitchell commanded.

Eleanor fussed, directed Bett to fetch witch hazel, lint and a bandage, until Mitchell felt it was prudent to withdraw. Lil, when she saw that he was planning to leave, called out her thanks and assured him that her ankle was not broken.

'How do you know?' asked her mother, 'wait until Dr Peters has seen it in the morning. Bett, there's no point in you hanging around. Late nights do not suit you, so away you go to bed.'

The unusual activity in the nursery had not gone unnoticed by Beatrice and Elsie, whose bedroom was along the corridor. They waylaid Bett as she passed their door.

'What's happened?'

Bett related the story.

'So Mitchell had to carry her up the stairs?' repeated Beatrice.

'Not carry, silly, just hold her round her waist and Lil had an arm on his shoulder.'

Beatrice declared that this was decidedly romantic, but Bett told her to stop speaking nonsense, and continued to her own room at the end of the passage.

'Elsie,' Beatrice said to her sister, 'Do you know what this means? This means that Lil can't go to Paris. Bett can't go, she can never go anywhere, so I could go instead.'

'Father would never allow that.'

'Why not? I'm nearly sixteen.'

'You're not.'

Beatrice ignored her as she developed her strategy. 'Flo would not be able to go on her own and if she says to Father that it's a good idea, then Father might agree.' She started to slip her feet into her slippers.

49

'Where are you going?' Elsie asked.

'To see Flo.'

Flo and Lil's bedroom was on the second floor. She was unaware of the drama and Beatrice was in a strong position to argue her case.

'So you see, Flo, you won't be able to go to Paris now that Lil's hurt her ankle, unless I go with you.'

'Go back to bed and don't say a word,' Flo warned, 'you will have to wait until I can speak to Father.'

Reginald, Eleanor and Flo gathered in the study after breakfast and the result of their discussion was that there was really no option but to allow Beatrice to take Lil's place. Reginald was mindful that Flo had delayed her wedding to accommodate him over Bett's marriage, and he did not want to deny her this exciting expedition.

'In your care, Flo, I cannot see that Beatrice poses a problem. You can curb her exuberance when she needs it, and she will be company for you. If Beatrice will listen to anyone, it's you. So be it.'

Those few days before their departure were a flurry of activity for the entire family. None of Lil's clothes were suitable for Beatrice but by picking the best of Bett's and Elsie's wardrobe, and with frequent forays to the shops with her mother, a large trunk was eventually filled with Beatrice's outfits.

On the evening before their departure as they were lying in their beds in the dark, Flo could hear Lil moving restlessly on the other side of their bedroom.

'Does your ankle hurt?'

'A little. I just need to get it in the right position. Can't you sleep?'

'I'm just thinking,' Flo answered.

'Yes?' Lil prompted.

'I'm sorry it could not have been you, Lil, going with us tomorrow. It's as if our lives have changed already.' Flo thought of this trip as the ending of her family life. When she returned she would be centre stage as a bride.

As it was the first traditional wedding in the family all their relatives had been invited. Tom's extensive family and many of those involved in the business and working at the mill would be there too. She was not sorry to leave Leicester because in many ways she had outgrown her role as eldest daughter. Tom had been understanding about the postponement of the date and had philosophically decided that perhaps it had been for the best, as it gave him more time to prepare their house. .

'What will you do, Lil, when I am married?'

'Take over your role, I expect,' Lil teased. 'I don't see the point in all these social occasions, but Mother and Bett will need me, and the young ones and Sheilagh too. I thought I'd ask Father if there is a way in which I can help him. I've been thinking about the catalogues, I feel I could improve on them.'

'That's true. Father will miss me and you'd fill the gap. You have such a flare for design.' Both girls were quiet. Flo was about to tell Lil that she would bring some catalogues back with her from Paris, when she realised that her sister was asleep.

The first leg of their journey to Paris was by train to London, where they would stay at the Metropole Hotel beside Marylebone station. They were due to leave on the 2.43 from Leicester. The hall was almost impassable with portmanteau and hat boxes where the paucity of labels advertised that the family were relative novices to long-distance travel. Dressing cases and umbrellas were strewn in a smaller pile. Members of the family milled around; Lil sat in a large chair beside the coat rack, Bett sat on the arm of her chair and the others gave them last minute pieces of advice or bombarded them with questions.

'Don't stand on my boots,' Beatrice snapped at Maisie who immediately looked ready to cry. 'Oh don't cry, Maisie. I'll bring you back a model of the Eiffel Tower, I promise, but please stand still.' Mollified, Maisie moved away and looked out of the window to watch for the carriage.

'It's here,' she called.

The short journey to the station was frustratingly slow and once again all the trunks and cases had to be assembled in the forecourt. Reginald advised the girls to go to the waiting room while he hired a porter and purchased their tickets. Although it was April there was little warmth in the sun and the wind funnelled along the platform. Flo and Beatrice sat near the fire in the Ladies waiting room and watched the other travellers. All of them, Beatrice thought, looked older than themselves and none, she was certain, was about to embark on a trip to the continent.

Beatrice grew impatient and Flo looked at her wristwatch. 'I think we should go and join Father now, it's not long until the train is due.' There were many passengers on the platform and they had some trouble in finding their father. He was holding three stubby cardboard tickets and checking each one. 'Good, good,' he said, tucking the tickets into his waistcoat pocket. 'The porter is dealing with the trunks and they'll be placed in the guard's van. Stand back now, here she comes.'

With slow heavy puffs of steam the engine came abreast and then slid towards the buffers. The porter they had engaged ran to the nearest door, and Reginald followed him to secure their seats and oversee the smaller cases as they were placed in the luggage rack overhead. The porter descended the steps and held the door.

'You can go in now, Miss,' he said to Flo and, once she and Beatrice were safely in the compartment, he closed the sliding door. Flo went across to the window reaching for the handles on either side and drew them apart to ventilate the carriage. 'I'll close it later if you wish, Father.'

They settled in, Flo and Beatrice on either side of the window and Reginald beside the door, pleased that they had the compartment to themselves. Later they were joined by three passengers and Reginald moved to sit beside Beatrice. He opened his Leicester Mercury and Beatrice wished that he had bought The Times so that the other passengers would think that they were from London; she did not know why she suddenly felt ashamed to be from Leicester because there was a time when living there had been the height of her aspirations. She sat very upright so that the fur collar of her coat, borrowed from Bett, did not ride up and upset the angle of her hat, and stared, without taking in any of the passing towns or countryside, out of the window. There was so much that she wanted to say to Flo, but she would have to wait until they were in their room at the Metropole.

The room allocated to Lil and Beatrice was at the back of the building, but the linen was clean and crisp, the heavy curtains in autumn colours protected them from some of the street noises, and the ewer and basin on the dressing-table were without cracks. A large radiator kept the room at a pleasant temperature and the rack beside it held two cotton towels. Flo and Beatrice unpacked their overnight cases.

'Do we change for dinner? What time is Aunt Helen coming? Do you remember her? Will I like her?'

'I think we'll just change our blouses, to silk ones, and you can pin Mother's brooch at your neck. We'll take our shawls in case the dining room is draughty. Aunt Helen arrives at seven, and I think you will like her.'

Downstairs in the lounge the girls were greeted warmly by Aunt Helen, who was Reginald's sister, a widow and childless. He beamed with pleasure when he saw her and watched her take stock of his daughters. He encouraged her as a raconteur and made every effort to indulge her as only a doting older brother could. She had an effervescent personality and took delight in disconcerting her country relatives with her cosmopolitan mannerisms and outrageously eccentric dress. That evening she was wearing a Moroccan kaftan with silver earrings and dark eyeliner.

'You're off to 'gay Paris,' said Aunt Helen, pronouncing it gay Paree, 'How I envy you. Perhaps your Father will take me later in the year?' Her eyes twinkled. Beatrice thought that her aunt was far too old to go on trips like this, it was different for her father because he had to go on business, but she was impressed that, unlike her mother, her aunt wished to go.

Aunt Helen continued, 'I hear that the grounds are so vast that you can get lost at the Exhibition, in places such as the souks of Arabia or the Temples of Asia!'

Beatrice warmed to her aunt and wondered whether this exhibition was so large that even Flo could lose her way. Their father was unlikely to leave them unattended but how delightful was the prospect. Towards the end of the meal her concentration drifted as her father and Helen discussed the well-being of various members of the family.

The maitre d'hôtel, who was keeping an eye over the crowded dining room and scuttling waiters, came over to their table. He paused until Reginald noticed him.

'May I present you with a millennium medallion?' He spoke to Reginald but indicated Beatrice. In his hand he held open a small box and a medallion the size of a sixpence rested on a square of blue velvet. 'We gave these to all our guests who were staying as the century changed and we have a few remaining.' Beatrice looked up and gave him one of her radiant smiles. 'Thank you, indeed,' said her father on her behalf.

'Thank you very much,' said Beatrice who took it from his hand, placed the box on the table and lifted the medallion. 'Marylebone Metropole 1900,' she read as she turned it between her fingers. She knew at that moment that this trip marked a turning point. She was no longer a child. She no longer felt like a child. She replaced the medallion and put the box in her reticule. Later she kept the medallion in the pocket of her skirt, and regularly turned it around through her fingers knowing that no one would suspect.

Later that night Flo and Beatrice clambered into adjacent beds.

'What did you think of Aunt Helen?' Flo turned down the gas lamp.

'I can't believe she's Father's sister.'

The room was in darkness except for a chink of light between the curtains created by the glow from the street lamps. At last she and Beatrice could speak freely and the two girls chattered long into the night.

Beatrice's knowledge of rail travel was limited to her rare visits to London. She was accustomed to the glass and metal construction of Marylebone station, where the horses stood patiently at the end of the platforms, where the kiosks were plastered in advertising boards for Bovril and Pear's soap, and where the workers and businessmen criss-crossed the forecourt, and she assumed that all London stations were similar.

Once they alighted at Waterloo station she was immediately aware of her error. Waterloo seemed to be the centre of the universe. There were numerous platforms and endless announcements calling for passengers to Paris or Boulogne or to destinations in the Orient. There were trolleys piled high with trunks covered with labels from all around the world, and passengers from many distant lands. The air was thick with accumulated smoke making the crowds seem endless as they disappeared into the murky distance. They were surrounded by noise. There were barrel organs and penny whistles with operators who vied for farthings, porters who slammed doors and conductors who blew their whistles. There was the sound of running feet as passengers caught the door handles and jumped on to moving carriages, and there was the explosive hiss of steam and crunch of metal as engines gained momentum at the start of their journeys.

From Waterloo to Dover was just seventy-seven miles but it felt much longer to Beatrice who sat willing the dockside to appear. Finally the train slowed to make its way through the town towards the harbour where it stopped at Admiralty Pier. The passengers transferred from the train to ascend the gangplank that was already lowered from the deck of the steamer. It was impossible to gauge the size of the ferry from the narrow wood-slatted walkway and the low-ceilinged reception area. It was not until they had mounted the metal stair with its wide wooden banister to the middle deck that the length of the ferry steamer was visible.

'It's going to be a breezy crossing, I have it on the best authority from the purser.' Reginald told the girls when he returned from purchasing their tickets. 'If you wrap up well, however, and find a place at the stern, you will not be uncomfortable and you will have a fine view of Dover as we leave. The white cliffs are quite a sight.'

The steamer got under way, its propeller churning the sea into foam leaving a trail of white wake as far as the dockside. Encompassed by houses and warehouses the harbour extended to a long esplanade which was used by only a few promenaders at this time of the year. On the hill above the town the keep and Constable's tower dominated the landscape. Beatrice saw the train that had delivered them to Folkestone appear and disappear into the tunnels which pierced the precipitous Shakespeare Cliffs as it headed back to London. Along the shore, the vast chalk cliffs which marked the coast of England, slowly receded as the steamer sailed into the main shipping route of the English Channel.

The sounds and sensations on board ship were unfamiliar. The rhythmic singing of the metal wheels of the train were replaced by the clattering of metal on metal as cleats on hawsers shook and rattled, and underfoot the vibration from the powerful engines permeated every area of the ship. As the land grew rapidly smaller and the distance from the shore increased, Beatrice felt the thrill of the traveller who enjoys the journey as much as the destination.

When the steamer approached Calais, Flo and Beatrice with their father went forward to the upper deck for their first sighting of France.

'The train circles the old town before stopping at the Gare Centrale where the local passengers join us, then we go all the way to Paris.'

Beatrice was disappointed with the dull grey houses and austere stone warehouses which seemed hardly to differ from those that they had recently left in Dover. When you arrived in a new country, especially one separated by sea, it should look and feel strange.

Beatrice imagined that she would leave a country that she thought of in shades of grey, black and white and enter one that was full of colour. She felt that somehow everything should feel alien, and so far it all felt familiar.

When the train stopped at the Gare Centrale, the compartment door slid open and with an explosion of incomprehensible French a family laden with purchases engulfed them. Three small children clambered to sit beside Flo, wriggling ever closer to allow their large, ample bosomed mother to ease her way on to the same seat. Meanwhile, their older brother and father stacked their parcels on the overhead rack and finally sat down leaving a box between them on the floor. The box was securely tied with string but moved of its own accord as some form of livestock rumbled around inside.

Piled on their laps were more parcels, one of which, judging by the smell, contained a quantity of cheese. Oblivious of the English family the younger children demanded 'goûté' which necessitated a rearrangement of parcels. Their mother extracted a long baguette and broke off sections which she distributed to her children, all the while scattering crumbs which she flicked with the back of her hand to the floor. The boy constantly shifted in his seat to check on his crate.

As Beatrice attempted to understand their conversation she wished she had made more effort at school. She could not know that her school French would not equip her to understand their Normandy patois.

The guard opened the door. 'Taissez-vous, le gendarme!' The mother gently tapped the hands of the three children who immediately obeyed, ceasing their wriggling.

'Billets, s'il vous plaît.' At last here was a sentence that Beatrice could translate. It was reinforced when her father produced their tickets from his inside pocket.

'Merci, Monsieur, merci.' Their tickets were clipped and then stowed away. The babble of the children and the energetic exchange of the views of the parents resumed.

The train made its way along the coast to Boulogne, and when the family left their place was taken by two elderly couples and a woman. They were remarkable because they lacked the foreign touch that Beatrice was searching for, and they were as plain and featureless as the Normandy countryside through which they were passing. While the monotonous chuntering of the train's wheels drew them ever closer to Paris, Beatrice did not dare to speak for fear of exposing her Englishness, little realising that their companions would have recognised the fact simply by their style of dress.

The Gare Saint Lazare, because of the language, the system of hiring a hackney carriage, and the press of people, seemed altogether more confusing than Waterloo. Flo spotted a carriage with the name of their hotel painted along the side and Reginald hailed it. Beatrice watched, bewildered, as her father called a porter and then disappeared to identify their luggage.

'What do we do now?' Beatrice asked, in a voice that betrayed her sudden nervousness.

'We wait for Father. I'll speak to the driver. We can probably sit in the carriage.' Beatrice listened carefully as Flo asked the driver in her flawless French if they could step aboard. She only caught a few words and was irritated with herself. She wondered if the whole trip would be like this, with her feeling as is she was in a vacuum. She started to practice simple sentences in her head.

Chapter Five

The Hotel des Marroniers on Boulevard Haussmann had an impressive exterior despite the grime and soot that engrained the brickwork. The uniformed commissionaire summoned two porters, one led the party to the reception desk where they were handed their room keys, the other carried their luggage.

An elaborate candelabra was suspended from the ceiling over the ornately decorated entrance hall. Rococo mirrors hung on the walls and vast enamelled pots filled with exotic plants were sited at the foot of every pillar. The porter, dressed in green serge trousers with yellow stripes the length of the outer seam, crisp white shirt, yellow bow tie and green satin waistcoat, opened the cross-hatched gates of the lift and indicated that the family should enter. The lift attendant, dressed in a similar uniform, operated the switches and the hydraulic apparatus cranked into action. As they followed their porter along the corridor Beatrice whispered, 'Does the boy live in the lift?'

'All day,' Flo replied.

'Le dîner est servi à sept heures et demi,' advised the porter.

'I'll see you in the dining room,' Reginald told the girls as he headed to his room.

In the dining hall there was not a table unoccupied, such was the attraction of the Exposition. Heads turned as Beatrice and Flo made their way to join their father.

'You look very nice,' he complimented. 'Glad to be shot of travelling?'

'A little,' admitted Beatrice. 'What time can we start tomorrow?'

'That's up to your sister.'

'We'll need to unpack our trunks and arrange for the maid to press our dresses. Shall we say eleven?'

Beatrice gave her father a conspiratorial wink, he was as impatient as she was to set off in the morning, but she received an answering look which suggested that they bow to Flo's decision.

The waiter approached for their orders.

'La truite pour moi,' said Flo.

'Le poulet s'il vous plaît,' said Beatrice, who was rewarded with an approving grin from Flo. Reginald struggled with his own pronunciation.

During the meal they planned their first day. Reginald brought out a pamphlet and, enlisting Flo's help, marked the exhibits that interested them. Occasionally he remembered to include Beatrice in the discussion, but he need not have worried that they were arranging their itinerary without her contribution, because she was absorbed with her surroundings.

At last she could study real French people, and real foreigners, and immerse herself in the lavish design of the hotel in her first introduction to the adult world. She paid scant attention to the details of the day ahead. Around her was the sort of life that she suspected existed and now was experiencing. She understood why she was so restless and dissatisfied with her provincial home and began to concoct ways to leave Leicester. Her reverie was interrupted by her father who suggested that they retire for the night.

The next morning, promptly at eleven, Flo and Beatrice joined their father in the foyer. 'The cabs go regularly to the Parc du Champs de Mars and you will have a grand introduction to Paris along the way. Have you your umbrellas?'

These vital accessories served for both rain and sun.

'I'm wondering if you will be warm in that outfit, Beatrice.' her father enquired.

Beatrice, whose dress with puffed sleeves, pleated waistline and full skirt would be spoiled with the addition of a jacket, declared. 'It's Spring in Paris'. Flo wore a small mantle over her shoulders which she tucked into the belt at her waist. They both wore fetching hats perched high on their heads and Flo's, as befitted her age, had an abundance of feathers.

Their cab left Boulevard Haussmann and travelled towards the river, negotiated the seething mass of carriages and wagons at the Champs Elysees, to turn along the Seine at the Quay D'Orsay. At this point they could see, surmounting the Pont L'Alma, a vast arch flanked by tall poles flying the red, white and blue flags of France.

Beatrice gave a gasp.

'We're not there yet,' Reginald pointed ahead along the river, 'look over there, the Eiffel Tower, that's the Exposition.'

Beatrice was unprepared for the sight of the majestic entrance gate. The carriages which queued in great numbers ready to deliver their passengers, were dwarfed by its enormous height. Topped with a statue of one of the muses on an ornate pedestal, the arched portal was shaped like a lady's bonnet, wider at the top than at its base. Filigree bands spread over a smaller arch which formed the public entrance. This was tiled in pale blue and white, with darker blue tiles for contrast.

On either side, on tall poles French flags unfurled in the breeze and flags of the participating countries stretched into the distance indicating a long thoroughfare. The Hefford family group alighted and joined the throng of people heading towards the ticket booths.

Very little was said as they walked, mesmerised, into the grounds of the Exposition. They gravitated towards the huge metal edifice that rose to dominate the landscape and which was the celebrated Tour Eiffel. Its four metal feet were each as large as a croquet lawn. From beneath the tower in every direction there were walkways leading towards different exhibitions. Beatrice promised herself that she would visit every one.

Reginald led them in the direction of the Dome and then on to the Pavilion des Beaux Arts. Their eyes were drawn ever onwards. There were exhibits from every major country in the world; pavilions from Algeria and Tunisia, South America and Europe, Russia and China. The first that they encountered was an Indian pavilion where Sikh attendants wearing white turbans with long white tunics and trousers, with colourful sashes around their waists, were serving small dishes of their specialities They were assaulted by the smell of spices and were encouraged to try curry and rice dishes.

'I think we'll visit the Histoire d'Habitation and then call it a day,' announced Reginald. 'The site will be one that will most interesting you girls.' It was an exhibition of houses from all over the world, from Byzantine to Japanese and from Russian to Arab.

Reginald found a bench facing the river. He had been sitting there for some time when he was hailed from a distance. Hurrying towards him, his top hat in one hand and his cane in the other, was a man whom he recognised as a fellow mill owner.

'Reginald, old fellow. What are you doing here?'

'Probably much the same as you, but perhaps not at this particular pavilion. My two daughters are planning their future homes.'

'Indeed. I only have sons. I was passing through looking for George. Both planning homes you say?' the newcomer asked.

'Not really. One is engaged but the other is still in school. That does not prevent them planning. Here they are now. Flo, Beatrice, let me introduce Mr Eaton. John, my daughters.'

John Eaton bowed to each in turn and inquired which country they were planning to live in.

'Arabia,' answered Beatrice at once, 'all those exotic carpets, and gold and silver-ware, and the lattice windows, and drapes hanging from the ceiling. The houses look so mysterious.'

'Not such a fine place for a woman,' Mr Eaton warned.

'Why?' asked Beatrice.

'Women are kept well out of sight. What you see is for the men.'

'Is that really true?'

'I'm afraid so. Now what do you say to my taking your father off to the gallery of the machines tomorrow, it'll take us most of the day for I hear it is a quarter of a mile long, and asking my son if he will accompany you? We've been here a couple of days and he knows his way around.'

Flo looked at her father who nodded in agreement.

'A capital idea,' Reginald said. 'No sense in taking these girls to see machines, not their style at all. Are you sure that your son is not otherwise engaged?'

It was all arranged. They would meet at the Trocadero.

The next morning Reginald asked the carriage driver to stop beside the Pont D'Iena which led in a straight line to the wide parterre which was the forecourt of the Trocadero. Set on a hill, the Trocadero was an impressive circular building in the form of an amphitheatre. Around its exterior were a series of pillars above which were numerous arched windows. Wide gleaming steps with fountains on either side led up to the palace, where the entire edifice was reflected in the water of the ornamental pool below.

"Look, Flo, there they are.'At the foot of the steps beside a tall Grecian urn overflowing with flowers stood two men. Beatrice hurried ahead down the steps.

The elder, sporting a trim beard and moustache, top hat, well-cut jacket, polished shoes and a black malacca cane was Mr Eaton, and the younger man was his son, George. There was no mistaking the resemblance between them but where the older was lean and rugged, the younger man was strikingly good looking.

George immediately escorted Beatrice and Flo, whispering that they could leave the old men to enjoy themselves. Beatrice decided that he might be amenable to some of her whims, one of which was to see Buffalo Bill from the Wild West, or even the Moulin Rouge. She was aware that there was something mildly disreputable about the latter, but could not discover the reason.

Rising high into the air the Grand Palais was made from thousands of panes of glass which glistened and glimmered in the sun.

'This is the sort of heat that you will find in the tropics,' George said.

'Except that we'll never go there,' Beatrice commented.

Plants and flowers grew in profusion and even in this early stage of the Exposition the large fronds of the ferns, and the drooping canopies of the palms, gave an indication of the lush vegetation such a temperature created.

Beatrice's stopped to take a closer look at a waxy yellow lily, when she felt a flutter. 'There's a butterfly on my shoulder. Have you ever seen such a beautiful creature?' Its wings were blue and looked like like satin and the movement was languid. She caught it in her hands. 'George, it's not like the butterflies at home, they fly too fast.' George pointed out others that had settled nearby. Soon an hour had passed as they searched for ever more unusual species.

The air felt cool as they emerged from the butterfly house and walked towards the Petit Palais. 'This is a real palace,' Beatrice remarked.

In white stone, the arched entrance was flanked with a colonnaded façade. On either end slate domes were inset with golden statues. Elegant gas lamps along its length, when lit at night, would cause the building to shimmer. George escorted the girls up the wide steps and through to the show rooms where he pointed out the ancient artefacts, mediaeval objects and rare manuscripts. Beatrice feigned interest until they came to the Egyptian treasures where she had no need to disguise her amazement and delight.

'The two palaces will stay when the Exposition is taken down in November. They are permanent buildings,' George said as they left the Petit Palais and began to walk towards the Pont Alexandre Trois.

'You mean all the buildings will go?' Beatrice asked. Just as she had never envisaged that the Exposition could be larger than a village she could not imagine how it could all disappear.

'Everything except the Eiffel Tower, of course, and the Champs de Mars which will return to being a park. The Pont Alexandre Trois was created especially for the occasion.'

They strolled over the bridge, its single span rose only six metres above the Seine so that no view would be impeded. The stone walls of the bridge gleamed white and the coloured glass lamps in the Art Nouveau style created a cheerful contrast. The parapet of the walls housed bronze and marble statues.

'Every ornament on the bridge is unique because each one is made by a different artist. They only just completed it in time, and it was created to celebrate the friendship between France and Russia.'

Beatrice hoped that George would offer to accompany them again the next day. She wanted to see entertainments which she suspected that her father would not think were appropriate for young ladies. In the foyer of their hotel before they parted company George said, 'I have a surprise in store for you tomorrow. Can you be ready for ten o'clock?'

Flo, Beatrice noticed, did not hesitate.

'Then I'll call for you here. If the weather is at all 'mauvais' be sure to wear a warm coat.'

Raising his hat, he strode towards the door which was immediately opened for him by an attentive commissaire. The girls entered the lift and mounted to their room in silence, but once they had closed the door, flung off their coats and removed their hats they looked at each other, elated by their day.

Beatrice impulsively wrapped her arms around her sister. 'Oh, Flo, wasn't that the best day in your life? Isn't Paris the most exciting place on the earth?'

'One of the best. George is certainly a very

considerate and amusing host.' Beatrice said nothing, because she thought Flo was being stuffy and too much like a grown-up.

The next morning George called for Flo and Beatrice in the hall of the Hotel. They left their father reading the paper, and followed George who hailed a cab and instructed the driver to take them to the river.

'We are going on a bateau mouche,' he told them. 'Don't tell her, Flo, she'll find out soon enough.'

They joined a queue of people of varying nationalities waiting to go on the excursion boats. Moored alongside the embankment the rigging of the tall ships flapped noisily as the wake from the bateaux mouches rocked them back and forth.

'There's no better way to see the Exhibition and some of Paris itself than by travelling along the Seine. You cannot leave thinking that the Exposition is synonymous with Paris because next time you come it won't be here, and you will have missed seeing Notre-Dame and Montmartre and the Louvre, which are some of the most famous sights in the city.'

'Do they have any real palaces?' Beatrice asked. She had been disappointed that the palaces that they had seen had been museums.

'There's been no royal family in France for years and they did not have a palace as we would think of one. The Palais Royal was built for a Cardinal and is now a state building. To see a real palace we would have to go out to Versailles.'

Sitting under the canopy on their bateau mouche they floated past buildings that had been especially constructed along the edge of the river, mosques with onion-shaped domes, churches whose exteriors were adorned with gold leaf and pink stone temples. The boat circled the Ile de la cité and on their return they saw, on the opposite bank, an Elizabethan gabled house juxtaposed to a wooden Norwegian chalet and, beside a Moor's homestead, an Arab tent.

'I think luncheon in the Moroccan café and then on to the food hall,' George proposed as they alighted. Flo and Beatrice were happy to comply, and Beatrice was prepared to forgo the wild west and Moulin rouge which George said were not suitable for young ladies.

'Are you on holiday or is this a business trip?' Flo asked George as they sat in their exotic surroundings.

'A bit of both I suppose, and more of one than the other. Father takes care of most of the business and I am meant to be learning the ropes, but I'm pretty much free to do what I like.'

'So what do you do?' She persisted.

'I travel quite a lot, sometimes seeing other colleagues for my father. There's the social round in London which keeps me busy. In the summer months we entertain at our family house by the Thames.'

Beatrice thought this a perfect life, and as Flo fell silent, she had a chance to ask questions of her own.

'Slow down, little chatterbox,' George said eventually, 'it's time to wake Flo from her daydream and continue our expedition.'

'Will you take us somewhere tomorrow?' Beatrice asked when they were delivered back to their hotel that evening.

'I have another trick up my sleeve, so be ready again at ten. Does that suit you?'

On that third day John Eaton and Reginald joined the younger members of their party. Beatrice's enthusiasm had given her father, who found the days long and tiring, renewed energy.

'So this is today's surprise!' George teased Beatrice as they boarded the railroad train, tracks for which had been laid to enable people to travel easily to and from the Exposition. The carriages were raised a foot above the street and each carriage was open to the air and divided into four sets of leather benches. The driver, dressed in a blue jacket with trousers to match, a blue flat-topped peaked hat, white belt, gloves and shoes, looked remarkably clean despite the copious amount of steam and smoke emptying from the engine's funnel. Other attendants, similarly dressed, ensured that everyone was safely on board before the whistle was blown for them to depart. The train went at a steady speed and since there were no doors or windows they had a good view of all the activities in the streets through which they passed. Beatrice noted the fashionable clothes worn by the Parisians, as well as the unusual, the outlandish, and the exotic clothes worn by the visitors. She had one over-riding wish however and decided that George would be her champion. This became more pressing once she discovered that he and his father were leaving for London the next day.

They spent the morning at the gallery of liberal arts. This building was surrounded by a lake where fountains tossed spray into the air sprinkling spectators with a spray of water. The group continued on to the giant globe for luncheon. During the meal their table was close to that of a French family, and John, George, and Flo struck up an animated conversation.

Hoping the others were engrossed in their exchange Beatrice said to her father. 'Can we climb the Eiffel Tower, only to the first stage, if you are tired.'

'Dis donc, que la petite est vive!' George remarked to his father.

Beatrice smiled up at George. 'What are you saying?'

'I said you were vivacious, 'vif' or 'vive' for a girl. I'll take you up the tower if you wish, while the others rest. Come on.'

It took longer than expected because there were over a thousand steps. Beatrice felt giddy when they emerged on to the balcony which surrounded the final pillar of the tower. They leant on the balustrade from where the whole of Paris was visible below them.

'I can see the lights of this tower from my bedroom. It must look wonderful at night, with the lamps lit in the walkways and on the buildings, and with all those bulbs alight on the Pavilion d'électricité'

'Électricité!' George repeated. 'That's good. It is a marvellous sight. You should definitely see it.'

A chill wind was rising and Beatrice lifted a hand from the parapet to grasp her hat. She looked up at George. 'But father would never come out at night.' She held her gaze.

'Now I see where you're heading. Would you like me to suggest it, Petite Vive?'

Beatrice could hardly contain her happiness. While

they descended the steps Beatrice's felt that she was floating and she squeezed the medallion in her pocket. Her wish had been granted. And then, almost immediately, another thought came to her. She had never had a pet name before, each of her older sisters were graced with one but she had always been cumbersome Beatrice. She would call herself Veeve, and when she arrived home she would announce it to all the family. She would return a changed person.

The exhilarating experience of being abroad at night was the part of the trip that she would always remember. Deprived of the visual impact of the exhibitions the streets had features that were missed during the day. The vibrations of the horses' hooves and the sound of cracking whips were heightened. When her attention was not otherwise distracted Beatrice saw with new eyes the shapes of the gas lamps and the outlines of the buildings. In the Parc du Champs de Mars the Tour Eiffel rose starkly in silhouette. The fountains, their spray caught by a myriad of electric bulbs, sparkled against the dark sky. Beatrice was aware of sandalwood and lemon grass as they passed the Indian pavilion and of musky incense from the Arabian pavilion. Musicians played, strange and exotic, the haunting tones issuing from one pavilion dying away to be replaced by the lyrical notes from another as they wended their way along the thoroughfares. It was an enchanted land.

The following day, the Heffords, now on their own, set off to visit the Pavilion de la Belle Epoque which was dedicated to exhibiting the most recent Parisian fashions and was a showcase for costumes from around the world.

'I'm meeting some colleagues today,' Reginald said. 'You'll be safe here and I'll collect you later.'

This was no hardship they were presented with the most recent fashions for the new millennium. Flo collected catalogues for Lil and leaflets with sketches from well-known couturiers. They looked at wedding gowns. 'None of these would suit you, Flo', Beatrice announced, 'but when I get married I'll come to Paris for my wedding trousseau because to be chic, Parisian designs are the most fashionable.'

That night, Beatrice asked Flo, 'Do you want to leave us and marry Tom?'

'I don't want to leave you but I do want to be with Tom, and he wants to be with me,' Flo said simply.

Beatrice had not considered the marriage from Tom's point of view. Her only experience was Bett's marriage to Brindsley-Smith and it was not a very satisfactory model and besides, Bett was still living at home whereas Flo was to leave. Their family was to lose a figure as important to her as their mother, the sister to whom she felt the closest. Beatrice knew that, one by one, they would marry but when she thought of Tom, whom they all knew and loved, she could understand that he would be as eager for the marriage as Flo.

Flo, Beatrice and their Father had a rapturous welcome from the family. Reginald gave each of his daughters a small parcel and then he disappeared to his study to regale Eleanor with his adventures. Ruth, Elsie and little Sheilagh gathered round Flo while Lil and Bett stood by. Maisie stood alone waiting hesitantly for

Beatrice to notice her. Beatrice was puzzled by this for a moment and then, full of remorse, began to fiddle with the medallion in her pocket as she remembered her promise. She went over to Maisie, put her hands on her shoulders and spoke clearly to enable her to lip read.

'Maisie. I'm so sorry,' she said, 'I didn't buy you a model of the Eiffel Tower.' She rushed on before Maisie could react. 'But I have brought you something special, it's in my overnight case.'

Maisie's face brightened with expectation and she followed Beatrice up the stairs, her clumsy feet contrasted with her older sister's mercurial ascent.

'Do not look.' Beatrice turned Maisie so that she faced the window then she delved into her case to find the small box with the velvet cushion. She took the medallion from her pocket, placed it on the cushion and closed the lid. She went across to Maisie and presented it to her.

'There will not be any more of these made for a hundred years,' she said impressively. 'You are the only one in the family who has a millennium medallion.' Maisie's eyes shone.

'There is something else important that I need to tell you. From now onwards I am going to be called 'Veeve.' Beatrice is too long and cannot be shortened because of Betts. Can you say Veeve?'

'Viv,' Maisie attempted.

'No, Veeve, it's French.'

This time Maisie managed.

'It means vivacious,' she added, not caring if Maisie could hear.

With this action Veeve justified her lack of forethought. She had given Maisie a better present than a model which anyone could buy. Perhaps she had been selfish not to have given her sister a passing thought when she had been away, but the sacrifice of her medallion amply made up for her sin of omission.

Chapter Six

On the Sunday before Easter, the family gathered outside the church and then followed one another down the aisle into the pews that they were beginning to adopt as their own. Reginald and Eleanor with the three youngest girls sat in one pew, with Flo and Tom, while Lil, Bett and Veeve were seated behind them. This was no ordinary Sunday because the attention of the congregation would be focused on their family, and more particularly, Flo.

How curious was the wording, Veeve thought, as she anticipated the solemn exhortation that she had heard on previous occasions but with no sense of their significance. 'I publish the banns of marriage'. It was almost as if the Vicar was attempting to prevent the marriage. Perhaps it was a test of their commitment. Veeve saw Flo blush and wondered if she was deterred in her resolve. Then she remembered Tom, as she had seen him on the day that he and Flo went for instruction from the Vicar. He showed no signs of doubt and their happiness had proved contagious.

Veeve had created an unpleasant scene which she now regretted, when her mother had suggested that she be a bridesmaid. It was not the dress that she objected to, although nothing would induce her to wear such childish clothes, it was that she had upset Flo and the realisation that she wanted her sister's wedding day to be perfect. Since then her attitude had changed and she wished with all her heart that Flo would have a trouble-free wedding and she vowed she would cause no more strife.

While she was singing the final hymn, one well known to her, Veeve looked around. The solid grey columns supporting the wooden arches of the domed roof carried the sound of the organ to all corners of the church. The sun slanted through the clear leaded windows of the Lady Chapel and lit up the colours of the stained glass windows in the chancel. The organist pulled out extra stops and added a descant to enrich the accompaniment of the last verse. The sidesmen in pairs placed the collection bags on the wooden plate held by the assistant curate, the tall wax candles on the altar table were snuffed out by a choir boy, and the rituals of matins drew to a close. This church would be a perfect setting for Flo's great day. Their time away together had cemented their friendship, and regardless of whomever Veeve pitted herself against in the weeks to come, Flo was her ally forever.

Everyone noticed the change in Veeve. Her mother was the first. When the fracas over the bridesmaids had been resolved, she broached the subject of Veeve's outfit for the wedding. Eleanor advised Veeve to wear a brown velvet jacket over a satin skirt with touches of yellow and orange and choose a hat by picking out one of the colours, and Veeve had acquiesced without a murmur. Without needing much self-restraint, Veeve was reconciled to Flo being the centre of attention and accepted that she had nothing to gain by usurping that place. She could foresee a time when she would need all her powers of persuasion to obtain what she wanted, although she was not yet certain what that might be, and until such a time she would be biddable.

Elsie was bemused by the change in Veeve when they returned to school for the summer term. When she commented on it to Ruth and Maisie, they shrugged. 'Veeve is always unpredictable. She usually ignores us because we're the youngest and our opinions don't count. Nothing's changed.'

However, Elsie persisted. Veeve used to complain to Elsie about their uniform as they dressed in the morning. They wore shapeless slips over combinations and thick black stockings. Their short-sleeved uniforms were made of green serge which was pleated above and below the waist and held by a wide belt. This, the only attempt at femininity, was then lost by the addition of a white sailor's collar. The overall austerity was only broken by large buttons on the belt and skirt and a white bow at the neck. Veeve's particular grouse was that even the senior pupils wore their skirts short, when on every other occasion she had now progressed to the longer length which was the prerogative of her older sisters.

As for their school, Elsie noticed that Veeve refrained from ridiculing the ornate building that was Wyggeston Girls' School and which her sisters secretly admired. In contrast to their almost military uniform, their school was flamboyantly Romanesque with gables, a crenulated roof, a dramatic spire and long sash windows with multiple panes of glass. The interior matched the exterior in elegance, with the rooms panelled in wood and the ceilings surrounded with heavy cornices.

'Veeve appears to have settled down.' Reginald remarked to Eleanor one evening.

'You can't take Veeve at face value. If she's quiet then you can be sure it's for a reason.'

Veeve was anything but settled. Paris had opened her eyes to possibilities beyond their provincial town. It had at the same time awoken a romantic trait and all her energies were concentrated on helping her mother with preparations for Flo's wedding.

Her first self-appointed task was to ensure that the bridesmaids had their hair coiffured in a style that reflected Flo's. She watched carefully as the dresser arranged Flo's hair allowing for her tiara and veil, and then compelled Ruth to sit for a whole afternoon while she attempted to create a similar style. Ruth, happy to read a book, sat contentedly while her long silky brown hair, which shone with hints of russet in the sunlight, was brushed and pinned and curled. Veeve then turned her attention to their shoes, persuading their mother to replace the bridesmaids' leather court shoes with silk slippers such as she had seen in Paris.

The task that required a herculean effort on Veeve's part was drilling Maisie how to walk up the aisle behind Flo. There was the risk that she would tug on the train or trip over it. The original suggestion that Ruth should take her place was reasonable, but the youngest was the traditional carrier of the train, and Maisie had assumed that she would carry Flo's. Veeve made Maisie practice walking slowly, which she was unable to do without losing her balance. Veeve walked in front of her, behind her, made her close her eyes, walk with no shoes, walk with her arms outstretched, until she was confident that, although she would not be graceful, she would not disgrace herself.

'Flo, has Tom seen your dress?' Veeve asked innocently. Tom had visited so often in the previous weeks that it was not such a strange question.

'Tom has not seen anything. It is all a surprise for him. The bridesmaids, the church decorations and the wedding breakfast. Just as the house he's preparing will be a surprise for me.'

'Do you know where you will live?'

'We've found a house but it needed renovating and Tom has been overseeing it. He says that his workmates have helped and that it should be ready in time.'

Here was an aspect of a wedding that was new to Veeve. There had been no similar air of expectation during Bett's sorry engagement. Bett's marriage had been conducted so hastily that there had not even been a display of presents most of which were still in their boxes. Eleanor had re-arranged her writing room so that, as presents arrived for Flo and Tom, they could be laid out for all to see. The girls would come in after school and vie with one another to spot the new additions, each with their neatly displayed labels.

With the preparations completed there was a lull on

the eve of her wedding and Flo decided to spend the time with her sisters. Elsie, Ruth and Maisie were in their night gowns too excited to sleep.

'Flo,' Elsie saw her first, 'have you come to say goodbye?'

'I'm not going very far,' Flo said, making herself comfortable on Ruth's bed. Elsie clambered up beside her, Flo put an arm around each of them and beckoned to Maisie, who rested her head on Flo's lap. 'You'll come and visit me, and Tom and I can take you on picnics like we did before.'

'Can we sleep at your house?' Elsie asked.

'If Tom allows it, I'll have to make sure that we have enough beds.'

'I'll miss you,' Elsie said.

'I'll miss you too, but you don't need me now. You're quite grown up.' Elsie beamed and with a contented sigh relaxed into Flo's comforting body.

Flo struggled momentarily to find something encouraging to say to the two youngest, who at eleven and nine were still children.

'Maisie, you need to practise your elocution. Elsie and Ruth will help. You will won't you?' Maisie's deafness impacted on her speech which was distorted. When she spoke, the words were delivered monotone and staccato. Maisie nodded sleepily and then rested her head again.

'Ruth, she does not always grasp what the teacher says and often she does the wrong homework. You could help Maisie in the evenings, you are doing so well at school.' She felt that she should have more to say to

Ruth who could be overlooked. At times Ruth injected an observation or comment into a conversation which reminded those around her not to underestimate her intelligence, but she was also moody. Perhaps she was preoccupied with her own thoughts and reluctant to join in idle chatter, but anyone who took the effort to be closer acquainted with her was well rewarded. Once she trusted you the smiles appeared readily.

'One day you will be such a help to Father. He likes us to be good with figures and he is very pleased with your school reports.' Flo saw that she was winning through Ruth's protective shield. 'You are going to look beautiful tomorrow. You all are. Is everything ready?'

The girls, remembering the reason for their recent high spirits, soon regained them and the magic of the moment's intimacy was dissipated. Flo saw this as a cue to leave and kissed each one in turn.

Flo opened Veeve's door to see her sitting on her bed, arms clasped around her knees, eyes bright and mischievous. Flo was grateful that, in contrast with her younger sisters' view of her parting, Veeve would not make her feel melancholy.

'It's going to be so romantic,' Veeve declared. 'You'll come down the aisle with Father, all mysterious with your veil over your face, and when Tom sees you he will swoon!' She laughed infectiously and Flo clapped her hands with delight. Veeve moved rapidly to kneel on the edge of her bed. 'When Tom has recovered, we will all have to endure that terrifying moment.'

She mimed the Vicar holding his prayer book and intoned. 'If any of you have just cause or impediment,' she broke off and looked quizzically at Flo. 'What is a just impediment, everyone says that Maisie's speech is an impediment, does that mean she is barred from being married?' Veeve stretched her legs and slid off the bed. 'When that awful silence has ended, we can all relax and enjoy the rest of the wedding service. I'm glad that I'm not a bridesmaid. I can watch everything and not worry that I'll make a fool of myself, by giving you your flowers at the wrong time, or wanting to rub my nose.' Veeve was unconvincing, Flo was sure that under no circumstances would Veeve fail to be in control.

Flo, who had been laughing along with Veeve, now felt a twinge of sadness. She would miss this incorrigible sister of hers. Veeve caught something of the change in Flo, embraced her, and then detached herself, misty eyed. 'It will be wonderful tomorrow,' Veeve said as she released her.

Flo and Bett had drifted apart in the last few months. Bett was often occupied with Sheilagh, who looked on Bett as her own mother, as if she sensed that she was to be the constant figure in her life. Bett would sail to Quebec and Flo had noticed that she had become both more mature and more distant, her married state, in reality only in name, causing a natural barrier. Flo wondered if she would feel different, or if her sisters would view her differently, once she had crossed that boundary. With these thoughts she was hesitant about saying goodbye to Bett. This time it was a genuine farewell because there would be only a few more occasions before Bett departed.

'Am I disturbing you?'

Bett was still dressed and was writing a letter at her desk. 'Not a bit. You'll be excited about tomorrow.'

'Weren't you, excited I mean, before your wedding?'

'More nervous than excited. You know Tom so well while I...' she bent her head and left the sentence unfinished. Flo sat on the bed and waited, but Bett did not continue.

'But it was all right wasn't it?' Flo had never before raised this subject with Bett. 'And your honeymoon?' She held Bett's eyes.

'Everything was fine. Are you having one?'

'Tom is taking a week's holiday and we'll spend it in our new house. That is honeymoon enough for me. What about yours?'

'Going to London was very interesting,' Bett said, 'but after dinner I was so tired that he kindly said I was to go to bed and not worry about him as he would go to his Club. He showed me all the sights the next day. We saw Buckingham Palace, and Big Ben, and other places, and I was introduced to his relatives at luncheon but I had one of my spells that evening and so he went to his club again. The next day we came home because he had to prepare for departing from Liverpool on the boat.'

Flo was anxious. 'You will like to go to Canada, won't you?'

'When I have Sheilagh with me I find that I enjoy almost everything. I'm sure I shall like Canada. I can't stay here at home for ever.' The last remark was spoken wistfully, but Flo, for whom the idea of a home of her own was her highest aspiration, chose to ignore it. 'You will have a very happy wedding, everything will be perfect.'

The next morning the younger girls were the first to leave for the church. Upstairs Flo and her mother spent a few minutes together while Lil fetched the wedding dress from the cupboard where it had been airing. Lil watched Eleanor lift the dress carefully over Flo's head and then move to fasten the hooks and eyes that were carefully concealed down the length of the back. They stood on either side of Flo to look at her in the long mirror. Her dress was made of cream satin with a bodice of Brussels lace. Folds of fine tulle formed bell-shaped sleeves. The skirt and bustle were also overlaid with tulle which increased in layers to create a glorious train, the edge of which was embroidered with heavy satin stitches.

Flo's hair was drawn up from her face and she wore a simple pearl necklace with matching earings. Eleanor fitted the veil carefully over the crown of her tiara.

'My Flo!' Eleanor said, too emotional to say more.

'We must go now, Mother,' Lil urged, 'Father will be waiting.'

After the church ceremony, and despite the short distance, Reginald arranged for carriages to transport not only the bride and groom, but all members of his family, to the wedding breakfast. He wondered whether any of those whom they passed in the streets were envious of his good fortune, and he felt himself blessed as the horses trotted homeward in the warm spring air.

It was Elsie who finally voiced what the family was feeling some weeks after Flo's wedding. They were sitting at the dining-room table and conversation was desultory. 'It has not been the same since Flo left. I miss her and I want to see her.'

Maisie heard Flo's name and tears began to run down her cheeks.

'Now, Maisie,' Reginald spoke more clearly than he might have ordinarily, 'none of that. How about I arrange a visit for you this Sunday? Let me see what I can do.' He turned to his wife. 'Eleanor, I can't think that Flo can manage everyone in one visit. She will want to see you and I can arrange for the others to go quite soon. I'm sorry, girls.'

Elsie persisted, 'Does this mean that I can't go?'

Reginald weighed up the options. The older girls would have to contain their disappointment but it seemed unkind, since Elsie had introduced the subject, to deny her a place. 'Your mother, you, Ruth and Maisie. How's that?' Reginald was rewarded with happy smiles.

Since Flo had left, the family had drifted into a dull acceptance. Each member had adjusted in their own way but none felt that there had been any gains from her departure, quite the contrary. To compound it there were no welcome diversions to the daily tasks which the preparations for the wedding had provided.

Reginald missed Flo on his visits to the mill and although he saw her on her breaks from her schoolroom, these short encounters were no compensation for her companionship on their journeys.

Eleanor had been irritable. Now that Flo was no longer sharing her maternal duties she had presumed that Lil would adopt her older sister's role. Lil felt awkward and was uninterested in the younger ones' schooling and squabbles. She had always had an ambivalent relationship with her mother.

Eleanor observed Bett's devotion to Sheilagh, and was secretly relieved that this gave her daughter a worthwhile occupation. Bett was probably the least affected by Flo's absence, since she had created her own life with the little girl within the family, yet without disrupting the smooth running of the household.

Veeve was not given to introspection and countered the change by transferring her affection to Ruth. The shift was subtle but she discovered in Ruth an admirer of her wit and sense of humour, while also finding someone who was not averse to calling a halt if she over-stepped the mark. Only Flo had commanded an equivalent control over Veeve.

While each of the older girls regretted that a chance to see Flo was not yet permitted by their father, he made a suggestion that they understood was a form of consolation.

'I understand that there is a Fair in Abbey Park for the Whitsun holiday. I believe it is worth attending and we should take advantage of the warmer weather to enjoy ourselves.' Reginald was pleased that he had found a way to cheer a household that had been dreary since the wedding, and even he looked forward to the outing.

The following Sunday one carriage arrived to transport Eleanor and her charges to Shepshed, and another to convey Reginald and the older girls to the park. It had been a considerably more animated group that had sat round the breakfast table that morning, and the usual groans that accompanied Eleanor's instructions for dressing for church were very much more muted in the light of the afternoon's promised expeditions. Elsie was not sure that the older ones had not the best of the bargain but her loyalty to Flo restrained her from saying so.

It did not take more than ten minutes to reach Abbey Park, and they heard the music from the bandstand even before they joined the crush of carriages and pedestrians around the entrance gate. The grassy stretches were carpeted with late daffodils and covered with petals from the cherry trees, and it appeared as if every person in Leicester was there. Lil was excited by the chance to be out and about and Veeve, although nothing compared in her mind to Paris, had not until this occasion felt the pleasant anticipation of seeing familiar faces. Bett, for once without Sheilagh, attached herself to Veeve.

A large area of the park was filled with stalls and amusements for children. Reginald and his daughters wandered along the paths to watch the participants at the coconut shies, skittles, shove halfpenny stalls, and the Punch and Judy Show. A path curved gently towards the river, tall trees obscured much of the water but an attractive arched bridge spanned a tributary to give access to the opposite bank. Veeve and Bett walked ahead and stopped in the centre of the bridge to watch the water flowing lazily beneath them. Some children with fishing rods were practising their casting under the tutelage of an elderly fisherman who was sitting on a stool with a container of worms beside him. He was attaching a worm on to a rod held by an impatient boy.

The girls watched a boat with two boys at the oars, pass under the bridge and join other boats whose occupants, with varying degrees of success, were manoeuvring into the centre of the river.

Veeve pointed out a small landing stage. Tied alongside were several rowing boats and a set of steps leading from the wooden platform to the water's edge. Wishing to join the rowers, she turned to look for her father and saw that he and Lil were approaching in the company of a stranger. Bett informed her that the man with them was Mitchell Devenick.

Lil made the introductions and Veeve asked Mitchell, 'Are your family here?'

'They're watching the Punch and Judy Show. I thought I'd come along to see if there were other amusements. The older ones are getting restless and I was going to enquire about hiring a boat.'

Veeve turned towards her father with a look that he knew well. 'We could go over and ask about hiring,' suggested Reginald, 'and then find Mitchell's family.' He enjoyed Devenick senior's company, and it would take little to persuade him to hand his daughters over to Mitchell, if he could enjoy some convivial conversation with his friend.

Veeve and Bett quickened their steps and hurried ahead towards the landing stage. They arrived at the platform well ahead of the rest and then had to wait, frustrated at the pace at which Flo, Mitchell and their father were walking. The boatman was engaged with two young people who were in so much haste to attempt what was obviously their first experience of rowing, that they paid scant attention to his instructions. Eventually the boatman waved them away so as not to lose his next customers.

'I'm sorry to keep you waiting, Sir. The young! They will have to find out the hard way, but if one of those oars jumps its rowlocks and lands in the water that young whipper-snapper is going to get very wet. What can I do for you?'

'We are looking for boats for my daughters and my friend's family, are they available?'

'It's first come, first served. If you are here and a boat is returned then it's yours. Sixpence a time.'

Reginald relayed the information but when he suggested that they all went in search of Mitchell's family, Veeve protested.

'Father, we don't all need to go. You know I can row, could you not leave Bett and me here while you go along. There's no way we can get lost.' She looked rather disparagingly at the river.

'Water is always water.' Reginald wondered if any of his warnings ever made the slightest difference to Veeve, but he had faith in Bett and trusted that Veeve would not put her at risk. 'You have a point,' he relented, 'I'll ask the boatman to give you the next that's available, and here's a sixpence.'

Neither Bett nor Veeve caused the boat to move more than a fraction as they stepped in. Bett sat on the bench facing forward, Veeve set the oars and began to row, barely creating a ripple.

Mitchell followed the path that took them back up the sloping bank, around a shrubbery and from there they could see quite a gathering of people absorbed in a show. 'There they are,' Mitchell waved, and one of his sisters alerted the rest of the family, who peeled off from the crowd.

'Mitchell, you should have seen the show!' His sister reproached him and then looked shyly at Lil. Mitchell made the introductions and explained that he had been inquiring about boats.

'You'll find them across the bridge, run ahead if you like.'

The older members walked at a more leisurely pace. Lil walked with Mitchell and his mother, while Reginald and Mr Devenick lagged behind.

'Are you missing your sister?' Mitchell asked.

'I am, but I am kept from moping because I now have to do many of Flo's duties. The difference is that I only have to look after four, where Flo had six of us.'

Mrs Devenick detected a touch of disenchantment. 'Is it good for you to be in the house all day? A girl needs other interests.'

'I know, but that is how it has always been.'

Mitchell remembered that Lil had mentioned drawing as a hobby of hers.

'I have designed some costumes which Father has taken to the office and they have used them on occasion.'

'Do you have any lessons?' Mrs Devenick asked.

'Lessons? I only had lessons when I was at school.'

'Did you know that an art college has recently opened in Leicester?'

They were interrupted by Michael, who ran up to his

older brother to complain. 'Clemmy wants me to go in a boat with her but when she rows but she's so slow. Won't you hurry? I want to be in your boat.'

They were soon surrounded by Mitchell's sisters, all of whom had their own ideas as to who should go in which boat. When they reached the landing stage a decision had to be made.

'Can I suggest,' said Lil, and the novelty of an unfamiliar voice had a gratifying effect on the childish rabble, 'that I take one boat with two of you and your brother takes the other?'

'We'll give them a race,' she said hoping to reassure them, 'let's see who wins.'

'We're going to win,' piped Michael. Mitchell glanced at the boatman who fortunately was distracted and then shot Michael a look which he hoped he would interpret as an assent combined with secrecy. Michael grinned and lowered his voice, 'Well, are we?'

Mitchell waited until they had been rowing for some time before he declared. 'If they want to challenge us, we're ready.'

Lil had become better acquainted with her passengers and they were prepared to pit their new friend's skills against those of their brother. 'We're ready.'

'I'll give you a fair start, we'll paddle upstream and then it will be the first to the bridge.' Lil realised that their chances were even since they were rowing with the flow of the river, but there was the risk of a disappointed Michael. She was glad that his brother would be dealing with the inevitable scene.

When Lil won, Michael was mollified by another challenge, this time against the current. Mitchell's boat reached the finish and by then Veeve and Bett had spotted them and all three boats chased each other as they returned to the landing stage.

'Lemonade and then home,' Mrs Devenick welcomed them and included both families in her invitation.

'Can we do that again?' asked Michael.

'Another day. Perhaps next Sunday?' Mitchell answered him but he was looking towards Lil as he spoke.

Chapter Seven

The proposed outing was temporarily forgotten when, a few days later, Bett received three large embossed tickets for the 'SS Haverford' which was sailing on the White Star Line from Liverpool.

'When are you leaving?' Eleanor asked in an unsteady voice.

'Ten days, Mother,' Bett answered, as if stunned, and it was difficult for Eleanor not to compare Bett's reaction, which seemed to be one of disbelief, with Flo's calm certitude towards married life with Tom. Bett's response was not one of a bride anxious to join her bridegroom. She felt unequal to the task of preparing her daughter for so major a journey.

'Wait until your father gets back, he will deal with

arrangements for passports and travel, and in the meantime you had better start sorting your wardrobe. You will need trunks for yourself, Sheilagh and the nursemaid. Ask Lil to help you.'

'What did he say in his last letter?' Lil enquired when she and Bett were together.

'He said that he had found us a house and would soon be sending for me.'

'You never said,' Lil reproached her.

'Soon could have meant anytime,' Bett countered, 'shall we do Sheilagh's trunk first? We can decide what toys she's grown out of and which clothes to take.'

'Quebec is warm at this time of the year, and you will have plenty of time to purchase winter clothes for her once you have settled in. We must remember to keep some toys for Sheilagh while on board ship.'

'There is a nursery. I almost forgot, we must tell Tilly, she will be excited.'

The irony that it was Bett, her least adventurous and least equipped sister, who was to embark on an overseas voyage was not lost on Lil. Canada was not a foreign country in the way that China or India were foreign, but for Bett the undertaking was momentous. Lil envied her sister the experience of travel but when she thought of Brindsley-Smith, she shuddered.

'How many days will you be on board?'

'About a week,' Bett answered. 'How do you think we will travel to Liverpool? Will Mother come?'

'Mother will see you off, and so will that dragon Mrs Brindsley-Smith,' Lil warned, teasing her.

'She won't will she? Perhaps we need not tell her.'

'She may be unfeeling towards Sheilagh but she is her grandmother and she will be saying goodbye for quite a while.'

'Would you come too? I don't think I can face her on my own.'

Lil had every intention of accompanying Bett, partly from selfish motives because she could not resist an adventure. When Reginald was appraised of the imminence of Bett's departure he had plenty of good advice although he had never travelled abroad on a liner himself. They would travel by train to Liverpool four days prior to departure, not only to ensure that Bett was not fatigued by the journey, but because Reginald could see no reason not to make the most of the trip. He had heard that Liverpool, that great hub of the shipping world and of the Empire, was a fine city.

Mrs Brindsley-Smith sent a telegram to say that they would be staying at the Central Hotel and that she and her husband would like to entertain the Heffords to dinner the night before the ship sailed.

Lil was thrilled by the journey to Liverpool with the changing landscapes, encounters with fellow passengers and the novelty of a new city, but her impulse to explore was tempered by her concern for Bett, knowing that she did not have the stamina for sightseeing.

On their last night together, at the dinner at the Central Hotel, Lil undertook to field questions from Mrs Brindsley-Smith and positioned Bett beside her husband who, as a man with an overbearing wife, was adept at recognising others needing to seek refuge. A fortunate encounter helped to relieve the inevitable tension on the evening before they parted. The Brindsley-Smith's discovered a family with whom they had a tenuous connection. The mother was travelling to Quebec to join her husband; she had made the voyage several times she told Eleanor, and reassured her that she would keep an unobtrusive eye on Bett.

The massive hulk of the TTS Haverford rose above the docks. Her two funnels, painted white with broad red rims dominating the upper decks were flanked on either side by masts, and rigging and rows of lifeboats were lashed to the stern. The gangway, which had been attached until the final few minutes to allow visitors to disembark, was removed and as the decks filled with passengers anxious to keep their relatives in sight as the ship prepared get under way, the pier was crowded with those who were waving farewell. Lil thought that she could identify Bett but she could not be sure.

Eventually the anchors were hauled up beside the prow. Lil stood with her parents hemmed in by the crowd and watched the deck hands as they scurried to perform their tasks and the dockworkers as they paid out the ropes, until the ship was drawn away from its berthing by a tug. Silently the majestic ship slid away from the harbour and gradually, under her own steam, disappeared into the distance leaving only lines of wake water on the surface of the Mersey river.

The Heffords had been in Leicester almost a year. Lil was lonely. Veeve was still inscrutably compliant, Elsie had joined her at the senior school, and Ruth and Maisie no longer needed an older sister to supervise them. Mrs Devenick's suggestion that Lil take some art classes seemed to offer her a solution, and she made the decision to speak to her father.

Reginald cleared the pile of papers off his desk, rested one elbow on the table and picked up a pen which he rolled over his fingers with his thumb. 'What can I do for you?' He was curious and a little amused at Lil's request for an interview.

'I need something to do other than help Mother. I'm not like Flo and good with children. I don't want to teach.'

'Have you anything in mind?'

'Mrs Devenick says that there is an art college in Leicester.'

'Mrs Devenick, you say?' He remembered that she had mentioned it, and even then had suspected that she had an ulterior motive.

Lil hesitated, wondering if the information would help or hinder her case.

'Mrs Devenick is a very astute lady. I am embarrassed that I never thought of it myself but somehow I imagined, pardon me my dear, that you would be married by now. I can see that you need to be kept busy. You don't fancy your mother's church work and so on?'

Lil shook her head and smiled at him now that she could see that he was not against the idea.

'Have you any new sketches? I have not seen your drawings for some time.'

'It's been the summer, Father, remember? Visits and outings and relatives. I can show you a few recent sketches.' Lil indicated that she would need to go to her mother's writing room.

'Ask your mother to come back here with you. We need to see what she has to say.'

Eleanor and Lil returned and stood on either side of Reginald as he looked at her work.

'Quite nice costumes,' he said provokingly.

Lil exploded with indignation, 'Father, don't tease. Are they any good?'

'I do not know, Lil. They seem fair enough to me and one or two of your ideas have already been used. You'll have to do some houses and landscapes and the like, because the college will want to see what else you can do.'

Reginald went along with Lil to enrol at the college and they discovered that there were courses taking place on four mornings. There were no requirements except for a small fee. Lil was delighted and her days sped by, and the evenings too, as she drew, sketched and painted while her sisters did their homework.

'I wish I had homework like yours,' Elsie grumbled.

'I wish I had no homework at all,' Veeve said, and grinned.

Maisie did not hear and Ruth, who was not averse to homework, did not contribute,

'Ruth, how can you be so stuffy?' Veeve riled, 'Where is all this studying going to get you? Do you need mathematics for household accounts and grocery bills, and who can enjoy the books we read for literature?'

'You're not meant to enjoy them,' retorted Ruth, 'they are to improve your mind.'

'Which needs a lot of improving,' quipped Lil.

'If you intend to travel then at least languages are worth it,' Elsie attempted to pacify Veeve, who was preparing to defend any stance that argued against schooling.

'That should be a good enough incentive,' Ruth confirmed. 'So why don't you put some work in now?'

'You are far too sensible. I can never get around to something until it is necessary - after all it might be a wasted effort,' Veeve retorted.

'But you've nothing else to do at school.'

'Ruth, you always have an answer and you are right, but it is all such a confounded bore.'

'I bet you wished you could speak French when you were in Paris.' Lil still felt a touch of jealousy when she remembered Veeve's trip.

'There's no need to be spiteful. In fact we hardly needed French because all the people we met spoke English.'

'Like George Eaton,' Maisie contributed. She had started to listen to the conversation once she realised that it was more than usually interesting.

'George Eaton, I'll have you know, Maisie, spoke perfect French.'

'I still wish that all I had to do was to draw,' Elsie returned to the original topic. There was a temporary truce.

Veeve broke the silence. 'Do you know, I even miss that scrap of a thing, Sheilagh.' It was true, Sheilagh had been an excuse to visit the swings in the park, feed the ducks under the bridge or take a walk down the street.

'It's all gone very flat.'

'Well, that will change,' Lil promised, 'Aunt Helen is coming to stay.'

Aunt Helen's arrival was accompanied by a frisson of excitement which affected every member of the Hefford family. Reginald enjoyed his sister's visits, which were prolonged but infrequent. Aunt Helen did not have his methodical and cautious approach to life but although unorthodox she was not outrageous.

Eleanor was in awe of her sister-in-law but enjoyed it when she was encouraged to try things that she was hesitant to do on her own, and Helen was an ally if she sought to prevail upon Reginald to accede to ideas that in usual circumstances he might ignore.

To Lil, Aunt Helen was a favourite whose influence was disruptive but welcome because she was entirely unpredictable. To the others she was a distraction from the dull school routine. She had brought with her several boxes and she invited the younger girls to help her unpack. Bett's room was now free and this became Aunt Helen's bedroom. It was next to the younger girls' room and they immediately felt proprietorial towards her taking it upon themselves to make her feel at home.

'Aunt Helen, shall I fold your shawls on to this shelf?' asked Elsie. The shawls were unlike any that they had seen, originating as they did from overseas destinations.

'Can I try one?' Veeve asked, running her hand over the smooth silk and stroking the gold tassels which hung along the border.

'Of course. Take one each. Maisie, here's one from Morocco, and Elsie, from Egypt.'

'And mine?' Ruth stole a look at herself in the mirror.

'Both yours and Veeve's are from India. You can almost smell the different countries, can't you?'

Aunt Helen's dresses were too old fashioned to attract any comment, but her hats were modish and for that alone were worth trying on.

Aunt Helen sat at her dressing table and enjoyed the spectacle. 'Everyone gather round.' She opened her jewellery box. 'Each of you take two things and put them on. When I'm gone all these will be left to you, I have no one else to give them to.' She said this as a matter of fact, not requiring or receiving any pity, the girls in any event were too busy choosing and rejecting from the collection of rings, bracelets, brooches and necklaces to react with anything other than a giggle.

'How do you have so many?' asked Veeve.

'I had a very generous husband,' Aunt Helen's eyes twinkled, 'and since your father does not need jewellery, I inherited all your grandmother's as well. This antique brooch I inherited from her.' Veeve made a face. 'It is not in fashion now but you'll be surprised how one day it might be all the rage.'

Aunt Helen surveyed her nieces, intrigued how each gravitated to jewellery that seemed to define them. Maisie chose a chunky pendant and a bracelet in beaten silver set with semi-precious stones from North Africa, while Ruth picked a simple pearl necklace and earrings that had been Helen's mother's. Elsie, on the other hand, was fastening a neat little diamond and sapphire brooch to her blouse and on her finger she displayed an exquisite diamond ring.

Veeve spent a few minutes at the mirror fastening a clasp at her throat which she then twisted around her neck to reveal a large ostentatious pendant. She turned with a coquettish flick of her head to show her aunt.

'Veeve, you look beautiful,' Ruth said in admiration. Veeve then wound a sparkling circlet through her hair and, well aware of the effect, gave Aunt Helen a mischievous but triumphant smile.

'Lovely.' Aunt Helen's eyes swept around the room. 'Now put them all back in my trinket box.'

Aunt Helen had been staying a couple of weeks when Reginald looked up from his dinner and remarked to Eleanor. 'The cook's been surpassing himself recently. We've had a very varied menu and these cuts of pork are most unusual.'

'Yes, it's the sauce. Tarragon, I believe,' Eleanor replied nonchalantly and received a wink from Aunt Helen. This did not go unnoticed by Lil who had also been aware that their meals had been uncharacteristically appetising.

The next morning Aunt Helen joined Eleanor who was seated at her desk and deposited herself in the armchair that was conveniently placed so that she could command Eleanor's attention. Satisfied with her success in the culinary department Aunt Helen was ready for her next crusade.

'Eleanor, these girls of yours. They're bored. I'm not saying that they are dull, but there's not enough for them to do.'

'I know,' answered Eleanor resignedly.

'Something needs to be done. With your permission I shall take Lil with me this afternoon and make enquiries on behalf of my nieces.'

'Would you?' said Eleanor hopefully. If Lil went with her they would surely choose sensibly. 'It was so easy when we lived at Shepshed, they were outside most of the day.'

'They were also younger,' she pointed out, reasonably.

She set off with Lil that afternoon and wandered up Gallowtree towards the clock tower. 'We'll start by asking at the library and failing that there are always the gossip shops.'

'What do you mean, Aunt Helen?'

'I mean the drapers, or butchers, or wherever wives meet and chat while waiting in a queue. Besides it's a long time since I was in the town and I want to see what has changed.'

The librarian was so alarmed by Aunt Helen's strident voice that when she answered their enquiry regarding activities, Lil thought the poor woman had lost her voice.

'I believe that Mrs Tyndale gives dancing lessons. Her sister, Miss Jones, has the sweet shop and you could ask there.' She whispered and looked pointedly at the sign beside her requesting all library users to respect the need for silence. 'The sweet shop is in Haymarket by the theatre.'

Miss Jones explained that her sister gave dancing lessons in the parish hall and could be found at home at this time of day. Mrs Tyndale was a talkative lady in her early forties who overwhelmed them with information not only about her dancing classes, but about crafts for girls and fishing and woodcraft for boys.

'We have no boys,' Aunt Helen stopped her, 'and I think we will be content with one activity at a time. Unless you happen to know about lessons in archery?'

Mrs Tyndale twittered and Lil raised her eyebrows until she understood that Aunt Helen could not resist the impulse to shock, however gently. As they passed the theatre Lil drew her aunt's attention to a notice at the bottom of the window. There was an announcement that auditions for the forthcoming Christmas Show were to take place the following week. Anyone over twelve was invited.

'Look at this,' Lil said. 'That would suit Veeve.'

'Or Elsie,' Aunt Helen added. 'We are doing well, Lil, your mother will be pleased with us. Let's celebrate by finding you a new frock and then we shall have some crumpets.'

Laden with three boxes, a frock that could not be bought without matching gloves, hat and jacket, according to Aunt Helen, they entered the busy tea shop.

'Tea for two and a plate of crumpets and cakes,' ordered Aunt Helen and then with no preamble questioned Lil on a subject that she had been puzzling her ever since she arrived. 'Tell me about Bett. Why the hasty marriage and why did she remain at home?'

Lil related the story and when she had completed it, Aunt Helen looked serious.

'Lil, there's to be none of that nonsense with you, do

you understand? Better not to marry at all than to go into a contract that you are not convinced is right for you.' Aunt Helen looked intently at her niece whose eyes did not flinch.

'But how do you know when it's right?' Lil challenged.

'It is surprisingly simple. You know because you don't have to question it. Why, is there someone?'

'There might be,' Lil glanced up at her and smiled.

'I won't pry, but just remember what I said.'

'Thank you,' Lil said, and Aunt Helen was touched.

News of the dancing lessons was greeted with a mixed reception which was only restrained because of an innate respect for their elders, and especially for a visiting aunt. Veeve answered for them, thanking their aunt kindly for her enquiries and affirming that they would all be going to the next classes that to be were to be held. Aunt Helen was mildly surprised at Eleanor's easy acquiescence, and offered to accompany the girls.

'Aunt Helen!' Veeve remonstrated on their return from their lesson. 'You can't make Maisie go again, she simply can't dance and she is miserable and she makes us embarrassed. You must have seen that for yourself.'

Aunt Helen was apologetic. 'I did, and I'm sorry for it. It was extremely thoughtless of me not to take into account Maisie's deafness. If Maisie can't hear the dance teacher properly it follows that she can't learn the moves.'

The next day when the girls were at school she walked through the centre of town to revisit Mrs. Tyndale. The latter opened the door.

'Was there anything amiss? Would you please come this way? What delightful girls!'

'Mrs Tyndale,' Aunt Helen silenced her, 'there is nothing amiss and I have come hoping that I won't cause you any distress.'

'No distress at all,' echoed Mrs Tyndale who began to suffer the first symptoms immediately.

'I need to withdraw one of my nieces from your class.'

'Indeed,' nodded Mrs. Tyndale cautiously.

'Maisie, the youngest, is hard of hearing and we were remiss in not being aware of how this handicap would affect her dancing.'

'Poor child. She is deplorably put together,' Mrs Tyndale affirmed frankly, 'but that explains everything. Poor child.'

'Which means,' Aunt Helen ploughed on, 'that I need to ask for your advice.'

'Mine? Can I help?'

'You mentioned crafts when I spoke with you last week. I need to find an alternative occupation for my niece.'

'Well, yes, that will be Miss Caldwell. Miss Caldwell has a great way with crafts and provides all the props that are needed for the Christmas Show which the amateur dramatic society put on each year. Do not look shocked, quite genteel people do amateur dramatics, you should not believe all you read in the papers.'

Aunt Helen smiled at the thought that she might be shocked, but none the less some more information about the society might be useful.

'Don't be stuffy, Reginald,' Aunt Helen remonstrated with her brother that evening. 'Quite genteel girls enter amateur dramatics. Elsie needs to be drawn out of herself, she's quite overshadowed by that Veeve of yours. Don't believe all you read about the stage.' She amused herself by quoting the somewhat ridiculous Mrs Tyndale, and felt unkind in the same instant.

'If Eleanor does not object,' Reginald capitulated.

Eleanor was persuaded, acknowledging that Aunt Helen had a wealth of experience and could be relied upon not to suggest anything that might be remotely improper.

Aunt Helen's final suggestion was the most daring of all. She introduced it once the novelty of dancing, crafts and drama had receded and become an accepted part of the girls' routine. Veeve gave her the opening she needed. 'What is the point of classes when we just dance with other girls?'

Eleanor braced herself to parry one of Veeve's diatribes when Aunt Helen forestalled her. 'You'll need them for a proper dance one day. Won't she, Eleanor?' Aunt Helen continued silkily. 'Such as when Lil turns twenty-one. That would be an ideal opportunity to give a dance, wouldn't it, Reginald?' Aunt Helen launched the idea and watched it gain ground. Eleanor and Reginald were only vaguely aware that they had been successfully manipulated, and only partially regretted it.

'On another subject,' Aunt Helen continued, and Eleanor felt a mixture of amusement and exasperation but waited expectantly, 'I would like to visit Flo and Tom.'

'That would be fine,' laughed Eleanor relieved, 'I'll send word any time you like.'

On the following Saturday the carriage was brought round and drew up some time later outside the door of a terraced house. Solidly constructed, smoke trailed from the chimney causing a light smog which made the sun appear hazy. All the houses had front gardens which looked sad at this time of year. Most were tidy with beds dug over for the winter, but some had an evergreen shrub or a clipped holly bush, and all had damp grasses and dead flower stalks. Aunt Helen walked up the path and Flo opened the door.

'I was watching out for you,' Flo exclaimed, inviting her aunt into her parlour where a coal fire was burning. 'I'll show you the rest of the house later when I've made us some tea. It's all ready. I only have to fill the pot.'

Aunt Helen looked around. The house was similar to her childhood home. Her parents had not moved to a detached house until she was twelve years old. The furniture was functional and Flo had hung pretty floral curtains in the windows. On the dresser was displayed her wedding china, and the kitchen was tidy and newly swept. Flo was simply dressed and her hair was loosely tied. She had thrown off the frills that she had acquired while in Leicester.

'Tom will work long hours,' Aunt Helen remarked, taking the cup that Flo handed her, 'how do you spend your Sundays?'

'We usually walk out along the lane to the river, or along the canal, and choose one of the paths into the countryside. Tom's family are close by. In fact his younger brothers and sisters often call in, especially during the week.'

'I'm sure they do, they will enjoy having someone like you to entertain them.'

'They help fill the time before Tom comes home.'

'Do you get lonely?'

'Well, I do miss not having the family around,' Flo countered loyally.

Aunt Helen refrained from the expected comment that when she had children her situation would change, particularly in the light of her own inability to have any. She endeavoured to find a way to give purpose to Flo's day.

'Come, show me the house and then we shall take a walk. I'd like to revisit old haunts.' Once the tour of the little house was completed she said, 'What do you know of the working of the mill?'

'Only what I saw from the schoolroom,' Flo told her.

'It's important to understand what happens, although never to interfere.'

They walked down the street and towards the bridge that spanned the Soar. Here the river narrowed, increasing the power to the wheels of the mill. On the opposite bank rose the impressive building of the mill itself. The rumble of the weir at the bend in the river made a soothing accompaniment to their walk and covered any awkward pauses.

'Folk are curious,' Aunt Helen observed, 'we treat a newly married couple as if they were likely to be tainted by our contact, and yet they are almost strangers to each other. We leave them to flounder alone.'

'I feel as if I don't fit in,' Flo confessed.

Aunt Helen knew that she had touched a chord. 'That's hardly surprising,' Aunt Helen laughed sharply, adding bluntly, 'since Tom has married the boss's daughter.' She halted, and they watched the water as it gurgled and tumbled below them forming waves where it was obstructed by the pillars of the bridge.

'Only you can solve this. People will be expecting you to make the first move.'

'You mean people think I am stuck up?'

'They will unless you prove them wrong.'

Flo's eyes welled with tears. She shook them away and fixed her eyes on an eddy which formed a circle that never seemed to join the main flow of the river. 'I would like to teach but that depends on Father, and I would like to start helping at the Sunday school, but that depends on Tom.'

'Have you asked?'

They retraced their steps. The notion of instigating ideas and putting them into practice had always been the domain of her father. Flo did not feel in a position to suggest alterations to their life. She had no experience except that of her mother's acceptance of her father's decisions. Could Aunt Helen's way, which seemed so alien to her, be one she could adopt without upsetting the delicate balance of her relationship with Tom? Or might it be interpreted as considering herself a cut above his family?

Aunt Helen, reading her mind, said easily, 'Tom is a sensitive man. I think you could talk to him without him taking it amiss, and it could even set the seal on your marriage.' She was aware of a change in Flo by a sudden quickening of her stride as they climbed back up the hill to the house, as if fortified with a surge of courage to tackle the situation.

Aunt Helen felt the quiet glow of a mission accomplished, and she would have been more than justified in her sense of satisfaction if she had entered the mill later that night. Tom had taken the large key from its hook by the door and, his eyes searching Flo's in curiosity and incredulity, asked her again if she indeed wanted to be shown over the whole of the premises. Flo had carried out Aunt Helen's suggestion and once Tom had completed the tour and explained his role as a foreman, she found that a gap in her life had closed. Now she would be able to share more of Tom's day to day existence and she felt a lift to her spirits and a new warmth between them.

Aunt Helen's visit was drawing to a close and the arrangements for a dance for Lil were under way. Reginald, absorbed by business affairs as an antidote to the female preoccupation with domesticity, enjoyed nevertheless, his sister's company. He was beguiled by her brash exterior to underestimate the subtle manner in which she undertook to guide the members of his family in directions to which they subconsciously yearned, but had not the courage or the knowledge to achieve.

'Aunt Helen, can I ask you something?' Veeve said on her last day. 'When we were in London with you before leaving for Paris, you said that I should beware of getting lost in the souks. When George took us around the exhibition we never saw any.'

'Of course you didn't, dear, no self-respecting gentleman would take a schoolgirl to the Oriental Bazaar!'

'George did not know I was a schoolgirl,' objected Veeve.

Aunt Helen responded with an affectionate but knowing smile.

Chapter Eight

There had been concern, but no undue alarm, when one wintry day at the beginning of the new year, the news reached the Hefford family that Mr Devenick senior had caught a severe chill. The two families, facilitated by the affection between Lil and Mitchell, who had been engaged since her twenty-first birthday, had spent many hours in each other's company. It was for everyone's entertainment that Lil and Mitchell devised excursions into the country for picnics, tickets for the theatre to watch Elsie performing, or support for the charity bazaars where Maisie's crafts were sold.

'Lil, you and Mitchell take the children skating. Your mother and I will visit Mr Devenick. Wrap up warmly.'

Each held their skates by their runners. They anticipated a great crowd in the park as not only skaters would be there to slide and play on the ice, but many curious onlookers who would be lured by the spectacle of the frozen river and the vendors of roasted chestnuts and hot beverages.

The children were competent skaters and needed no encouragement to step on to the ice. They snaked away from the river bank, creating shapes on the surface of the ice, sure footed and expert, competing with each other to race to the opposite bank.

Mitchell had challenged them to play a form of hockey using broken-off branches and a suitable pebble. After a while Lil skated to the river's edge to catch her breath. It had been a pleasant year. Lil reflected on its contrast to their first year when she had serious doubts about her ability to enjoy the town. She was surprised at how happy she had been. Her studies at the college had evidenced itself in some competent art work and her father had felt emboldened to approach his partners with some of her designs. Her mother had been reluctant to subject her daughter to the rigours of a workplace but Lil was undaunted.

After a while Lil skated to the river's edge to catch her breath. Mitchell had finally reached a position within the firm whereby he could support a wife. She and Mitchell had borne their long engagement with patience and had enjoyed a relationship that had inevitably included their sisters and Mitchell's younger brother Michael. She stood with her hands clasped behind her head and looked into the distance. The sun was low in the sky with a touch of pink, warning that the short day was nearing its end. The scene resembled a photograph. The black outlines of the leafless trees and the distant figures of the skaters were silhouetted against the white frozen river and frost-covered grass bank. Yet unlike a picture there were sounds, the scrape of blades, crackle of ice and the undulating calls of the skaters.

Her gaze travelled to the familiar figures whose lithe bodies dressed in vivid colours were playing their improvised game of hockey. Lil gave a sigh of contentment and picking up a stick prepared to join the children's game when she saw a man further along the bank beckoning to the group and a skater detach himself to speak to him. She watched as the skater then made his way purposefully towards Mitchell, who after a hasty discussion crossed with him to the edge of the ice where he proceeded to remove his boots.

Lil skated along the river's edge to where Mitchell was now in conversation with a carriage driver. 'What's happened?' she asked.

The grave faces of the men told part of the tale. 'It's my Father. He has taken a turn for the worse. The doctor has diagnosed pneumonia and Mother has sent for me. Can Michael and the girls stay with you? There is no need to disrupt their afternoon.'

Lil agreed and Mitchell rested a hand briefly on her arm. 'Thank you Lil, that was a grand afternoon.'

Once Mitchell had departed the skating expedition lost much of its appeal. Lil was unable to rekindle their former enthusiasm and suggested that they bought some roasted chestnuts and went to Granby House for tea.

When it came time to return the Devenick children home it was accepted that Lil would accompany them and enquire on behalf of the family as to Mr Devenick's condition. The news was grim. It was unlikely that he would last the night.

The next morning the news of his death was brought while they were still at breakfast. Eleanor spoke first. 'To think that we saw him only yesterday.' Their visit had been curtailed by the arrival of the doctor. 'Those poor children. And their mother will be devastated. We will miss him too.' She was thinking of her husband, who had lost a friend.

Three days later Lil stood at the nursery window and watched as the funeral cortège passed below. Mr Devenick had been a well-respected lawyer in the town, and behind the hearse the family was followed by many bare-headed mourners walking in stately rows. The procession was almost hidden by the multitude of people who stood in the street. She could see Mitchell, who looked dignified but older as he supported his mother, and felt more forlorn than at any time in her life. A dull heaviness enveloped her, which she interpreted as an empathy with Mitchell for his loss, and her body throbbed in response to the mournful tolling of the church bell.

The cold chill persisted and Lil went about her daily tasks from mere habit in an effort to stave off her despondent mood. It was many days before she saw Mitchell again. One day word reached Lil that he was in the study speaking with her father. She waited until she heard the door open and then descended the stairs. Her father was standing in the hall.

'Lil, dear, he said,' his voice strained, 'you're to see Mitchell in my study. I'll leave you to go in.'

Mitchell stood with his back to the door with his head bowed. He turned an anguished face towards Lil. She hastened forward and took his hands in hers. 'I'm so sorry, Mitchell.'

He nodded, then slowly lowered her hands to her sides and gently guided her by her shoulders to the nearest chair. Lil looked up at him. He seemed to shake his head.

'It cannot be,' he forced the words, thickly.

'What cannot be?'

'Our engagement, our marriage. I have to break it off.'

Lil was silent, fixing him with her eyes.

'We were able to marry because I finished my articles in the summer. Now there is no one to support my mother, my sisters and Michael. They rely on me.'

'I can wait, Mitchell.'

'Michael is only fourteen. Lil, it will be years before I'm free.'

Lil grasped the seriousness of their situation. Perhaps she had already prepared herself. She saw there was nothing to be gained by arguing against his decision. His duty and his resolve were plain. She admired him even as she relinquished him.

'We were good friends,' Lil faltered. She stood up and went towards Mitchell who held onto the mantelpiece with one hand as if to let go would be to crumble. She kissed him lightly on one cheek and, light-headed and bewildered, went out into the hall.

Lil kept mainly to her room and during the course of the day each member of the family visited her. On subsequent days they were intimidated from offering sympathy or expressing regret as Lil resolutely repelled all advances. The household adapted to a new rhythm, the only interruptions to the round of lessons and homework was a sortie to wander around the stalls that were set out on market days. This dismal state of affairs might have carried on indefinitely except that, late one afternoon, a carriage drew up at the front door and a young man was shown into Reginald's study. Maisie saw the carriage and relayed the news to Elsie and Ruth, who were delighted to be involved in any event which disrupted their now mundane existence.

'A knight in shining armour,' proposed Elsie.

'No, he was small and plump and wore a great coat and cape,' retorted Maisie.

'Young and handsome,' Elsie continued.

'He may have been a friend of Father's,' Maisie countered.

'Are you sure he was not just a businessman?' asked the more pragmatic Ruth.

'No, he was too smartly dressed and he had his own carriage.'

Veeve joined them. 'Someone has called for Lil,' she announced enjoying the surprise on her sisters' faces, 'I heard Father sending for her.'

'Shall we ask Horace?' Elsie said, and received a scornful look from Veeve and saw incredulity in Ruth's face.

'Why do you want to inquire of Horace something that we want to discover for ourselves?' Veeve said.

In his study Reginald was saying to the stranger, 'I

appreciated that this was probably the only method in which you could have enticed Lil out, Mr Lewis. It was very thoughtful of Mitchell to give you the concert tickets. If you had given her any warning she would probably have refused. It will be good for her to go out. We are at our wit's end not knowing what to do for her.'

Once seated in Henry Lewis's carriage Lil stated. 'I thought you were in London.'

'I've been there since we met at the lantern lecture, remember? I have come back to the Leicester offices. I saw Mitchell again at his father's funeral. I am sorry, Lil, I really am. Mitchell told me about your engagement being called off and that was when he gave me the tickets. I am a poor substitute but I could not bear the thought of you imprisoned at home.'

He refrained from saying that she was moping and besides he gave her more credit than that of succumbing to such weak female emotions. Lil, who had accepted the invitation because she felt it would be churlish to refuse, realised that it had taken some courage on Henry's part to invite her. She determined to make an effort. 'Why did you not send word earlier in the day?'

'I thought it was likely that you would refuse.'

'I probably would have,' Lil smiled ruefully.

'Or forgotten who I was,' added Henry.

'I hadn't forgotten you,' Lil told him frankly, and Henry was pleased and relieved that his gamble had paid off. He was no match when compared to Mitchell, but he had felt the want of friends since returning after so many months in the City, and had been less disconcerted by Mitchell's request than he might otherwise have been.

The concert was unexceptional. Lil recognised a few faces in the audience and the return of Henry to the area was acknowledged by others. In such a close-knit society most people would know of her broken engagement, or soon would do once the news of her being escorted by Henry circulated. She had to emerge from the cocoon of her home eventually, and being in Henry's company prevented even the most forthright of acquaintances from conveying their condolences or remarking on her circumstances, neither of which she felt strong enough to endure.

'I did enjoy that,' Lil said at the end of the evening, 'I did not expect to, but I did. That sounds ungrateful, but I'm not.'

'Don't mind me,' said Henry affably, 'I'm always happy to escort a pretty girl.' Hurriedly he added. 'I don't mean that glibly either. There's more to you than just looks. Would you allow me to arrange another evening sometime?'

'Another provincial performance with outstanding singers from the West End,' Lil mocked gently. 'Yes, anything. I must.'

'I'm not a sportsman,' Henry paused and they both understood that he was comparing himself to Mitchell, 'you only have to look at me.' He laughed and emboldened by Lil's answering spark of amusement, he added, 'I have an idea. Do you have anyone you can stay with in London? I could take you to some top notch shows. I spend a night each week at my club and report to head office. It would be ripping if you could come up to town.' His enthusiasm for the idea dispelled his previous formality. Lil was infected by his good humour.

'There's always Aunt Helen. I could stay with her.'

'Good for Aunt Helen. Let me see what I can arrange.'

Delighted with himself for finding a solution to the task that Mitchell had set him, one that did not require him to look ridiculous on skates, he had to prevent himself racing ahead with plans for the future.

Henry could not have engaged Lil's interest in a manner more likely to capture her imagination. She had, for some time, felt the need for activities beyond those of entertaining her sisters, albeit with Mitchell. Her work absorbed her but she had begun to outgrow the intellectual stimulus offered by Leicester. Philosophically she had accepted the situation, but the opening that Henry described would help her overcome the loss of companionship that she had so valued in Mitchell, while widening her cultural education.

Her first excursion to London was a success. Aunt Helen welcomed her as a guest and was curious to meet Henry Lewis. Interaction with the younger generation added a spice that was otherwise missing in her life. There had been a time, she mused, when she had had her fair share of excitements and if she had not felt Lil's sadness so acutely, she thought it would be amusing to see a new relationship bloom.

When Henry arrived to collect Lil for the evening's entertainment, Helen was disappointed. She had envisaged a friend of Mitchell's to be as athletic and handsome as he had been. Henry had a good natured face she admitted but no real presence. His manners were impeccable however, and he was considerate and uncomplicated in his rapport with Lil. For the time being, she decided, Lil had been sensible in agreeing to meet him.

Late in the spring an event occurred which was to dispel the pall that Mitchell's disappearance from the family scene had created. Bett, her husband and Sheilagh were due to return from Quebec. The family expected that when the ship docked Brindsley-Smith would inform them. However, when the telegram arrived it did not announce, as they had expected, that the ship had docked in Liverpool, but one which stated, 'Bett unwell, request arrive tomorrow'. The household was spurred into a flurry of activity without being at all certain what they should be preparing for. Lil sensibly suggested to her mother that some arrangements should be delayed until they had ascertained the state of Bett's health.

The family all congregated in the hall when they heard the carriage draw up but were a rather a subdued gathering in view of their worry for Bett. Brindsley-Smith mounted the steps to the house with a jaunty air and forestalled Eleanor who was anxiously hurrying towards the door of the carriage.

'Mrs Hefford,' Brindsley-Smith addressed her, blocking her path and forcing her to stop. 'Thank you for receiving Bett and Sheilagh. Bett's in a poor way but she'll perk up now that she's home. I need to continue on to London. I'll book into a hotel tonight and take the early train in the morning.' Eleanor was discountenanced by the unexpected proposal and remained silent as she pressed on past him to the carriage.

'What's the meaning of this?' Reginald asked.

Brindsley-Smith was unabashed. 'Best place for a girl is with her mother when she's under the weather, you know.'

Reginald was prepared to argue with his son-in-law, but the sight of his sick daughter in pain and needing assistance, overcame any wish to contradict him. Bett's plight was his priority. 'If that is what you need to do,' he said, almost glad to be shot of him. 'Take the girls upstairs,' he instructed his wife unnecessarily.

Sheilagh dismounted by herself and stood uncertainly at the bottom of the steps. Lil went down and took her hand. 'I'm Lil, you won't remember me I'm afraid, but come on into the house.'

By nightfall Bett was ensconced in her own room and Lil arranged to keep Sheilagh with her to settle the poor frightened child. Eleanor stayed with Bett during the night, sponging her forehead to reduce her fever, and assuring the other girls that they would be able to see her once the doctor had called.

Veeve held court in her room that night when the sisters met to discuss the events of the day. 'Brindsley-Smith's a rotter,' she declared,'why is he in such a hurry to go to London?'

'Has he done something wrong?' said Elsie.

'It's probably catching,' predicted Ruth.

'I'm just glad Bett is here again,' Maisie declared.

Maisie was not to be disappointed. The doctor diagnosed an acute episode of rheumatoid arthritis requiring rest and careful nursing. Maisie was charged with ensuring that Sheilagh was made to feel welcome but the little girl oscillated between speaking French and English which somewhat complicated Maisie's task, but for Bett's sake she persevered.

When next Lil went to London to meet Henry he surprised her with his opening question.

'You write that your sister was married to Brindsley-Smith.'

'Why do you mention that?'

'I saw him at my club. I guessed it was him, the name's unusual, but when I heard that he had returned from Canada, I knew it was the same. Can I speak frankly?'

Lil wondered what Henry knew. She had gleaned very little from Bett.

'He's a bit of a bounder. There's a lot of talk, mostly about himself and what a big shot he was in Quebec.'

'Oh,' Lil said doubtfully, 'Veeve calls him 'the rotter'.'

'She may be right. The word is that he made the devil of a mess of business over there and he has hot footed it to head office to say his piece first.'

'His father is one of the partners,' Lil was puzzled.

'His father sent him to Canada because he was an embarrassment. I expect he hoped he would learn something. It's my belief that he threw his weight around until someone convinced him that he should return.'

'Poor Bett, do you think she was all right?'

'No one knows. In fact there was no mention of a wife or child. I pray it's all a rumour.'

'So what happens now?'

'He is going to be what he terms a scientific salesman. He bored us all with how the market is studied, on the strength of the competition, on possible consumption, and how a salesman bases his selling plans on opinions formed from such expert study. It's all talk.' Henry finished.

'He can't do much harm by talking,' Lil commented.

'Ruth,' Veeve confided one afternoon as they were walking to their dancing class, 'can I trust you?'

'It depends what this is about,' answered Ruth cautiously. Veeve was almost grown up and seemed, to Ruth, both sophisticated and knowledgeable. Her sister was pretty and all the boys noticed. Ruth had only her innate good sense to prevent her from idolising Veeve, who was courageous and daring, attributes with which Ruth did not credit herself. Ruth enjoyed the walks to and from the dancing class as much as the class itself, and they were the best days of her week. Veeve treated her as an equal and did not bracket her with Elsie and Maisie, the children as she insisted on calling them, although Elsie was now fifteen and Ruth herself was thirteen.

'The minute Lil marries Henry...'

Ruth interrupted her, 'Who says she will marry Henry?'

'I do, I can see it.'

'But Henry's not at all like Mitchell.'

'That's the whole point. He is different, so she will marry him.'

'How do you know?' Ruth persisted.

'Because he makes her laugh.'

'So what? What if he does marry Lil?'

'Then I am going to live with Aunt Helen. Nothing will make me stay at home and help Mother.'

'How do you know she will have you?'

'I've written to her already. I intend to leave school as soon as term ends and go to London.'

'What will you do?'

'Go to parties, of course. Why do you think I have stuck it out at Mrs. Tyndale's dancing class?'

Ruth was saddened. She had hoped that Veeve enjoyed the afternoons as much as she did. Veeve saw her look. 'It's been good being with you. We do have fun, don't we?'

Ruth was only a passable dancer but Veeve excelled and, despite what she said, enjoyed being the star of the class. There was something exhilarating about executing a dance correctly and stylishly, but its attraction was lost on Ruth.

'Don't you want to go to proper dances and dance with proper partners?'

'What, boys?'

'Well, yes, and men. That's why we are learning,' Veeve rationalised.

Ruth blushed, 'I shan't go once you've gone.'

Veeve did not try to pretend otherwise. 'You can swot away at school and get wonderful results and be given all the awards,' she said airily, but she saw that Ruth was pleased.

When Henry Lewis proposed to Lil and she accepted, Veeve was gracious and allowed Elsie and Maisie to express their own reactions before she engaged Ruth's support and claimed that she had already predicted their engagement. She listened with amusement.

'How can Lil want to marry Henry Lewis?' expostulated Elsie, 'I thought she would pine for Mitchell forever.'

'She couldn't wait forever,' defended Ruth.

'Why not? If she had loved him with all her being,'

'What other choice did she have?' chipped in Veeve.

'I like Henry Lewis.' Maisie's voice with its harsh lisp was not attractive but it gained their attention. All three girls stared at her, surprised by her sentiment and her conviction. 'Why shouldn't she marry him? Flo married and she hasn't even had any babies, Beth married and she has been abandoned. At least Henry and Lil are friends and they have fun.' Veeve never had her moment. They digested Maisie's observation and each agreed, privately, that she there was some truth in what she said.

'Well, it's not very romantic,' sulked Elsie.

'Why should you mind, you're not marrying him,' Veeve said testily.

'Whatever we think,' Ruth said, 'Lil has had a miserable time and we should be happy for her. Lil is not so foolish as to marry because she thinks no one else will ask her.'

'I think it's horrid that all women can do is get

married,' declared Maisie.

Elsie looked shocked. 'Maisie, where do you get your ideas?'

'I'm not the only person who thinks like this.'

When Flo arrived later in the day she asked what Bett had thought about the news, and they realised with embarrassment that they had forgotten to tell her.

Veeve shrugged her shoulders. 'Flo, you better go,' she suggested.

Bett had made a good recovery and Eleanor was pleased that her return to their home proved so little a burden. Maisie was, on occasions, glad to have a younger child to play with, and all her sisters drifted towards Bett when they needed a sympathetic ear. Bett raised her head when Flo appeared, her cheeks pale, her dark hair swept from her face but loose on her shoulders, her habitual stillness accentuated. It was as if she braced herself against contact with the outside world, represented at this moment by Flo. Beside her sat Sheilagh who looked up from her book, and sprang to her feet to give Flo a vigorous embrace.

'Flo, Why are you here?'

'Good news.' She sat Sheilagh on her lap and addressed Bett. 'Lil is to marry Henry Lewis.'

A mixture of emotions crossed Bett's face. 'I'm glad for her, Flo.'

'Do you like him?' Flo asked.

'I don't know him, but Lil does and I trust her judgement.' Perhaps, thought Flo, she does not trust her own. Sheilagh took the opportunity to sidle out of the door.

pleased.

When Henry Lewis proposed to Lil and she accepted, Veeve was gracious and allowed Elsie and Maisie to express their own reactions before she engaged Ruth's support and claimed that she had already predicted their engagement. She listened with amusement.

'How can Lil want to marry Henry Lewis?' expostulated Elsie, 'I thought she would pine for Mitchell forever.'

'She couldn't wait forever,' defended Ruth.

'Why not? If she had loved him with all her being,'

'What other choice did she have?' chipped in Veeve.

'I like Henry Lewis.' Maisie's voice with its harsh lisp was not attractive but it gained their attention. All three girls stared at her, surprised by her sentiment and her conviction. 'Why shouldn't she marry him? Flo married and she hasn't even had any babies, Beth married and she has been abandoned. At least Henry and Lil are friends and they have fun.' Veeve never had her moment. They digested Maisie's observation and each agreed, privately, that she there was some truth in what she said.

'Well, it's not very romantic,' sulked Elsie.

'Why should you mind, you're not marrying him,' Veeve said testily.

'Whatever we think,' Ruth said, 'Lil has had a miserable time and we should be happy for her. Lil is not so foolish as to marry because she thinks no one else will ask her.'

'I think it's horrid that all women can do is get

married,' declared Maisie.

Elsie looked shocked. 'Maisie, where do you get your ideas?'

'I'm not the only person who thinks like this.'

When Flo arrived later in the day she asked what Bett had thought about the news, and they realised with embarrassment that they had forgotten to tell her.

Veeve shrugged her shoulders. 'Flo, you better go,' she suggested.

Bett had made a good recovery and Eleanor was pleased that her return to their home proved so little a burden. Maisie was, on occasions, glad to have a younger child to play with, and all her sisters drifted towards Bett when they needed a sympathetic ear. Bett raised her head when Flo appeared, her cheeks pale, her dark hair swept from her face but loose on her shoulders, her habitual stillness accentuated. It was as if she braced herself against contact with the outside world, represented at this moment by Flo. Beside her sat Sheilagh who looked up from her book, and sprang to her feet to give Flo a vigorous embrace.

'Flo, Why are you here?'

'Good news.' She sat Sheilagh on her lap and addressed Bett. 'Lil is to marry Henry Lewis.'

A mixture of emotions crossed Bett's face. 'I'm glad for her, Flo.'

'Do you like him?' Flo asked.

'I don't know him, but Lil does and I trust her judgement.' Perhaps, thought Flo, she does not trust her own. Sheilagh took the opportunity to sidle out of the door.

'What about your marriage, Bett?' Flo and their mother had failed to elicit an explanation either of her life in Quebec or the circumstances of her apparent abandonment.

'I just want to stay here, Flo, with Sheilagh.' Bett seemed reluctant to enlarge on the subject and Flo felt a twinge of guilt and promised that in the future she would include this undemanding little family more often. Sheilagh returned holding Lil's hand. Lil embraced her sister. Surrounded by warmth and happiness, Lil berated herself for being so preoccupied with her own affairs that she had not considered Bett's plight. How fortunate she was that despite the sadness surrounding her broken relationship with Mitchell, she had found Henry Lewis. Sheilagh, with a shy questioning look, took Lil's hand and rolled the ring between her finger and thumb so that the diamond twinkled.

Flo watched her sister and Sheilagh playing with the ring, and slowly broke into a smile as a memory floated back to her. 'Who was never going to marry a toff?'

Chapter Nine

1902

If any of the family had known that Veeve had planned her escape for nearly two years they would have been astounded at her patience. As it was, Veeve had concealed it so well that when she announced to her father that Aunt Helen had invited her to stay indefinitely, the news was greeted with total surprise.

Veeve, positioned in the middle of the family and neither mature and responsible like her older sisters nor childlike and naive like the younger, was Reginald's most irresponsible but irrepressible daughter. Vivacious, to match her name, and witty, she livened a household inclined to be serious. In Veeve's character Reginald could see traces of his sister Helen, and thought that the combination could be detrimental without being able to articulate how that might manifest itself. However, he knew from the start of the interview that Veeve would achieve her goal, and when he viewed her future, staying at home, even he knew that she would be unhappy, fret and cause trouble.

'Veeve, how can you leave when Lil and Henry are now engaged? Have you given no thought to your mother?' Reginald asked.

'Father,' Veeve argued, maintaining a light-hearted manner which from practice she knew he could not be angered with, 'there are no children left, Maisie is twelve, and, besides, Mother has Bett.'

'And Sheilagh,' he countered reasonably. Veeve decided to ignore this since it was established that Bett had sole charge of her step-daughter.

'Father, what do you expect me to do? Just stay at home and wait for my turn?'

He promised to speak to Eleanor but both knew that permission would be granted.

Reginald admitted that Veeve had a certain justification to her request and was nervous of the effect of inactivity on his middle daughter. She had been less troublesome of late but such calm was ominous and Veeve could erupt at any time.

'Eleanor, I believe it would be pleasant for Helen, since she has no children of her own and Lil's visits would now be ending, to have Veeve to stay for a while. Helen has many acquaintances from her colonial past to whom Veeve could be introduced. They are certain to have offspring of their own of Veeve's generation.'

Eleanor was not long in recognising the advantages and shared Reginald's belief that this could be a suitable solution. She could then direct all her energy to arranging Lil's wedding.

Veeve saw no reason to delay her departure. The lure of the city which beckoned her, and the longing to leave home which she had hidden so masterfully, now overwhelmed every consideration. She was superfluous to the wedding plans for Lil. She and her older sister had never been close. Flo had been Lil's confidant and once her visits had become less frequent Lil had transferred her affection to Bett. Veeve liked Henry Lewis but the details of their wedding failed to engage her attention now that she was absorbed in her plans to live in London. Mentally she had been packed for months.

Even as a child Veeve had been striking, but she was developing into a beautiful young woman. Her only fault, if she had one, was her lack of height, but her exquisitely proportioned figure was ample compensation. She had bronzed brown hair and dark eyes set widely apart and framed by soft eyebrows. Her rounded cheek bones gave her an impish air, which, far from detracting from her looks, intrigued people. Her mouth did not have the full lips associated with classical good looks, but she had a generous open smile and her expression constantly moved, reflecting her moods. It was hard for Reginald to refuse any request from this pretty upturned face, and he succumbed.

Elsie stepped seamlessly into the role of elder sister and became a constant companion to her mother in a way that none of the older girls had done. Flo had seemed to replace her mother, Lil had had no real wish to emulate Flo, and neither Bett nor Veeve had been contenders. Eleanor began to enjoy her smaller family.

Although Ruth had been privy to Veeve's plans she was unprepared for the effect of her departure. Veeve had never been a friend, the difference in their ages precluded this, but she felt the loss of a champion and protector and was experiencing a sense of boredom now that Veeve's mercurial spirit was no longer in evidence. Ruth was naturally studious and retiring and Eleanor hoped to draw her out now that she had more time.

Maisie was becoming more headstrong and Eleanor wondered if this was to counteract the effect of her deafness which tended to isolate her. She had made a group of friends, giving her the opportunity to visit and receive visits, but Eleanor was concerned about their influence.

'Maisie does have the oddest notions,' Elsie said to her mother. 'Yesterday she declared that she would rather work as a weaver in Father's mill than be at home once she has finished with school. Another time she said that she wanted a bicycle.'

'Where does she get such ideas?' asked Eleanor.

'It must be in the crafts group. She is very friendly with that Sally Pevey whose Mother has to work because her father died. Do you remember?'

Eleanor did not but she felt alarmed. 'Perhaps Maisie should change her evening activity. What else could she do?'

'There are the first-aid classes. These are more practical and there would be less time for idle chatter,' Elsie suggested.

'And what should we do about Ruth?' asked her Mother.

'She will not return to the dancing now that Veeve has gone.'

'She can't hide with a book every night. She needs company.'

'Why don't you suggest that she joins the crafts group, she is not easily influenced, like Maisie, in fact she might challenge their ideas.'

Summer in London was relatively quiet and Veeve was disappointed that much of her time with Aunt Helen was spent making calls on elderly ladies. However their topics of conversation included subjects that she had previously dismissed as uninteresting, and she began to read the papers that were delivered each morning, and to become familiar with the leading figures of the day. She found that they became more than names and that the accounts of the activities of Lloyd George and Asquith, the announcements of the daily engagements of the Royal family and the reviews of the new plays, became relevant now that she was in London. Aunt Helen took her to the theatre and art galleries and planned when Parliament re-opened to visit the Strangers Gallery.

Invitations to social events started fitfully and gradually gained momentum as the large country houses emptied of their summer visitors. It was to a small dinner party hosted by a friend in the Diplomatic Service that Veeve had her first taste of the eclectic group amongst whom Aunt Helen moved.

Count Von Kuder from Lübeck, Pierre Dupont from Paris and an American called Sam Blair, with an older Englishman and two other young ladies were selected as company for Veeve. She said very little as they sipped their cocktails, but watched the interplay of conversation as the banter ricocheted from one speaker to another, no one person dominating the subject. The variety of topics covered was stimulating and the wit and sparkle of the repartee excited her. She determined that she would find a part to play.

At dinner, conversation became more intimate and Veeve was able to engage with the men seated on either side of her. The Count, a jovial bewhiskered man in his mid-twenties was the first. After some conventional opening questions which she quickly decided had nothing to recommend them, Veeve took the initiative. 'Why are you in London, Count?'

She was surprised at the effectiveness of this simple strategy, and gaining in confidence ventured to question him about his country. Far from finding that her ignorance was an embarrassment, she discovered that it was the magic ingredient that allowed the Count to shine in her eyes, and his own.

'Germany is going from strength to strength,' he told her, his strident guttural accent lending an exotic menace. 'Since the great Bismarck united all of our countries, our population has increased by one million a year. Can you imagine that? We have been for many years envious of your industrial prowess but now we are catching up. We have infinite resources of coal, and we can build and build, and export too.'

Veeve was beginning to sink out of her depth. Concepts such as imports and exports had never featured at Wyggeston, and she switched to safer ground. 'What is it that you like about London?'

'We in Germany have a great respect for Kultur. Our education, you know, is very thorough. Here in London you have fine theatres and excellent concerts. They almost rival Berlin,' he joked.

'Do you enjoy parties?' Veeve asked hopefully.

'Of course. Where else can one meet delightful creatures such as yourself but at parties like this one. What would be the pleasure in going to concerts and theatres without the company of an enchanting lady.' He gave her a wide smile which embraced her along with his other acquaintances.

Veeve was emboldened to tackle the guest who sat on her other side. Sam Blair was a clean shaven, healthily lean young man whose blond hair and blue eyes fitted Veeve's picture of an American; however she had been warned that Americans and Canadians disliked being mistaken for each other and advanced cautiously.

'I can tell that you come from across the Atlantic,' she began.

'I'm from Washington,' her neighbour said and added, 'U.S.A.' This was fortunate for Veeve whose geography was hazy, and who made a quick mental note to do some homework. She was prepared to admit some ignorance but not to be considered stupid. Her American continued smoothly. 'I've been in your capital for some while now, it's a neat place. Have you lived here all your life?'

'I used to live in a place called Leicester, but I'm living here now.'

'Lester? I don't know it. Is it anywhere near Oxford? I've been to Oxford and it's a fine little University.'

Veeve hoped that if she smiled encouragingly he would rattle on until she could contribute again. Finally she was rescued by her host who suggested that the ladies retire and she welcomed this tradition with relief.

Aunt Helen arranged several dinner parties on these lines and Veeve became more adept. With a quick glance at the morning paper and some anecdotes from previous encounters she was able to beguile her fellow guests. She started to enjoy her ability to amuse people but she was impatient to be invited to her first dance. A real dance, she told herself, not just the harvest hop in the local hall. The round of balls and dances traditionally started in the autumn and eventually the long-awaited invitation arrived. To mark the occasion her Aunt proposed that they set forth that very morning to find a gown.

'How will we know if we choose the right one?'

'What you wear is fashionable if you wear it with confidence. Besides, the patrons of the stores to which I shall introduce you would not permit you to wear anything that is not totally 'comme il faut'.' Aunt Helen answered unwaveringly. She, whose own dress sense was flamboyant and daring, was aware that whatever Veeve chose would cause a stir. 'It is how you wear your clothes rather than what you wear that counts.'

On the evening of the ball Veeve sat beside her aunt bewildered by the scene before her. She was wearing a dress of grey tulle with ruffled sleeves decorated with pink rosettes. The deep neckline, edged with frills of pink lace was matched by a large bow at her waist. Smaller rosettes were scattered over an overskirt of countless gossamer-like folds. She wore pale pink gloves which reached above her elbows, pink slippers peeped from below her skirt and her hair was decorated with tiny flowers and mock pearls. Candles flickered, ladies floated and men in black and white hovered, but before she was aware that she had been noticed, Pierre Dupont had taken her by an elbow and guided her towards the centre of the floor.

When Veeve stepped out for her first dance and Aunt Helen saw the effect on a group of young men standing nearby, she felt a nostalgic thrill. Veeve, like herself many years ago, would be a social success. She contemplated her niece with satisfaction.

That night was a whirl of music and rhythm as Veeve exchanged one partner for another in a succession of dances. Never had she experienced such elation and enjoyment. As the evening was drawing to a close Pierre brought her a lemonade.

'Your name is French, is it not?' He said.

Veeve could not decide whether to explain the story

or to laugh it off with a shrug.

A hand rested on Pierre's shoulder, 'When I knew her she was called Beatrice,' a newcomer leant forward and caught Veeve's eye with a challenge.

'George?' Veeve queried.

'None other. Pierre, would you permit me to ask this lady for the last dance?'

Veeve had never forgotten George Eaton, and in his formal evening dress he appeared more striking than any man in the room. His elegant movements, attentive manner and evident charm captivated Veeve. When the orchestra played the national Anthem announcing the end of the evening, George returned her to her original party and gave no indication that he intended to seek her out again. Veeve felt that midnight had struck and she had been left in rags.

It was two days later that a card was sent up. Aunt Helen and Veeve were sitting in the drawing room, and a few minutes later George was shown in. He enquired, if her aunt permitted, whether Veeve would like to accompany him on a drive in the park.

'How did you arrange to be in London?' George asked her with a sidelong glance as they set off in his carriage, and before she had a chance to answer he continued, 'and where do you want to go?'

'Anywhere. I hardly know London. Anywhere where the horses can go fast.'

'Then it's out to Richmond park, the horses can have their heads there. Tired of the pace of London already?'

'I love everything in London but no-one else has taken me for a drive. It's just been social events like tea and dinner parties, and the theatre sometimes.'

'I can see that I shall have to liven things up.'

Veeve's eyes sparkled. George, who had recently felt a strange ennui at the thought of another winter in town, found a renewed sense of adventure as he considered taking the recently arrived young girl under his wing.

'How would you like to come to the theatre and a spot of dancing?' Veeve was on the verge of accepting when a shadow of doubt crossed her face.

'I'll square it with your Aunt Helen and have her eating out of my hand.'

Veeve believed him capable of fixing anything. The theatre production was more amusing than any she had attended with Aunt Helen and the dancing afterwards was less formal, conversation and communication among his friends less inhibited, and Veeve felt that this was the London she had been looking for.

When George was out of town Veeve had no shortage of escorts. Her earlier acquaintances moved swiftly to offer a variety of entertainments. Count Von Kuder arranged an excursion to visit Windsor Castle, Pierre Dupont invited her to an evening on the Thames and Sam Blair, keen to explore London, encouraged Veeve to accompany him to the British Museum and National Gallery.

Aunt Helen welcomed this diversity. She was uneasy about Veeve's obvious preference for George so early in the season.

'Veeve, give yourself time to explore the wider field before making a hasty commitment, you've only been with me for a few months.'

'They are many commendable young men,' Aunt Helen went on, 'the Count, the American and Pierre, but there are others. You have only turned eighteen. Have you met anyone else to tell me about?' Veeve would regale her aunt with snippets of gossip but never mentioned George.

One evening Veeve admitted to Aunt Helen that she had an admirer. 'There is this naval officer but he has returned to his ship. George said not to become entangled with a man from the sea, because they spend most of their lives imprisoned on their ships, and are notorious for having a girl in every port.'

'George is reputed to have a history himself,' Aunt Helen commented.

Veeve, who thought she understood what her aunt meant, replied, 'That does not interest me. I'm only concerned with the present.'

'Although,' Aunt Helen continued, almost as if Veeve had not spoken, 'what else can you expect of a man of twenty-eight?'

Both were silent for a few moments and then Veeve, who disliked it when her Aunt became serious, proposed that they play cards which always distracted her and amused them both on the rare occasions that they had an evening to themselves.

Veeve's letters to her family were infrequent although she did not consciously fail to communicate. When a letter of hers arrived for Flo it caused her older sister some disquiet. She waited until Tom had settled into his chair by the fire.

'What is it?' Tom asked.

'Veeve has written to me.'

'And is she fine?' Tom could not see how there could be any problems since Veeve had achieved her goal and moved to London. Flo had seemed to be in favour of the plan at the time.

'She's fine,' Flo answered, 'that's not what is worrying me.'

'How do you mean?'

'Veeve is mixing with a much older group, and Aunt Helen gives her licence to do anything and go anywhere. It cannot be right for an eighteen-year-old to go around unchaperoned.'

'How do you know she is unchaperoned?' Tom challenged.

'It seems that Aunt Helen allows her to go to the park or to the theatre,' Flo searched for a section of the letter. "because Count von Kuder or Sam Blair can look after me.' That does not sound as if Aunt Helen is there with her.'

'Why are you so concerned?'

'Veeve knows what she wants but never knows what is good for her. She is impetuous and dislikes being thwarted. This can lead a girl like her into all sorts of trouble.'

'How come Veeve is so headstrong? She is not like you and your sisters.'

Flo described how Veeve was always eager to be included with the older girls but was a misfit, wedged between all the sisters. She told Tom that she needed to talk to her mother.

'If Veeve came home for a while she may go back to

Aunt Helen with her feet more on the ground.'

'You mean when you have had a word with her?' Tom teased. 'Are you trying to say that Aunt Helen has introduced Veeve to a racy set?'

'I fear so,' Flo assented. 'It is not our style, and that is why it will be so attractive to Veeve. None of us expected this. When Aunt Helen comes to stay everyone brightens up and she has the right thing to say for each person.' Flo remembered her aunt's gentle advice to herself when she had been a lonely newly-wed. 'Mother is livelier and Father of course adores her and her aura of sophistication. I suppose even Father could not know that Aunt Helen was so emancipated. I'll need to talk to him and perhaps show him this letter.'

Tom looked across at his wife with understanding. Flo would always be a second mother to her sisters. A better mother even than their own, in a practical sense. It would be good for Flo to visit her home for a few days.

'Go and stay. See what you can do,' Tom urged, 'a word from a big sister may be all that is needed.'

'I fear for Veeve,' Flo mused, 'people who think only of themselves are rarely happy.'

'But they tend only to upset their own lives, Flo. Veeve cannot harm anyone else. She cannot touch us.'

Flo was not so certain as she contemplated confronting her parents with the situation and then challenging Veeve. She saw the fabric of their family shaken by Veeve's possible indiscretions, and shivered.

'Do not be too sure,' Flo warned.

When she asked her mother if she could speak to her without the younger girls present and mentioned that she needed her father too, Eleanor wondered what her daughter could have to say of such importance. After dinner Ruth and Maisie went upstairs as was usual to complete their school work, while Elsie followed her parents and Flo into the drawing room.

'Elsie, dear. Flo wants to speak to us on our own.'

Elsie was unused to being excluded and resented Flo's return. She had school work to do but her mother usually allowed her to stay with them in the evening. Flo thought that Elsie was too young to take such a position in the household, a place that Bett could have filled and was conscious that Elsie was annoyed, but pretended otherwise.

'I have had a letter from Veeve,' Flo began. Reginald looked mildly interested while Eleanor showed some surprise.

'Veeve wrote to you? We'd been hoping for a letter from her. In fact I said to Reginald that he must go and visit her at Aunt Helen's. But you know your Father, Flo, he said that we should not interfere.'

In truth, Reginald was not sure what he would have been looking for were he to go to London, nor, if he disliked what he found, how they would manage their daughter should she return home.

'She is fine, Mother,' Flo hastily reassured her, 'but, do you think that Aunt Helen's is a suitable place for Veeve?'

'Why ever not?' Reginald was quick to defend his sister. 'What have you got against Aunt Helen?'

'Nothing Father, but Veeve has been given licence to do what she wants. There are no restraints on her,' Flo continued. 'It is not good for her,' she added limply.

'Whatever do you mean, Flo. Aunt Helen is perfectly respectable.'

'She does not chaperone her, Mother. She lets her go out in the care of her friends.'

'Is that not reasonable?'

'Except that her friends are young men, foreigners too. They are older than Veeve, Mother. She could so easily make a mistake and bring misery to herself and shame on you.'

'Now, Flo,' Reginald said firmly, 'Veeve will be home for Christmas and in the meantime we will decide what to do.'

When George was in town Veeve's social diary filled and her life became a whirl of activity as she continued to accept invitations from all and sundry while spending every available minute with him. George would ask her how she had filled her days and was amused at her account of visits to the museums with the studious American.

'So, this fliberty-gibbet of a girl has a serious side to her, I'm pleased to hear it. And what did you take a particular fancy to, I wonder?'

Veeve was not sure if he expected a flippant answer or a genuine one, and chose the latter.

'I loved the Egyptians. It all happened so long ago and they look so elegant and their designs are so beautiful. I would love to dress as they did instead of these cumbersome and restrictive frocks.'

George nodded pensively and Veeve wondered if he

would tease her for becoming a tedious scholar, but instead he answered, 'You are right, they had style. I have an idea. I give a ball every year in December. This year it shall be in fancy dress and I'll arrange for a dressmaker to turn you into an Egyptian. Royalty not slave!'

Veeve tipped her head to one side, constructing the image in her mind and then gave a peal of laughter at this unexpected outcome.

'Don't you like my idea?' asked George, mildly puzzled, certain that Veeve would be delighted with such a suggestion.

'It's wonderful. When can I meet with the dressmaker?'

The excitement generated by the Fancy Dress Ball continued to be one of the prime topics of conversation until the evening itself arrived. Veeve's dressmaker had designed a beautifully simple silk dress in gold and turquoise with touches of ruby red. Her hair was swept into a tall turban. George had found her some gold sandals with a small heel in Paris and gave her wide gold bangles to wear on her bare forearms. He was pleased with his creation but had no intention of wearing an Egyptian costume, himself. As host he reserved the right to wear a more formal outfit and chose that of a soldier from the Napoleonic War.

Aunt Helen felt both alarm and admiration for Veeve's audacious figure-hugging attire. She wondered whether she was wise to be seen in an outfit so outrageous at so young an age, but Veeve looked stunning and had the wit to carry it off. The ball was the culmination of a series of parties before everyone dispersed for Christmas.

Veeve, too, was returning home. On her last afternoon George called in and suggested a drive. She gathered her fur coat, replaced her day shoes with her warmest boots and chose one of her favourite hats while George assured her aunt that they would not be gone long since the light was fading and the air was chilly. Veeve and her aunt were to spend their last evening quietly together.

'I'm coming,' she called to George as she ran down the stairs, 'Aunt Helen says that you promised that I will not be late.'

'Nor will you be. I do not have much time.'

George drove them around all their familiar landmarks. To Oxford Street to watch the Christmas shoppers and the cheerful window dressings and then along Pall Mall and past the Palace which looked larger and more impressive when dimly lit, to return through Kensington gardens.

'Tell me,' George said, 'this name of yours, 'Veeve'.'

'I changed my name when I came back from Paris.'

Veeve looked at him and watched a smile play around his lips and a glint appear in his eyes. 'There was something else that I remember from France. I remember a schoolgirl who said that when she got married she wanted her dress made in Paris.' The only sounds were the hooves of the carriage horses as Veeve held her breath. 'Would you come to Paris, Veeve? Would you marry me?' He stretched out an arm and wrapped it around her shoulder drawing her towards him. 'And, my joie de vivre, shall we honeymoon in Egypt?'

The following day Elsie found herself in the position of being the bearer of extraordinary news. This privilege mollified her only a little when she realised that they had all been excluded from the recent developments in Veeve's affairs. There had been voices in the hall and Eleanor, who was impatiently waiting for her middle daughter to return for Christmas, asked Elsie to enquire who had arrived.

'Someone called Mr. Eaton. He wants to speak to Father and has been shown into the study.'

Not very many minutes later Elsie reappeared, with her beautifully dressed and exquisitely pretty sister beside her at the entrance to the drawing room where the rest of the family had gathered, and hardly containing her triumph at being the first to impart the news, declared 'Veeve's going to marry George Eaton.'

Chapter Ten

George and Veeve spent an increasing amount of time in Paris returning there each year when the Parisians flocked back after their August exodus. The city was airless and dusty and congested with tourists who filled the cafés and shopping streets to indulge in the warmth of the late summer, or to promenade in the parks before they were driven inside by the colder weather. For many tourists, and the British were no exception, not only was the weather clement but the exchange rate was favourable and people were able live more cheaply than they could at home.

This was not a consideration for George and Veeve. The main attraction for them was the recent purchase of a four seater Type 77 Peugeot which could do twenty-seven miles an hour and which George had seen in the Paris Show. The French were less restrictive regarding motoring than the British, considering a twelve mile-an-hour limit officious, and were actively encouraging road races to improve the speed and reliability of this new form of transport.

George was not particularly interested in racing but enjoyed being in the vanguard of the motoring world by owning the most up-to-date machine, and it was not long before Veeve was begging to be allowed to take the wheel. George duly drove them out of the centre of Paris into one of the quieter arrondissements where they changed places and Veeve put on her goggles. George smiled tolerantly when Veeve engaged the pedal, and stalled. He climbed down, took hold of the starting handle and cranked the engine back into action. Veeve had one more false start, George showed extraordinary patience, and then she found a feeling for the pedals. After driving the length of the tree-lined road, devoid of traffic, several times, George waved from the grass verge indicating that she should take the car on her own. Even cumbersome goggles failed to detract from her allure, and with a determined but exhilarated expression on her face, Veeve gave a flamboyant answering wave of her gloved hand. George reflected on his luck in finding such a spirited companion. He had had the freedom of a playboy before meeting Veeve but somehow that life had begun to pall, and he realised that sharing his exploits and his home with her made every day more pleasurable

One morning, when George had planned an early expedition into the countryside for some of their friends who also owned motor vehicles, Veeve seemed less enthusiastic than usual. She was game for an outing and enjoyed the company of these friends. He said nothing and as the day progressed Veeve regained her normal spirits. However Veeve had several more mornings when, despite her efforts to disguise it, George saw that she was pale and wan and quickly recognised the symptoms.

'Veeve, have you something to tell me?' he asked.

She looked at him defiantly but then seeing his expression of concern, she could not lie. She turned away to brush her hair in front of the mirror, but then swung round on the stool and looked at George, misery all over her face. He felt a pang of anguish, partly because he could see that she was not well, and partly because of the memories of two similar episodes.

'Veeve, you can't risk your life again. You are not able, like other women, to ignore your pregnancy and continue as if it is not happening. This time you need to take care. I do not want to lose you, nor this time can I bear to lose our baby.'

He walked across to Veeve and held her but he could

not lighten her distress. Veeve, who was so easy to please, who delighted in all the travels and the parties that they had shared over their years together, was having to face a curtailment of these pleasures and he knew that she was ill prepared to do so. George had to make a decision and immediately, knowing that his life also had changed.

'We need to return to Maidenhead. I can trust Doctor Andrews to look after you. Our staff will make sure that you rest and are comfortable.'

'And you George? What will you do?' She hesitated to ask him to stay, he never settled in one place for any length of time.

'I'll arrange for sedate company for us both. No late nights and no gadding about in motor vehicles, just cards and croquet.' George spoke in a slightly mocking tone but his intention was to cheer her. 'I will be with you as often as I can. You could ask one of your sisters to come and stay.'

Veeve could see no alternative and acquiesced meekly. She could not see past the decisions regarding their travel. The future looked bleak and the possibility that a healthy baby might be the outcome did not afford her any consolation.

George cancelled their engagements and informed the hotel staff of their impending departure. Veeve loved the Hotel Impérial. They had stayed there often and she had become a favourite of the maître and adored by the bell boys and waiters. She looked around the suite which was always reserved for them. The inimitable French stamp on the interior design had endeared it to her. She appreciated the long mirrors, generous sized bed and abundance of upholstered armchairs, the elegant porcelain washstands and the capacious wardrobes, the discreet gentleman's dressing room and her gloriously proportioned dressing table on which there was always a display of cut flowers. Spacious, with high ceilings, the walls broken up by tall windows, she now had to leave this room, the views from whose balconies were as familiar to her as those from the drawing room of their home on the Thames. Ahead, there was only the prospect of many dull months.

While her trunks were being packed and arrangements finalised word had circulated among their friends and when Veeve went downstairs a group awaited her. The repressed energy of the young socialites, ostentatiously fashionable, representative of Veeve's set, emphasised the pitiable state to which she had been reduced. She listened to them half-heartedly, but it was a subdued party, all treating her pregnancy as a misfortune, embarrassed to talk about it or engagements of their own in which she was unable to participate. There was a tangible feeling of relief when George said it was time to call a cab.

The maître ushered them towards the door with the fondness of a father, and the porters scurried helpfully when the news had carried that this was a family matter of some delicacy. They showed an amount of concerned excitement for Veeve and George which was shared by neither Veeve nor her friends. George sensed the warm anxiety of the hotel staff and tipped them handsomely. He escorted Veeve to the cab and clambered in beside her to begin their sombre journey to England.

When Eleanor was handed a telegram she hurried to Reginald's study, fearing that it must bear bad news.

'Please Send Ruth. Doctor Says Rest. Veeve,' Reginald read. 'She can't be ill or George would have sent for you, my dear.'

'The girl is most likely going to have a child. How it will irk her to have to rest.' Eleanor divined with a mother's intuition. 'Perhaps this is the answer for Ruth for I really do not know what to do with her and she and Veeve used to get along.'

Ruth had finished school that summer and had proved academically accomplished. Her father encouraged her to help with the accounts of a couple of charities that he administered, and discovered that he could trust her with most of the work.

'My little Misery.' Ruth's smiles were rare now. 'What are we going to do with you?' he would say. Ruth would not countenance teaching and with Elsie established at home, Ruth's natural ability with sewing and mending was not necessary. Elsie had become maternal, altogether no fun at all and Maisie exasperated them with her obstinate behaviour. She had taken to wearing masculine-style clothes, as the more slimline fashions were called, and dashing off on her bike to attend meetings with her friend Sally, who was proving an inflammatory influence which constantly upset her mother.

This plea from Veeve was timely. Although they would never have suggested this had she been well, they felt Ruth might benefit as much from Veeve's company as Veeve would hers. When Ruth was told by Reginald that Veeve had requested her company his 'little misery' looked genuinely happy at the prospect.

'She's not ill, is she?' Ruth voiced her sudden misgivings.

'No, most probably just having a baby. You'll be a tonic for her and help her pass the time.'

Ruth had visited Veeve's luxurious house on the edge of the river and was thrilled at the idea of an extended stay. She could read whenever she wished and more than anything she would have a friend again. It would be her first taste of independence.

Eleanor had always felt inadequate where Ruth was concerned, the girl was so self-contained and undemanding and if she had spells of unhappiness it would not have been to her mother that she would have confided. She regretted it, but Ruth would have gone to Flo or Bett. Ruth had always seemed to gravitate towards Veeve, whose strong presence enabled her to stay in the shadows. Eleanor wondered if this reserve was the essence of Ruth's character. She was neither melancholy nor particularly cheerful and it appeared to Eleanor that Ruth assumed that her life would continue in this way.

Eleanor misjudged her. Ruth was more excited than at any other time in her life, and she left the family home without a backward glance.

A few days after Ruth's departure Elsie was passing

through the hall when she saw a policeman leaving by the front door. She assumed that there had been an interview with her father and as the study door was open she looked in.

'Elsie, come in, shut the door.' Her father sat motionless at his desk and his voice was unsteady. 'I'm not sure I want your Mother to hear this. Maisie has been arrested.'

'Arrested?'

'It seems that her friend Sally is mixed up with the women's movement, the one they call the suffragettes. There is a by-election in two weeks time and there were demonstrations about the women's vote. It appears that Maisie tagged along. We won't know more until we speak to her. We need a lawyer, Elsie, and I want to keep this hushed. Could you go along to Mitchell Devenick's office and ask if he will accompany you back here? I'll arrange with Horace to call you a carriage. If I go it will set tongues wagging.'

Elsie thought that the reverse could be true, but her father was obviously shaken and as she had encountered Mitchell intermittently since the break up of his engagement to Lil, she was not intimidated at the prospect of requesting his help. It was market day in Leicester and despite choosing a route to avoid the square, Elsie's driver experienced endless obstructions.

In an effort to distract herself from the shock of Maisie's predicament, Elsie leant forward to watch the bustling scene out of the window, but her mind was preoccupied with the question of how a member of their family could end up in custody. She could not forgive herself for not being more alarmed by Maisie's increasingly radical stance on women's issues. She wondered whether it was because of her age that they had dismissed any extreme views as attention seeking. Although they had attempted to thwart the friendship with Sally, it seemed that the girl had started to do the first-aid course alongside Maisie, and that they had both come under the influence of the girl's mother. It was embarrassing for their family to be associated with unruly behaviour in public, and detrimental to her father's standing in the community. She was grateful that Mitchell was a family friend, because it would be awkward to describe her sister's disreputable conduct to a stranger.

A receptionist showed Elsie to a chair in the waiting room which also served as her office, and enquired whom she wanted to see. Her aloof manner made Elsie feel as if she had committed a crime.

She had not long to wait. Mitchell, observing her pale tense face, nodded abruptly to the receptionist, while he hastened towards her and hurriedly ushered her away from the public area. He asked her, solicitously, to sit, and allowing Elsie time to compose herself, collected papers and replaced some files before finally settling at his own desk opposite her.

Mitchell was no longer the boyish playmate that he had been when engaged to Lil, but an established lawyer who had stepped into his father's shoes and did so with a suitably grave air. Despite leaving in a hurry, Elsie had selected a leaf green cloche hat and wore a wool coat which neatly fitted her slim figure, and her pleasant face, if not striking, showed evident distress. 'Tell me what's happened,' he encouraged her.

'I've been trying to decide how to tell you why I'm here, but the fact is, Maisie's been arrested.'

'Maisie? But she's only a schoolgirl.'

'She's sixteen. She was caught up in a demonstration. It will be in the Evening Standard and Echo tonight. Father asked me if you could come immediately.' Elsie suddenly lost her bravado and looked pathetically vulnerable. Mitchell felt a wave of sympathy that he did not usually associate with his professional work.

'Have you a carriage waiting?'

Elsie nodded.

As they were driven back to Granby House Mitchell said. 'Now, tell me what you know.'

Elsie told him about the recent change in Maisie's behaviour and how they had not envisaged that it would be anything more than a passing phase. When they came abreast of the house, Mitchell suggested that she remain in the carriage while he persuaded her father to come with them directly to the police station.

'Do you think it is a suitable place for Elsie?' Reginald asked as he and Mitchell descended the steps.

'I think it would help Maisie if her sister were there.'

When asked if she was prepared to go with them to a Police Station, Elsie, not wanting to miss out now that she was part of the drama, and feeing safe because Mitchell was with them said, 'Maisie might need me.'

None of them spoke during the short ride, and once they arrived Mitchell took control. He held Elsie's arm as she stepped from the carriage and continued to hold it as they entered the large gloomy building. Reginald followed.

A police officer came forward and demanded their business. He then led them to a desk where a second policeman read the charge; 'Malicious damage and breach of the peace.' Cell number three,' he announced gruffly.

Elsie had not been prepared for the noise that emanated from the cells. She assumed that this was how people would behave if they were drunk, but she was surprised at the way the inmates shouted out, and used obscenities. Mitchell kept a firm hold of her and whispered that she should ignore the outbursts and avoid looking into any of the cells.

The police officer found the correct key on his chain and opened the heavy door. 'She never seems to hear us. Quite oblivious when we come and go. She's been no trouble.'

'The girl is almost totally deaf.' Mitchell felt it was only fair to elucidate the officer.

'Very good, that explains it, Sir.'

Elsie was relieved that the officer did not appear to be rough or unkind. Maisie was sitting motionless with her hands together and clenched between her knees. Her clothes were dishevelled and dirty and her hair also. Elsie went forward and only when she prized Maisie's hands from their fixed position and held them in her own did Maisie raise her head. Her eyes were swollen from crying. She registered Elsie and seemed to hold herself together, but when she saw Mitchell and her father her face crumpled.

'I'm sorry, Father,' she said in her rasping speech, a catch in her voice.

'What did you do?' Reginald asked.

'Not very much. It was quite fun to begin with, marching and singing and everyone watching. I was just carrying a placard.'

Elsie sat beside her and put an arm around her.

'Was Sally there?' Elsie asked.

'She was when we reached the town hall but someone threw a bottle which smashed one of the windows, and Sally disappeared.'

'What happened after that?' Mitchell prompted.

'Everyone around me suddenly got very agitated. The placard was wrenched from me and I fell. It was difficult to get up because people around me were running and I did not know why or where they were going. Then there were a lot of policemen and these women that I did not know were pushed across to where I was, and then we were all made to walk here. Elsie, I was so frightened. Can I come home now?'

Mitchell explained that he would have to complete some formalities and that she would then be given back her belongings. He offered to sort out the paperwork while her sister and father remained with Maisie, and returning with a brown paper bag containing Maisie's personal items Mitchell removed the shawl and wrapped around her shoulders. 'We can go now. There's time enough to talk about this once you're home.'

When they arrived at the house Elsie took Maisie upstairs while Reginald and Mitchell headed for the study. 'I can't stop the papers reporting this, I'm afraid, Sir,' Mitchell said. 'It's unlikely the magistrate will do more than admonish her but it's important that we show that it will not happen again.'

'It's all the fault of that mother of Sally Pevey. I shall have to stop her seeing the girl. The trouble is that they are at the same school and they socialise together.'

Reginald and Mitchell waited for Elsie, and Reginald lit up his pipe.

'Mother's with Maisie,' Elsie reported when she joined them. 'She is having a bath and getting changed and Martha's making up a tray. What will happen next?'

Mitchell told her the usual procedure and added that these affairs usually took some time to come to court. In the meantime they needed to redirect Maisie's interests because a second offence would be serious. Reginald was restless while they discussed the implications of the news locally and the effect on Eleanor. Eventually he excused himself. 'Do you mind if I go and see how Eleanor is bearing up?' Then he remembered that it had been a long afternoon for them all. 'I'll send Martha in with some refreshments. Perhaps you could discuss what you have in mind for Maisie with Elsie?'

In Mitchell's judgement Elsie had maintained a greater composure during the event than her father and decided that it would be of some benefit if he discussed the situation with her, in the absence of her parents, with the object of reducing their anxiety.

'You'll have to be prepared for Wyggeston to send a polite letter asking your parents to withdraw their daughter from school.'

'Expelled?' Elsie looked horrified.

'They have their reputation to guard. It is possible that you could persuade your parents that in one way this could be a good thing.'

'Limiting her contact with Sally?'

Mitchell was pleased that she had grasped the point without him having to appear to be harsh.

'Was Sally arrested?' Elsie asked.

'That is what I need to find out_ that, and when the case is likely to be heard.' He tried to reassure her that Maisie's reputation would not be marred for life, and asked her to think of an alternative occupation that they could present to her father. He said that he too would think on the matter. He stood up to go. 'I have accomplished all that I can for today. Please excuse me to your parents. Remember, some people admire what these women are doing. I'll call in and see you tomorrow.'

When Mitchell arrived the next day Elsie made sure that she was informed of his visit and knocked on the door. 'Can I listen in, Father?'

'We could probably do with your help. Mitchell tells me that the incident was covered extensively in the papers but a young girl called Maisie was too small fry to be mentioned.' Elsie moved to her father and he placed an arm around her shoulders. 'I cancelled the papers yesterday as I didn't want to upset her or your mother. The damage to the buildings near the town hall caused by the women on their march was quite considerable.'

Elsie wondered how Mitchell viewed her sister's behaviour. 'I do believe that Maisie had only a hazy idea of what was happening, with all the noise she would have heard nothing distinctly and even if Sally had tried to warn her, I doubt that in the confusion she would have heard.'

By Mitchell's third visit the anticipated letter had arrived from the school and he found Reginald, with Elsie's support, trying to gain some benefit from the fact that she would have to leave the school. Eleanor joined them, and despite the miserable situation Mitchell caught Elsie's eye and they exchanged a wry smile at Eleanor's rather predictable reaction.

'Mother, none of this will help Maisie,' Elsie withheld her exasperation. 'There's no point in blaming Sally and Mrs Pevey. We need to decide what Maisie is to do, now that she is forbidden to see her friend and has been expelled from school.'

'She was not expelled, as you put it, Elsie, she was just asked to leave. It really is most unfair because she hardly did anything.' Eleanor's voice was sharp and directed at Elsie in particular. She then addressed the room in general. 'It's most unreasonable.'

When Elsie saw Mitchell to the door she said soberly, 'If Maisie had not been caught this time, she might have ended up doing something really dreadful.'

'That is my thought exactly. I'll have a talk with my youngest sister, Clementine, and see if she has any ideas. Come over to the house when I've finished work tomorrow and bring Maisie. She must get out. I'll arrange it all.'

For the first time in several days Elsie's spirit lifted as she watched Mitchell go down the steps into the street.

She would enjoy the change of scene too, she decided. When she informed Maisie of their invitation she hoped that she would be receptive to the idea. Maisie may not have welcomed it but her mood was such that she agreed, and implied that anything was better than sitting alone in her room or enduring her mother's reproachful looks.

'I don't at all mind leaving school. I wasn't much good at lessons anyway, and apart from Sally and her group I don't have any friends. Sally said that the work we did should be everything to us. But it was nice of Clementine to ask us.'

'Well, it was Mitchell who asked us, but Clementine will be there too, and it will be good to get out.'

'Will Father let me go?'

'I think that 'lawyer' Mitchell Devenick's house is most suitable.' Elsie laughed in an effort to cheer her. 'I'm coming too, it could be fun.'

Clementine was cheery and eager to put the girls at their ease. 'Mother says that we don't want fuddy-duddies like her around so we are on our own. You know that Michael is at boarding school and that both my sisters are married. So it's nice for me to have company. I'll ring for tea. Mitchell will be home shortly.'

It was a relief to sit in another drawing room without mention of the incident that had dominated the last few days, and they began to enjoy themselves. After a while Clementine slipped a suggested course of action so subtly into the conversation that only Elsie perceived her intention.

'They're looking for leaders and helpers to set up the

new Girl Guide movement and I've recently enrolled. Do you know about it?' Clementine described the aims of the guiding movement and their activities, and Elsie could see that Maisie was interested since it was a practical course and specifically for girls.

When Mitchell arrived he found Clementine was more than half-way towards achieving her goal and pressed the two girls to continue their discussion while he took Elsie aside.

'Maisie's friend Sally escaped scot-free, but her mother was arrested and imprisoned for a few nights. The demonstration went severely out of control and people in the hall listening to speakers for the Election were injured. How is Clementine succeeding?'

'Wonderfully,' Elsie smiled happily.

When they returned to join the girls it was to hear Clementine saying that there were fundraising events which Maisie could help with straight away, and were rewarded by seeing some signs of animation after days of watching her sunk in apathy.

'You know, Maisie,' Mitchell said clearly, standing in front of her and looking down at her compassionately, 'women are more likely to be recognised for the valuable people that they are by proving themselves in movements such as the Girl Guides, than from any amount of irresponsible acts of civil disobedience. This new guiding association may be the very best way forward.'

Maisie beamed at Mitchell as if she had been awarded a prize. He had given her a new goal, yet one that sought the same ideals as she had been encouraged to believe in.

'Thank you, Mitchell,' Elsie said quietly, while Maisie and Clementine arranged their first meeting.

Mitchell recognised, with some surprise, that he had been enjoying himself while helping them through the incident and was reluctant to lose contact. 'Would you be interested in accompanying me on Saturday afternoon?' He asked impulsively.

'I would,' Elsie looked amused at the idea, 'what are you doing?'

'I haven't thought yet,' he answered, 'I'll call for you around two o'clock and you can find out.'

Chapter Eleven

The day after Veeve sent her telegram, Ruth stood in the hallway of their house in Leicester and waited for her father. She was dressed in her Sunday clothes. Her hat, a dusky brown felt with a small brim, and with a coat of light-weight wool also of a sombre hue, she often managed to appear inconspicuous. Ruth had an ability to close her face so that all vitality was drained from it, and this, more than any other of her characteristics, ensured that she avoided uninvited scrutiny.

Reginald was to accompany Ruth and to oversee her safe deposit on to the branch line. Eleanor voiced a few qualms on the subject of Ruth travelling on her own from London to Maidenhead, but Reginald told her that there were only a few stations to her destination,

Ruth was unaware of the outward impression that she portrayed. Her hands were clammy and she was tense with anticipation. However she was not frightened and as she examined her emotions she was almost embarrassed at her keenness to undertake the journey. Until this opportunity had arisen, she had accepted unquestioningly that she would stay at home. Now she feared lest circumstances might change and Veeve counter her first request, and send a second telegram which would prevent Ruth from departing. She was relieved that her father was to go with her because she felt unequal to the task of crossing London, but the onward journey, alone, was a distant hurdle that she assured her father she would manage.

Reginald had been anxious on Ruth's behalf, knowing that he had not much to offer her in the way of stimulation and this unexpected opportunity to break the monotony of her life seemed to him an answer, if not a perfect one. Reginald distrusted the influence of Veeve's acquaintances, but could rely on Ruth's good sense. She needed to be among young people and George, despite his hedonistic lifestyle, was good-natured and would be kind to Veeve's young sister. He allowed a rye smile as he pictured Ruth's disapproving assessment of Veeve's liberal lifestyle. The two girls were good for each other. Veeve to draw Ruth out of her retiring and somewhat puritanical personality, and Ruth to restrain some of Veeve's excesses. Not that there would be many of the latter if Veeve was now confined to her sofa. Ruth was the ideal sister to send under these circumstances.

In the event, once she was alone in a carriage leaving

London, Ruth was happy to be left with her thoughts. Alone she may have been, without the reassuring presence of her father, but in the same carriage were a young couple who paid her no attention, and a business man who opened his broad sheet newspaper and was hidden from view.

Veeve was almost a stranger to Ruth and her family. In the four years since the extraordinary occasion that had been Veeve and George's wedding, Veeve had rarely visited Leicester. Ruth could not remember much discussion or organisation prior to the wedding. Eleanor had not been involved except in so far as to find outfits for her younger daughters and herself. George had arranged a London wedding which gave them a glimpse of the kind of society that Veeve inhabited. Ruth and her family arrived at the fashionable church of St Mary Le Strand and been lost amongst the sophisticated friends and relations that Veeve and George had invited. The reception at the Savoy Hotel following the ceremony had been a further source of wonder.

Remembering that occasion Ruth felt inadequate. She contemplated Veeve's entourage with trepidation but hoped that, with Veeve indisposed, she would not be required to socialise. She also hoped that she and Veeve would enjoy a semblance of their old relationship because, although Veeve's exploits had always alarmed her, she had to admit that life around Veeve was never dull.

Her own life, since leaving school, had been decidedly unexciting. Elsie was content to have animated conversations with their mother on a multitude of domestic issues in which Ruth was not included. She found no particular consolation in Maisie's company because, when she was not attending a rally she was organising one, and was rarely at home.

Her greatest pleasure was to sit with her father in his office. There were times when he would interrupt her work with a comment from the paper leading to a welcome discussion. Her father appeared to gain as much enjoyment from these interludes as she did. He made a habit of ending these lengthy conversations with a twinkle in his eyes saying, 'Shall we join the ladies?' Ruth had trained herself not to look ahead and plan for herself, unlike Veeve and Maisie who seemed to have an inner driving force. She was not gregarious and without someone to encourage her to join their parties or to go to the theatre, Ruth could see no future for herself beyond her home.

Ruth's rapport with Veeve was not shared by any of her other sisters and she wondered if this would be rekindled. She was conscious that Veeve, albeit often reluctantly, used to listen to her counsel and ask for her advice. Upright and solemn Ruth lifted her chin and, if her travelling companions had troubled to notice, gave a ghost of a smile. Something had finally happened to disturb her humdrum existence and Ruth felt a surge of courage as, for the first time, she looked ahead and wondered where this episode might lead her.

It was not a long journey and George told Reginald that a driver would be at the station; he had only to send a telegram. Ruth was uncertain how long she was expected to stay and had only packed a small suitcase.

Once they left the station which served the village of Maidenhead, the driver directed the carriage through the main street lined on either side with small family shops, the parish hall and the church, until the surface of the road became rougher and narrower. Hedges took the place of cottages and pastureland rose on either side of the lane. Finally they turned towards the river. The area had been discovered by affluent families seeking an escape from the City, taking advantage of the proximity of the river and the railway station to build houses with landing stages and boathouses. Recently planted woods and fields could be seen between houses which, set back from the road by lawns and gardens, were grandiose in style with spacious grounds.

The carriage turned through a pair of iron gates and swung on to a gravelled drive edged with well kept lawns. Elms and beech gave leafy cover and obscured any nearby habitations. The curve of the drive continued until it swept on to a circular forecourt on which two motor vehicles were parked. The carriage drew up underneath an arched porch where George stood to welcome her.

Immediately inside the solid oak double doors was a slate-floored entrance hall. To one side were branched coat racks on which hung a variety of jackets and hats. Trophies from hunting expeditions were displayed on the walls, and on tables under the windows were stuffed animals in glass-covered cabinets. A second set of doors led into a central panelled hall. George strode ahead but Ruth stopped to gaze upwards at the chandelier, at the balcony which surrounded the hall on three sides and at the wide wooden staircase which divided to left and right under three long windows through which the sun was streaming.

'Come this way,' George said as he reached behind him to take hold of a door handle concealed in the panelling.

'Here she is, Veeve!' He announced as they entered. The drawing room was light and airy and dominated by a fireplace with a substantial marble surround. Veeve was resting on a settee. When she saw her sister she threw aside the magazine that she had been reading.

'I've been looking forward to seeing you all day and haven't been able to settle to anything. George, isn't this wonderful? Now you will be able to gallivant off and I will always have company.' Ruth went across towards her sister unsure how to approach, now that she was pregnant. Veeve grasped her hand and drew Ruth's head down so that she could give her a kiss.

'Now sit over there and tell me all the news from home.' This was a new sensation for Ruth, who was accustomed to be the recipient of all Veeve's exploits, and she enjoyed the sense of importance that it gave her. For the first time she felt that she could become, if not her equal, a good friend to Veeve.

Time passed pleasantly. George came and went. In the afternoons Ruth walked to the village or explored the surrounding area. Veeve held small lunch or tea parties but was forbidden by the doctor to exert herself.

One evening when Veeve had set out the cards on the table to play at patience, Ruth opened a small bag containing some wool and knitting needles.

'What are you doing?' Veeve asked.

'I'm going to make a matinee jacket for the baby.'

Veeve looked astounded. 'Whatever for?'

'When I was in Pritchards I saw some knitted baby clothes, and I thought that I could make something. Do you want to?' Ruth added, worried that she might have offended Veeve.

'No I certainly don't. But you can if you want. I hardly think about the baby. I'm glad that I am confined to the house because I could not be seen in company in these shapeless garments.' She looked disgustedly at her carefully designed dress which dutifully concealed her expanded waistline.

'Veeve, how can you say that?' Ruth had never been as particular as Veeve with her clothes but neither had she had the licence that Veeve had been given by George to squander money on a vast wardrobe. She could not understand how Veeve could take so little interest in the baby.

The next time George came down from London he introduced the topic of a nurse. 'Veeve, have you thought what you will need for the baby?' he asked.

'There's plenty of time for that,' Veeve answered.

'I've arranged for a prospective nurse to come and see you,' George disregarded her comment. 'She's had plenty of experience. See if you like her.'

'If you think she is fine, and used to babies, then hire her. I'm sure she will be able to look after one of ours. Where will she sleep?'

'I'll arrange with an architect to alter two rooms

overlooking the herb garden for a nursery and a day-room. Has Dr Andrews seen you this week?'

'As usual. When do you go to Paris?' Veeve seemed to think that she would take up her hectic social lifestyle the moment the birth was completed and enjoyed discussing George's plans with him. Ruth took out her knitting.

'What a splendid little sister you are,' George smiled encouragingly, 'you are lucky, Veeve.'

Ruth returned home briefly to gain her parents' approval to extend her stay until the birth. She arrived back at Veeve's house in much the same manner as on the first day, but this time she needed no one to meet her at the main door. She took off her travelling cape, hung it in the porch and ran up the stairs to her room to tidy her hair. Ruth had been exhorted by Elsie not to allow Maisie's story to become generally known, and Dr Andrews had given strict instructions that Veeve should not to be excited. However, when they were having coffee by the fire after dinner, Veeve reopened the subject.

'So Maisie has been allowed to leave school because she joined the women suffragettes, and I never put a foot wrong and had to stay until the bitter end,' she commented, only half in jest.

Ruth went on to tell how Mitchell had become a regular visitor.

'Mitchell?' Veeve repeated, 'I suppose that they would need a lawyer.'

'And now his sister has encouraged Maisie to join the Guides.'

Veeve made a face. 'Who would have thought that it would be Maisie to cause the family such an upset. We never took much notice of her opinions and now we know that underneath she was a veritable firebrand. I confess I am impressed.'

'What is your mother's reaction?' asked George, mildly amused that the youngest could have succeeded in disrupting the family's equilibrium so completely.

'Mother blames everyone except Maisie. Maisie has already put the whole affair behind her. She says that she is glad that she has left school, and that she is better off with Clementine as a friend.'

'Clementine?'

'Mitchell's sister. They're as thick as thieves, and Maisie says that if it hadn't been for her, Mitchell would never have noticed Elsie.'

The climax to Ruth's story had the desired effect. Veeve reacted with incredulity and explained to George. 'Lil was all set to marry Mitchell and then when his father died he had to break it off. What about Lil?' She turned to Ruth, almost scandalised.

'I'm sure she'll be very happy with Henry,' Ruth said primly. She had grown to like Henry.

'Well I'm sure it is still very strange for Lil,' Veeve persisted.

Reginald must have been of the same opinion when he invited Henry for supper. On their arrival he sent Lil upstairs. 'Your mother is anxious to have a word with you,' he told her, 'Henry and I will disappear into my study.'

He looked forward to Henry's company but today he was uneasy, unable to predict whether the recent developments between his old friend and Elsie would be disturbing.

'Have you seen much of Mitchell Devenick?' Reginald began as he leant forward uncomfortably in his chair. He had to have this conversation before the others arrived downstairs knowing that Eleanor was having the same discussion with Lil.

'Not much. It's different when you are engaged somehow. It is awkward for Lil too. I imagine that Mitchell has put in some hard graft to take over from his father and establish himself. I hope he's doing well.'

'You may have heard about Maisie's little incident?'

'Some scrap with the women's movement!' Henry laughed affectionately at the exploits of Lil's youngest sister.

'A bit more serious than that,' Reginald was able to talk about the affair with more detachment now that it was resolved. 'We needed the services of Mitchell to extricate her from the law.'

Henry raised his eyebrows as he realised the implications. 'She did get into trouble, didn't she? Is she on the straight and narrow? Seen the error of her ways?' Henry's attitude was that this was a mild rebellion on Maisie's part and not a threat to the fabric of society.

'Since then Mitchell has been seeing our Elsie. They are quite taken with each other.' Reginald watched the effect of his words.

'Lil and I,' Henry said slowly, 'are very happy. I don't

think she has any regrets now about Mitchell. However, you never know do you?' Reginald was sad that he had to cause Henry to speak so wistfully. Henry, who was invariably confidant and robust, showed the vulnerable side of his nature for the first time.

'If I know my daughter,' Reginald strived to find some way of comforting him and yet remain strictly honest, 'she is happy.'

Reginald played with his pipe and Henry gazed into the fire.

Eleanor disturbed them when she opened the door. 'Reginald, can I have a word with you?' She looked at him meaningfully and beckoned with her hand to encourage him to leave with her.

Lil entered the room and Henry, still sitting, raised his head, tipped it to one side and waited with a questioning look.

'I've heard, Mother told me,' Lil interpreted his look correctly, 'they'll make a good couple.'

Henry stood up but stayed where he was. Lil sat down in her father's chair.

'Any regrets about our engagement?' Henry looked down at her with such an expression of sadness and longing that Lil realised that he had misunderstood her easy dismissal of Elsie's and Mitchell's relationship.

'Henry,' she chided him, 'we were so young. Elsie is much more suited to Mitchell than I am.' She rose and lifted her face to be kissed. 'I need a man of substance.' And Henry, who accepted the double entendre as confirmation that his affection was equally reciprocated, gathered her to him with relief and gratitude.

Eleanor reassured Reginald that Lil had long ago outgrown Mitchell and judged the moment to return to the study to a nicety. She found the couple, Henry with an arm around Lil, planning Elsie's future for her.

'Elsie will know all our secrets,' Lil speculated, 'since Mitchell is lawyer to all of our family. We will have to watch our step, we can't have Mitchell intervening for any reason on our behalf, he has already had to rescue Maisie and sort out maintenance between Brindsley-Smith and Bett.' Lil smiled at Henry. 'Any news of 'the rotter' by the way?'

'I see him on occasions at the Club. He travels a good deal and from his accounts his sales are the reason that the House of Whitehorn is riding high. He has no end of an opinion of himself. I don't seek him out but our past links entitle him to clobber me for a glass of port after dinner. I console myself that he might have information that could be useful one day.'

With the atmosphere restored and the two couples in agreement that the new addition to the family would be very much welcomed, they went into dinner to enjoy the effect of their news on Bett, Maisie and Sheilagh.

Meanwhile, the event gave Ruth and Veeve many hours of delicious gossip as they discussed whether Lil was devastated, or Elsie embarrassed, or if Mitchell had any regrets and they would have been disappointed if they had full cognisance of the facts, which were that all the individuals involved were convinced that they enjoyed the happiest outcome.

As Veeve neared her time she became less

demanding and this meant that Ruth's role as a companion was easier. She hoped that this change in Veeve was a precursor to a more maternal attitude. Veeve seemed to have lost the restlessness which caused her to tire quickly of a pastime and need company whenever she was not compelled to rest. She watched Ruth as she performed her small tasks and lay stretched out on a chaise-longue in the wintry sun to enjoy its warmth through the south-facing windows.

The two sisters settled into an easy routine. The nurse had been engaged to arrive when the baby was due, and George had seen to all the arrangements. He had no engagements that would prevent him from being at home for the birth of their child.

One afternoon, a week before George was due home, Ruth heard a clatter of hooves and the rumble of wheels on the gravel below her bedroom window. There was only one person who arrived with such panache, since guests would draw up with more respect for the raked gravel and awaiting servants. Her suspicions were confirmed when she leant out of the window and saw George walking briskly from his carriage and under the porch.

Ruth had mixed feelings about his arrival. When George was around Veeve was animated and the tempo of their lives increased, even with the strictures on her activities. Word would travel fast around the neighbourhood and a succession of visitors would call. Some to drop in their cards in expectation that George would return their visit, some to enquire after Veeve and stay to entertain George, and some to join them for a meal or spend an hour in idle chat. Ruth endeavoured to make herself scarce during these social visits but George would entreat her to stay and was mainly successful, except in the evenings when Ruth would steadfastly refuse all invitations and would retreat to Veeve's bedside. She did welcome the change to their routine for Veeve's sake, but for her own she preferred it when there were just the two of them.

Since his arrival was unexpected, Ruth felt that it would be considerate of her to go out in the afternoon. Wrapping up because there was a sharpness to the January air, she took a walk through the woods and on returning she dawdled. The aconites were out and she gathered a large bunch for Veeve since none of them grew near the house. She knew that she was deceiving herself and that Veeve took little interest in wild flowers, barely noticing which was in season and only appreciating the bowls of cut flowers around the house as one might value a recently purchased picture, but it was her way of expressing her sympathy with Veeve's confinement. However, with the exhilaration that would accompany George's unexpected reappearance, Veeve was unlikely to appreciate them and Ruth decided to keep the flowers for her own room. She changed her dress, partly in case there was a visitor for tea, but also because George always chided her for looking 'missish' if she wore her every-day dress when he was there. Veeve always looked stylish, even in her eighth month, and George was keen that Ruth was not considered a poor relation.

Having allowed Veeve and George a reasonable

amount of time together, Ruth descended the stairs and joined them in the drawing room. Veeve's cheeks were glowing and George, releasing Veeve's hand, stood up as she entered.

'Even Paris could not keep me one week longer,' George began by way of explanation, and indicating a chair went across to the trolley and poured Ruth a cup of tea. 'How are you, little sister?'

He then turned with a beaming smile to both girls. 'I've told cook that we are to have a celebratory dinner, just the three of us, to congratulate Veeve on her magnificent patience. I'll be able to help you entertain her now, Ruth, as I've cancelled everything. You could have a few days at home if you wanted. There may be some more scandals.'

Ruth looked shocked.

'Only joking Ruth, I admire Maisie for her convictions.' Seeing that Ruth was unappeased he went on. 'She seems to be a model daughter again, and I'm sure Lil doesn't care a toss who Elsie marries because Henry is such a good sport. I've little news to report but I've promised Veeve that I shall purchase her a car that we can keep here. I can't see Veeve spending all day nursing a baby, can you?'

It was the happiest afternoon. Ruth was fond of George and he had a knack of making her feel at ease. Veeve glowed with delight at his return and shed the veneer of affectation she sometimes felt obliged to adopt so that she lived up to her reputation as the glittering hostess. George too seemed to take pleasure in their simple, cosy evening. After dinner Ruth left them and had to stifle an unforeseen pang of loneliness. These were her friends, but they were greater friends to each other and had no need of her. She resolved to leave the next morning and to spend some time, as George suggested, back with her family. Everyone was pairing up except Maisie, and she determined to give her younger sister more of her time, if Maisie had any time to spare for her.

Ruth woke in the night to hear noises coming from below her window. She lay for a moment listening and then saw lights playing on the curtains. When she heard the horses' hooves, the rattle of carriage wheels and the sound of muted voices she crossed the carpeted floor and, more curious than fearful, parted the curtains. George was giving instructions to a driver, speaking earnestly, and without his usual composure. Without thinking of the propriety of her action Ruth took her shawl and, wrapping it around her, fumbled for the handle of the door. The passage was well lit, nothing had been extinguished for the night, and when she reached the balcony she looked down into the hall. George was standing alone. He looked up and saw her and took the stairs two at a time. At the top he stopped and ran his hand over his eyes.

'The baby's coming, Ruth. I've sent for the doctor and the midwife. The first baby often takes a long time. I'm going back to be with her.' He seemed to take control of himself. 'Nothing to worry about, go and make yourself some hot milk, then go back to sleep, there's a girl.'

In bed, Ruth sat in the dark warming both hands as

she clasped her cup. She sat until she heard the carriage return, and be met by George. She sat and listened for the footsteps to retreat down the passage to the opposite wing of the house.

She woke late, dressed, and went downstairs to the dining room. She ate alone, following her usual routine until, instead of going to see Veeve, she made her way back to her room. She wondered where she should go and if there was anything she could do. There was silence in her part of the house. She wandered along to the nursery and tried to imagine a baby in that cot. How strange it would be to have other occupants in her wing, as she thought of it, trying to picture the nurse and the baby.

'There you are,' George exclaimed. Ruth felt guilty, as if she was trespassing, but the moment she saw him, with his collar open, without his jacket, his eyes red from lack of sleep and his hair rumpled, she knew that she had no need.

'Can I do anything?' she asked.

'If you would, I'd be grateful. I don't want to leave Veeve, she's having a rough time. Could you meet the nurse when she arrives, sometime this afternoon? Her name is Mrs Summers. Could you do that?'

'Of course,' said Ruth, 'is Veeve all right?'

'I think this is normal. No place for a young girl like you.' He spoke almost bitterly. 'I must go now.' He stood indecisively, and then strode away towards the other wing.

Wherever Ruth went there was a deathly calm. The servants seemed like ghost figures, silently dusting or carrying sheets, continuing with their domestic duties. In the kitchen there was an air of lassitude. Water was kept boiling on the hob. Ruth was invited by the cook to sit with them and was given a mug of tea. Cold ham and other meats were laid out, freshly baked bread cut into thick slices sat in a basket, and Ruth could see a saucepan of soup ready to be heated. No one spoke.

She went outside. The gardeners were talking in a group together, one resting his foot on a spade, another had abandoned his wheelbarrow and was sitting on the steps of the ornamental fountain. Ruth avoided them and picked some flowers from the woods for the nursery. It was when she re-entered the house that she heard the scream. She ran up the stairs and halted on the landing. As she set off for the nursery she heard another. She racked her brains to remember what had been said about babies. She was too young to remember Maisie being born. Flo said that she had an easy birth with her daughter so Ruth surmised that some were difficult and painful. She had promised to wait for Mrs Summers. Mrs Summers would tell her. She went down to the drawing room hoping to be insulated from her sister's ordeal, and here she waited.

Some time later a maid asked if she would like some tea and Ruth nodded, not trusting herself to speak, yet she had so many questions. Later a servant came to say that Mrs. Summers had arrived. Ruth dreaded the moment when she would have to take her up the stairs but Mrs Summers took control at once.

'Take me to my room, dear, and fill me in on the way.' She gave directions for her luggage and headed for the stairs.

'I don't really know,' faltered Ruth, 'I heard screams.'

'That's to be expected,' Mrs Summers said dismissively.

'But they seem to have stopped now.' Mrs Summers made no comment and they proceeded to the nursery. 'Flowers. Very pretty. Did you pick them? Thank you. Now I'm just fine and I'll make myself at home. I take it your sister is along the other passage? I'll go along and see what is happening.'

Ruth began to say that no one could go along to Veeve, but in reality it was she who did not want to. She was frightened by the mysterious horror of the day and did not want to know more. She went to her room, shut her door, and taking a book, lay under her bed cover. When the sun went down she was hungry. Without looking in the mirror or having any regard for her clothes, trailing a hand along the banisters to lengthen the time, she walked slowly down the stairs, avoiding anyone who might bring her unwelcome news. In the kitchen were the remains of a cold spread and the soup tureen was simmering. Ruth helped herself and wished that she had brought her book. She continued to sit despite her plate being empty, stupefied into inactivity by the turn of events. Her reverie was interrupted when Mrs Summers bustled in.

'Your sister has had a boy. He's small, as is to be expected, but he's fine.' She saw Ruth's worried face and softened.

'Your sister will pull through, dear. It was touch and

go, but the doctor says that she has a strong heart and that given time she will recover.'

Ruth felt sick. She wished she knew what questions to ask. 'Veeve?' was all she managed to say.

'She's lost a lot of blood. She's sleeping now. I'll make sure the baby is cared for. Don't fret. Childbirth can be like this.'

'No one told me,' Ruth said weakly. She wished she could leave the table but felt constrained to stay and sit while Mrs Summers ate heartily. Then she was glad that she had stayed because George arrived.

'Ruth, the doctor says that Veeve will live.' He seemed to have been searching for her and temporarily forgotten Ruth's age. 'It was terrible. I just had to sit and wait and wait, not knowing. Everything's all right now. It's over.' George then turned to Mrs Summers. 'I'll go and lie down, Mrs Summers, if you don't mind. Thank you for coming so promptly. Will that be all right? If I sleep?'

Mrs Summers attitude to George was maternal and a surprise to Ruth. 'Leave everything to me and the midwife. Ruth can help me if I need it, can't you, dear?' Ruth smiled gratefully. 'It's too early for you to see your sister but would you like to see the baby?'

In her preoccupation with Veeve, Ruth had barely registered that there was now another person to be considered. They were passing through the hall where they met the doctor.

'The midwife will stay until I send a nurse for the mother.' He spoke in a grave voice. 'Complete peace and quiet. I will call in the morning.'

They continued on to the nursery and Ruth wished that she did not feel so resentful towards the sleeping baby. He was very small and crinkled and defenceless. All those months of waiting without knowing what to expect, but nothing had prepared her for this.

Chapter Twelve

The following morning, when Ruth went downstairs to find some breakfast, George was already in the dining room. He stood and greeted Ruth eagerly, the previous day's ordeal behind him now that he had a night's sleep, a shave and a change of clothes.

'How have you been? The doctor's not due until later this morning and I suggest that we go for a walk to stretch our legs. Veeve is still sleeping and the nurse said that she's not to be disturbed. It's best to wait and be advised by the doctor, although I appreciated that you'll be anxious to see your sister.'

The early mist that hung over the river had begun to lift, evaporating as the sun rose and gained strength. George and Ruth kept to the path avoiding the damp grass. After the agitation of the previous day the still air and steadily flowing river soothed them. They spoke intermittently, content to listen to their footsteps as they crunched on the gravel. Above them the leafless trees were showing early signs of swollen buds, and on the ground surrounding their trunks a profusion of early snowdrops had opened overnight. Ruth wondered whether yesterday, while Veeve had been in labour, she had been looking without seeing and that the flowers had been there all the time. They followed the path along the river and sat on a bench by the boathouse. The warmth of the sun penetrated their clothes and it was tempting to indulge themselves by watching the ripples and eddies and shut out any thoughts of Veeve's suffering. It would be so much easier just to stay, Ruth felt guiltily, and sit there forever. Veeve would recover and the baby would eat and sleep. George would come and go and then Veeve would come and go but what would happen to her.

'Will you stay until Veeve is better? She gives the impression of being so independent and strong willed, but it's a veneer. It's a lot to ask because you have already spent so much time here.'

'I'll stay,' she tried to express more than just a simple acquiescence, 'I'd like to stay, more than anything.'

The doctor permitted Ruth a short visit to her sister. 'Five minutes,' he warned. Veeve was a very small figure lost in the large bed. Her slim body was covered with a white cotton blanket and her face was as pale as the pillows. Ruth sat on the chair vacated by the midwife and held Veeve's hand. It was lifeless.

'I can't stay long,' Ruth whispered. Veeve slept.

Closing the door she made her way along corridor. George was saying goodbye to the doctor. She went down the stairs and joined him in the hall.

'Dr Andrews says we need to be patient.' He put a hand affectionately on her shoulder. 'Can you amuse yourself, little Ruth? You can see Veeve again tonight. I'm just going out for a bit.'

Ruth passed the next two days in a haze. She wrote to her mother without alarming her, picked up her knitting, read a little, went for walks and was allowed short visits to Veeve.

On the third day, however, everything changed. Veeve became very ill. She developed a fever and Dr Andrews organised a second nurse so that she could be attended night and day. Mrs Summers took sole charge of the baby and George was distraught. Day after day they waited to see if Veeve would pull through. Finally the crisis passed but Dr Andrews warned them to expect a prolonged recovery.

George went away for a few days and when he returned Veeve seemed to rally, only to have a relapse a day or two later. Dr Andrews suggested to George that he limit his visits. His absences became longer. Ruth's presence, on the other hand, appeared to soothe the invalid and she spent more time in the sickroom. One nurse was dispensed with and eventually the day came when Veeve sat by her bed and then began to move around the room. Ruth could feel the effect of her recovery on the whole household and a few weeks later when Veeve was able to come downstairs, it felt as if everything was returning to normal. At the end of August George came back to Halswell. He told Ruth that she should visit her family and he would ensure that Veeve was not neglected.

There was plenty to tell her family. Ruth relayed a warning from Dr Andrews that they were not yet encouraged to visit. No-one could imagine Veeve confined for a year, nor were they aware that the first four months had been so critical. She told them that she spent many hours reading to Veeve and generally keeping her company. George was not often there, Ruth explained, for what could he do, and the baby was fine. She tried to describe the baby but could think of no remarkable traits. She told them that the baby's name was Ronald. George had named him because Veeve had been too sick and there had been no discussion regarding a Christening.

For once Ruth was disappointed with her home. So very little had changed and yet there was no place for her. Maisie cycled regularly for meetings or to perform her Guiding duties and was obviously establishing that she could be as independent as if she were a suffragette. She even told Ruth that she intended to earn her own living. She implied that Ruth led an aimless life in comparison to her own.

Bett spoke of the baby with such longing that Ruth felt ashamed she had ignored Ronald in favour of staying by Veeve. Bett hinted that Veeve needed to take an interest in the baby for the child's sake and Ruth resolved to initiate this.

Reginald, Ruth discovered, was preoccupied with a recent accident at the mill. A woman had caught her fingers in a machine and would be left maimed, and he was in frequent discussion with Tom, in whose workshop this had occurred. He would closet himself with Henry, for financial advice on the case, or Mitchell for legal advice and had no spare time.

Flo and Lil, however, were anxious to see their sister and to talk about Veeve.

'It is ironic that Veeve of all of us, should have been the one who has been virtually bed-bound for a year,' commented Lil.

'Can she really be going to learn to drive a motor car?' Flo asked.

Ruth was amused at being the focus of attention. 'George is buying her a new one to have at Halswell.'

'Won't she have to look after the baby?'

'Not if I know Veeve. She has a nanny, Mrs Summers, and another girl who helps her. Mrs Summers is excessively overbearing and only George is good enough for her. She will do anything for him. Not that there is anything to do as there are plenty of servants. She doesn't notice me.'

'So what do you do all day, Ruth, if there are servants for everything?' Flo asked, awed by this talk of a houseful of servants.

'Veeve has been very ill. The doctor at one point said that it was touch and go if she would live. I stay with her most of the time.'

'But when she's better?' persisted Flo.

'I don't know,' admitted Ruth, 'I couldn't live as she does with house parties, and Ascot, and Paris and London.' Her voice trailed away.

'It sounds glamorous,' said Flo doubtfully, 'but I like my home and having my daughters with me.'

Ruth sighed, she felt groundless. She did not belong at home nor at Veeve's.

By the end of the week Ruth was ready to leave. She was surprised at how defensive she felt towards Veeve, despite understanding Flo's and Lil's views of what appeared to be an idle existence lived for pleasure. Veeve managed to extract so much fun out of life that it was not easy to condemn her.

It was becoming apparent to Ruth that there was no right way to live. Flo and Elsie were content with domesticity. For Lil there was the intellectual stimulus of her design work and an outlet for her talents. There was the woman with a mission which was her youngest sister, and then there was the social butterfly that was Veeve. None of these lifestyles appealed to her and she wondered falteringly if she would have to find her own path or whether a path might ultimately be laid out for her.

For Ruth, there was an air of wonder at every stage of Veeve's recovery, and indeed, at the daily development of her nephew. Ruth took Ronald in his perambulator on her daily walks. He was a chubby, red cheeked little boy with a predominately cheerful nature given to bouts of enraged crying but which never occurred when being pushed outside, much to Ruth's relief as she had little faith in her ability to cope with an upset baby.

Sitting in his black leather chair, legs covered in a blanket and his hat askew he seemed to enjoy everything he saw and Ruth began to extend her walks to the village where the little chap's earnest expression attracted people to approach them. The perambulator and its cheery occupant was the key that opened the door to making friends, and people that she had passed regularly in the street now came to speak to her, admire her nephew, and comment on his beautifully upholstered pram. He was a healthy looking child, when many, especially those in the cities, were not, and this too encouraged exchanges of views with mothers and grandmothers that she met while making her purchases in the nearby shops. She began to linger in the nursery to watch Mrs Summers change and feed the little boy, although any attempt to do the task herself would have been foiled by the possessive nanny. Ruth was not upset, she had no wish to take over these essentially messy tasks.

Ruth found, however, that her efforts to interest Veeve in Ronald's progress met with quiet resistance. She reasoned that it was only a matter of time and patience before Veeve would show some affection for the child, but in the meantime Veeve resented the loss of Ruth's company while her activities were still restricted.

Throughout September Veeve grew steadily stronger. The household became more active as Veeve received callers whose visits were carefully monitored, and then was permitted to return a few of those calls.

George wrote from Paris to say that he would return towards the end of October when the weather would still be mild enough for him to take Veeve to the south of France to continue her convalescence. This spurred Veeve to be conscientious about her rest and to limit her walks to short strolls through the gardens. Gradually Ruth introduced the idea of taking Ronald in his perambulator with them on their walks and she would catch Veeve looking at her son with curiosity, or smile occasionally at his babyish antics.

She should have guessed that this idyllic period with the prospect of a steady return to health and normality could not last. She went to the drawing room one morning to find that it was empty. She heard a gramophone playing upstairs and followed the sound to Veeve's bedroom. When she entered she saw Veeve being tied into a new bustle by her dressmaker. Veeve had lost weight and the bodice, combined with the padded bustle, gave her some of the shape that she had lost. In the wardrobe hung a new dress made from deep purple satin. Ruth watched as the dressmaker lifted the garment over Veeve's outstretched arms and then began to close the new-fangled press fasteners. It was a day dress of exquisite workmanship; layers of pleated fabric encased Veeve's narrow waist, and material from the gently scooped neck fell to the ruched edging of the sleeves and bodice in effortless lines.

Veeve's face was flushed with the exhilaration of seeing herself in her new clothes. 'It's the height of fashion, I'm told. What do you think? I've another dress to try on, and a suit for travelling.'

'Why do you need travelling clothes?' Ruth asked.

'I'm going to Paris. George is coming back in a week but I feel so good that I want to surprise him. Can you imagine his face?'

Once Veeve had fixed upon a course of action she was unlikely to be dissuaded. 'Veeve, that is wonderful. I can help keep an eye on Ronald. You will be careful, won't you?'

'I'll spend the night in London, and then continue the journey from there. I'll be in Paris by late afternoon.' The dressmaker approached with a garment draped over her arm. 'Stay and see this one. I'll wear this on our first evening'

The second dress was olive green with coffee coloured stripes, but cut in so many panels and interspersed with so many layers overlaid with lace that the effect was harmonious rather than fussy. The neckline was square and the bodice tapered to the waistline with narrow darts. At the level of her hips, folds of material were gathered into the side seams to accentuate the curve of her back.

However, while she observed her, Ruth realised that Veeve had over-exerted herself. Her face became pale and her forehead to glisten. 'Let me and your maid do your packing for you, I know your wardrobe.' Veeve accepted without a fuss.

Later that evening Veeve rallied and packed the last of her belongings while moaning at her dowdy wardrobe and despairing that the styles were out of date.

'What will you do if George was not in Paris?'

All kinds of potential mishaps flooded into Ruth's mind.

'Most people show courage because they ignored their doubts, your fears are only a reflection of your nature. I'll soon be shopping for the latest fashions with George, who loves taking me to the very best boutiques that Paris has to offer.'

'You will give instructions to the housekeeper,' Ruth said, because she was not sure of her own position, 'and send a telegram when you're due home.'.

'We'll be back within the week, but I can't think of that now. George will organise it all.'

The next day the carriage arrived, Veeve's trunk was

stowed, and only Ruth watched her leave. She sensed disapproval from the housekeeper, and dismay from Mrs Summers, but put this down to annoyance at the disruption of their routine, rather than censorship of Veeve's decision. Ruth stood, a lonely figure under the porch, until the carriage was out of sight.

At last the train conveying Veeve to Paris drew into St. Lazare. Veeve, despite taking two days over her journey, felt drained of energy and light-headed. She wondered whether her sense of unreality was the legacy of her recent illness. It was as if she was floating through a mist and only when instructions were demanded of her did the fog clear to allow her to concentrate.

She had travelled the route countless times, sometimes leaving Halswell to arrive in Paris on the same day in time to join a party in the evening. She could not believe now, that such an itinerary was possible, so weak did she feel. It was true that previously she had travelled with George who handled all arrangements so that she was only required to step from one conveyance to another, yet she had been so profoundly tired following the channel crossing that she had almost begged the first porter she encountered on disembarking to find her a room in the nearest hotel.

When Veeve engaged with porters, hotel commissaires, bellboys or train conductors, she met with unstinting kindness and consideration. The effect of a well dressed, but obviously frail young woman elicited solicitous concern at every turn. Veeve was used to attention, usually because she actively sought it and enjoyed the interaction, but this unconsciously provoked care for her well-being was a sensation totally new to her. She had not the energy to assert herself and accepted help wherever it was offered.

At no point did Veeve contemplate returning home, nor did she regret her decision. As she neared her journey's end her spirits lifted and she felt as well as she had on leaving Halswell. She and George always stayed in the Hotel Impérial and she greeted all the familiar landmarks during this final stage of her journey with a small smile playing around her mouth. She looked out of the carriage windows at this city that she had come to love and which held so many treasured memories.

The driver slowed the horses as they approached the steps of the hotel's grand entrance. Veeve opened her travelling bag and took out her hand mirror. She was somewhat unnerved by the face returning her gaze and hastily touched her cheeks and lips with rouge, but there was little she could do to change the telltale dark shadows beneath her eyes. Tucking her cosmetics away, and glad that the jaunty set of her hat distracted from her wan complexion, Veeve took a deep breath and felt a surge of excitement. The carriage door was opened for her, she stepped confidently on to the pavement and then steadily mounted the steps to the foyer. She had no need to ask for her baggage to be collected, knowing that the hotel staff were exemplary. The commissaire gave Veeve a formal nod of acknowledgement, and led her to the reception desk where he rang the bell to summon Gaston, the maître d'hotel.

Veeve was momentarily dismayed that it was not

Gaston himself, but a younger man who came to the desk. On the last occasion that Veeve had been at the hotel, with her set of friends gathered around her to say farewell, Gaston had surrounded her with paternal solicitude. At that time she had firmly resisted his gentle administrations, but she wished that this kindly man had been there to greet her today.

'Is Mr Eaton in his usual suite? I would be grateful if you would tell him that his wife is downstairs in the lobby.' The boy looked confused.

'Un moment s'il vous plaît, Madame,' he said as he disappeared into the office closing the door behind him.

A few seconds later Gaston emerged. 'Madame Eaton, quel plaisir, it has been such a very long time since you were here. How delightful. Your husband is not, perhaps, expecting you? This calls for a celebration. Allow me, Madame.'

He led her across the hall and through a door to a corner seat in an alcove, where on a small round table a lamp emitted a subdued light. Veeve was a favourite of Gaston and she responded gratefully for the chance to sit down. He fussed for a few moments over the lamp, arranged for Veeve to be comfortable with a cushion and then stepped back to bestow his customary smile.

'Madame, I will order champagne and inform your husband myself.'

Before long a waiter brought two glasses and opened the champagne bottle. Veeve indicated with a nod that he should fill them. She watched the bubbles filter upwards in the fluted glasses, recalling the many evenings when she and George had shared champagne in earlier carefree days. She shifted forward in her chair to look towards the door which at that moment was opened by the maître, followed by George.

Veeve half rose then, feeling light-headed, sat down again. She saw George's face lighting up into a bright eager smile as he hurried towards her with hands outstretched.

'George! I was asking for the key to your room but you are here already.'

George looked over his shoulder to the reception area where Veeve could see a woman was standing leaning back against the highly polished desk. A look of intense irritation crossed his face which he corrected as he drew nearer to Veeve. Veeve saw a tall woman dressed in a light wool coat of autumn colours, leather ankle boots and a matching hat of deep tangerine.

Gaston stepped forward and appeared to try to prevent the encounter. Veeve stood but feared she would faint. 'Take me to another hotel,' she said shakily.

'George!' The woman called again from beside the reception desk, 'That dratted hair dresser was late again...what is it?'

George responded to this second call and when he returned Gaston was escorting an almost lifeless Veeve through the hall, requesting the Commissaire to call for her luggage and helping her into a carriage. Gaston accompanied Veeve the short distance to a nearby hotel, the area was plentiful with establishments of good quality, and supervised her removal to a suite.

For two days Veeve lay in bed, cried and slept, and ate a little. She soaked in a bath and cried some more and refused to see George on every occasion that the bell boy brought a message from him. She emerged once, dressed soberly, her hair in a simple chignon, and went into the lobby to send a telegram to her father.

Request Bring Devenick. Paris. Hotel Bourget. Seek Divorce. Veeve.

Chapter Thirteen

Not long after Lil's engagement to Henry, three years earlier, he had taken her to a restaurant where he told her he had some thrilling news for them both. Unfortunately, that very day, Lil had been to see her doctor. Henry was too engrossed with settling Lil into her seat at the table for him to notice that she was more subdued than usual. She looked enchanting, with her unconventional manner of dressing, a hotchpotch of designs which somehow seemed to work and resulted in her flair for anticipating the next fashion. He was eager to impart his news.

'What do you know about tea?' Henry asked as the waiter filled Lil's glass with a small amount of wine.

'China? India?'

'In this case, India. Production is increasing which means an increase in plantations, shipments, sales and distribution.'

'I thought you were in finance?'

'I am,' Henry was pleased that he had confused her. 'Let me explain. The larger the company, the more assiduous must checks be on cash flow. What we expend on development must be balanced by our production. I don't need to elaborate on this, since you can see it for yourself. What a company needs is someone to oversee the expenditure and returns, and for that it means beginning at source.'

'India?'

'Yes, India.' Henry scanned her face but he was unable to decipher how she was processing the news. 'A three-year posting with two home trips to England, to ensure that the company is on a secure footing. I have been offered the post as chief financial adviser, based in Delhi, but the summer months will be spent in Darjeeling and the foothills of the Himalayas, where most of the plantations are situated.'

Henry was still unable to get the measure of her reaction. 'It would be a great opportunity for us, Lil. Many people bring up their families in India, and the social life is reputed to be second to none with ayahs and servants. You want to travel, don't you?' Henry's voice trailed away when he saw Lil's expression. She avoided his gaze while he waited for her to come to a decision.

'I can't come, Henry. I can't live that sort of life. I can see that you have set your heart on it. I won't stop you.'

Slowly she twisted her ring and then held it in her forefinger and thumb. 'Go, Henry. If you find someone during that time, I'll understand. If, when you return you are still alone, then write to me, but not before.'

'Three years, Lil.'

'I understand. I can wait, but you must take this

chance.' She handed him the ring.

Henry wondered if she referred to the chance to work in India or the chance to find a different wife, but he did not want it clarified.

'Can we enjoy this evening?' Henry felt deflated yet he saw in Lil's eyes that she was saddened and irresolute.

'Henry, we will always be friends.' Her voice choked and she lifted her glass, tears brimming. Henry took her hand, removed her glass and placing it out of reach, leant forward to kiss her. 'I'll always love you, Lil.'

Henry was not sure why Lil had broken off their engagement, nor, despite plenty of opportunities, did he find anyone with whom he wanted to replace her. On his second furlough he made his way to his club because, although he took no particular pleasure in Brindsley-Smith's company, he was nevertheless related to Lil's family and this was his best chance of hearing news of her.

'Hello, old boy. Back from dust-ridden India?' Brindsley-Smith, looking as self-satisfied as on previous occasions, hailed Henry from an armchair in a commanding position by the fire. Henry, who had hoped for a more discreet encounter, swept his eyes across the room where several unfamiliar faces were turned in his direction. He did not wish to be associated with one of the least popular members of the club, and his annoyance was compounded by Brindsley-Smith's assumption that he would disparage India.

Henry's time in that vast country had been a revelation. 'No more dust-ridden than we are fog-bound,' Henry retaliated. 'Nothing can compare with the Himalayas.' Henry shook Brindsley-Smith's hand before sitting in an armchair on the opposite side of the fire. He was not going to be embarrassed into pretending a superiority that he did not feel towards the Indian peoples that he had met and worked with. On the other hand he suspected that Brindsley-Smith would be incapable of grasping this concept and would be impervious to persuasion.

'I'm glad it suited you, not my line at all.'

Henry's deduction was confirmed and the topic closed, but Brindsley-Smith continued in his overbearing manner. 'I expect you'll be catching up on events here, gossip, who's doing what and why. For myself, our company, we're still staying afloat. Ups and downs, as is to be expected.'

'I'm pleased to hear it. And Reginald is he well?'

'He slogs along. With all those women at home Reginald needs a break. Like that distressing bother with Lil.' Brindsley-Smith stopped suddenly. 'Sorry, you were engaged to her weren't you, before you left for India.'

Although he instinctively resisted giving Brindsley-Smith the opportunity to disseminate gossip, Henry asked, 'What bother was that?'

'The poor girl can't have children. It'll ruin her chances of finding anyone, now that they know.'

Very little of the subsequent conversation did Henry remember, once he had extricated himself from Brindsley-Smith's company, but much that he had not understood was now clear.

Several months later, returning from his final tour,

Henry wrote to Lil without admitting that he knew her reasons for breaking their engagement. He quoted a passage from the marriage service and then wrote. 'If you feel the same, even now, there are no obstacles to prevent us being together. I'll take you on any terms, you can continue to work, if you wish. We are sufficient for each other, if you wish. I will work in Leicester, if you wish.' He enclosed an invitation to a concert and dinner, and after a few days he received a note from Lil accepting.

'I should have told you that we can never have a family,' Lil said with Henry's hand clasped tightly in her own.

Henry did not answer but with his other hand turned her face to him. Lil's expression was troubled.

'I could not have lived in India, what would I have done?' she asked. 'What would you have done, if I had told you then?'

'Stayed here with you,' Henry saw tears in her eyes. 'Yet, perhaps, one day we'll see that it was for the best. I learnt much, I am humbler, and more grateful for the gifts back home,' he wiped a tear from her cheek, 'and you, my dear one, are a celebrated designer.'

Chapter Fourteen

Reginald, wearing his hat and coat, was leaving Granby House having had lunch at home with Eleanor, when a post boy met him on the steps and handed him Veeve's telegram. He turned into the house, hung his coat and hat back on to the coat stand and entered his study. In those few seconds his mind conjectured several scenarios all of which were of a morbid nature.

He rang the bell and arranged to be taken immediately to Mitchell's office. Mitchell ushered his father-in-law into a private room, so as to avoid the ignominy of sitting in the waiting room. Reginald turned the piece of paper over and over in his hands. What was the girl doing in Paris when he thought she was convalescing at Halswell? George had always appeared to be a nice man, and they had, even if he did not particularly approve of it, a carefree existence. He did not know what to make of it. Despite his exasperation on many occasions with Veeve, he did not like to think of his girl in trouble.

'Mitchell, there's the devil to pay,' he began. 'It's Veeve. She's in Paris. Here, read this for yourself.'

Mitchell read the note. 'We can only respond to her request. Can you be ready to leave tonight? We could travel as far as London.'

'Call for me when you're ready. What shall I tell Eleanor?'

'A crisis meeting of the Board in London. Something vague. I'll have to tell Elsie but I'll ask her to say nothing at this point.'

'I don't like to keep Eleanor in the dark, it tends only to make matters worse, but perhaps I'll wait until we have more information. I can't shield her from everything although I could wish to spare her.' He would have wished to spare himself, but failing that he would have liked to share this upset with Eleanor.

Mitchell and Reginald arrived in Paris late the following evening and it was after nine o' clock when they finally booked into the Hotel Bourget. They sent word to Veeve to meet them in the lounge, where Mitchell ordered brandy and coffee.

Now that they had arrived, they found that Veeve was reluctant to talk. She had had three days alone and it was beginning to appear that she might have convinced herself that she had imagined the entire scene.

After unsuccessfully attempting to gain access to Veeve, George found himself in an intolerable position. While Reginald and Mitchell were travelling to the Hotel Bourget, George had arranged at the Impérial for an early call and explained that he would be away for two to three days. He would keep his room, and he reserved a second room for his return. The next morning he boarded the train, took the ferry and by crossing London without stopping he arrived at Halswell late in the evening of the same day. The telegram that he had sent ahead of him had been a catalyst for a household which had been uncertain what to do since Veeve's departure. George apologised to the housekeeper for giving her so little warning but he found supper on the table and his room ready.

Ruth was party to none of these events, no-one seeing it as their place to inform her, and she spent her day with Mrs Summers and the baby for lack of any other company, in ignorance of the reason for the household's activity.

When she discovered that George had arrived, Ruth knew that some disastrous misunderstanding had taken place. Instead of seeking her out, George had closed the door of his study. Ruth stayed in her room and only later went down the stairs and sat on the bottom step. She was still sitting there when George emerged. He was so self-engrossed that had he not been heading up the stairs, he would have missed her.

'Ruth, what are you doing?'

'Veeve's in Paris,' she said dully.

'I know,' he answered. He took her hand and helped her to stand, opened the door to his library, and indicated that she should follow.

'She won't talk to me,' he began, 'I have been so foolish. How could I know she was coming? I had arranged everything for her next week, everything.'

Ruth was naively unaware of the implications of what George was telling her.

'So you have seen Veeve?' she asked.

George pulled himself together. 'Yes, I saw her. But this woman, I'd known her a long time, long before Veeve, well she came back to the hotel and Veeve saw her. Ruth, will you come back with me to Paris and persuade Veeve to talk to me?'

Ruth nodded, prepared to do anything. She did not even, at that moment, consider Veeve's emotions, those of being alone and betrayed, that came later as she tossed, sleepless, at night. She had breakfast and then went to the nursery to see Ronald. George was already there and since Ruth could not retreat she stood transfixed, party to a scene that she did not want to witness.

'Mrs Summers, will you not come with me? I need to take Ronald. I have to get her back.'

'Mr George, I am very fond of you, but whatever scrape you have got yourself into is your affair. I have my respectability to think of. Not only will I not go to a foreign country, I shall be leaving your service altogether.' She signalled to Ruth who was hovering at the door. 'This girl is perfectly capable of feeding and changing a baby. He's eight months old and his mother should be looking after him, not gallivanting off.'

Ruth looked at George appalled, and he returned her look with another, beseeching her silently to acquiesce.

'So I'll thank you to allow me to pack my bags. I'll pack a case for the child.' She softened briefly.

By midday a carriage had taken Mrs. Summers to the station and had returned for George, Ruth and the baby.

'I don't know anything about babies.' Ruth attempted to foil George's plan but he was determined and she embarked on her first trip abroad with a baby on her lap and a distracted man at her side, and had no time to feel either fear or excitement because of the misery that she felt about the forthcoming reunion with Veeve.

Mitchell and Reginald managed to extract very little information from Veeve. She related the brief encounter in the lobby but apart from that she had no further evidence to give them and even seemed to be playing down the incident. Mitchell wondered if this was because she was sick, while Reginald was of the opinion that she would probably forgive George anything given time, and he was anxious to avoid any irreparable state of affairs.

Early the next morning, after they had breakfasted together and before Veeve came down from her room, Mitchell left Reginald and went round to the Hotel Impérial. He questioned the receptionist tactfully and ascertained that 'Mrs Eaton had been staying for most of the previous month with Mr. Eaton in the first floor suite.' Mitchell thus had the proof that, as a lawyer, he would need when drawing up a case.

'And George? Did you speak to him?' Reginald said when they met again.

'George has left the hotel. The maître was discreet and would only say that Mr Eaton had checked out and would return in a few days.' Reginald looked crestfallen, the prospect of solving this lover's tiff was becoming less likely.

'I did however have a confidential conversation with the receptionist who in an unguarded moment told me that Mr Eaton has engaged a second room for his return. I do not know what that signifies. Nor do we know where he has gone, or why, or for how long.'

Reginald sighed. 'We can't hang around here indefinitely. I'll see that Veeve is looked after, and when

George returns we will have to come back, and challenge him.'

'In the meantime I shall verify what facts I can in England,' Mitchell said.

'How will you do that?'

'Go to Halswell. Speak to a few people there.'

The full force of the ramifications for himself and Veeve began to dawn on Reginald. He had not seriously contemplated a divorce settlement until that moment.

They returned to London the next day, leaving Veeve none the wiser as to her fate, but with her father's assurance that until he returned, he would guarantee her hotel bill.

Early the following morning Mitchell took the train to Halswell while Reginald fretted in his London hotel and informed Eleanor that he was delayed. Mitchell's news when he arrived back in London was both disturbing and confusing. 'George has been home, the nurse has taken off after a row and George, Ruth and the baby have gone to Paris. They have no intimation when any of them might return.'

'He's taken Ruth?' echoed Reginald.

'I then spoke to the doctor. George has hardly been at home since the birth. In the early days Dr Andrews noticed that Veeve relapsed after his visits and so he advised him to leave her alone for a while. George seems to have taken this literally. It looks bad,'

'What do we do now?'

'Decide in the morning. If George has returned to Paris we should receive a telegram from Veeve.'

There was indeed a telegram and Reginald sent

Mitchell on to Leicester to begin arranging the legalities while he, with a heavy heart, set off back to Paris alone.

Mitchell, too, felt oppressed. Not only did he have the task of initiating divorce proceedings for his sister-in-law, but he would be the one bearing the news to the family. Elsie's reaction gave him a flavour of the effect the news would have.

'It's a scandal, Mitchell,' she exclaimed once she had heard his tale. 'Veeve has been ill for months, George hardly at home. What does he think he has to gain by dragging Ruth and Ronald out there? Do you think Veeve sent for them?'

They discussed how much the family should be told, but, as a lawyer, he knew that all the details would eventually be common knowledge and they were entitled to have the facts as he knew them.

'No, Veeve has had no communication with George, she refuses to speak to him. George could be hoping that she will change her mind, but the damage is done.'

'Poor Veeve,' commented Elsie, 'but then perhaps she is better off without him. It's shocking, Mitchell. What will she do? We'd best go and see Mother.'

The reaction to the news of Veeve's divorce at Granby House was much as Mitchell had anticipated, having witnessed its effect on his wife. He suspected, correctly, that this was an indication of how Eleanor would receive the news and wished that he could have told her himself.

Elsie, whose house was within walking distance, arrived at Granby in the late afternoon at a time that Lil was often at home. Maisie's presence was erratic but

Elsie did not count on her for support because she was unpredictable and her views contrary.

Mitchell's communication had, of necessity, been an incomplete account of Veeve's predicament, but there was no softening the impact of divorce. Elsie fidgeted, neither able to introduce the subject nor to concentrate on her mother's observations on her day.

'What is it, Elsie? You're not listening to a word that I am saying.'

'Sorry, Mother. You see, I've had some news from Mitchell. It's not good.'

'Reginald?' Eleanor asked alarmed.

'No, not father,' Elsie was relieved that at least there was no unpleasant news except in so far as he was involved in the drama, 'no, it's Veeve.'

Eleanor gave an exasperated shrug, 'I can believe anything of Veeve, the way she lives, and she barely communicates, so what can she have done that affects us?'

'She's the reason that Father has gone to London. He's been to Paris. Veeve's in trouble.'

'What's Veeve doing in Paris, she's meant to be gaining strength at Halswell. How can she get into a scrape, isn't Ruth with her?'

'Veeve's asking for a divorce.'

Lil arrived in time to hear Elsie's announcement. The distraction gave their mother a chance to absorb the information. Lil understood at once the wider implications of that statement. 'Veeve's suing for divorce? Oh, what has George done?'

Eleanor roused herself, 'It's not a matter of what

George has done or not done. Veeve is placing her family in an intolerable position. Why did she want to go and demand a divorce?'

Lil turned to Elsie to enlighten them.

'Mitchell said that Veeve has asked for a divorce, he did not say what happened.'

'I hope that she doesn't do anything too hastily,' Lil commented.

'It's too late,' Elsie asserted, 'it's already underway.'

As if both girls knew that when their mother gave her opinion they would not be able to reason with her, they looked towards each other. It was not often that Elsie, the contentedly married housewife, and Lil, the energetic working girl, were in tune with each other. They waited for Eleanor who shook her head and sighed.

'No one will want to be associated with a family embroiled in a divorce scandal. Now you'll never be married, Lil, nor will Ruth.'

Elsie's wispy hair seemed more than ordinarily dishevelled and her pallid blue eyes, meeting Lil's, gave out a signal of resignation only matched by the slump of her body. She arranged the folds of her skirt, the action, so futile as a response, kindled a spark of defiance in her sister.

'Not everyone thinks like you do, Mother.' Lil, while shocked at her mother's remark, managed to smile at her omission of Maisie for the marriage stakes. However, she was sobered. Three years previously she had broken off her engagement to Henry, and had it not been for Henry's precipitate proposal their relationship would have been in jeopardy with convention and society again dictating her future. Yet, seeing her engagement through the eyes of her mother and Elsie, she wondered whether the ensuing scandal might influence Henry, who might after all not want to be associated with their family.

The next day Henry called in at his club where he was waylaid by Brindsley-Smith at his most pompous. 'The cat's among the pigeons now.'

Henry steered him to a table some distance from a rowdy group of members. 'You obviously have something to tell me.'

'Your precious Lil. Her family's caught up in a divorce scandal. George Eaton, he has quite a name around here. It'll be in all the papers.'

'Veeve?'

'Reginald's back and forth to Paris and Eleanor's overwrought about the girls' marriage prospects and the slur on their position. They are saying that you have had a lucky escape.'

Henry could not remove himself fast enough from his gloating informant. 'Excuse me,' he said.

Two hours later Henry knocked at the imposing front door of Granby House. 'Horace, thank God it's you. No, I won't come in. Could you find Lil? Ask her to come down, and be sure to give her a coat.'

Almost roughly Henry took Lil's arm and pulled her through the door. 'Thank you, Horace. Tell Mrs Hefford not to worry. Lil is with me.'

'What's going on, Henry? Where are we going?' Lil found herself striding alongside Henry towards the High street.

'You're coming with me, Lil, to the station. We'll just make Aunt Helen's before ten. I've heard about Veeve.'

'How?'

His face set, he hurried her through the station forecourt, produced two tickets at the barrier and reached the first class carriages as the doors were being slammed and the whistle blown.

'Henry, what are you doing?' Lil was not sure whether to be exhilarated or angry.

'Tomorrow I'm arranging a special licence. Nothing is going to stop us marrying. We are both of an age to determine our own lives. Aunt Helen's a sport and she'll be a witness.' His only thought was to spare Lil the repercussions of any scandal.

Lil began to laugh, slightly hysterically. 'How romantic! Are you sweeping me off my feet?'

Henry was relieved to note her amused elation. 'I am. I am going to place another ring on your finger and you are not going home. You're mine.'

It was fortunate that the carriage was empty because Henry wrapped his arms around a still bemused Lil, and allowing not one word of defiance to escape, sealed his pledge with an indecorous and prolonged embrace.

While Elsie and her mother were speculating on the implications of Veeve's divorce, Reginald was travelling, and George, Ruth and Ronald were arriving in Paris. Veeve had been on her own, and apart from her one interaction with her father and Mitchell, had spoken to no one. Feeling stronger once they had left she had taken courage and descended the stairs for her evening meal.

She ignored the stares that she perceived she was receiving with the pretence of haughty disdain. She would not be browbeaten by anyone, she resolved, and the next day had all her meals in the dining room and ventured outside into the grey cold streets for some air. She wondered how long she could sustain this solitude and agonised over the silence from George. She could not believe he would abandon her, the look on his face had been one of joy, the disgust had been for the other odious woman. She felt that if she waited long enough he would seek her out, her refusal to see him was only to show her disapproval. But where was he?

She dressed in a suit of antique white silk. The bodice had silk covered buttons and hand-worked button holes from neckline to waist. Each seam of the bodice, and each seam of the matching eight-gore skirt, was oversewn with piping. The raised Chinese collar and fitted cuffs were also edged with piping. George had given her the antique white silk as a present for her trousseau and together they had chosen the design. It had been his favourite.

The bellboy brought a message to her room. 'There is a visitor for Madame.' Agitated, Veeve instructed that he should be sent up immediately.

'Madame, it is a lady by the name of Ruth Hefford.'

Shocked, Veeve answered abstractedly, 'Bien sûr. Of course.'

'Why are you here?' she asked as soon as Ruth came through the door.

Ruth was taken aback. 'Because George asked me. He said you wouldn't see him.'

Veeve seemed to have forgotten, in her change of heart, her initial intense rejection of him. 'I'll see him.'

'Shall I send him up then, Veeve?' Ruth asked in a feeble voice. 'I'll look after Ronald.'

'What do you mean? Ronald's here? Why did you bring Ronald?' Veeve looked irritated as if this was an irrelevance.

'Because Mrs Summers left. She wouldn't stay if there was a scandal.'

'What scandal?'

'Your divorce. There was a telegram from Mitchell waiting for us at our hotel. He is setting everything in motion as you requested.' Ruth walked away.

Veeve's elation at the thought of a reconciliation with George deserted her. Had she embarked on a course that was irrevocable? George would put it all to rights again. He always managed to, for her.

She greeted George with relief and affection.

'Veeve,' he said gently holding her at arm's length, 'you said that you did not want to see me.' He then seemed to recollect something. 'Veeve, you've started divorce proceedings.'

She looked at him with disbelief. 'You don't want to divorce me do you?'

'No., Veeve I don't, but that is not the point. The scandal is out.'

'But I can stop it if you want. Do you want it,

George?'

'Veeve, all I want is to be with you. What I did was foolish, but what is a man to do when his wife has been ill for a whole year? I just picked up with a few friends that I knew before we were married. I never saw them until you were ill. But it's too late.'

'Why is it too late?' She ran her hands down the sides of her skirt and knowing how she used to look, drew herself upright, rescuing some of her former defiance.

'Because we will never be a respectable married couple again.' He seemed irritated. 'In my circles these things are brushed under the carpet, everyone knows, no one says anything and respectability is maintained. But in your bourgeois world, white has to be white or you sue for divorce. Can't you see what you've done, Veeve?'

Veeve could only just grasp that she had been the instigator of a process that was set to destroy her future with George. They stood opposite each other and through her tears she saw George gaze at her with a combination of compassion and despair. Then he turned and left the room.

When Reginald arrived the next day Veeve stormed at him. 'Father, George won't see me, please make him take me back. Please stop the divorce.'

'Stopping the legalities is not the answer. Everyone knows. Halswell is empty. People talk.'

'Who?'

'Well, Dr Andrews for one.'

'How dare he?' Veeve fumed.

'But it was true, Veeve.' Reginald was weary and exasperated with his daughter. He was upset for her, and for himself. How could he have another daughter at home, the first at least had a show of being married, but divorced? He shuddered. She would have to take the consequences of her actions. Mitchell had telegraphed that George was more than able to settle Veeve financially, so he, Reginald, had no obligation there. Nonetheless he felt overwhelmed.

'Veeve, it's going to happen. George will provide very handsomely for you but don't think you can come running back home. I'll have no scandal to upset your Mother or to spoil your sisters' chances. You seem to like France, so stay here.'

Some of Veeve's innate resilience returned. 'Nothing will induce me to go back home. I'll stay here. I'll get George back.' But even at that moment Reginald sensed the emptiness of her conviction.

Reginald saw his daughter again that afternoon and brought Ruth and Ronald with him. 'Veeve, I am leaving in the morning. I've spent long enough away from business dealing with your affairs. I'm sorry for all this, I really am.'

'How shall I manage?' Veeve looked small and vulnerable and Reginald found it hard to keep his resolve.

'You can get a nurse for Ronald.' Reginald wondered if she had allowed for Ronald when she contemplated her future. She would be alone, but with a baby.

'Come Ruth,' he clasped his hands together, 'you'll

need to pack your things, we leave early tomorrow.' He stood up, but, delaying his moment of departure walked across to the window, as if for a last look.

'I'm not coming,' Ruth's voice hung in the air and she spoke so clearly that there was no mistaking her intention. Reginald turned, mystified.

'I can't leave Veeve, Father.' Ruth stood very still.

Reginald seemed to crumple. 'What will your Mother say with both her daughters exiled?' He asked dramatically, and looked from one to the other: Veeve, a tragic figure as pale as her white silk suit, her sister quietly defiant, whom he was obliged to leave. What future awaited these daughters that he now had to abandon? He felt defeated, his shoulders slumped, and distraught he said, 'You'll come back one day,' and left the room.

The departure of their father left a silence. The room felt empty as the door closed, echoing the sense of finality to the end of a life that they both had known.

Ruth waited for a reaction from Veeve, her future determined with that one clear statement. Why did she say that she would stay? Perhaps because, for once, Veeve had not deserved the deal that fate had dealt her. Ruth was piqued at the injustice. Although she liked George she did not understand his lifestyle. She was prepared to make allowances for him and was saddened that what he had done had led to this. If only Veeve had not seen the other woman, they might have resolved their relationship. If only events had not progressed so fast, the situation might have ended differently. Young as she was, when she observed that Veeve's affection for

George had not changed, she was deeply moved. Moreover she was a silent witness to George's agony, knowing that he did not want to leave Veeve. Yet there was no chance now of a happy outcome. Ruth's decision to stay with Veeve had been instinctive but already doubts assailed her. The two sisters looked at each other. Neither said anything. Veeve sat, her colour heightened, her fingers drumming on the arms of her chair while Ruth waited. She could not gauge her sister's reaction, but was relieved that Veeve had not dissolved into helpless tears. She went across to Ronald who was sleeping in his bassinet. Here was another complication. Ruth never doubted that Veeve would take control but would she realise that there were now three of them to consider?

'Father won't see us short of money,' Veeve began. 'Mitchell spoke of a settlement. George will have to support us.'

Ruth was shocked that Veeve's first thoughts were about money. She had never had to think who would pay for her food or clothes, but Veeve had run a household and understood. Money would be Veeve's first preoccupation. She waited, her mind racing with questions about their future. Where would they live? What would it be like living in France? What about Ronald? At that moment he gave a cry, as if to emphasise her concern. Veeve's head jerked around, surprised by the unexpected noise.

'What about Ronald?' Ruth asked.

'You can pick him up. You understand about babies,' Veeve answered. This was not what Ruth was asking.

'Won't you need a nurse, or a nanny?'

'We'll stay here while I organise everything. We can't stay in Paris, there are too many of George's friends here. People go to the south of France, don't they? I shall think of something.'

Veeve suddenly looked less sure of herself and slumped back in her chair. 'We don't have to leave immediately. Tomorrow I'll take advice from the maître d'hotel. He can arrange train reservations and a hotel in Cannes. There is probably an overnight sleeper.' Veeve rang the bell. There was a quick exchange in French.

'I've asked for some lunch and some milk for Ronald. What else will he need? There must be an agency that supplies nannies. I take it that you can manage, you know, to feed and change him?'

By the following morning Veeve had a booking on the night train for the next day, and a reservation at the Station Hotel. While Veeve rested in the afternoon Ruth entertained the child. Ronald was now able to pull up on furniture, babble and smile. She found that the simplest things, an ashtray, her slippers or the doorstop, along with the few toys that she had brought with her, were sufficient to amuse him. For the first time since she had left Halswell Ruth felt happy.

The next day Veeve was ill. The recent excitement had overstretched her nerves and weakened her body. Veeve lay listlessly on her pillows, her hair soaked from perspiration, with dark rings around her eyes, her arms motionless on the coverlet. 'Ruth, you need to be brave and strong. This is what you must say to the maître. He'll understand enough English. Tell him that we can't leave. That I need a doctor. Go now!'

Ruth was alarmed but knew that she had no option but to relay the message.

'Madame est malade. Entonces, I will send up some light meals for her. And some nourishment for yourself. Et le bébé, bien sûr.'

An hour later there was a knock at the door. Ruth opened it. She did not want to call out for fear of disturbing Veeve.

'Mademoiselle. Le Docteur. Je m'appelle Docteur Thiel. Y vous êtes?'

'I am Ruth. Veeve is my sister. Elle est très malade.'

Ruth stood back to allow the doctor to pass. Veeve raised her head.

Dr Thiel was dark haired, of slight build, tidily dressed with alert darting eyes. Quickly he moved to the bedside and took Veeve's wrist to feel for her pulse. He indicated a nearby chair. 'Asseyez-vous, Mademoiselle Ruth.'

Dr Thiel proceeded with his examination, careful not to tire Veeve with questions, he nodded to himself after each procedure. Ruth went to pick up Ronald. She wanted the doctor to be aware of her other concern.

Finally the doctor beckoned Ruth over to the window. He spoke softly. 'This is exhaustion with a mild temperature and fever. Rest will suffice.' He made no mention of the circumstances causing Veeve's relapse and Ruth wondered whether he had been informed. She presumed that he had. Two English ladies and a baby could not fail to generate some speculation.

'Le bébé!' Dr Thiel smiled for the first time. 'Quel

joli!' He reached and took the sleeping bundle from Ruth. 'I will send a nurse to help you. Give me a few hours. Mademoiselle you are looking after the baby well. Ne pas avoir peur. Bon courage!' His eyes twinkled and he tickled Ronald under his chin. 'A demain. I will return tomorrow.'

Now that their stay had been extended Veeve became pettish and fretted that George had not been to see her. Ruth refrained from offering her opinion that George's visit, should he decide to call, would only upset both him and Veeve and cause an even greater relapse.

The next morning there was a knock on the door. Ruth felt anxious and unconsciously her hands went towards her stomach. The doctor and nurse had already called that morning.

'Mademoiselle. A visitor in the foyer.'

'You had better go, Ruth,' Veeve said, suddenly animated. Ruth descended to the hall. Sitting with her back to her was a woman. She was wearing travelling clothes and an extravagantly large hat. As she heard Ruth approaching she turned and Ruth recognized Aunt Helen.

Aunt Helen hurried to embrace her. 'You poor girl. Your father has told me everything.'

'Oh Aunt Helen, I can't tell you.'

'You don't have to. Now take me upstairs to Veeve. You and I will sort this between us. Don't look at me like that. You had the courage to stay and not desert your sister.' Ruth smiled weakly. 'We none of us know what we are capable of until we are tried. How old are you now?'

'Eighteen.'

'Perfect. You have a great capacity to learn when you are young. Look what I did.'

Ruth was not at all sure what Aunt Helen had done, but there were not many women who would impulsively take a train and travel to Paris. What was more, Aunt Helen did not appear disconcerted by the situation.

'I feared that Veeve would land herself in trouble,' Aunt Helen said as they climbed the wide mahogany staircase, 'but I had not anticipated this. I can stay for as long as it takes Veeve to get back on her feet and for you all to be settled.'

For the next week Veeve remained in her room while Aunt Helen took over. She engaged a permanent nanny for Ronald, and arranged for Ruth to explore Paris. For the first time in her life Ruth felt that she was not just one of seven sisters. Aunt Helen did not treat her as if she was an awkward accessory. She was asked for her views on books and current affairs and Ruth, who had always listened but had rarely been consulted on any of these subjects, discovered that she had her own opinions.

'It will take several days for your trunks to be sent from Halswell, and at least a week until Veeve is strong enough to travel. Paris is at our feet. It is impossible that you should be in the most avant-garde city in the world and not see the sights. The Champs Elysees, the Tour Eiffel, Sacre Coeur, Notre Dame, it is too exciting for words. Besides, I have a surprise.'

In the foyer of the hotel. Ruth saw a young man, tall and angular with hair which he attempted to control with the discreet use of hair cream, but which had a tendency to curl giving him a boyish look. He had high-coloured cheeks and his wide mouth was almost too large for his face. He broke into a cheery grin.

'I am Pierre, a friend of Veeve's from a long time ago.' He shook Ruth's hand before she had time to be embarrassed.

'And how is Veeve?' He asked, and when he heard that she was unwell, exclaimed, 'Oh, la pauvre,' and turned to Ruth. 'But I can entertain her sister. It is a beautiful day so we will go to the Bois de Boulogne, where I am assured there are bands playing and all manner of interesting entertainments.'

Pierre seemed very mature and assured although he was only a little older than Veeve. Ruth liked his mix of brotherly concern and impish humour. He promised that he would cheer life up for Veeve once she had recovered.

'It will be a wonderful excuse for me and my friends, many of whom know Veeve from the old days, to come to the south coast. I understand that is where she is planning to live.'

Aunt Helen advised that if there was a choice of Cannes or Nice, Veeve's money would go further in Nice. 'The smartest sets go to Cannes, but you would be out of your depth.'

Pierre agreed. 'Besides,' he added, 'it is convenient for us to drive there in our motor vehicles. Even your sister will want a motorcar once she is recovered. She might even teach you to drive.'

Ruth thought that this was unlikely. Although she was unwilling to admit it, she knew that Veeve would not want her sister to overshadow her. She was justifiably concerned about Veeve's reaction to her day out with Pierre.

On their return Veeve was particularly querulous. Aunt Helen winked at Ruth. 'Veeve, you can allow your sister one day of pleasure. She has been extremely loyal and unselfish and how can you deny her an outing? I do not know how you would have managed without her.' Veeve gave a weak conciliatory smile. 'Pierre has made you a marvellous offer. He says that he will accompany you to Nice. He tells me that he has to go south on business.'

Veeve made a rapid recovery. She began to sit out for longer periods and to take short walks in the hotel garden, some of her vitality returned and Aunt Helen felt that she had achieved her goal. It was time for her to leave for London.

'Are you not coming with us?' Ruth asked.

'No dear. All the plans for you, Veeve and Ronald have been made and your new life is in your own hands. I am not sure what this will be, but with Veeve it will be anything but uneventful. I trust you to watch out for Ronald, and I hope that his nurse is reliable. Although she needs it, I don't think that you will have any influence over your sister, but her interest in Ronald needs fostering.'

Aunt Helen wished Ruth good fortune, and in the evening she left.

Book Two

Madder Red

1914-1929

Chapter Fifteen

For many months, following her divorce Veeve had to act a part. She bitterly regretted the departure of George and those who knew her would have observed a brittle edge to her high spirits and frenetic activity. The steadfast friendship of her closest and oldest friends, chiefly her old flames, Sam Blair, the American, Count von Kuder from Germany, and Pierre Dupont, the Frenchman, combined with the companionship of her faithful sister who shared her unoccupied hours, supported her as she fashioned a new life.

Travelling had, in some measure, broadened Veeve's horizons and generated an interest that fascinated her for several years. The North African coast was predominantly under the protection of either France or Britain and Veeve, like a chameleon, changed her identity to suit her geography, adopting Moroccan customs on one trip and Egyptian on another. Her magnetism drew people to her and she was never without a lively entourage keen to join in whatever expedition she organised. When not travelling she chose to reside in one or other of the resorts along the French Mediterranean coast where she held court by virtue of her considerable wealth and her liberated status. While the English at home were pursuing their sporting activities with gun and fishing rod, the English abroad toured the Sphinx on camels, explored the picturesque Cities of Fez or Casablanca, or yachted around the coast.

The south of France was inhabited in the winter months by those, like Veeve, who had the leisure and the income to escape the northern climes. However, this last winter, Veeve felt herself abandoned and had based herself in Monte Carlo in the tiny state of Monaco where she had been drawn into the halls of gaming and cards and to which she had all but become addicted.

One April afternoon Veeve returned to the hotel where Ruth was spending the afternoon alone. Ronald had been taken for a walk and Ruth had taken the opportunity to catch up on some reading. Veeve wore the shorter style of dress that was becoming fashionable, and her hair was swept up into a saucy little hat. She looked groomed and soigné, and projected a slightly false air of jollity, one which Ruth suspected hid some underlying anxiety.

'Refait, again!' She said breezily as she started to take out her hat pins and placed them on the table below the mirror.

'I don't know what you are talking about,' said Ruth. She refused to take any interest in Veeve's games of rouge et noir, nor her triumphs at the roulette table. She knew better than to voice her disapproval of Veeve's losses in the hope that her lack of disposable income would dampen her enthusiasm. Instead she said, 'While you were out the laundry woman brought her bill. It's on your desk along with the account from the milliner.'

They were staying in a small but select hotel decorated in the art nouveau style. Ruth liked the clear bright airiness of it after the heavy décor of their previous hotel, but even its lofty design did not mitigate the unseasonably hot weather. This undoubtedly contributed to Ruth's testiness.

'Don't bother me with this now, Ruth. I'm stifled and I need to change. I don't suppose you want to come out with me this evening?' There was an aggressive edge to the question. Ruth reverting to the subject of the bills.

Veeve asked with uncharacteristic concern; 'When is Ronald due back?'

Veeve, having found that a nanny on a permanent basis for the seven year old Ronald proved difficult, had resorted to employing local girls when needed. Unfortunately the quality of nanny prepared to work for a divorcee was below the standard that she would have liked. Ronald was turning into an attractive boy with a mass of fair curly hair and a solemn but affectionate nature who adapted easily to these arrangements.

'The girl's bringing him back at six o' clock. I'm going to the library.'

'Well, I have an evening engagement so tell him goodnight from me. Children do at least become more interesting as they grow older.'

Ruth once again retreated from a confrontation. She found the idea of gambling repugnant, even more so because it was outlawed at home. In many ways Ruth had absorbed the French outlook on life, but some of her home grown morals remained. It was not only that Ruth found Veeve's gambling demeaning but she was also aware that they relied on Veeve's annuity and had no assets against which to borrow. They could hardly turn to earning their own living.

Fortunately a letter arrived that resolved the situation. Sam Blair wrote to say that he was entering the Paris to Nice motor race the next week. Veeve seized on this face-saving solution to her financial predicament and decided that they would move to Nice to be there for the finish. Prices in Nice were not so dear and with care she could pay her bills and start to entertain again. Ruth was equally relieved for almost all the same reasons, but particularly because she had not had to be the instigator of the move. Nice was the town that they had first moved to from Paris. It had been Ruth's introduction to France, and she had an affection for it as of a first love. Veeve moved them all into the Hotel Suisse within the week.

The race had also been entered by the Count Von Kuder and Pierre Dupont, the common interest in motorcars had brought the friends together for the first time since Pierre's marriage. Veeve had been disconcerted by his marriage because she had somehow expected loyalty to her to be sustained despite frequent absences and the passage of years. While others found stable relationships that she was denied, because a divorcee was acceptable as a friend but was a liability thereafter, she endeavoured to make sure of her friends. She had discovered, from hints that were dropped into the conversation, that the Count had a wife to whom he had no intention of returning, and this gave her a measure of security. As far as Sam Blair was concerned she had never had any illusions. For him, home was America and anything that happened in France was merely a diversion.

The road race marked, Veeve hoped, the beginning of another summer of frenzied social activity. The addition of Pierre's wife, Armelle, their young widowed friend Hortense, and Pierre's friend Jean-Paul, added a spice that had been lacking the previous year. Veeve, always the natural leader, discovered a renewed energy and an urge to surprise her friends with new ideas. She had experienced spells of boredom on occasions during the winter, which was unusual for her, but conversely she had a sense of excitement for the forthcoming summer that was unexpectedly high.

Two factors contributed towards her restored vitality. One was the arrival of Jean-Paul. Veeve could never resist the challenge of attracting another, if not suitor, certainly admirer, to her entourage.

The second factor was some felicitous news from her lawyer. Veeve's settlement depended in part on provision for her son, Ronald. She knew that once he became of age, or in reality when he attained eighteen, twenty-one and again at twenty-five, Ronald had the prospect of a substantial personal allowance which increased as he matured. She was unaware that the settlement for

Ronald during his childhood would reflect his educational needs. It transpired that since he had reached the age of seven it was anticipated that his allowance would increase. In fact, had she remained in England, it would be expected that he would be sent to a boarding school or at the very least require the employment of a tutor.

Veeve did not apprise Ruth of the contents of her letter, nor of her now, much increased, income. It did not seem necessary, at Ronald's young age, to disrupt their lifestyle in the French Riviera because of the dictates of the educational requirements of a small boy. She was cognisant that Ronald was bright, but she believed that Ruth was more than amply competent to supply his needs. Travel and exposure to the Arts and Music, readily available in Nice, were more than sufficient stimulation for the child for another year.

The idea of travelling re-ignited Veeve's imagination. Travelling was something that she enjoyed above everything, and the considerable increase in her income fuelled a project that she had been nursing for some months. She invited her friends to dine at her hotel on the evening following the race. Veeve took especial care with her 'toilette' prior to the dinner. She also suggested to Ruth that she choose her prettiest dress. She would randomly take an interest in her sister's appearance, especially when she was devising one of her more lavish affairs.

'I've placed you beside Hortense, who I think you'll adore, and Pierre because you know him so well.' Veeve whispered to Ruth. Her rapid speech denoted the level of excitement that she was experiencing and her fevered whisper was to prevent Ruth from making any adverse comment. Her sister was easily silenced.

The meal was of the best and the company was merry. As the dishes were removed and the dessert wine replaced by port and brandy, Ruth began to sense that Veeve was on the brink of revealing a hidden purpose to the gathering.

She suddenly aware that Veeve had created a stir. Although she thought she knew her sister tolerably well, she was curious. There was a lull in the conversation and Ruth heard Veeve say to those around her, 'And so what do you think?' Immediately all heads turned towards the head of the table.

'What about Egypt? I'm inviting you all to join me on an expedition. Who knows what the future holds with the Balkans in turmoil and Russia flexing its fists and gnashing its teeth? Why shouldn't we explore that mysterious country while we can and before the heat of the summer?'

There was a sudden outburst of ideas and opinions, each person talking over the other. Veeve's enthusiasm was contagious and, as Ruth sat isolated amongst all the chatter, a maelstrom of thoughts whirled through her mind, the over-riding impression of which was that Veeve was likely to plunge them into debt. It was much later that she was able to tackle Veeve and ask how she was planning to finance such a trip.

'Don't look all censorious, Ruth,' Veeve said once they were alone. 'I can explain how we can afford it, but just think, Ruth, how exciting it will be and such a lark.'

Ruth had yet to be convinced. 'I received the annual audit of my allowance. My shares have been doing excellently and because the capital has remained the same the trustees decided to add the profit that has accrued to my annual allowance. I can amply afford this trip.'

Ruth was about to produce further obstructions to her plans which included Ronald's education, but Veeve raced on with her argument.

'Egypt has not had such a peaceful period for years. It is administered by a British agent and so we'll feel quite at home. It's a healthy climate and Ronald will simply love riding on a camel.'

Ruth's astonished expression caused Veeve to peal with laughter, which had the unlikely effect of catching her unprepared. Before she knew it Ruth, too, was laughing at the outrageousness of Veeve's irresponsible project. This was hardly the response either of them expected but both were delighted to find that they were in harmony.

Within the month the expedition was organised and the party assembled ready to board the cruise liner to Alexandria. Their baggage was piled high on the pier and Ruth was perplexed at the amount that they appeared to have accumulated, since her own and Ronald's valises contributed only a small proportion of the whole. Not having travelled in a large group before in this manner and because no one else seemed surprised, she presumed that it was normal.

On arrival in Egypt the chaos, noise, congestion and

variety of modes of transport was confusing. Ruth kept a tight hold of Ronald's hand and sheltered at the rear of the group to take her cue from them. Soon, however, Ronald's childish enthusiasm infected her and she began to enjoy the strangeness for herself. At the station the party climbed into a first class carriage which took them to Cairo, where the entire party and all their baggage was transferred to a Hotel in the centre of the City. Here they stayed for a few days to sightsee before they set off for the pyramids.

The camel knelt for her to mount, and from her elevated viewpoint Ruth could take in the vastness of the desert. From here she could absorb the unique atmosphere of the extraordinary landscape. Its majesty caught her imagination and she absorbed the history and architecture of the ancient civilisation around her as one who has thirsted for knowledge for years. To the slow plod of the camel's stride, drawn by the stark contrast between the arid desert and the green fertile valley that spread on either side of the Nile, she forgot the present and absorbed her surroundings.

The fellaheen, blue cotton cloth covering their slim wiry bodies, turbans their only protection against the sun, worked tirelessly on the land to produce crops of cotton and maize. Egrets followed the grazing buffalo and sheep. Exotic shrubs and trees grew in profusion; date palms, sycamore, tamarisk and milk trees. There was little that resembled the hedgerows and wild flowers that she was used to in England, but instead there were groves of oranges, lemons, cloves, mulberries and pomegranates. Pungent scents of hyenas, or hare foxes, jackals and desert rats filled the air at dusk. In the groves of Indian figs and olives hid horned viper, hooded snakes, lizards, spiders and scorpions.

Finally they reached the Pyramids, the Sphinx and the Temples. Ruth was transported to a bygone era that had fixed itself in the young mind of Veeve all those years before. None of the party knew the significance of Egypt, the place where she and George had begun their courtship. It had been the destination of Veeve's dreams, and its influence on her infected all her guests, including her younger sister.

As a finale to their expedition Veeve had organised a camp in the desert. Servants travelled ahead to prepare, on the outskirts of Cairo and in sight of the pyramids, a collection of lavish tents hung with rich cloth and carpeted in deep pile. Oversized cushions instead of chairs and low tables were the only furniture, and further tents with airy drapes and raised beds provided their sleeping quarters. Out of sight were tents for the cooks and the servants, and accommodation for the camel drivers. Veeve encouraged her guests to dress in the style of the Bedouin in long robes, Arabian jewellery, the men in fez hats and all wearing soft embroidered slippers. An inspired addition to their entertainment during their last night was provided by a group of musicians.

The desert could be a quiet place, when not punctuated by the snorting of camels, or the barks or shrieks of night animals, and the eastern music had a soothing quality uniting the party in a way that marked it as distinct from any of their previous evenings.

Ruth enjoyed her growing friendship with Armelle and Hortense, which had the advantage of enabling her to share the care of Ronald. She lost her reticence and became, in a manner that she had not managed before, a member of the party and entered into the spirit of the event.

Pierre and Sam had known each other for many years but had been unable to spend so long together and discover areas of mutual interest. The Count, Veeve and Jean-Paul were therefore naturally thrown together.

The Count had been Veeve's constant companion. He understood Veeve's predicament, and what is more, understood her need for excitement and adulation. At times he had been the long suffering friend who watched Veeve's flirtations, knowing that nothing would ultimately result from them. However, even he noticed that there was a change in Veeve since Jean-Paul had been introduced to their group. It was not that he felt threatened, he knew that this relationship like the others would not last, for he suspected that Jean-Paul assumed that she was a widow, like Hortense, yet for once he felt mildly inadequate. Jean-Paul possessed a charisma to which Veeve not unnaturally responded. The Count was aware of a rival. Veeve, he suspected, was looking for a more permanent and settled life and was making tentative moves in that direction, and because he could not provide it he wondered if she might be hoping to inveigle Jean-Paul into doing so.

'Very beautiful you are looking this evening, my dear,' said the Count as he and Veeve found themselves sitting alone in one of the tents set up to appreciate the

Egyptian sunset. The rest of the party had gathered in the main tent where the musicians were playing and refreshments dispensed by silent and attentive servants. The Count smiled to himself as the veracity of his observation occurred to him. Veeve was as attractive and vivacious and her wit as sharp as at any time since he had known her.

Veeve caught his eye and gave a familiar lift of her eyebrows as she tipped her head. She stretched out an arm so that the bangles that adorned her wrist clattered and the glass pieces embedded in them glistened. This gesture embodied the Count's assessment of Veeve's state of mind. He was aware of an underlying restlessness to her mood. Although some of his concern was on his own behalf, a greater measure was for Veeve herself, but he needed to be more firmly convinced of Veeve's motives before he acted. Jean-Paul would never marry a divorcee, as a catholic this was a bar to marriage that even Veeve in her most sanguine moments would acknowledge, but Veeve could be obstinate and was capable of self-delusion once determined on a course of action.

'This expedition was a splendid idea, Veeve. It has given everyone an escape from the rumblings of discord in Europe and given us as friends some wonderful memories. Even your little sister has settled into the group. That was inspired of you, she has for too long been allowed to hide in the shadows. I had no idea that she had such a quick mind or wealth of knowledge. It must be all that book reading. To see her relaxed and animated is welcome.' The Count was not sure that

Veeve wanted to hear this glowing report.

At twenty-five Ruth had become, although in a less striking manner than her older sister, a pretty girl in the Rossetti style. The Count feared that Veeve might resent any comparison, but it would be skirting the truth to pretend that Ruth's development into a personable young woman was not now being remarked upon by their friends.

'I've been impressed by Ruth,' Veeve said defensively. 'It's time that she made a life for herself. You will have to help me find a suitable husband for her. Ronald will be boarding next year. Come, Count, you are looking serious. What is it?'

The Count took her hand and kissed it. 'Just be careful, Veeve.' He gave her a wistful smile that was almost disguised by his gesture. 'Sometimes we have to allow life to take its course. Not all aspects of our lives, or other people's lives, can be moulded to our wishes.' He hoped that, although he appeared to be referring to Ruth, Veeve might understand his caution and apply these principles to herself. 'While we are here we can dream and hope, but events have a way of taking over.' The Count was alluding to the political situation in the countries to which each of them belonged where, even then, events were leading towards an impasse that could set one against the other.

'Don't be so dismal. It may never happen. Why should it affect our lives? If we try hard enough to be happy, we can survive outside conflicts.'

Veeve was more resolute than the Count was prepared for, and rather than disturb the evening's ambience, he continued in the same flippant manner.

'We shall overcome. Is that it, dear? I do believe that you will, and I will be there with you.'

Veeve took his hand and kissed it in return. 'I shall always be able to rely on you. It has been a marvellous expedition, hasn't it?'

'No-one could have arranged a better party. Shall we join the others?'

The main tent now held, not only Veeve's friends and the musicians, but a troupe of dancers, all of whom were awaiting Veeve's arrival. The dancers had been hired by her friends and they were delighted with her reaction. It was not often that they could turn the tables and have the chance to show their appreciation.

Although the night air was cool, the tent was warm and conducive to conversation, dancing or quiet contemplation. Veeve was rarely quiet and Ruth rarely danced, but they and all of their friends were conscious of a precious time suspended.

Once the dancers and the musicians departed people drifted off to their tents for the night until only Jean-Paul and Veeve remained. Jean-Paul suggested that they sit and listen to the desert sounds, an experience that was only possible once all had settled for the night, and which was an occasion that might not be repeated. For Veeve, whose life never allowed for peace or silence, this was a novel idea and she had almost exhausted her stock of novel experiences.

For a while neither spoke. Their eyes became accustomed to the dark. The silhouette of the pyramids was depicted by the light of the waxing moon and only the sounds of desert animals broke the silence. Veeve was lost for words, but her emotions were heightened. The character of Jean-Paul intrigued her as no man had done for some time, and she was unsure of her ground. Almost imperceptibly Jean-Paul began to speak.

'This has been an amazing journey for me, Veeve. You may not know this but I was born on a hillside farm in Alsace. My parents were traditional farmers and they were not much influenced by who owned our country, whether France or Germany, because the dictates of the soil are stronger than that of politics. I left to join the French Army for two years of National Service, and I could not go back because I was considered to be French and Alsace was still under German control. It was contacts that I made during those years that gave me an introduction to the silk trade. I have worked my way up in the industry to a good position and now with friends like Pierre I also have a sympathetic social circle.'

Veeve for once had nothing to say and allowed Jean-Paul to continue without interruption.

'I little thought it would involve an adventure such as this, and with such convivial company. I think that the addition of your little boy has enriched us by reminding us to notice things, and to wonder, where we might not have done otherwise.'

In the heady atmosphere of the evening Veeve saw her son in a new light.

'Did he ever know his father?' Jean-Paul asked.

'No, he was only six months old.'

'Ronald is lucky to have the Count, and others, to fill that role,' Jean-Paul commented. 'And your sister seems devoted.'

'Ruth is invaluable,' acknowledged Veeve with relief at the turn of conversation, 'to me too.'

They were sitting on a pair of embroidered cushions, Veeve was resting on one elbow, her hand placed on the rug, with her other arm raised behind her head. Absent-mindedly Jean-Paul ran his index finger along each finger of Veeve's resting hand. 'You must have needed her,' Jean-Paul observed, before withdrawing his hand as if he had taken a step too far. 'I think it's time to turn in. Thank you, Veeve, this has been a memorable evening to end an unforgettable holiday.'

Veeve did not stir. She was uncertain how to interpret their interchange. Jean-Paul made a mock formal bow without any apparent embarrassment and stepped softly across the carpeted floor, lifted the side of the tent, and disappeared.

Chapter Sixteen

At the end of June a few weeks later there was another motor race from Paris to Nice. Veeve left Ronald with Ruth by the barrier to watch the cars pass, while she made her way to the finishing post. The first few cars came in close together and the rest straggled in over the next two hours. Ronald was learning to identify the different models and was happily engrossed in the noisy atmosphere when Sam drove by in his Ford followed by Pierre in his Peugeot. The latter spotted Ronald with Ruth and engaged the brakes to a stop beside the barrier. Jean-Paul, his driving companion, called to Ruth.

'Do you think Ronald would like a ride?'

Ronald nodded excitedly when he heard their proposal and dragged Ruth by the hand. She helped him over the barrier and he stood in awe by the side of the motorcar. The steering wheel blocked the driver's side but Jean-Paul leaned across and lifted him onto his shoulders placing his legs astride his neck so that he could have a clear view. The motor was dusty from the long journey but only Ruth noticed. Ronald waved and grinned, Pierre shouted over his shoulder to say that they would meet at the hotel, and Ruth watched them weave their way through the press of cars that thronged the streets.

Ruth took a short route through the back streets to the hotel outside which several motors were parked. Hortense, Armelle and Sam were there with Veeve. The Count's driving companion was also part of the assembled company. Soon Pierre drew up with Ronald still riding on Jean-Paul's shoulders. Everyone gathered at the steps of the hotel gravitating towards Veeve who, before anyone had a chance to do otherwise, invited them to a private dining room in the evening. She was back at the centre of her circle and each member of the party was eager to be drawn in.

The Count's co-driver was an addition to their party that evening and was a relative stranger. Hortense and Armelle were both lively and intelligent and had quickly been accepted by the group, as had Jean-Paul who was a ready and willing listener. It was obvious, to Ruth at least, that Jean-Paul had awoken a spark in Veeve, although it may just have been that she had a new audience to dazzle. The Count's co-driver, on the other hand, proved to be truculent and monosyllabic, which might have been an advantage on a long drive, but would be a disadvantage at dinner.

Towards the end of the meal Sam commanded everyone's attention. 'We're a curious bunch of people around this table,' he observed. 'The newspapers are daily announcing that France and Germany are vying with each other to stockpile arms and build up their Navy, and yet here I see before me an entente cordiale. Then there are the British, sorry ladies I forget your country of birth, who are finally coming down off their high horse and thinking that splendid isolation is not perhaps the thing. Now it is us in America who are the ones who are isolated. What do you say, Count? How does it feel for you?'

The Count had for some years been seconded to the Embassy in Paris. 'I'm more than aware how tenuous my position has become, and there are plans for me to move to Madrid. Spain does not seem interested in the stand off between the other nations of Europe. You don't think it is all a bluff and, however much each country arms itself, so long as power is balanced we can preserve the peace?'

'France has never stopped smarting since the last war,' provoked Sam.

'Germany has never stopped smarting since we wrested Morocco from under their noses,' added Pierre, with a friendly dig to the Count's ribs.

Ruth heard the previously insignificant co-driver suddenly snarl, 'It's all to do with power, especially Africa. You French and British carve up the continent between you, and the Belgians they are in there too, and what about us in Germany?'

Ruth feared that he was turning the gentle banter into a battleground, but Jean-Paul stepped in; 'I can't blame Germany for feeling frustrated, even the Russians are ganging up with Britain. I pray that everyone realises that we are sitting on a tinderbox and draws back.'

'Not while the Kaiser keeps striking matches,' persisted Sam, but he seemed aware that the co-driver could become obstreperous and diverted the conversation to discuss with him the excellence of the German machines and the Count began to regale them with his flying exploits.

Ruth listened to Jean-Paul as he described an incident at Zabern the previous year where German Officers had ruthlessly attacked some local people near their garrison. 'It was dismissed by the Paris papers as a border incident but, it happening in the part of the country where my parents live, it left us with a sense of menace.'

The co-driver joined in, and the conversation continued in German.

'That incident, the Reichstag totally condemned their action.'

'So they might have done,' Jean-Paul answered steadily, 'but the Kaiser upheld the military party, and the officer who had attacked a maimed man was acquitted.'

'That was a purely German affair,' blustered the co-driver.

'It may be in your eyes, but there are many who still consider themselves to be French.'

Ruth understood the gist of the exchange, but did not know to what they were referring. She understood that Jean-Paul was trying to prevent the evening from being spoiled and refrained from asking for more information. She watched Veeve, impatient at the turn of the conversation, manoeuvre to divert everyone's attention.

'Before you all return to Paris, I want you to visit the house that I have taken for the coming summer. You cannot believe its location. It is a real find. You must all come for a picnic in the grounds.'

The house was in the hills above Monte Carlo in Roquebrune. She had taken possession of the key and was due to move in at the beginning of July.

On the morning of the expedition Veeve had commandeered rugs, cushions, and provisions along with a set of boules for Ronald, which were all loaded into the motors.

The journey took them along the coast until they reached Monte Carlo. They then turned up a steep road which snaked and twisted until it led high into the mountain above the town. From various vantage points they could see, far below them, the sea stretching to east and west. The road led them inland along a rutted lane and through woods of pine trees until they reached a pair of gates which marked the entrance to the property.

The house appeared ahead of them and there was not another dwelling in sight.

Extending around three sides of a courtyard the house was a two storey building of rough stone with central pillars of the same material on either side of a weather-worn wooden door. The circular gravelled area was bordered by low brick walls which served the dual purpose of containing the drive on the one side and the encroaching vegetation on the other. Some attempt had been made to cut back the undergrowth, but the trees grew close to the house providing shelter on that aspect from the sun. The pink stone of the walls and the terracotta tiles of the roofs gave a feeling of warmth despite the cooler air at this height. Windows were set at regular intervals, with small panes enclosed by stone frames. Climbing roses clung to the walls and their tendrils draped across the windows confirming the impression that, although the garden had been well maintained in the past, it had recently been given a free rein.

Doors from the various rooms led directly onto a terrace so that it was often easier, if going from one room to another, to cross the gravelled forecourt outside than to use the corridor inside. There were a few bedrooms on the ground floor, which consisted predominantly of reception and the dining room. Numerous bedrooms on the upper floor could easily accommodate twenty guests. The kitchen and the single bathroom had only cold water taps but this would be a minor inconvenience in the heat of summer.

From a low balcony at the rear of the house, steps led

down to a lawn that could be used for tennis and croquet and beyond which were untended flowerbeds and an extensive orchard. Stone tables and benches had been constructed on the terrace, so that guests could enjoy the view across the gardens and towards the forest. Pine trees, through which the party had travelled on their route to the house, covered most of the mountainside and followed the contours of the hills before the land dropped away to the coast. Roses and climbing honeysuckle filled the flowerbeds and in the orchard early apples grew on gnarled fruit trees, deep red plums hung in profusion and shiny crimson cherries dangled invitingly. A short walk through the woods from the house was a gorge where a river cut into the hillside and there they would find water holes deep enough for bathing.

Soon after they arrived everyone dispersed. Pierre and Jean-Paul amused Ronald with a ball while the co-driver, from one of the stone seats erected at random around the garden, moodily watched their game. Ruth joined Hortense, Armelle and Sam where they had arranged rugs on the grass below the steps. Veeve and the Count sat apart from the others perched on the wall of the balcony, holding wine glasses and surveying the scene.

'Why do the French fear the Germans?' Veeve asked. She had come to identify herself with France rather than Britain, her ease with the language, her familiarity with the customs along with her French name made many assume that she was French, and it troubled her that her friends should have fundamental differences that could one day lead to irreparable rifts.

'It all stems from the last war. We beat France soundly and occupied Paris for some terrible months before they surrendered. I have huge admiration for the French, they paid the reparations in three years and regained their self-esteem, but that was forty years ago and we are a new generation. Now we have become a strongly industrialised nation, and know that they could not fight us and win.'

'It would be horrible, to think that you and Pierre and Jean-Paul could be fighting on opposite sides. Surely we are too civilised for war.' Veeve, who always viewed a situation as it related to her own position, then asked, 'Besides, what would I do?'

'When it happens, I'll tell you,' laughed the Count.

'Now, enough misery,' said Veeve, determined to turn to more cheerful subjects.

'I thought that is what you called Ruth,' the Count observed.

'What do you call Ruth?' asked Jean-Paul as he and Ronald, who had finished their game, joined them.

'Little Misery. Well that's what Father always called her because she is so serious.'

'Misérable, oui?' Jean-Paul looked across to where Sam was entertaining the girls, including Ruth, who were laughing in response to his antics. 'I think not.'

Ronald tugged at Jean-Paul's sleeve and whispered in his ear.

'Ronald asks if you will come and play, but I told him it was time to eat,' he told Veeve.

Veeve had long ago decided that playing vigorous

games with small boys was not elegant and she hastily accepted Jean-Paul's excuse. 'Ruth will play with him later.'

'I thought English boys played cricket,' commented Sam once they were all gathered around the lunch picnic.

'What's cricket?' asked Ronald, causing the group to laugh indulgently.

'Cricket is played with a hard ball, a wooden bat and wooden sticks called stumps,' explained Jean-Paul, 'you try and stop the ball from hitting the stumps by hitting the ball with your bat, and then you run towards another set of stumps. I have, however, never seen it played.'

'And since you are a thoroughly French boy you can't be expected to know anything about it either,' Pierre said, to ease the boy's confusion. 'Later we will all play an excellent French game called petonque.'

Ruth was silent while the others explained the game to Sam, thinking that here was yet another decision that should be made for Ronald. He was not French, both his parents were English, yet he barely spoke a word of the language and had never visited England. What was Veeve planning for this boy? She could only teach him for another year and then he must go to school and find friends of his own age. It was a wonder that he was not more precocious considering the life he led.

Hortense and Sam had gone to prepare the game when Ruth was startled by someone speaking to her and using her father's old pet-name, but in French. 'La Misérable! Is this what they call you? Why so serious?'

Jean-Paul asked as he joined her on the rug.

'Not miserable,' Ruth smiled, 'just thinking, about Ronald and schools and friends.'

'When the time is right, decisions can be made. Not many children have a chance to develop in such ambient conditions. Besides, he has a teacher, I hear.'

Ruth blushed, 'I'm no teacher, not a proper one.'

'What is a proper teacher but one who cares?' Jean-Paul said smoothly, but it comforted her that her efforts warranted approval. 'Come, we are going to play petonque. Everyone can play, even Ronald.'

Ruth enjoyed the game. She easily adopted the wrist action used to throw the heavy ball and she was never so far from the jack as to feel conspicuous, nor so close that she would be noticed. Ronald was allowed to stand a couple of paces closer to the jack and managed commendably. He remembered the order of play and, flitting from one to another as their turn came around, was keen to see where their balls landed.

Veeve threw herself into the game. She and Jean-Paul began to stretch ahead with the winning points and finally it was a battle between the two. Ruth wondered if Jean-Paul would allow Veeve to win and hoped that he would not, because she disliked it that Veeve always got her own way. Jean-Paul must have come to the same conclusion because he made quite certain, with his considerable experience at the game, that he won.

Veeve lost gracefully, but not without challenging him for a return match on the next occasion that they met.

'Then Mother can win,' said Ronald loyally. Ruth noticed, because it was so rare, Veeve run her hand over the boy's head and give him one of her dazzling smiles.

The afternoon passed pleasantly but when moves were made to return to Nice, Veeve proposed that some of them should drive further up into the hills. The group was divided with Hortense and Ruth wanting to leave and Veeve for continuing. Sam suggested that he drive one party home, including Ronald, while the others followed later.

Ronald whispered to Ruth that he would like to travel in the front seat of the motor and Sam, to whom Ruth relayed this information, was happy to oblige.

Shielded by the wind from having their conversation overheard, Hortense and Ruth were able to discuss the afternoon's events, and more particularly, Veeve's interest in Jean-Paul.

Hortense had rarely been alone in Ruth's company. Close to her in age, Hortense was a tall, elegant woman with chestnut hair fashionably swept off her face. Her eyes often had dark rims which gave the impression that her make-up had seeped below her lower eyelashes giving her a wistful look. Although she was lively and joined in all activities she managed to hold herself aloof.

She had not consciously, until that day, considered Ruth other than as a self-effacing sister with little to recommend her other than her devotion to Ronald. Side by side in the rear of the motor she watched Ruth's animated face as she drank in the scenery and relaxed her vigilance of Ronald, and she was struck by the dissimilarity of their lives. Commendable as it was to commit oneself to a child, her sister's child at that, surely Ruth was entitled to a life of her own.

For the first time Hortense began to be critical of Veeve where before she had been captivated by her. Perhaps Veeve still thought of Ruth as her little sister, Hortense argued generously. With Ruth unaware of her study she considered her with new insight and was surprised that she had failed to see how pretty she was, imagining that with a fresh wardrobe and with attention paid to her face and hair she might even rival Veeve. Hortense smiled at the prospect of Veeve having an equal.

Hortense could not draw Ruth out to the extent that they could speculate on Veeve's motives for encouraging Jean-Paul, but keeping her suspicions to herself she turned the conversation to her other area of interest, Ruth's future.

'Do you not want children of your own one day?' Hortense's question, so logical to herself following her train of thought, seemed to catch Ruth unawares.

'Don't you?' Ruth countered.

'Of course, but it is not always possible,' Hortense answered, 'for you, it is possible.'

'Perhaps. I am happy with Ronald.'

Hortense could understand that this was true. Ronald was an endearing and intelligent child, and unspoilt due to Ruth's calm discipline and undivided loyalty. Many a woman devoted themselves solely to the care of a child.

'But one day,' Hortense persisted, 'you may return to England, or you may meet someone, or you might be on your own because Veeve might...'

'Veeve would never...' she flared up angrily.

'Would you not want to return to England?' Hortense asked intending to placate her.

'What would I do? Besides, I have been in France for seven years now, everything will have changed.'

Hortense decided to pursue the topic no further, but she hoped that she might have sown a seed if not of discontent, then of self-interest, that had not been planted before. She turned to other matters such as the coming summer and new fashions in Paris. Ruth, with her upbringing and innate curiosity in clothes began to inquire what was in vogue.

'Do you think Veeve is up to date,' asked Ruth, 'it is important to her.'

'How about yourself?' Hortense hoped that she would not embarrass Ruth since she had no way of knowing her financial circumstances.

'I don't need very much.'

'No one needs very much,' Hortense laughed, 'but it is 'très sympatique' to wear new and beautiful clothes, don't you agree?' She wondered if all Ruth needed was a friend. 'I would adore to go shopping with you.' She saw that Ruth was not offended. 'Would you enjoy that?'

They made a plan to visit the shops the next day and Hortense rather childishly relished the moment when she would inform Veeve. Veeve however, was not discountenanced.

'Very nice idea, Hortense,' she agreed, 'What prompted this?'

'I'm planning to match-make. Sam is needing to be married off!'

Hortense steered Ruth through a range of shops with a variety of prices until she gauged her budget. Ruth was obviously careful with money but not short. Hortense told her that the choice in Nice was not large but it was certainly the equal of Paris. She derived enormous pleasure from dressing Ruth, guiding her from her habitual brown and dull maroon to soft blue, deep yellow and subtle emerald green. She passed over shapeless coats and matronly skirts in favour of the simply cut and the stylish. Hortense was pleased at the transformation from governess to young woman and she wondered if she would witness a change in Ruth herself.

She called for a carriage and directed the driver to deliver the boxes to the Hotel, and then invited Ruth to stroll with her along the promenade to a café to revive themselves.

'I'm not tired,' Ruth said.

'But I am,' maintained Hortense, 'it's not every day that I have to set my mind to dress someone. It has been a revelation.' Ruth looked nervous. 'It has also been a great pleasure.'

'How do you know what looks right and how things match?'

Hortense grinned. 'My husband was well off.'

Ruth noted the past tense. Hortense had spent the whole day focused on her and she felt guilty that she had never enquired after her friend, yet she did not like to probe into her past.

'What about when you were young?' Ruth skirted around any reference to her friend's adult life. 'We had to wear hand-me-downs and serviceable clothes most of the time.' She was able to be honest with Hortense.

'So did we. I was brought up on a farm and there were many of us. Life was not easy and we all had to help, but although it was hard it did us no harm. I was sent to the city to be a maid but very quickly I found that the men noticed me. I chose such a wonderful man, but just two years later he died. Now I live like the people that I used to serve. For the time being it suits me.'

Ruth, sitting upright with her hands resting on her lap while absorbing the story, did not know how to respond, and tried to imagine how someone of her own age could already have so much history.

Hortense broke the silence. 'I think it's time to return to the hotel. Don't be shy. Wear that blue dress tonight. We are all leaving tomorrow so there may not be another occasion for a while.'

Jean-Paul had mentioned earlier in the day that he wanted a private conversation with the Count and they agreed to meet in the lounge. At this hour it was usually empty. The two men spoke quietly.

'We can speak German if you like,' said the Count. He gave Jean-Paul an amused smile, 'Is this confidential?'

'In a way, it is,' Jean-Paul answered in German, 'I am afraid it's a business proposition. I hope this is not an inappropriate time to discuss it?'

'Not at all. Business or pleasure, it is all one to me.' The Count was intrigued and eager to find out Jean-Paul's proposal.

'Allow me to stand you a drink.' Jean-Paul nodded

towards the bar. 'What will it be?'

'My usual.'

The bar tender reached for a bottle of white wine from the bucket of ice.

'And a dry sherry.'

The Count sat in one of the wicker chairs, swung one leg over the other, and waited. 'So what is it? How can I help?'

'I am in an awkward position.'

'Yes,' the Count was amused.

'Pierre tells me that you have connections with the dye industry, with chemical dyes.'

'That used to be my line of work, certainly, it's the family business.'

'Our company has the contract for supplying the material for Army uniforms. I have a problem. Our natural dyes are expensive and time-consuming.'

The Count smiled, 'Your famous blue coats and red trousers?'

'For the cavalry and the infantry, that is correct.'

'We favour more subdued colours.'

'So would many of our soldiers because they are rather too conspicuous in modern warfare, but the conservative element of the Army oppose it. With the rapid increase in numbers due to the recruitment drive, we are struggling to meet the demand.'

'And we have the dye you need?' The Count finished the sentence for him. 'What is it that you are needing?'

'Madder red.'

'Madder red? It's true, it's not easy to produce

enough of the natural dye but we have the chemical equivalent. I understand your predicament. Perhaps in a few months our countries could be at war yet Germany has the supply of dye that you need. It might be best if we work through an intermediary. I can think of an agent in Switzerland. I'll send you a sample and if it is satisfactory we can do business.'

'That is more than I could have hoped for.' Jean-Paul picked up his drink which he had barely touched. 'So you are with the Embassy?'

'I needed work that took me away from Lübeck. My domestic situation was not satisfactory.' Jean-Paul's quiet manner encouraged the Count to confide. 'Shall I say that my wife was taking too great an interest in a young officer.'

'I thought the Embassy favoured married couples.'

'They do, but I pleaded my case. My wife is of a delicate and nervous disposition and needs to remain near her family. They accepted it and that left me free. The life is agreeable to me.'

The two men shook hands and as the Count turned to leave the bar he said, 'Despite what might happen between our countries, I shall always think of you as a friend.'

Hortense, pleased with her excursion with Ruth, had sought out a comfortable chair on the Hotel veranda where there was a cool breeze, before changing for dinner. She was rarely disturbed by other guests at this time of day and she enjoyed the peace. In another room she heard the murmur of voices and was unable to distinguish what they were saying but she thought the conversation was in German. She closed her eyes to soak up the late afternoon sun and drifted off to sleep.

She was mildly irritated to hear footsteps approach and bent her head to appear engrossed in a journal. She wished to deter any intrusion on her privacy, however the footsteps did not retreat, they merely stopped. They stopped at some distance from her but remained unmoving for so long that ultimately her curiosity was aroused.

Jean-Paul walked towards her. 'I was thinking of taking a turn in the Jardin Publique, and was wondering if you would accompany me. I have never really explored the gardens and it is dull doing so on one's own.'

'I know it reasonably well and I would be more than happy to join you.' She placed her magazine on the table was swiftly on her feet. 'Let's go.'

'You are ready?'

'No need for a hat at this time of day.'

To reach the Park, Hortense and Jean-Paul had to walk a short distance along the Promenade des Anglais. Already it was filling with people taking advantage of the cooler air to stroll or walk their dogs. The park was extensive and since the trees were well established, when a visitor meandered from path to path it was possible to lose one's bearing.

'Keep the fountain as our landmark and we can't go wrong,' said Hortense, 'we don't want to be late for Veeve's dinner tonight.'

'No, that would not be diplomatic, or desirable,' Jean-

Paul answered, 'besides it would set tongues wagging.'

Hortense laughed companionably and led them in the direction of the rose garden. The blooms were abundant and, as many of the petals had fallen, there was a carpet of pink, red, yellow and white creating a heady perfume.

'That reminds me of home.' Hortense bent to pick up a few petals which were in perfect condition. 'My grandfather looked after an estate. The house was not unlike Veeve's house in Roquebrune. He would take me, even as a young girl, around the gardens and through the woods and tell me the names of the flowers and trees. I remember the wild flowers. There were aconites covering the ground when it was cold in early spring and carpets of bluebells in April. I remember the excitement of finding cuckoo's spit or lady's mantel and ox-eye daisies and bryony and old man's beard in the autumn. I wonder if the same flowers grow here in the south.'

'Where is home?'

'Not far from La Rochelle in La Vendée. It was always royalist, whoever was on the throne or even if there was no king, we are a rebellious lot by nature.'

'Are you? You appear peaceable.'

'I suppose I rebelled when I married, or Etienne did, when he married me.'

Jean-Paul's quiet empathy prompted Hortense to elaborate. 'My father was bright and, unlike my grandfather who worked on the estate, he was employed in the Mairie in Fontenay-le-Conte, our nearest village. I spent every holiday with grandfather. The estate owners had four daughters, younger than myself, who my grandfather adored, and he was popular with them. I helped look after them. Grandfather and I would take them hunting for mushrooms, filling our baskets, or go down to the river where we could bathe. He attached a rope from a branch of a tree, from where we would swing out over the water and then, when we let go, fall into a deep pool. We never made a mistake. The family entertained regularly and when I was eighteen I was asked to help serve at dinner or hand out drinks.'

Hortense took a deep breath. 'I knew their cousin, I'd seen him in previous years, but that year we became friends.' Hortense looked searchingly at Jean-Paul for approval. 'I fell in love with him.'

Jean-Paul and Hortense started to retrace their steps towards the fountain. 'His family allowed us to marry. It was a fairytale Wedding. All the guests assembled in the Notary's office where my father worked for the civil ceremony, but on that day of course, he was my proud father. Then Etienne and I led a procession of all our friends and relations through the village to the church. It seemed that every one wanted to throw flowers in our path, and the bells rang all the way.'

'You paint quite a picture.'

'And then within two years, Etienne was gone. Consumption.' Hortense looked squarely at Jean-Paul to challenge him not to show pity in case she became emotional. 'The family made sure I was safe. It is difficult to refashion a life of one's own. I don't want anyone else yet there is this emptiness. That is why I enjoy being with Veeve and her friends, there is always entertainment and good company.'

'You are excellent company yourself, Hortense.'

She smiled up at him gratefully, and refrained from placing a hand on his arm to emphasize her affection for her, although she was tempted. She did not want to upset the delicate balance of their friendship.

'There's a herb garden over there,' Hortense pointed to a part of the garden under a wide-spreading cedar.

'You seem to know your way around,' Jean-Paul observed.

'Ruth and I have brought Ronald here a few times. There's a swing and a see-saw beyond that shrubbery which we always aim for. I must admit that I haven't always taken as much notice of the gardens as I should. It's good to have time to appreciate them.'

They circled the herb garden whose perfume was pungent at this time of the evening.

'Why does Veeve take so little interest in Ronald. It seems unnatural in a Mother.' Jean-Paul asked.

'Don't be too harsh on Veeve. She had a tough time for the first year of Ronald's life, during which he really only knew Ruth. It's not surprising that Ruth is like a mother to him.'

'When did Ronald's father die?' Jean-Paul asked.

'He didn't die,' Hortense looked at Jean-Paul and saw his slow, dawning comprehension, 'Veeve's divorced.'

Chapter Seventeen

Despite the fact that the newspapers had for months warned of an escalation of arms production by the leading European countries, or perhaps because nothing had resulted from it, most peoples' lives continued unchanged. For those in the privileged position of not having to earn a living, and who had copious amounts of leisure time, there had never before been so many forms of entertainment. The age of the machine meant that, for the male of the species in particular, there was a new phenomenon every year in the motor car or aeroplane industry, while many of the women were, thanks to the suffragette movement, experiencing a freedom that had not been seen for over a century.

Yet it was at this juncture that Veeve began to contemplate the possibility of domesticity. She had reluctantly heeded Ruth's reproach that Ronald was going to need some schooling, and she was viewing more favourably a residence of her own. Without perceiving herself as calculating, she foresaw a situation where she might remarry and in which Ruth too might be attracted to one of her acquaintances. With the advent of the summer months Veeve planned to enlarge her circle of friends to include some suitable men for Ruth. She could see the wisdom of Hortense's whim to encourage Ruth to dress more fashionably and a well-dressed sister reflected favourably on her. The only drawback, which Veeve was reluctant to admit except when she was wholly honest with herself, was that Ruth at twenty-five was in her prime, while she at twenty-nine was drifting into that of a mature beauty. Veeve had been amused and then intrigued by the more frequent appearance of Jean-Paul in the Riviera, especially now that Pierre was married and had consequently to spend more time in Paris. She thought she knew why his visits were more frequent and although she still saw the Count as regularly as ever, she planned accordingly.

There was, however, soon after she took possession of the house in Roquebrune, a glamorous proposition from the Count to fly in easy stages to Madrid which Veeve accepted.

'You must go out and about while I am away,' Veeve told Ruth, 'Ronald will be content with the girl and I shall feel guilty if I am having a high old time and you skulk around on your own.'

On the day of Veeve's departure Ruth and Ronald accompanied her to the airstrip where the Count kept his Fokker. Ronald held tightly on to Ruth's hand as they followed Veeve towards the hanger. The Count emerged carrying his and Veeve's flying gear and a map on which he had plotted their route. Since the weather was fine and there was a clear sky Ruth had few qualms for Veeve's safety. When they were beside the aeroplane the Count lifted Ronald so that he could see the wings and the tail and then he was allowed to sit in the cockpit.

Ronald and Ruth watched the propellers revolve ever faster, churning the air around them and stirring up the dust. Ronald looked up at Ruth, smiled bravely, and then with wide arm movements waved to his Mother as the plane taxied the length of the runway, turned into the wind, and took off.

'What shall we do now?' Ronald asked.

'First of all we'll ride back into town and then you might enjoy a play by the sea.'

Ruth sat on a bench and watched Ronald create an aeroplane from driftwood and a runway with pebbles. She heard her name called and saw an open car with its driver removing his goggles and cap, while shaking his hair free.

'Hello Ruth,' Jean-Paul clambered out of the car, 'is Veeve around?'

'She's away. She's flown to Spain.'

'Well, I am here for a few days, so you and Ronald will have to entertain me instead.' He did not appear to be disappointed, on the contrary, and despite having asked them to amuse him, and much to Ruth's relief, he suggested a diversion for Ronald straight away.

'What is he playing at, with those stones?' Ruth described the aeroplane and runway. Ronald came towards them stumbling over the uneven pebbles. 'There's a cobbler I know who whittles away at wooden toys. Let's see if he has an aeroplane for sale.'

Ruth never asked Jean-Paul why he came to Nice or what line of work meant that he travelled so extensively around the country. She knew that, like her family, Pierre and he were in the textile business, but no details were ever discussed. Yet during those days she came to learn a little more. It happened one evening when she referred to a trip that she and Veeve had made to Morocco. Everything had been so easy, she commented, Veeve had a knack of choosing a place and then the household seemed to gravitate around her.

'That's the colonial in her,' Jean-Paul observed.

Ruth asked what he meant.

'The French and the English, wherever they go are the conquerors so to speak. You annex, subdue and dominate.' Jean-Paul stopped.

'But you are French, why do you say that we do that?' Ruth was piqued into engaging in a discussion.

'Because I was born as the underdog. We were dominated, subdued, annexed. You see, I'm from Alsace. Alsace and Lorraine were French territory until my grandparents' time. When my parents were just schoolchildren we became part of Germany. I was brought up going to German schools and where everything that was French was frowned on.'

Ruth attempted to form the image conjured up. Remembering her trips to India and Ceylon where the British were trying to influence those countries she understood that it was impossible to make India or Ceylon part of Britain. However, Jean-Paul was referring to Europe. Did countries change hands. Could you be part of one country and then find yourself belonging to another?

'This could never happen in England. It can't happen to an island.' She said cautiously, unused to voicing her observations.

'Germany is a very new country, you need to understand that and see her actions in that context. In England you have been free for long over a thousand years. We, by this I mean France, too are an old country, but Germany only came into being during the last century. They just did not know when to stop.'

'I thought you said that they behaved in a nasty manner in Alsace and Lorraine?'

'They could be brutal at times but as a child I was never picked on, they liked to assume that I was German.' He smiled ironically.

'Why was that?'

'My surname was the same as one of their revered composers. That helped. But seriously, just recently near my own home, in Zabern, there was ill treatment of Frenchmen. You may have heard me talking about it with the Count.'

Ruth said that she had heard but she had not seen the significance. 'Why did your family not leave? Were you allowed to leave?'

'Many did leave, almost a third of our people left for France, but some could not.'

'Why was that?'

'Because of their occupations. We are farmers. If you are a teacher or a plumber you can emigrate and take your skill with you, but not if your livelihood is linked to the land. So we stayed. However, my parents encouraged me to leave once I had finished school. The farm is small and would not support more than one family.'

'So that is why you can speak German with the Count?'

'Yes. Only recently have our people gained the right to be taught French in schools. We only spoke French at home.'

Ruth said nothing for some time. In her mind the

boundaries of a country were fixed and not due to some arbitrary arrangement, or treaty or war. Boundaries gave its society stability so how unnerving it must be to see your homeland change hands, and by force. She tried to imagine not being English. It was impossible, even though she had absorbed many of the French ways, her home and identity would never change.

On this and on successive occasions while Veeve was in Spain, Ruth found herself in discussion with Jean-Paul and she was a captive audience. She had been the silent observer for all the years that she and Veeve lived in France yet had absorbed much of France's history and even appreciated their ambivalent feelings towards her own countrymen, but now she had an ear for all her observations.

Jean-Paul took a particular interest in Ronald and in the education of the younger generation. He claimed that the education that children obtained in France produced the most intelligent children in Europe. The French cherished children with a fervour that was alien to the Englishwoman in Ruth. There was a good reason for this and for the resultant care that the country took over their education. France's population had not increased for fifty years, partly due to the reduced size of families necessitated by land inheritance where land was divided between all the sons into smaller and smaller parcels until it eventually became unsustainable, but partly due to the recent wars.

'If Ronald were to be educated in France it would be no handicap and he could return to England when he was older.'

Veeve arrived home from Spain fired up with plans for their summer in the hills. Her experience in Spain had sickened her of city life, she said, and they needed fresh air and space. She had enjoyed her time there, she told Ruth, but the hothouse of parties in which the same people revolved from one Embassy to another, and the need to be a dutiful addition on the Count's official engagements had been wearying, even for Veeve. They had had few opportunities to do what they wanted and she was ready to entertain at her house in Roquebrune.

Summer was well established. In the garden the bushes were laden with fruit, the shrubs ablaze with colour and the flowers were cheerfully unabashed by the untended condition of their beds. The grass had been cut but the tennis court needed marking out and the paths weeding. Veeve soon organised her house staff and the groundsmen to prepare the property and then to fill the house with friends. It was not long before they started arriving.

Towards the end of August, Veeve arrived back at the house from one of her forays into Monte Carlo. There had been a short interlude without guests and there was only a limited amount of time that she could endure with Ruth and Ronald as company before searching for further amusements. Despite the scorching heat and without removing her driving helmet, Veeve hurried across the forecourt and called through the open doors.

'Fetch as many baskets as you can. Bring aprons for myself and my sister. Call for Benoit to bring the cart.

The soldiers have been mobilized and all the reservists are being called up. Everyone is pouring into the town to see them off. We'll gather all the peaches and distribute them on the station.'

It did not take long to assemble the household and they descended the steps from the terrace to the orchard. With the promise of a trip to town the maids applied themselves to the task of picking the fruit with enthusiasm. Veeve handed Ruth an apron and a basket, and tying her own apron around her pushed her sister towards the peach trees.

'There are rumours that Germany is amassing troops along the border, and the papers say that despite Belgium and Luxembourg being neutral, troops are entering there too.' Veeve related all her news excitedly to the girls.

'They are brave men, Madame, but some may never come back.'

'Don't be overdramatic!' Veeve's spirit was festive, caught up by the unexpected frisson that accompanied the sight of hundreds of young men being called away from their jobs because their country needed them. When the baskets were full and loaded onto the cart she packed the maids off to change from their working clothes and she instructed Ruth that they should do the same. 'Wear your cream skirt and jacket and your pink hat with the wide brim.' Veeve was in no mood to be refused. 'I'll wear my olive set and beige cloche with its plumed feather. We need to look good. Everyone is dressed to the nines to see the boys off.'

When all were ready the maids clambered onto the

back of Benoît's cart and Veeve set off in her motor with Ruth. At the station Veeve and Ruth blended in with the fashionably dressed crowd of well-wishers. Anyone who was free, young and old, workmen and children, who wanted to be part of this momentous occasion, gathered along the railway line and on the platforms of the railway station. Veeve, as she carried her basket of peaches flanked by her helpmates somehow managed to create the perfect rustic picture, and a passage opened up to enable them to reach the front of the platform. They were fortunate that it was well into the afternoon and that the fierce midday sun had abated, for there was little overhead shelter for those waiting for the train to draw in.

Eventually the engine came into sight with soldiers leaning out from every carriage window, shouting and waving their hats to the crowd. The mobilised troops were marshalled onto the platform and allocated their divisions.

'Walk towards the front of the train,' Veeve ordered, 'we'll start distributing the peaches there and even if the train moves off we can still hand them out.' She drew appreciative smiles from the onlookers, and elicited flattering comments from the young men in uniform.

She sent the maids back to replenish their supplies of peaches from Benoît, and was having a mild flirtation with a group of soldiers at one of the windows, when above the noisy babble around her she heard her name called in an insistent and disapproving manner.

'Veeve! Ruth! Veeve! Come away. What do you think you are doing?'

Veeve was so intoxicated by her role of lady bountiful that this angry interruption hardly checked her. Ruth instinctively shielded herself by stepping behind Veeve as Jean-Paul threaded his way towards them, his face glowering with displeasure and a sort of despair. He did not wait for Veeve to speak but took her arm brusquely and steered her away from the platform. Ruth followed. They emerged into the street and he growled, 'Where's your motor? Get in and drive home.'

Ruth said, 'The maids, they are with us.'

'Leave them to me.' Jean-Paul pushed Veeve away from him in the direction of her motor car and nodded, with a flick of his head, for Ruth to go with her.

Once on the road, it was not long before Veeve reacted.

'Who is Jean-Paul to gainsay us?' She fumed. 'Who is he to question what we were doing?' She put her foot on the accelerator and hooting and muttering under her breath carved a path through the crowds, forging her way towards the quieter roads in the direction of the hillside and Roquebrune.

Ruth made no comment. By the time they arrived back at the house Veeve had decided that Jean-Paul must think that it was unbecoming for them to be seen alone and in such a throng of people and that he needed to be brought up to date regarding the acceptable boundaries of a modern woman.

Veeve ordered dinner for three as if there had been no disagreement. To diffuse the tension of the encounter with Jean-Paul when he returned with the maids, she informed him that a room was ready for him, and that he was expected for dinner at the usual time. It seemed that she managed to regain mastery of the situation.

As they sat at dinner Veeve was gracious and alluring, 'Jean-Paul, now that we are all friends again, I only want to say that there is no necessity to worry about two attractive English ladies abroad.' She played the 'innocents abroad' card knowing that this usually softened any faux pas on her part.

She did not receive the response she expected. Jean-Paul, usually so charming and courteous, grunted. ' Ce n'est pas ça. That is not it.' He presented a calm exterior but finished eating in silence. Veeve, the consummate hostess, upheld a one-sided conversation, dispensed the wine, and enlisted Ruth as an accomplice until the meal was over and they had moved onto the terrace where coffee had been laid out for them.

In the semi darkness lit by a few flickering candles the anxiety on Ruth's face was not apparent. In these more intimate surroundings Veeve relaxed her guard, and Jean-Paul, in the softened atmosphere of the evening finally spoke, almost hypnotically.

'War is not a glorious thing. War is going to happen. It is brutal and indiscriminate and everyone is affected. In your country you send your men to war but they do not fight on your soil. Your families and loved ones stay safely at home. In France this does not happen. It invades every part of our existence. Our livelihoods are destroyed, our fields are turned into battle fields, there is shortage of food and fuel. Veeve, those peaches, they are not a luxury to be given away. They will be needed to see us through the winter. People starve in war.'

Ruth sat motionless. Veeve, by contrast, wrenched herself from his spell. 'I see no reason to fear the worst when it might never happen, but I can see that this has upset you. You can't really believe that those soldiers will actually be at war. Surely it is enough to present a show of strength.'

'Veeve,' Jean-Paul said sadly, 'already along the border in Alsace and Lorraine the Germans are deploying troops to set up barbed wire fences and to establish batteries. The German troops are amassing all along the frontier.' Veeve was subdued under Jean-Paul's air of authority and dared not question him, and he continued. 'It all started in Sarajevo. The Austrians could not countenance an attack on their sovereignty, and the assassination of the heir to their throne gave them the excuse that they needed to subdue the Serbians. Germany backed them and whatever they said after that meant little as they prepared for war. Now Germany insists that Russia demobilise and as she is unlikely to do so, Russia is being drawn in as well. Everyone is poised.' He paused and looked from Veeve to Ruth. 'In any event, the question is, what are you ladies going to do?'

'Oh, that's simple,' Veeve said, on the brink of being flippant, 'If the war was to break out then we would go home.'

Jean-Paul lifted his head at that moment and happened to see Ruth's expression. An incomprehensible look passed across her eyes which Jean-Paul tried to fathom in the dim candle light, and from it he deduced, that for once, Ruth's own sentiments were at odds with her sister's.

Veeve had confidence in her own judgements, and now, unexpectedly, Ruth seemed ready to challenge them. They sunk into their own thoughts and watched the insects as they were attracted by the flames of the candles and then, repelled by the heat, disappear into the darkness.

The next morning when Veeve joined Ruth and Ronald for breakfast they discovered that Jean-Paul had left at first light. Veeve was irritable with Ruth and short with Ronald and it was with some relief that after a couple of days she said that she had to see about some money transfers in Monte Carlo. If the country was in turmoil, she grumbled, she needed to speak to her bank manager.

In the late afternoon Ruth was supervising Ronald over his meal when a motor drew up and Ruth, thinking that it was Veeve returning, paid little attention. Ronald's face lit up as he looked beyond her and slipped from his chair. Ruth was about to remonstrate, when she heard him call 'Jean-Paul!'

Jean-Paul held Ruth's gaze with studied gravity before he swept Ronald off the ground and carried him towards the terrace. Ruth rose slowly, sobered by Jean-Paul's expression, not a little puzzled by his reappearance, and followed them outside.

Jean-Paul picked up a ball and seemed to shake his head to rid it of thoughts, like a dog emerging wet from a pool shaking its coat. With a grin he entered into the child's world. He lobbed the ball unexpectedly to Ruth, who caught it, was infected by the carefree atmosphere, and instinctively propelled Ronald into a game of 'pig-in-the middle'. As one game progressed to another Jean-Paul put aside, as if to enjoy for the last time this uncomplicated interlude, whatever disturbing news he had brought with him. Ruth, aware that his visit was for no frivolous purpose, joined in the conspiracy so as to delay its inevitable revelation.

Ruth was animated. Gone was the governess and gone was the retiring sister, and in her place was a young woman laughing and unselfconscious, who enjoyed the games as much, if not more, than Ronald. When Jean-Paul finally called a halt and declared that it was time for a young man to go to bed, Ronald was naturally disappointed. He reached for Ruth's hand and walked with her across to Jean-Paul.

'I have a special place I want to show you,' he said. With his other hand he took Jean-Paul's and walked, one on either side of him, for a short distance along the drive. At this point he turned up a narrow path between the fir trees. In a small clearing, with cones, pieces of bark, stones and ferns, he had made an airfield with hangers and a runway. In the centre of the runway was the aeroplane that Jean-Paul had given to him in Nice.

'That is a very special place,' said Jean-Paul, 'we will leave it just as it is and come back and play here another day.'

Ruth steered Ronald to his room while Jean-Paul said, 'I'll stay for supper and the night, if you don't mind. Let me go and talk to the kitchen staff.' He made no mention of Veeve's absence. It was understood that there would be a meal prepared for her should she return before nightfall.

Jean-Paul was sitting on the terrace when Ruth had settled Ronald and she approached quietly. His former exuberance had left him and he indicated that she should sit beside him.

'The news is not good,' he said without preamble. 'Germany and France are at war. Germany has backed Austria who have declared war on Serbia. Russia has mobilised against Germany. What I have come here to tell you is that Britain has declared war, as our ally. Germany never thought she would, but once German troops marched into Belgium, Britain was drawn in.'

Ruth took some time to absorb the information.

'German troops are moving fast towards Paris but the Belgians are resisting hard and may allow us more time to meet the advance.'

'How do you know all this?' Ruth asked, hoping that perhaps it was not true and that the papers were exaggerating.

'I've been working with the military for some time, in one capacity, while continuing to work for our silk business.' Ruth looked perplexed. 'Silk has other uses than fine clothes and furnishings.' Jean-Paul smiled. 'The military use it for their clothing, and parachutes,' he paused, 'and for packing armaments. Silk is non-combustible and the perfect medium for transporting any form of explosive. It's better that you know no more than that, but it will explain why I travel as much as I do, and the veracity of the news that I am bringing you. I am already involved in the war.'

'Do you wear a uniform?' Ruth asked.

'If I need to.'

Over dinner Jean-Paul told her of the hardships that his family and their neighbours would be enduring now that the German troops were active in their area, and how theirs would be the first terrain on which hostilities would be seen. 'It will be almost impossible to communicate with them.'

Ruth was a realist and was grateful that he made no attempt to lighten the impact of the news. Unlike Veeve she did not dismiss what he was telling her with optimistic conjectures. When the meal ended Jean-Paul looked remorseful. 'Now I have made you 'misérable' but I've brought you something to bring a ray of sunshine. The news I have brought you has placed a cloud over your face. I have brought you a present from Saint Cloud.'

Ruth heard 'Saint Clue' and did not know the place nor did she see the connection with the cloud he referred to.

'Saint c-l-o-u-d,' Jean-Paul spelt it, 'a cloud in English pronounced 'clue' in French. It seemed apt for you.' He smiled and picking up a parcel from the sideboard led her through to the drawing room.

Ruth had never experienced such a feeling before of elation mixed with fear. She had so rarely received presents that she had no conditioned response. Jean-Paul stood beside her chair and watched as she untied the string.

'In Saint Cloud they make the most beautiful Sèvres porcelain. The factories will close for the duration of the war. I purchased these knowing that there would be no more made for a while. No-one buys fine ornaments when lives are at stake.'

Ruth opened the brown paper to reveal two further packages, identical in shape, and each wrapped in newspaper. She removed the first item from its paper and gasped. In her hand she held a vase about twelve inches high with a vivid turquoise glaze whose ornate stem and handle were embossed in gold and whose spout was also embossed with gold. Around the spherical bowl of the vase was an intricately depicted rustic scene. She unwrapped the second package and gazed in awe. The pair were exquisite pieces. After a few minutes Jean-Paul took both vases from Ruth and placed them on the mantelpiece. He then he stood back to admire them.

Ruth was confused by a conflict of emotions.

'There is also, to make up the set, a mantel clock.' Jean-Paul stopped until, feeling his eyes on her, she returned his look. 'I have the clock on the mantel piece in my apartment in Paris. I was hoping that one day your vases might join my clock.'

Ruth blushed, she was intelligent enough to understand what Jean-Paul was implying but her temperament was against her.

'I'm asking you if you would marry me, Ruth, when this war is over.'

Ruth stood up and turned away from him with her elbows bent and her fists closed against her shoulders. She was disorientated by the awesome consequences yet flooded with happiness.

Jean-Paul moved behind her and she felt his hands on her shoulders, turning her towards him. The firm pressure helped her to control her emotions. 'Go and fetch your wrap, Ruth, let us go for a walk.'

Ruth shook her head, 'I don't need a wrap,' and seeing his outstretched hand, took it in hers.

It was mid-morning the next day before Veeve drove up to the villa and parked her motorcar beside Jean-Paul's. She sprang down lightly from the driving seat, steadying her hat with one hand and grasping a newspaper with the other. Ronald ran out onto the gravel when he heard the car but when he saw his Mother, he hung back with Jean-Paul and Ruth.

Veeve, heady from the recent news and ready with new plans, paid no attention to Ronald but smiling coquettishly at Jean-Paul said. 'Have you come to rescue two damsels in distress?'

She swept ahead of them towards the drawing room. She then noticed that neither of them were sharing her exuberance and instead called across to Ronald. 'And what have you been up to while Maman has been away?'

Jean-Paul told Ronald that he should go out and play. 'Veeve. Did you know that Britain has declared war?'

'Why do you think I spent so long in Monte Carlo? Once I heard the news I knew there was no question of returning home.' She saw Ruth looking at her expectantly. 'So I telegraphed the Count and had to wait until this morning for his reply.'

'What do you mean?' asked Jean-Paul.

'You don't think I'm staying in France while there's a war on. The Count says we can go to him in Madrid.

We'd be refugees. It would only be until Christmas. Everyone says it will be over by then.'

'Who says? The Germans or the French?'

'The papers. Everyone.'

'And you intend to be on which side?'

'The winning side. Spain is neutral.'

'But courtesy of the Germans?'

Veeve looked defiant. They stood in a circle seemingly at an impasse.

'I won't be coming with you,' Ruth said.

Suddenly a myriad of possibilities ran through Veeve's mind. She turned to Jean-Paul for explanation and received it when she saw Ruth exchange a glance with him which he acknowledged.

'Why, what's happened?'

'I've asked Ruth to marry me, Veeve. It seems she's willing to do so.'

Veeve rounded on Ruth. 'And where will you go? Who will look after you? How can you think...' She made no effort to control her anger.

Jean-Paul reacted with studied silence. Ruth said nothing. At that moment Ronald ran into the room and passing his mother went to speak to Ruth.

Veeve, as she had many years before, calculated without Ronald. She could go to Madrid but her life would be insupportable if she was hampered by a child, and besides, this child hardly noticed her.

'And what about Ronald?' She could not bring herself to say that he seemed to treat Ruth as his mother.

'Ronald can stay,' Jean-Paul intervened, 'it is only, as you say, until the end of the war. I can make arrangements for him.'

Ronald looked from one to another. No one spoke to him but he slipped his hand into Ruth's.

'I'm not staying here a minute longer,' Veeve said coldly, and started to walk away. Then she turned and addressed Jean-Paul. 'You can send my things to the Hotel Mirabelle. Do not expect to hear from me until the war is over.' Without another word or gesture she left.

Ruth watched Ronald press his lips hard against each other, his eyes staring with fear and she pushed him gently across to Jean-Paul. He put his arm around the boy and over his head he instructed Ruth.

'We leave as soon as possible. Ask the maids to help you to pack. Do you have much? I'll arrange for Benoit and the cart. We must hurry to Paris, which means boarding a train, and from there send you on to England. The rest we can discuss later.'

'And Veeve. What about her affairs?'

'We do nothing. Veeve can make her own arrangements and she cannot leave without closing up the house. You can be sure that when we have gone she will return.'

Two hours later Ruth and Ronald's valises were assembled on the terrace. Their worldly possessions made a somewhat pitiful collection. The significance of their small pile of belongings was not lost on Jean-Paul. He sent Benoit on ahead with the luggage in the cart but placed the two carefully wrapped and boxed Sèvres vases safely in his motorcar. He was about to go back into the house to advise the staff to remain until Veeve returned, when seemed to remember something.

'Do you have a passport? You are going to need some form of identification.'

'No. If I have needed any I have used Veeve's old one. It's in her maiden name.'

'Do you know where it's kept?'

Ruth nodded.

'It's no use to Veeve, and could be invaluable for you.'

Throughout France, people would be on the move. Some, like the soldiers, moving towards the war, some moving away, families regrouping or taking in refugees. Tradesmen and businessmen would be gauging their chances of survival in a wartime economy and assessing what changes they would have to make. A camaraderie not known before was already prevailing, even among their small household where petty differences were buried in the face of a greater threat. Veeve's eccentric behaviour would be excused by her staff on account of the extraordinary circumstances.

Ruth retrieved the passport and joined Jean-Paul. He placed his hand on her arm and said earnestly. 'It will be a long journey, many people will be travelling and the trains will be crammed. Are you ready for this?'

'Yes, we'll be patient, won't we Ronald?' She turned to the boy but he was not there. 'Ronald's gone!'

'We'll start the engine, and if that does not bring him then we will search.'

Jean-Paul made a slow sweep across the gravel, pressed the horn as he waved to the staff, and started slowly up the drive. Ahead of them they saw Ronald emerge from the woods. He was holding his toy aeroplane high above his head flying it as he ran towards them.

What were they to say to this child? How explain a war? How to explain the months until his mother returned? How were they going to look after him? Soon all questions were put aside in the practicalities of buying tickets, boarding the train, securing seats and stowing luggage. Then there was the transfer from the coastal line to the larger rail line and finally to the mainline train whose destination was Paris. This train left late at night and as Ronald fell asleep with his head on Ruth's lap and his tired little body on Jean-Paul's, they finally had a chance to discuss their plans. Their conversation was muted but their privacy ensured by the rhythmic rumblings of the train.

'Once we reach Paris your onward journey to England should be to Cherbourg and then across the Channel. I envisage a great exodus of English people by that route because the German army is advancing from the east. You can stay with your family while you prepare for our wedding. That is what you would like?'

'What about Ronald?'

'You can't take Ronald. It'd be impossible to explain Veeve's desertion, for that is what it is, and it would place you in a compromising position. Leave Ronald with me. I believe he likes me and this is no time to confuse the lad by introducing relations that he does not know.'

'But you'll have to work and travel.'

'And Ronald has to go to school, remember? I shall ask Armelle, Pierre's wife, if she will look after him and send him to the lycée until you return, or Veeve returns. Once I'm in Paris I will see you onto the train to Cherbourg and you'll have no difficulties after that. I'll explain everything to Ronald as it becomes necessary and he will come to no harm. Rest your head on my shoulder, and sleep while you can.' Jean-Paul shifted his body on the cramped seat until Ruth was comfortable.

Many hours later, Ruth stood on the deck of the ferry unwilling to leave the security of the wooden rail. She strained her eyes in the twilight to seek out the dark outline of the coast and she fixed on the fast dimming lights of the harbour to give her a focus. The air was colder than she had experienced for a long time. The summer nights in England were never as warm as those in Southern France and she shivered as the ferry gained speed. She felt in her purse, took out a piece of paper and read again the address that Jean-Paul had given her, and then she memorized it. It was that of his apartment which was in the seventeenth arrondissement, an area of Paris, Jean-Paul told her, near the Arc de Triomphe. Ruth was none the wiser. It was not the time to tell him of those few sad days which were her only experience of Paris. He had asked her about her family and she told him about Flo and Tom and the mill, about Lil and her dependable Henry, how Elsie had married Lil's beau and the curious circumstances of Bett's marriage.

'It does seem to me,' commented Jean-Paul, 'that Bett's husband is unreliable. He does not seem trustworthy.' Then he asked if that was all and was delighted to discover that Ruth had yet one more sister and said how fortunate she was, because he had neither brother nor sister. He had been saddened to hear of Maisie's deafness but admired her plucky independence.

'You, too,' he had said affectionately to Ruth, 'have the ingredients to be both brave and self reliant.' Ruth had glowed with pleasure and smiled at the recollection, and with it came the courage to descend the steps to the lower deck, despite the throng of people who were all escaping,l ike herself from France, to secure a chair for the night.

Ruth found a seat in the crowded London bound train, and heartened by the helpfulness of a fellow traveller, underwent a strange sensation. It was a sense of exhilaration that she had never experienced before. Could it be the taste of freedom now that she had a legitimate status? She was engaged to be married. She was a daughter coming home to arrange her wedding and as such her mother's approval was guaranteed.

Her father could now be proud of her, and her adventures abroad would give some credence to her life which should gain her sisters' recognition. Her spirits rose as the train carried her towards her home town which she had last seen when she had been just out of school uniform. Jean-Paul had promised to send a telegram to prepare them for her arrival. She remembered the excitement that she had felt when her sisters returned home; Veeve and Flo when they returned from the Paris Exposition, Bett when she returned from Canada, Lil from her trips to London and the drama surrounding Veeve's wedding to George. Would they be anticipating her return with the same suspense? Perhaps it was because she had been young and lived a secluded life their forays into the wider world had created so strong an impression. She thought of her sisters with affection and realised with a jolt how much she had missed them. Over-riding everything, she perceived herself, having turned away from them to cleave to her wayward sister, returning contrite to be welcomed and forgiven.

Chapter Eighteen

It was evening when Ruth stood on the threshold of her home. She walked slowly up the steps, savouring the moment, then took hold of the handle of the large brass knocker and struck the plate. At the same instant the door opened. Horace must have been hovering and from the size of his grin Ruth suspected that he had. The commotion in the Hall caused by Horace as he carried in her cases summoned the family from the drawing room. Ruth hesitated, undecided who to approach first, until she saw her Mother.

There were exclamations of amazement and happiness, solicitations over her journey and entreaties to come into the drawing room so that, as her Mother said, 'they could have a proper look at her'. Ruth found herself in the centre of the room in the largest chair by the fireplace, with her Father sitting opposite her, Maisie and Sheilagh on the settee, her Mother arranging for Bovril and biscuits and Bett sitting on a separate chair with her feet resting on a stool.

It was a curiously subdued evening with each person brimming with questions, yet the sheer enormity of their emotions seemed to cause a barrier to communication. Since her family could not begin to imagine Ruth's life and since they assumed that she had returned due to the outbreak of the war, they enquired little of her apart from the details of her passage home. They seemed surprised that there were so many English people abroad, and were concerned at her travelling such a long way on her own. Maisie reminded them that Ruth was now quite capable of looking after herself.

Ruth, while listening to her Mother recount the changes to their neighbourhood, and extol the delights of her grandchildren, thought how much her parents had aged. Their movements were slower and they looked to each other for reassurance more than she remembered. The family allowed Eleanor to dominate the evening while they adjusted to the new member in their midst. There were many days ahead when they would be able to gain Ruth's attention for themselves and eventually Maisie took charge and dispatched everyone to bed declaring that Ruth was tired. It was as if she was a visitor in her own house. She would have to learn the routine that they had established, and the tempo of the household.

She woke early and made her way to the dining room. There she found Maisie who had clearly finished her breakfast and was ready to go out.

'I'll see you to-night. I'm on a driving instructor's course. We're likely to need many more women drivers if the lads are all off to fight. What will you do with yourself? Find your feet for a few days and then I'll tell you the sort of jobs where women are volunteering.'

Once Maisie had left, Ruth helped herself from the sideboard. She had eaten little over the previous two days and was grateful for the selection of cooked meats and eggs. Shortly afterwards Sheilagh joined her.

Sheilagh was almost eighteen and in many ways resembled Maisie more than Betts, not that she was related to either in the strictest sense of the word. She had adopted Maisie's brusque movements and purposeful walk, and, once she began to talk, had obviously been much influenced by her aunt. She was concerned, however, for her mother, Bett.

'She's not very well at the moment. She will be so happy that you are here. She talks about you frequently. I wonder what you will do now you're here. I want to ask you about France. What was it like?' Ruth assured her that they would have plenty of occasions on which to talk and she then learnt that Maisie had arranged for Sheilagh to attend a first aid course with a view to joining the St. John's Ambulance Corps in case the war escalated. Everyone, it seemed, was doing something.

'I usually refill Bett's hot water bottles before I leave for the Town Hall, but I am running late, would you do that for me?' Ruth was grateful for the chance to be useful.

She spent most of the morning with Bett. The rheumatoid arthritis which had brought Bett home from Canada, flared up regularly and this was one of those episodes. Bett's swollen joints needed rest and warmth and she delayed joining the family downstairs until the afternoon. Her room felt like a safe haven. She would listen without judgement and was unlikely to divulge anything that she was told. This was not because she was secretive, it was merely that nobody asked her, yet they all used her as a repository for their confidences

Bett learnt that Veeve had gone to Spain and then gently inquired why Ruth had not gone there as well. Ruth moved from her chair and rearranged Bett's pillows before she told her with a shy smile that she was to be married once the war was over. While Bett rested her head against the back of the armchair, her painful swollen hands placed on the arms for support, she listened as Ruth related her story.

Jean-Paul was taller than their father and of a slight build. He had a thin angular face that was serious and preoccupied until he smiled, and then you felt singled out for his especial attention. He spoke, unlike other men that she knew, to both men and women without discrimination, imparting his thoughts and knowledge to anyone who would listen and relishing discussion. There was no situation in which he would find himself out of his depth. His war work meant that he would not be called up like other men summoned to serve in the armed forces. She explained to Bett that she had no qualms about waiting for the war to end while she arranged her wedding.

Bett was entranced. A Wedding! How long it had been since there had been one in the family, for Elsie had married soon after Veeve and Ruth had left. She inquired if Veeve was happy, and Ruth said truthfully that she thought Veeve was as happy as she was capable of, but that no-one would ever replace George. She then recounted the sorry saga of those days in Paris and Bett understood why Ruth could not have left her.

When Bett grew tired Ruth read to her, and when she needed anything Ruth fetched it for her. It was so peaceful that Ruth felt guilty at denying her Mother the interview that she knew she so anxiously awaited.

'Married?' Eleanor was ecstatic. She had the perfect piece of material for her dress. 'When the war was over? Why that was just until Christmas. Not long at all.'

Reginald waited until Eleanor's maternal exuberance had abated before he allowed himself to voice a father's concern. 'This man. Can he support you?'

'I should think so, Father. He has his own car and his own apartment. He's in the silk business.'

This seemed to mollify her Father as did Ruth's insistence that there was no need to rush into organising the event. He then gently probed about Veeve and looked somewhat wistful as he pictured her so far away.

'In Spain? She will at least be safe. And the boy too.' Reginald added, once again including Eleanor with a reassuring nod in her direction. 'This lad you are to marry. What's his name?'

'Jean-Paul.'

'But that's a French name,' Eleanor was quick to interject.

'I know, Mother. He is French. I'm sorry that I didn't make that clear.'

'How can he be French?' Eleanor was shaken.

It was useless for Ruth to describe the cosmopolitan

society in which they lived. For Eleanor there would always be pockets of English people abroad untainted by the foreigners around them. She immediately envisaged all manner of problems and started to enumerate them, when Reginald interrupted.

'In due course we will meet the young man, this Jean-Paul. All in good time, my dear. He does speak English I presume?' He turned to Ruth for confirmation. 'It is nice to have you home again. No doubt it will feel strange to begin with and we are living in turbulent times, there's no knowing from one day to another what will happen.'

If he or Eleanor thought that the war might thwart Ruth's intention to marry a foreigner, they kept it from each other, and from Ruth.

Ruth enjoyed the novelty of being back in Leicester, revisiting the town and the prospect of visits from her older sisters. Lil and Elsie with their husbands Henry and Mitchell, and Elsie's two children, were due to join them for the traditional Sunday lunch.

It was Elsie who upset everything when the children had been taken away by Sheilagh to play in the nursery. 'How can you marry a Frenchman, Ruth? He'll be a Roman Catholic. Don't you know what happens when you marry a Catholic? For a start you have to promise bring up your children as Catholics. Nor can you be married in St. Mary's.' A glance at Mitchell confirmed that her sister was correct but Ruth could not understand the antagonism in Elsie's voice.

'I always used to think of the French as our enemies,' mused Eleanor, 'but now I suppose that our enemies are the Germans.'

Lil seemed uncomfortable with the exchange but it was Henry who rescued Ruth. He was sure that there were ways in which Protestants married Catholics, Mitchell could look into it, but for the time being they were not even sure that Jean-Paul was a Catholic. The atmosphere of happiness that had pervaded the reunion was somewhat marred. Elsie excused herself to go and see whether her children were behaving and Lil took the chance to mitigate the effect of her objections.

'I'm sure he is very nice and we all want to meet him. What does he do, is he working for the war effort?'

'He's not a regular soldier,' Ruth admitted.

'Nor is Henry,' said Lil comfortably, looking happily at her husband. 'He has been declared unfit for Military service. He has a weak heart that we never knew about.'

'Have you enlisted already?' Mitchell asked Henry amazed.

'On the first day,' Henry replied.

Mitchell did not like to be upstaged and found an excuse to join Elsie in the nursery. Lil took the opportunity to say to Ruth. 'It's so romantic. Just imagine, your children will grow up speaking French naturally. We spent so long labouring over all that grammar. We hear that the German troops are moving towards Paris, is Jean-Paul in any danger?'

'He supplies cloth to the army so I suppose he could be.'

'What an extraordinary coincidence,' remarked Henry, 'it seems that it's an ill wind and all that. Brindsley-Smith has leapt on the band wagon, my apologies Bett, and made himself very important. He's arranged with the War office to supply all the uniforms. In so doing, to be fair, he has secured the prosperity of your father's mill for the duration. He liaises with the recruiting officers and then ensures that your father supplies the materials. You have to take your hat off to him. If only he wouldn't blow his own trumpet, it makes a man want to avoid him at the Club.'

Henry then appeared to remember something. 'Except that last time when I saw him the poor blighter was quite shaken. He took me to a booth and pressed a brandy on me. He already had a large one in his hand. 'What do you think happened to me on the way here?' he asked me. I was dashed if I knew but the poor fellow's face was so white that I felt for him. 'I was handed a white feather by two women on the bus.' He had been accused of being a coward although how they knew he had not enlisted goodness only knows. I told him there was only one solution. To make the army give him a commission. It's strange. No-one has tried to give me a feather. Must be something in my face.'

Henry and Lil viewed Ruth's engagement with an ease that reassured Eleanor. However when Henry mentioned a Civil Wedding as a solution to the Catholic conundrum, she saw her aspirations of a white wedding for the older of her two unmarried daughters begin to slip away.

It took a while for letters to cross the Channel because military correspondence took precedence but eventually Ruth received a reply from Jean-Paul regarding his religion. It was not one that he had anticipated because the issue no longer arose in France where all marriages were licensed by the State, and his answer was, obligingly, that he could be either. His parents were Catholic but Lutheranism had been encouraged by the schools and he had been confirmed in neither. With this hurdle seemingly surmounted the family was anxious for the war to end so that they could all indulge in preparations for their beautiful bride and her enigmatic groom. Even Elsie became slightly mollified although she still muttered darkly about separate schools and first communions, both of which she regarded with suspicion.

Ruth had been home a month when, sitting around the dinner table, the family could see that Reginald was cogitating over whether to share a piece of news with them. He would start a sentence and then drift off the subject until Eleanor, who knew the signs, asked him directly the reason for his distraction.

'I'll tell you frankly. Tom has joined up. Flo says that he could be called at any time. What the dickens am I to do with the workshops? There will be no men available to take his place and it's like a contagion, they are all doing it.'

'You can hardly be surprised, Father,' said Maisie. 'Everyone wants to do their bit, even Sheilagh.'

'So who am I to find to run my workshops? We have many new contracts to fulfil, from the army and the ancillary services, and no one to supervise.'

'Why not Flo?' Maisie with her usual bluntness. 'She'll know more than most. Ruth can go and help her and she can learn Tom's work.'

Reginald was not as averse to the idea as he might have been a few years earlier. Maisie's drive to be independent had enlightened him and he saw the sense in Maisie's proposition. He would rather trust Flo with his workshops than anyone else. Ruth, too, was taken with the idea and they agreed to set out the next morning to present it to Flo and Tom.

Ruth's sojourn with her sister was a revelation. Flo taught her how to wash their clothes, to put them through the wringer without damaging her fingers, and to iron without burning either her hands or the fabric. She learnt to tend the range and to make nourishing soups and stews, and Flo took her to the market where she began to understand how to plan meals and gauge quantities of ingredients. Every afternoon Flo went to the mill, donned the uniform so that she blended in with the other women, and began her apprenticeship under Tom.

It left little time for the sisters to be together, but Ruth found the days sped by and she did not feel lonely. The letters from Jean-Paul were encouraging; the French troops were fighting well and holding the Germans back from the passes of the Vosges in his home territory. The battle line was from the Channel to Switzerland but the Germans were being hampered by unexpectedly strong resistance from the Belgians in the north, and the British troops had thus been given time to come to France's aid.

Flo became more and more anxious however, knowing that at any moment Tom could be called away. 'There was no need for him to enlist.' Flo confided to

Ruth one day when they were walking to the haberdashers. 'There seems to be some invisible magnet that draws them. We had gone to the pictures with two friends. Instead of the usual screen and music playing, there was a desk, two men in army uniform and a singer. They spoke of the glorious opportunity that our generation had to serve our country, and of the gratitude that would be felt by all the wives and mothers as they defeated the scourge that was sweeping across Europe. The singer sang patriotic songs and smiled encouragingly at the young men. First one and then another stood up and made their way to the table to sign up. She came near to our group and laid a hand on Tom's shoulder. I didn't want him to go, but it was as if he was mesmerised by the moment and he joined the line. When everyone was back in their seats they put on a different picture from the one we were expecting and showed us what splendid lads there were in the army. Tom says he's worried it will all be over before he has a chance to be involved.'

Tom was not disappointed. Within a week of that conversation he was gone.

Ruth knew that she was invaluable to Flo as her sister adapted to her life as a working mother. Before she had a chance to question whether in fact she could sensibly remain with Flo for an unspecified length of time, a letter arrived from Jean-Paul that made the decision for her.

'I shall have to be married in France,' Ruth told Flo. 'Jean-Paul has been in communication with his parents. They do not want him to marry a foreigner. He is their only son, you understand.'

'When they meet you they will change their mind,' said Flo defiantly, 'why does it depend on them where you marry?'

'In French law Jean-Paul cannot marry me in England without his parents' permission. Only if we marry in France is it a legal marriage.'

Ruth thought over her options and decided that there were only two. She could hope that Jean-Paul's parents might like her, but her natural pessimism argued against that possibility and besides it would be some time before they could travel to Alsace in the centre of a war zone. Alternatively she could be married on French soil. If this was her choice might she not as well leave for Paris sooner rather than later?

Jean-Paul wrote that, after the hostile reaction of his parents, he feared that she might want to call off the wedding and he was overjoyed at her response. He could not expect her to travel while there was a risk that the Germans might reach Paris and occupy it. Flo found it hard to understand that Ruth was prepared to travel voluntarily into a country where Tom had been sent to fight, but she failed to take into account that France was as much Ruth's home as Leicester was Flo's, and that apart from reservations about the war she had no fears about returning.

'As soon as I can, I'll go back to France. I can stay with a friend until I am married. It can't take long to arrange a civil wedding. I was never someone who wanted the limelight and all the fuss that Mother insists on.'

Eleanor and Reginald were mystified by Ruth's decision. Reginald asked Mitchell to verify the legalities of the marriage. Eleanor hoped that the war would continue for a very long time and that Ruth 'would get all this nonsense out of her head.' Bett was quietly supportive knowing that no amount of time or distance would change Ruth's mind. Sheilagh decided that it was highly romantic of her aunt to pine for her future husband across the sea separated by a war, and plied her with questions about her life in France in case this mysterious relative disappeared without trace in much the same way as she had appeared, as if from nowhere, into her life.

Ruth took the ferry to France in mid-December. She stood on the deck where the heat from the engines and the wooden housing of the lifeboats gave her some protection from the elements and hoped that by staying on deck she might prevent the sea sickness that already some of her fellow travellers were suffering. She did not feel remotely unwell and was exhilarated by the raging sea. She watched with fascination the swells as they approached in their serried ranks, and the spume that was whipped up by the wind to form a crest on every wave. As the ship rose and fell and took each onslaught with a sort of majesty, Ruth had the impression that it was invincible. Even when an unexpectedly monstrous wave crashed against the bow and threw spray the length of the decks sending people scurrying from the railings, her reaction was one of delight.

Ruth revelled in her isolation. Wrapped in her Mother's fur coat, she leant against the outer wall of the saloon and knew that the howling wind would prevent any unwelcome approaches. She wanted to savour her feeling of daring as she faced a new adventure. She stayed on deck until she was so cold that she was driven to find some corner where she could sit out the journey.

Early in December the British in general, and her family in particular, began to understand that the war was not a minor affair to be dispatched by Christmas. Preparation for the festivities were subdued and in some quarters were viewed as inappropriate. The newspapers which had been so confident of British supremacy and natural domination in the early weeks of the war, were now sowing seeds of doubt which pervaded every section of society. Businesses were cautious, families were careful, the government was undecided. And men were being killed in their thousands. At the battle of Ypres three quarters of the men that Britain had sent to fight were lost.

Then news came from Jean-Paul that the fighting in northern Europe had stalled, bogged down in mud. Horses, the usual vehicles for transport, were unable to drag the guns and equipment through the sodden terrain. Supplies to the front line were hampered and fighting had ground to a halt on both sides. The expected lightening encirclement and isolation of Paris had not happened. General Gallieri had, it seems, anticipated Germany's tactics and fortified their city. When he heard that the situation was critical he sent his troops to assist those already on the Marne river by taxicabs. The line of confrontation had been taken up sixty kilometres from Paris but access was possible, as were supplies, to the inhabitants of the city.

Unwittingly Jean-Paul had fed Ruth with the information that she needed to convince herself that she could as easily help the war effort in France as in England. Maisie had told her of women who had already crossed the channel to work with the Red Cross teams and assured her that she would find work in some capacity even if she had no nursing skills.

Eleanor and Elsie had originally been up in arms at Ruth's decision to travel to France insinuating that she was being unpatriotic, but later were genuinely distressed for her welfare. Elsie, ironically, when she heard that the French prohibit the marriage to foreigners except on their own soil, reluctantly felt the stirrings of some kinship with the erstwhile object of her derision. She had been certain that it would have deterred her sister from any rash decision and when she considered her feelings for Mitchell, she understood that if Ruth felt similarly, her need to be with the Frenchman was not to be questioned. Had Ruth not felt totally committed then Eleanor too, when she realised that Ruth was prepared to face untold dangers, removed her censorship and parcelled up the material for her wedding dress. The tears in her eyes when she thrust the gift into Ruth's hands and said a choked farewell betrayed her true feelings.

Reginald, who had stated regularly over the recent years that he did not understand his daughters, only had his sentiments confirmed when Ruth announced that she was returning to France. He was too old and tired to attempt to convince her to do otherwise and a part of him recognised a stubborn streak when he saw it. He took the view that Ruth would have to live with the consequences of her actions, yet there was a tenderness underneath his rationality and he could not deny that he experienced a wrench every time he handed over a daughter to another. Reginald could not imagine, especially with France in the grip of war, what sort of life Ruth could be entering, but he respected her intelligence and the innate female ability to adapt to a situation. He decided, like a father escorting his daughter up the aisle of a Church, that he would accompany Ruth to the coastal port where she was to leave Britain's shores. That much he felt that he owed her, and Ruth was touched by his gesture and grateful that she had not had to leave her home quite alone.

Now that she had said her final goodbye she examined the future. She would stay with Hortense until Jean-Paul was able to fix a date for their wedding. She had, for as long as she could remember, been the recipient of advice and instruction from all around her and had felt a strong obligation to please and do her duty. She had no ambition for herself until she met Jean-Paul. Now, like the independent Hortense, she could start to make decisions regarding her future life with him unfettered by consideration for others. She had broken all familiar ties so as to join a man to whom she felt drawn, but in which logic played no part.

When she arrived at Gare St. Lazare Ruth made her way to the station hotel and took a seat by the coal fire. For all her bravura she felt conspicuous, and picking up one of the magazines that lay on the table, flicked through the articles unable to concentrate on any of them. She would very much have liked some tea but this English habit had not crossed the Channel and she felt a momentary pang of homesickness. She was certain that the minute she ordered a drink Hortense would arrive and then it would be awkward. In the interests of staying awake she would have a coffee, she would have been mortified to have been found dozing, and almost as soon as she had made up her mind, Hortense entered the lounge. She gave her a kiss on either cheek, and called a taxicab.

Although it was dark, by the dim light of the street lamps Ruth glimpsed the avenues and alleyways, shuttered windows and balconies, of the quintessential Parisian town houses that they passed as they headed towards the 17th arrondissement.

Hortense had been overjoyed, she told Ruth, when she had been asked if she could help. She was delighted to be instrumental in enabling her to come to Paris to marry their friend Jean-Paul. The reason for her happiness, she explained, was that it was so distressing if friends married and moved away, or chose someone that was not much liked, but Ruth and Jean-Paul had done neither. She said that her apartment was small but comfortable, and since she had sent her young maid back to her family, the little room was free. It was plain but serviceable and she told Ruth that she could stay as long as she wanted.

Hortense's apartment had an old world charm with many pieces of fine furniture and pictures which she would never have aspired to had she not inherited them from her husband. The maid's room was no more austere than a child's room in her own home and the house was warm because the apartment sat snugly in the centre of the building.

'There's no knowing when Jean-Paul will be in town again, but he knows you are here and he is relying on me to introduce you to the area. As for Ronald, he is with Pierre and his family. I am not free until Sunday but you will have a chance to visit him tomorrow after school.'

'Where will you be?'

'I am working at a munitions factory. Jean-Paul found me the job. I've been there for two months. I can introduce you to the manageress and find a place for you too.'

'I should like that. I was keen to do something to help the war effort when I was in Leicester.'

'Can you ride a bicycle?' Hortense suspected that Ruth could not and watched with glee a look of consternation pass over her face. 'Then I'll have to teach you. We'll go to the Bois de Boulogne on Sunday and I'll give you a lesson.'

'Why do I need to ride a bicycle?' Ruth could see no connection between munitions and cycling.

'To get to work. Horses are being requisitioned by the Ministère de la Guerre and transport around the city is a problem. Motor factories have converted to producing bicycles and it will be easy to purchase one for you.'

Ruth found sports of any kind a pleasure and

although she never excelled she managed passably. She admired Maisie who, despite her poor coordination which made any physical task taxing, had been determined to master riding a bicycle and this knowledge gave Ruth some incentive. The wintry afternoon had repelled the faint-hearted and only a few families were to be seen scattered around the park. Here and there a child played with a hoop or ran with a ball, a few dogs were being exercised, and young couples meandered along the gravel paths. Hortense found a spacious area of grass between some rhododendron bushes and handed Ruth the bicycle.

'Don't pedal too fast. I'll hold on to the saddle.' Hortense was strong and Ruth was light but they quickly gave up because Ruth could not keep the handlebars steady, took her feet off the pedals, and leaned onto Hortense

'Pedal faster this time,' Hortense ordered. The two girls were engrossed, oblivious to the casual walker who would stop at a respectful distance to watch.

'Pedal much faster and keep going, I'll give you a push and then don't stop. It's speed that gives you control.' Ruth looked fiercely ahead and gripped the handlebars to prevent them from throwing her off her balance. Hortense placed a hand behind the saddle and, coat flapping and hair flying beneath her hat, as the bicycle gained momentum Ruth pedalled furiously. She travelled at speed for some twenty yards and then a rhododendron bush reared up in her path. Suddenly another hand was on her handlebar and had seized the brake, and there was someone running beside her to lessen her fall.

'Well done, Ruth,' said Jean-Paul breathlessly. Covered in confusion and tangled with the handlebars Ruth was elated by her achievement, but could have hoped for a more dignified reunion with her fiancée. Jean-Paul detached Ruth from her bicycle, let it fall to the ground, and enveloped her in a long embrace. Hortense gave them a few moments and then ran over to greet him.

He retained an arm around Ruth's waist. 'Veronique, in the apartment below you, saw you leave with the bicycle, so I hazarded a guess that you might be here.'

Hortense mounted the bicycle and started along the path. As she turned on a bend she looked back over her shoulder and smiled. How typical it was of Jean-Paul who, instead of linking an arm through Ruth's in the traditional manner of a suitor, had an arm around her shoulder and with his head forward and turned towards her was talking earnestly.

Ruth and Hortense set off together for work each morning and discussed Ruth's wedding in the evenings. They felt guilty at ignoring the war that was so close and affecting everything around them, as they managed to extract some semblance of normality. When Hortense discovered that Ruth had material given to her by her mother she insisted that she use it. Jean-Paul deserved a beautiful bride and she was not to disappoint him or her mother.

Each day it became easier to accept the changes that her decision to return to France entailed and which determined her destiny. Ruth tended to be mistrustful of leaps of faith, yet she had an unwavering conviction that the marriage that she was embarking on was right. She remembered the advice that Aunt Helen had given to her sister Lil, that she should have no doubts. Ruth had none.

Only Pierre, Hortense and Ronald attended Ruth and Jean-Paul at their Civil Wedding ceremony in the Mairie. Ruth, with Hortense beside her, surveyed the old building with its classical proportions and stamp of authority. Although she was not taking part in a traditional religious service, the ancient splendour of the ornate vestibule, the wooden panelling of the interior and the leaded glass windows gave a solemnity to the proceedings that resonated with her mood. It would have been insensitive, given the present dire circumstances in France, to have had a wedding with all the trappings that society demanded against a backdrop of imminent and encroaching danger.

Jean-Paul, so negligent as a rule about his clothes, was resplendent in the latest model of morning dress and young Ronald in his first suit was transformed from a small child to a young boy. Hortense wore a silk dress of pale magenta which had been the height of fashion the previous winter, under a mink coat of exquisite tailoring.

At the door of the Mairie, Ruth shed her fur coat to reveal a wedding dress that celebrated her slim figure. She wore no veil and the round neckline was free of frills or ornamentation. The effect was of gossamer folds of material flowing from neck to floor, and Ruth, as she paused in the doorway, seemed ephemeral.

The flow of words, one part familiar, the legal part

not, pronounced by the Notary in his sombre Parisian accent wove a spell around Ruth that enmeshed her in a safe cocoon. It severed her from her family and offered her the security and serenity for which she yearned. She drifted through her wedding in a haze of unreality, struggling to believe her happiness.

Ruth and Jean-Paul emerged into the weak winter sunlight, their faces nipped by the cold, but their hearts beating fast. They were only dimly aware that those joyful moments, timeless and sacrosanct, were to be short lived. A horse-drawn carriage waited to convey them to Pierre's house. Ronald sat between Hortense and Pierre and, looking around from one face to another, settled his gaze on Ruth.

'When am I going to see my mother?' he asked.

Ruth, who held Jean-Paul's hand, gripped a little tighter. Jean-Paul caught Pierre's eye, but it was Hortense who answered.

'Maman cannot come home until this nasty war is over. Until then you will stay with Pierre and go to school, and Ruth and I will see you every Sunday.'

'What about Jean-Paul?'

'Whenever this horrid war allows me, I shall see you too, just like I used to.' Jean-Paul said, and then gave the young boy a playful dig in his stomach.

Ronald smiled briefly and then wriggled back into the seat between Hortense and Pierre and placed his hands together in a sadly adult fashion. For them he was the first casualty of the war.

Jean-Paul introduced Ruth to the Paris that he loved during their short honeymoon. Having the city on their doorstep was no reason for not spending their holiday there, Jean-Paul pronounced exuberantly. Many people travelled for days to visit this magnificent place, and it would be, in their case, a matter of making the very best of their only option. Ruth was swept up in his enthusiasm, curious at last to explore a city which had so affected Veeve and which was held almost in reverence by many of their acquaintances. Even more than London to the English, Paris was the epitome of any Frenchman's aspirations as a place in which to live, or failing that, to introduce to a newcomer.

Jean-Paul reserved their last day together to introduce her to his apartment. It was a dull morning, a thick mist of cold damp air was rising off the Seine and percolating along the narrow streets when Jean-Paul, holding Ruth's hand, precipitated her along to Boulevard Malesherbes. His speed was partially because they were driven to shelter indoors by the inclement weather, but more particularly because Jean-Paul was impatient to conduct Ruth to her new home. After the frenetic itinerary of the previous days they both relished the thought of peace and privacy.

'I shall not expect you to stay here, that is unless you want to, when I am away,' Jean-Paul said solicitously. 'Hortense assures me that she is happy for you to remain with her and you should not be alone too much.'

There was a gaiety to Jean-Paul that infected Ruth as they walked through the windowless vestibule and then into the lift. He drew the double gates with an iron clang and pressed the button for the second floor.

'Let me go in first and light the lamp. Wait a

moment.' Ruth glanced along the passage, there were no other doors.

'Entrez!' Jean-Paul stood in the open doorway and made a lavish gesture of welcome. He then slipped an arm around Ruth's waist and walked with her across the entrance hall towards one of the two doors facing them. The light from the windows revealed a dining room. It was spacious and well furnished with upholstered chairs, a polished dining table, pale patterned wall paper and a deep pile carpet. There were several unobtrusive prints on the walls and dark green velvet curtains with full valances hung either side of the windows.

Ruth had not imagined that a bachelor's apartment could be so homely. In the adjacent room bookcases filled every wall and books overflowed onto the desk. Beyond the study the drawing room was larger and lighter, on either side of the three windows hung pale pink brocade curtains. The carpet, patterned with swirls of pink and brown, made the room feel warm, as did the reading lamps beside the armchairs. On a table under one of the windows was a new gramophone. The centre of the room was taken up by large fireplace with a marble surround and a substantial mantelpiece.

Still keeping his arm firmly around Ruth, Jean-Paul gave her time to absorb everything before he directed her to the mantelpiece. She turned towards him, a smile spreading across her face.

'No 'cloud' on the horizon for a long time, I hope,' Jean-Paul said. 'Your St Cloud vases have joined my clock. What do you think?'

Ruth scrutinized the Sèvres clock and the two vases.

At each end of the mantelpiece were her vases with their turquoise glaze, embossed rims, handles and stems, and there between them in pride of place, was a magnificent clock. It was the same height as the vases but its generous proportions allowed the craftsman to add scrolls and embellishments to three ornate domes, and to make extravagant decorations of gold filigree to the base.

'It's wonderful.' Her exclamation extended to encompass the whole room. Jean-Paul, his mission accomplished, lifted her so that her feet cleared the ground, swung her in a half circle before setting her down. Gently he wrapped his arms around her as if he would never release her.

'Ma chère Ruth,' he said.

Chapter Nineteen

The year passed and as winter turned to spring a pattern developed. To save heat and to reduce bills Ruth shared Hortense's apartment and each day they cycled together to work. When Jean-Paul was in Paris, Ruth would return to their apartment, spending more time there on her own in summer months when the demand for fuel was reduced. Almost imperceptibly items of food and commodities began to disappear from the shops. As autumn turned to winter these shortages, which beforehand had been an inconvenience to be circumvented, had a stronger impact and the deprivation suffered by the populace increased.

News, brought by Jean-Paul or disseminated by their fellow workers, augmented the censored reports that they read in the newspapers, and kept them abreast with the war, yet whenever they had a free day Hortense and Ruth, no differently from other Parisians, attempted to defy its restraints. Musicians met and arranged concerts, actors maintained morale, shops kept their windows filled even if their shelves became depleted. In the temperate weather families went on picnics or congregated in cafés. As clothes became scarce styles changed with designs that maximised the use of the fabric and which tended to flatter the thinner figure. Women wore more cosmetics and continued to keep their hair fashionably cut so to maintain a semblance of femininity in an increasingly austere world.

Ruth never knew when to expect Jean-Paul. Sometimes his visits were short but frequent, on other occasions he would be away for weeks at a time.

'Fighting started again as soon as the weather improved. There have been battles at Neuve Chapelle, Arras and Festubert. The casualties are so great it is hard to comprehend,' Jean-Paul related. 'There were nearly one hundred and fifty thousand casualties and twice as many have been wounded. The hospitals are at breaking point.' Jean-Paul hesitated, uncertain whether to continue. His recent experiences had taken their toll and his eyes had the haggard look of someone haunted by what they had seen.

'Both sides are using gas. They are trying to poison the air. As if it isn't bad enough to try and shoot to maim and kill, they now mean to inflict even more misery. How can they do this?'

'Is it worth it?' asked Hortense. 'Are the Germans being pushed back?'

'Not enough to make much difference. Only a trifling gain in ground, but at least it means that my two girls are still safe here in Paris.'

One day, when several weeks had elapsed since his last visit, Ruth returned home to find Jean-Paul asleep. He was dishevelled and travel-stained and his only concession to the furniture was that he had removed his shoes. Eventually he stirred and Ruth watched from the doorway until she was certain that he was awake. One glance at the evening sky should be enough for him to know that she would have finished work. He sat up and looked around for her, then beckoned her over. He asked her to sit beside him and then lay back with his head on her lap.

'Forgive the state of me.'

Ruth did not answer but removed a section of unruly hair from his eyes.

'There has been another offensive. It has been difficult to ensure the movement of supplies. I had to oversee the goods right to the troops at the front. It's dreadful, Ruth, what those men have to suffer.' Ruth rested a hand on Jean-Paul's and he took hold of it. 'This all could have been avoided. France had the upper hand at the beginning, we only had to have the will and the courage to press on. We faltered, and now there is a deadlock. We made a tragic miscalculation. We calculated that the Germans would attack France by entering through Alsace and Lorraine because Belgium and Luxembourg were neutral. We placed our army ready for an attack there. We weren't in place to stop their advance further north.'

'Why should France blame herself? If a country is neutral then Germany should have respected that.'

'There were plenty of people who warned us that Germany would use that ploy,' Jean-Paul said ruefully. 'After all if you are going to war you are hardly going to abide by the rules. We were foolish not to anticipate that Germany would violate Belgium's neutrality.'

'Could France do nothing about it?'

'We did, we switched troops to the north, but they had many more soldiers than us.'

'I thought the British troops were fighting alongside us. Don't we outnumber the Germans?' Ruth asked

'They have such an efficient rail network and such well armed reserves that whatever we throw at them they can absorb. They were hoping to surround Paris.'

'What stopped them?'

'Luck I suppose. We had to retreat, but that extended their line. While they sent for more reserves, we regrouped. That's why we had stalemate. Your Kitchener warned that it would be a long war. We are only now bringing our factories up to speed producing guns and ammunition and the British, who took some persuading to increase their output of arms, are undertaking a massive construction of submarines and battleships. But now that Italy has joined in, and Bulgaria and Turkey have come in with Germany, the fields of fighting are enlarging. There are active battlefields all around the globe and soon the whole world will be at war.'

Jean-Paul took himself off to wash and change as if to throw off the gloom that he had introduced to the evening, and Ruth went through to the kitchen. He made no reference to his work or the war again and instead asked Ruth about the factory and nodded approvingly when Ruth told him that both she and Hortense had been given more responsibility. Hortense was now supervising many of the workers, interviewing new employees and organising rosters, while she was in the office keeping records and allocating pay packets.

'You'll do that well. How sensible of them to allow you to use your brain rather than leaving you as a packaging operative. How do you like the change?'

Ruth was more than content to change from the monotony of the production line but, she admitted to Jean-Paul, she felt somewhat guilty that she was being paid more for work that she infinitely preferred.

When Ruth woke the next morning Jean-Paul had already left.

As one year ended and another began it was as if normal life had been suspended. Whenever the girls discovered that Jean-Paul was in Paris they would press him for information.

'The overriding difficulty last winter was the inability for any transport to move through the glutinous mud that constitutes the terrain of the battlefields. The trenches were effectively gulleys full of water.' Jean-Paul managed to bring a reality to a war that seemed distant when their only information was through the newspapers, but he spoke too soon about the girls being safe.

The arrival in the skies overhead of Zeppelins which, contrary to all previous engagements in the history of battles targeted civilians, meant that both French and British civilians were under threat. This was not the only unusual feature of the war. The extent of the fighting and the length of the battles were unprecedented.

For Ruth and Hortense however, small events predominated because the wider world had temporarily taken leave of its senses. In the summer Ruth became certain that she was pregnant. One Sunday, when she and Hortense were spending their free day together, Ruth told Hortense of her suspicions.

'Of course you are,' Hortense laughed, 'I've known for weeks and was only wondering when you were going to tell me. People change. It's as if they retreat into an inner world, I've seen the signs often enough with other women at work. I am happy for you.'

Ruth blushed. She remembered the day when Hortense had suggested that she might have a child of her own. It was not into a world such as this that she had envisaged bringing up a family. She had imagined a small child on a sunny day in the carefree south of France.

'A baby will be good. We will have a reason to survive the winter. When do you think it is due?'

'February, March,' said Ruth vaguely.

'What about Ronald?' Hortense asked.

'What about Ronald?'

'Well he thinks of you as his mother, he doesn't realise it but that's the case. He needs to know he's to have a new cousin, and the sooner the better. There's no knowing how he will view this new arrival. I feel for the poor abandoned lad, I really do.'

There was a winsome vulnerability about Ronald that brought out a protective instinct in all those who came into contact with him. The more setbacks he faced the more this trait became apparent. Hortense feared that he might lose his erstwhile optimistic nature if he was to see Ruth's attention divided between him and a baby.

Ronald stayed with Pierre and Armelle, and Jean-Paul and Ruth tried to visit him regularly. Ronald had become a serious little boy and Pierre said that he caused him and his wife no trouble. However their second child was due and Pierre explained that they only had a 'bonne' and there would be enough work for her and his wife with the two children. They regretted that they could no longer manage to look after Ronald as well. Jean-Paul and Ruth arranged to discuss with Pierre and his wife what should be done. When Ronald left to go and play outside in the small courtyard that led off the kitchen, Ruth suggested that perhaps the solution was for her to leave work to care for him, but Jean-Paul was dubious that this was the answer. Ruth left the table thinking it was easier for the others to make a decision if she absented herself.

She walked across the flagstone floor of the poorly lit scullery and was almost blinded by the setting sun which was directed through the doorway onto one half of the yard leaving the other in deep shadow. It was a warm evening and Ronald had chosen to play in the shadowed area. When Ruth's eyes adjusted to the dim light she saw Ronald, who had a piece of paper propped up against the wall where a lintel projected, concentrating on his hands. Ruth had the impression that he was pretending to play the piano. She stood and watched for a while and then quietly moved to stand behind him. Ronald looked up at her, continued moving his hands while looking at a page of manuscript paper handwritten with base and treble clefs and a multitude of quaver and semiquavers.

'Monsieur Cuanez gave this to me,' he stated.

'Monsieur Cuanez?' Ruth was slow to respond.

'My music teacher.'

'Can you play this on a real piano?' She asked.

'Of course. Monsieur Cuanez says he will find me a piano if you agree.'

'Why haven't you asked me?'

'Mother never liked to hear a piano.' Ronald picked up the manuscript paper and they both went back into the house.

'Ronald has something to show you.'

Jean-Paul took the piece of paper. 'Why, this is Mozart. Can you play this?' Ronald nodded. 'Well, my boy, the next time I come and see you we must find a piano and hear you play.'

Once Ronald had gone out of the room the friends continued their discussion. They were intrigued by the discovery of his musical ability. Pierre's wife, Armelle had often seen him playing in the garden but she said that she had dismissed it as make-believe.

'Why had he never told you?' Jean-Paul asked Ruth.

'Because of Veeve,' she explained, inadequately as far as they were concerned. 'George's brother is a musician. He was making his name as a composer and pianist. It must have been too painful a reminder for her.'

Soon after this meeting Jean-Paul spoke to Monsieur Cuanez who not only confirmed that Ronald had an exceptional talent for a nine year old but on hearing of their dilemma regarding his accommodation, the kindly schoolmaster insisted that he move to live with him and his wife.

'Then I can play the piano every day,' Ronald said contentedly.

Towards the end of the year Jean-Paul became steadily more anxious for Ruth and the baby. The war showed no signs of letting up. Although much of the action had been deflected to Austria, Germany was becoming deeply entrenched on the Hindenburg line, three lines of trenches, each twelve feet across, with wide belts of wire in between. Jean-Paul predicted that it would effectively stall the war for the winter months and cause severe misery to the civilians trapped in the area, but that eventually the Germans were certain to break through.

'You seem to be keeping well,' Jean-Paul said, remarking that she had not missed a day at the factory.

'Why shouldn't I, it's only a baby,' Ruth seemed amused.

'It's just that Pierre's wife had an unpleasant

pregnancy and was quite sick.'

'But that isn't until the last three months,' she declared. Jean-Paul realised that she genuinely believed this and was alarmed by her innocence.

'Where did you get that idea?' He laughed affectionately.

Nearer the birth he was no longer so light-hearted and sought out Pierre's advice. Pierre directed him to a Clinic run by a Marie Thiel where mothers could be looked after during their lying-in. Once he had arranged for Ruth to attend he felt easier. There was no one that she could call upon to help, and it was unreasonable to expect Hortense to be responsible.

When Jean-Paul was next home he told them that he could not believe the rate that ammunition was being used. 'In seventeen days they used what was expected to last a month. You cannot comprehend the scale of the fighting around the Somme, the German defences and fortifications are insuperable, it is like a siege. We have air superiority and have managed to destroy their balloons, but the death toll is enormous. Britain lost ninety thousand men in the first fortnight, and we've probably lost the same. The mechanical tanks have a wide base and their caterpillar tracks can surmount most obstacles but, although they're defeated by water, they're able to travel over barbed wire and concrete platforms.'

Jean-Paul enjoyed watching Ruth's and Hortense's understanding of the awesome new invention. 'The British invented the idea but both sides have tanks. The soldiers manning them are less likely to be injured since only a direct hit can really damage them. The advantage of tanks is that soldiers can shoot as they move whereas previously all guns were fixed. Just one crew caused the surrender of three hundred and seventy Germans. The Germans are falling back. That's the good news.'

Various factors, occupying the minds of those not contemplating a birth, began to emerge that winter which proved that, although the stalemate continued to be no different from the previous year, there were some indications that change was possible. America became infuriated at the German blockade of food and provisions for Britain, and the Allies began to hope that they might come to their aid. The Germans were settled behind the Hindeberg line and so were further from Paris. Yet, inevitably, every Parisian was preoccupied with finding enough food and fuel to survive from day to day.

Ruth existed in the pleasant euphoria of a pregnant mother and placidly continued to work while enjoying the extra warmth that her pregnancy gave her, giving little thought to the event itself.

Marie Thiel ran the lying in hospital in part of the house that she and her brother, a doctor, had inherited from their parents. Many babies were born at home but any mother that Henri felt needed to be monitored, or any mother who was on her own, could book into the clinic. Ruth liked the energetic Marie who, with her slightly bulbous eyes, and cheerful manner, exuded an atmosphere of competence. 'The first baby always takes its time to arrive,' Marie announced genially, 'You'll know, dear, there's no mistaking contractions.' Ruth looked confused. 'It might be an idea for you to come and stay. You will be cold and lonely once you stop working. I can find plenty for you to do here to help.'

Marie helped Ruth deliver a healthy boy, in what she described as a routine delivery. No sooner is it over than all memories of the birth process fade, Marie had promised. She had been allowed some sleep and by the time she had eaten, been congratulated by Hortense and Henri, and had the swaddled bundle placed in her arms, she was prepared to agree with them. Ruth never knew how Jean-Paul heard about the baby's arrival.

The baby was due for a feed before being taken to the nursery for the night. The light was dim, the windows blacked out, and a single lamp burned in her room. Ruth held her baby feeling lost and ill at ease. She heard Marie's footsteps in the corridor, followed by a slower, slightly heavier step. Marie stopped at the door to Ruth's room. Behind her stood Jean-Paul. He approached almost reverentially and she searched his face as he gazed down at the baby. In her relief at his arrival a large tear fell on the baby's head. Jean-Paul kissed her, wiped her tear-splashed cheek and carefully lifted the swaddled bundle from her arms. He looked at his son with pride.

'How wonderful. C'est merveillieux.' Jean-Paul said as he took the baby over to the lamp. 'A boy. Un garçon.' There was a pause. 'Could we call him Bertrand? One day my Father will acknowledge his grandson. How would that be in English?'

'Bertram.'

'Almost the same.' There seemed little more to say. Jean-Paul had dark rims around his tired eyes, he looked thinner than usual, his cheek bones were more pronounced and his hair was matted. 'I need to go straight back. I've been travelling since I heard the news.' Ruth knew better than to ask where he had been or where he was going.

Marie brought in a tray of food and then took the little boy from his arms. 'Do you need to sleep?' Jean-Paul shook his head. 'Even a couple of hours can help,' Marie insisted, 'there's the settee downstairs and you can let yourself out. Think about it.'

Then they were alone. Ruth and Jean-Paul were conscious that no one made plans in this climate of uncertainty, but this baby gave them a reason to survive.

The days soon merged into a routine of feeds, sleep and laundry. When Marie decided that Ruth was strong enough, she presented her with the plan that Jean-Paul had put in place. Ruth was to go to Hortense's family in the country where she would be among friendly, experienced people and be better fed. The food supplies in winter were particularly poor in the city and the queues were too long for a mother with a new born baby. The journey out of Paris was an ordeal, with crowded trains and icy compartments, and even the attention that a baby attracted was unwelcome to the shy new mother. Hortense thought that it would be a miracle if the child survived, but trusted that with her own mother to care for Ruth, the baby had a chance.

Chapter Twenty

Even in La Vendée, where Ruth and her baby were being looked after, news was filtering through of a new lethal gas that was being used at the front line of battle. When Jean-Paul visited Ruth he showed her the helmet that he had been issued to wear in the event of a mustard gas attack, as the poison was called.

'It goes like this,' he demonstrated by putting the clumsy helmet with its elongated snout over his head and face. 'I look like a large weasel. The gas has a blistering effect on faces and lungs and breathing is agony. The enemy uses the direction of the wind to blow the gas towards our troops, but it is indiscriminate and consequently civilians also suffer. Ruth, I am not happy about you returning to Paris. Not only because of the gas, but because the German aircraft are now powerful enough to fly over the city.'

Ruth, however, as the months progressed became restless and ready to leave the country regardless of the danger, and Jean-Paul admitted that he would prefer his family to be closer. When America finally declared war against Germany on the side of the Allies, he was tempted to sanction their move. Britain was in a desperate situation, it was said that they only had three weeks food left on the island., however, Clemenceau had taken charge of the French government, and Lloyd George had taken the reins in London, and there was a more optimistic feel in the air which revived people's resolve.

Jean-Paul was one of those people. A sense of gritty determination had returned. He moved Ruth and Bertrand back to Paris. Bertrand was a thriving boy and the decision to move to the country had undoubtedly contributed towards his survival.

The sultry air sapped energy, the windows of Jean-Paul's apartment were open, desultory sounds rose from the street below. In the drawing room Jean-Paul sat with Bertrand nestled in the crook of his arm and with Ruth beside him. He drew her to him and cradled her head on his shoulder.

'We need to plan ahead for the autumn and I am worried at the thought of you struggling with Bertrand on your own. Would you not be better if you were occupied. What do you think?'

Ruth turned up the palms of her hands as if to say that she agreed but what could she do.

'Marie Thiel needs help. She is struggling with housekeeping, finding food, organising laundry and keeping the accounts. I suggested that you might be able to help, I know how capable you are, and it would be company for you.'

'But, Bertrand?'

'Marie says that there'll be plenty of people around to keep him amused. How can anyone not want to play with Bertrand?'

Every day Ruth pushed Bertrand in his pram, the well beneath his mattress filled with toys, napkins and bottles, to the clinic. She began to enjoy the work and having others to help look after Bertrand. Marie was enchanted by the boy that she had delivered only a few months previously.

'Henri,' she said one day to her brother, 'isn't it charming to have a child that responds and plays? Although I love my work with the newborn, they are very demanding. This little chap gives so much pleasure. Look how he is playing with that spoon and saucepan.'

There was no doubt that Bertrand enriched the lives of those within the walls of the clinic and it was possible at times to forget the war.

Henri Thiel was small in stature and of slim build. He invariably wore a suit and bow tie with his stethoscope around his neck, as other men would wear their fob watch, and fiddled with it constantly. He was meticulous regarding cleanliness and had a tidy mind.

'Do you think you would be able to help me too, Ruth?' Henri asked diffidently. 'I find the task of sterilising all my instruments so time consuming and I am always running late.'

Ruth was prepared to take on any task so long as she was not required to nurse. She was squeamish with physical disabilities and was intolerant of illness but was keen to help in any other way. Henri showed her the steriliser, a double pan with a perforated inner section. The latter she should uplift onto a steel tray which was an operation that had to be undertaken with great care due to the scalding hot steam. All the scissors, scalpels and tweezers had to be lifted out with a pair of long handled wooden tongs and then laid out in a certain order onto a sterilised tray and covered with another.

Henri was unfailingly courteous and kind and when

he discovered that Ruth had been working in the wages office at the factory, he asked her to relieve him of various tedious tasks involved with ordering and record keeping. Due to the demand for regular doctors by the hospitals, and therefore an increase in the number of mothers in the district needing his attention, he described Ruth's arrival as a godsend.

Marie too found more work for her, and when Jean-Paul was away Ruth began to stay at the clinic later each day. One evening when Ruth said that she would darn a sheet with a tear, Marie suggested that she join them for their evening meal. Bertrand had a cot set up where he habitually spent his midday nap and Ruth was persuaded. This soon became a habit. Bertrand's presence cheered everyone from the nurses to the kitchen maids and Ruth suspected that part of her invitation was due to the fact that Marie and Henri also cherished the entertainment that he gave them.

One morning in early in November Ruth was working in the study. It was a spacious room with a tall window which looked out onto the boulevard. At this time of year the leaf-less trees were mere skeletons, dust swirled in eddies along the edge of the pavement where a few people, hugging their coats around them, hurried home to the shelter, if not the warmth, of their houses. In Henri's study the semblance of protection from the wintry cold was provided by the book-lined shelves on two of the walls. A large desk was placed between the door and the window and on opposite sides of fireplace were armchairs where Marie and Henri would sit in the evenings.

Ruth was balancing the accounts when Henri interrupted her. 'Marie and I have had a discussion, she says that her drawing room is unused except in the summer months. We plan to have a bed carried down and placed against the wall which, with a cover and cushions will serve as a settee. It can become your room. We would like you to stay with us until it is all over.' There was no longer any need to qualify his reference to the war.

Jean-Paul was enthusiastic about the plan. 'It would take a great weight off my mind. Air warfare is increasing and no civilian is safe.'

Ruth had less contact with Hortense and needed companionship. Their lives differed and they had drifted apart. It was easy, therefore, for Ruth to see the benefits of staying with Marie and Henri Thiel when Jean-Paul was away.

On Bertrand's first birthday, Ruth unreasonably, as she repeatedly told herself, was on tenterhooks all day. She was certain that Jean-Paul would arrange to be with them. Fortunately for Ruth everyone had decided to mark the small boy's birthday and no-one noticed her agitation. The nurses and kitchen maids donated some of their sugar and butter rations for a cake for 'goûtez' and when they were all gathered around the kitchen table Ruth carried Bertrand to place him in his high chair at the head of the table. Jean-Paul walked in. Bertrand swung round in his mother's arms and stretched out to reach for his father. Jean-Paul gathered him up and lifted him onto his shoulders while everyone exclaimed what a perfect day it had become. None more so than Ruth.

This occasion, in these austere times became incomparably special. In wresting some happiness from the misery around them, Bertrand's birthday became as significant as the most lavish of celebrations.

Later that night Jean-Paul was sombre. Ruth sensed that the cheerfulness that he generated when surrounded by people who needed enlivening, was spent. She waited for him to articulate his thoughts in his own time.

'I don't think morale has ever been so low. I fear for France. No European county has had as many conflicts as we have had in the last hundred years. Never has life been lost on such a scale. I don't think France will ever again be able to face the sacrifice of her men. We would be on the brink of annihilation as a race.'

'Do you think we will lose?'

'Nothing is certain, but the Germans must be feeling as demoralised as we are because the blockades are now being felt by their civilians. We are now dependant on the Americans.'

'Why have they not helped us before? It is over a year since they declared war on Germany.'

'Because their troops could not be safely transported across the Atlantic. Britain has been fighting to secure the sea for the passage of American troops. Hostilities will recommence as soon as winter is over. It will then be a race against time, between the German forces who will be attempting to clinch victory and the arrival of sufficient American troops to support us. Everything is in the balance.'

When life is at a low ebb there is little energy to spare

for extremes of emotion and the transient euphoria of the tea-party had resulted in a pervading mood of depression. Bertrand had been put to bed and Jean-Paul and Ruth stood together for a long while looking into his cot as the small boy slept. Jean-Paul slipped his fingers through Ruth's, words were unnecessary as they shared their child's peace and contentment. He lifted her hand to his lips, kissed it and then slowly released his grip. 'Oh Ruth,' he said with a sigh.

A few months further into the year and the change was palpable. Paris in the spring painted an image of beauty and inspired a promise of hope. That year, although there was little to commend Paris in the ordinary sense, its people allowed themselves to consider an end to the conflict. They were emaciated and bowed, their buildings were uncared for and damaged, their clothes were drab and worn but the troops were pouring in from across the Atlantic and German soldiers were deserting. Having recalled all her troops from the front against Russia, Germany planned to throw the might of the army against the Allies, and to drive a wedge between them, but they had been checked.

In June Jean-Paul manoeuvred to secure some leave and his spirits reflected the general optimism. Marie packed the small family off saying that they should make the most of their time together. Their first port of call was Ronald.

When they arrived at the house in the banlieue of the city Monsieur Cuanez ushered them into his parlour. He called his wife and she in turn summoned Ronald. The room was cramped but any awkwardness was deflected by focussing attention on Bertrand. Ronald greeted Ruth and Jean-Paul but immediately took hold of one of Bertrand's hands. Bertrand reached out and grasped his other hand. Responding with a chuckle Ronald swung the child's arms from side to side in a game understood only by the two of them. Bertrand's laughter unlocked Ronald's shyness, and that of the adults as well.

Ronald, animated and amused by Bertrand, turned to Jean-Paul. 'He is my cousin, yes? He is not a baby any more,' and looking round for a plaything Madame Cuanez handed him an empty cotton reel. He gave it to Bertrand who immediately put it in his mouth. Ronald retrieved the wet object, rolled it along the ground and received an encouraging smile from his Uncle. While the adults talked he fetched a few of his old wooden toys and played with Bertrand until the child grew tired and began to whimper.

Monsieur Cuanez suggested that this might be a good moment for Ronald to play to them on the piano, and it was obvious that he set more store by this than Ronald, who played unselfconsciously and with total concentration. It was apparent that he had a gift, the music flowed effortlessly. Jean-Paul thanked Monsieur Cuanez, but the old teacher waved away his thanks.

'He'll soon be beyond my teaching skills, but it has given me enormous pleasure. Another year, and I will have exhausted my ability.' He sighed. 'We cannot plan for the future but in the meantime there is plenty of work for Ronald to tackle. He is a studious lad and never any trouble.'

They continued to speak to Ronald about his music

as they walked to the park. Jean-Paul wanted Ronald to know that he, too, valued his talent as a musician. 'Music is a gift. You are lucky to have it and to be able to bury yourself in it. One day you may even use it as an escape.' He went on to explain to the puzzled lad. 'It can be your ticket to independence and a career. Few people are as lucky.'

Jean-Paul asked if he was lonely and what he did when not at school.

'I play the piano. I practise every day and I compose. I have extra lessons from another teacher and next term I shall be starting the violin. That is, if I am still here.' He faltered and Jean-Paul registered his lost look. He wondered what question Ronald was asking him. Was he referring to the war, or to his mother, or even if the Cuanez were prepared to keep him. He felt saddened for the boy.

'Are you unhappy?'

'No, but I should like to be with you more often.'

Jean-Paul placed his hand on the boy's neck affectionately. 'So would I like to be with you, but none of us, and I include you, can do what we want, especially now, and boys have to turn quickly into men. It's your birthday soon isn't it?'

'I'll be eleven and move to the senior school after the summer.'

Jean-Paul nodded. The Cuanez must be managing well. Ronald was sturdily built and did not look undernourished. He had stretched and was tall for his age but when he studied him carefully Jean-Paul saw that his expression was guarded, and only his thick blond hair softened his appearance.

'I like it that you are my real uncle now,' Ronald said after a while. 'Two of the boys in my class don't have fathers. They were killed. I am not so different from them, except that I have you.'

Ronald paused as if to wait for Jean-Paul to confirm this. A child grabs at a family like a kitten after a ball of wool. No matter how tangled or tenuous the connection he wants to belong, and in Ronald's case the need to love someone was as strong as his need to be loved.

'You have me,' confirmed Jean-Paul. 'How would you like to come for a drive? We could drop Ruth and Bertrand at home and then I could drive you back to Monsieur Cuanez. We might even find somewhere selling sweets.'

On the return journey Jean-Paul drew up in a square and halted the car.

'I have to go briefly into my office. Stay in the car, I will not be long.'

Jean Paul was away for ten minutes and then for twenty and Ronald became bored. He watched cars come and go and people arrive and leave the building, but Jean-Paul did not re-emerge. Ronald opened the door of the car, closed it carefully and looked up at the building. It was four stories high and there seemed to be activity at every level judging by the silhouettes that he could see in the windows. He meandered up and down the pavement and then crossed the road and stood at the foot of the steps by which Jean-Paul had entered the building. He hesitated before taking hold of the iron railing and then slowly climbed the steps. There was a brass plaque beside the door. He traced the engraved letters with his finger. 'Marcel Durand Importer-Exporter'. The door opened and a man pushed past Ronald without appearing to see him, giving him no opportunity to ask him about Jean-Paul.

He sat on the step and waited. It must have been another half an hour before his Uncle came through the door. He seemed surprised to see Ronald, as if he had forgotten about him, then he hurried with him to the car.

'I'm sorry. A crisis came up.' In this climate of uncertainty a crisis had heavy implications. He saw Ronald's worried face. 'Nothing unusual.' He said unconvincingly, and started up the engine.

'What does it mean, Import-Export?'

'The firm imports and exports silk and textiles. Well, it does in peace time, but it has a completely different function while we are at war.'

'What is that?'

Jean-Paul tapped his finger against his nose and gave Ronald a conspiratorial wink.

Ruth, Marie and Henri anticipated Jean-Paul's visits eagerly for current news. Progress at the front still seemed frustratingly slow.

'It seems to have taken so long,' Ruth said.

'It does,' Jean-Paul agreed, 'but finally it should be worth it. To be honest, without the Americans, Germany just about had us on our knees. So much so that some people have resigned themselves and have been tempted to join the winning side.'

'Go over to the Germans?' Ruth was scandalised.

'Not in so many words, but there are ways of helping such as giving information that can be used for a better deal should we be conquered.'

'How can they do that?' Marie asked.

'How do you think that we know what the German army's plans are, and the state of their ammunition, and the position of their guns?'

'Spying for France seems acceptable but the thought that French people could inform the Germans is unthinkable.' Henri commented.

'There are people who want to hedge their bets,' Jean-Paul explained, 'to be on the winning side whatever that side may be.' He thought briefly of Veeve and her exile in Spain. 'We are perilously low in ammunition. One or two people in our firm are concerned that there have been leaks.' Ruth looked alarmed. 'That is why I was late returning Ronald. I am investigating further.' Then he added so as to deflect their questions. 'Now that the American shipments are arriving we will have the superior strength. There is a build up again on the Marne. A million American troops have been pouring into France and Foch has been able to repel the German onslaught that had created a bulge into our allied front.'

Early in August, Haig used a hundred tanks and surprised the Germans at Cambrai. Jean-Paul was able to report the biggest defeat of the German Army so far. The allies began to sense victory. They knew, partly because of the successful British propaganda behind their lines, that the soldiers in the German army were undergoing a change of heart.

It was the beginning of what was afterwards called

the hundred day battle. Haig called upon a seemingly bottomless supply of munitions, and he unified command. He attacked the German line relentlessly. Throughout August he pressed forward gaining ground and capturing prisoners in violent attacks until the Germans were thrown back on their Hindenberg line. German troops were becoming exhausted and their civilian population were giving them less and less support.

In October Paris came less under threat and the Allies momentum gathered apace. Britain pushed through the northern end of the Hindenberg line with a concentration of over four thousand guns. Once the allied forces captured Cambrai the whole German line tottered, they abandoned Flanders and began to retreat. Foch prepared an attack which would have led to the capitulation of two million German troops. The danger of such a move led Germany to sign for Armistice. The war was over.

Chapter Twenty-One

Bertrand played on the floor. He was an active child, steady on his feet and with a reasonable vocabulary of childish words. A friend of Henri's made rudimentary jigsaws and Bertrand concentrated on slotting wooden shapes together.

'My little son, are you the first person to greet me on the day of Armistice? Where is everyone when we all need to celebrate?' Bertrand pressed the piece that he held in his hand into place and then ran to Jean-Paul's outstretched arms.

'Papa,' Jean-Paul swung him onto his shoulders and father and son went in search of Ruth.

'Maman, Maman,' they called playfully.

Marie appeared dressed, not in her usual clinician's uniform, but in a suit that had not been seen in four years. 'You'll find that Maman is changing. Henri told us the news and said that we should go out and savour the atmosphere. He will join us with some friends later. It is wonderful.'

Everyone wandered aimlessly along the boulevards and in the avenues smiling at each other or conversing with strangers. Despite the November weather people wore their best clothes. Shabby by pre-war standards and ill suited for the cold, they looked festive. For one day euphoria reigned. The war was over. The killing was over. They could only guess at the final tally for already six or seven million had been counted as lost and then there were many wounded and maimed. Today they would not think of the cost of lives but celebrate their survival, and the survival of their beleaguered country. Their city would be rejuvenated, it would fill again with civilians, and uniforms, reminders of the conflict, would disappear. Today they could rejoice that their city was standing, that the streets were filled with survivors, and every soldier was a hero. Although their bodies were thin, malnourished, ill-clad, aching and tired, their hearts beat with pride, relief, joy and hope.

How difficult it was to wake up the next morning,

and the one after, and the one after, and to find that nothing had changed. There was no extra fuel to mitigate the bitter weather, the shelves in the shops were still sparsely filled and food supplies had not increased. Where people had been working in the munitions factories, or in clothing or transport for the army, or those who had taken the place of the men folk, the situation worsened. The hardest blow was reserved for the men who returned from the front to find that there was a dearth of jobs. Motor factories had converted to producing bicycles for which there was no longer any demand, and investment would take time. Compounding the difficulties was the unstable political climate and the immediate need to seek reparation. Now that they had won the war, the Allies had to oversee the peace, but in the meantime the populace waited for change.

For the first month the news that the Germans were slowly being driven out of France made the uncomfortable realities of the Peace bearable. By mid-November they had been driven back to a line between Antwerp and Strasbourg and by the beginning of December to the original French-Luxembourg border. By mid December they had secured a line between Düsseldorf and Koblenz and Mainz and had bridgeheads at each. Jean-Paul brought them the news that Alsace and Lorraine were to be returned to France, under one of the peace agreements, on the thirtieth of January.

'We will go and witness this historic occasion, Ruth,' Jean-Paul said. 'You, Bertrand and I will drive to my homeland to see this happen. We will need to take our warmest clothes and a supply of food as we do not know what we will find.'

What they found was devastation. As the Germans were forced back to their own land they wreaked havoc on villages and towns. Buildings were destroyed and the land, occupied for over four years, was denuded of crops and woods. There was no winter barley, no fields had been ploughed for the spring, there were no vines, olive trees or orchards. Jean-Paul and his family drove across a dismal landscape of ruins, mud and tree stumps. Few could survive living in such terrain under foreign control, especially the old and infirm.

On the route they passed abandoned tanks and guns, evidence of military engagements and dugouts that until now Ruth had only seen in photographs. In the newspapers or in propaganda postcards these regions and the troops had been sanitised to show men in clean uniforms with habitable shelters. The reality had been quite to the contrary and Ruth recognised Jean-Paul's descriptions of the mud, filth and rats, the obstacles that had been in the way of supplies reaching the front, and the misery of enduring such conditions. It was hard to see how the land would ever regenerate. They drove along roads reconstructed by the victorious army as they pushed further and further to the east, and Ruth could be forgiven, in the horrors of what she saw, for forgetting that their pilgrimage was to be present at the climax of the victory.

'We will have to enable this land to recover,' Jean-Paul said passionately, 'Germany will be made to pay dearly.' He feared for his parents.

Strasbourg symbolised for the French the final chapter of the 1871 war when Germany annexed Alsace and Lorraine. The town had been a permanent reminder of their ignominious defeat. Strasbourg's position marked the restored boundary, and the French General Hirschauer with his troops were to make a public ceremony in which Germany would formally hand back the city.

Jean-Paul and Ruth arrived in a town that was seething with men in uniform. The military had been billeted in every available hostelry and household and it struck Jean-Paul that they might find nowhere to stay. They made their way through the centre of the town hoping that they might find some household with a vacant room. In a street close to one of the canals they found a family who were happy to receive their first French guests. It confirmed for their hosts that their ordeal was over. They were anxious to hear news from France that had been denied them for so long, and to relate their own experiences and sufferings to sympathetic ears. It was a salutary experience to see how pathetically grateful they were for the food that Ruth and Jean-Paul brought with them and which they all shared. If Ruth, and others like her, had considered that they had been ill fed in Paris, it was hard to imagine what it must have been like for this family in occupied territory. They talked into the small hours of the morning and the next day, joined the crowds and headed towards the town square.

Strasbourg had suffered less damage than the other towns that they had passed through because the

Germans had occupied it continuously throughout the war. The main street followed the course of the river towards the Kehl bridgehead where the ceremony was to take place. Flags had been erected from poles the length of the main street. Despite the day being cold and overcast not only were the pavements filled with onlookers, but every window was flung open with people waving hats and scarves as the procession led by the cavalry marched solemnly passed.

How moving it was to see fellow bystanders, with tears pouring down their cheeks, welcome their countrymen who were returning in triumph. Ruth did not like crowds, being small in stature she easily became engulfed, but she found that people gave her space when they saw that she and Jean-Paul were with their young son. She looked at the faces pressed closely around them and listened to snatches of conversation. She had expected anger or hate but, perhaps because they were too tired to express emotions that they must have been harbouring for years, they seemed merely expectant. Some indeed seemed too weary even to be any more than dispassionate spectators. Many were there, along with Jean-Paul like a doubting Thomas, not satisfied that this event was real unless they saw it with their own eyes. Only then would they believe that their homeland was restored to France.

As the troops moved through the street the onlookers erupted with wild cheers. Jean-Paul, clutching Ruth's hand, wove his way through the crowds until they could find a vantage point from which to hear the proclamation. Flags hung from the steel arch of the bridge from which the imperial eagle had been torn down. The crowd was silent in recognition of the historic event. General Hirshauer, the newly appointed military Governor of Strasbourg, impressive in his uniform, braided cap, great coat and cape, his craggy face and white moustache adding gravitas to the occasion, turned his horse and delivered his declaration. He read the words in a stern voice to the German notables, who stood to attention before him, and then he and his military entourage took possession of the Kehl bridgehead.

Chilled and hungry, Jean-Paul and Ruth moved with the dispersing crowd.

'Johannes!' They heard a voice shout. The crowd was muted and the call was easily heard. 'Johannes!' The voice hailed again, and Ruth saw Jean-Paul's head whip around.

'Max!'

To Ruth's astonishment he clasped the man in a great embrace. He was thin and his back was bent, his smile revealed broken, missing and discoloured teeth, his skin was sallow and his eyes were dark rimmed and sunken.

'Max is my old school friend,' Jean-Paul told her, excited.

They kept walking since it was too cold to stop, until they reached the house where they had been staying. Max entered with them. It seemed that after such a day anyone was welcome.

Once back in the car and on the road it was some time before Jean-Paul, who held the wheel as if for support and with his eyes fixed ahead, recounted to Ruth the conversation that he had with Max. The two friends had talked almost until dawn.

'Max says that my parents have died. Starvation. Starvation or illness or maltreatment, who knows? It is hard to survive in those conditions when you are old. Max had many tragedies within his family and friends too. He would not have spoken if you had been present.'

'I guessed,' Ruth said, 'it was natural that you would want to know, even if it was very bad.'

Jean-Paul drove through the day and through the night. Ruth dozed and Bertrand slept and Jean-Paul pulled off the road and slept when he needed to, but by the time that they arrived in Paris early in the morning his mood had changed. It was as if the night vigil had allowed him to mourn and the morning light brought a resolve; a resolve that mourning was a crime when so many had died to enable them and their children to live. It was as if Jean-Paul wanted to start the change that very morning. Instead of heading for their apartment he drew up outside Henri and Marie's house in rue Cardinet.

'They will want to hear our news, and besides, they will probably give us breakfast.'

Marie opened the door and greeted them rapturously. 'My family. Come in, I must call Henri. He will not want to miss a word. Give me Bertrand.' She took the boy's hand. 'Let's find Oncle Henri. Where is he?'

'You would think that I had no work to do today, but the nurses can cope.' Marie fluttered around happily unable to settle, cooking eggs and encouraging Jean-Paul to cut large slices of bread. Jean-Paul related their story. Finally Marie said. 'Now I do feel that the war is over. That is if we can get through the rest of this winter. Food should be more accessible if we can now import it, fuel too once our mines work again.' She looked at Jean-Paul, acknowledging that this might not apply so soon to his former home in Alsace, she added, 'Things will get better.'

She sat back in her chair to contemplate the three travellers. 'Henri, we need a photograph. Henri has looked out all his photographic equipment. He wants to make a record of the aftermath of the war so that we never forget. We also need to celebrate the joyous moments. Henri, take one of Jean-Paul, Ruth and Bertrand in their car before they leave.'

'Johannes.' Ruth repeated the name with which Max had greeted Jean-Paul the previous day. 'Jean-Paul, why did he call you Johannes?' They were sitting and dusk had fallen leaving the drawing room in a half light. Ruth could not make out Jean-Paul's features.

'It's Jean in German. We had to be called by German names when I was growing up in Alsace. Max was lucky, his name translates into most languages. I was always called Jean at home.'

'Wasn't that odd?'

'Not really. We never knew anything else. In your country I believe that boys are called by their surnames in school. You adapt.'

Ruth understood. 'So if you had come to England you would have been John?'

'Yes, and Juan in Spain.'

'And Iain in Scotland.'

'Really? What a mixture of personalities I could have had.'

Ruth then grasped another aspect of his upbringing in Alsace. 'So were some of your friends German?'

'Of course.'

'And you could have been fighting against your school friends?'

'That is the sadness of war. For nearly fifty years Germans were encouraged to live in Alsace and Lorraine and now, I suppose, they will be forced to leave. They are the innocent victims.'

'And the French will return?' Ruth surmised.

'Except that there will be little to return to, every village was decimated as the German army retreated. Only Strasbourg and a few other towns where the German army was based have been left unscathed.'

Jean-Paul sat and stared into the fire and Ruth, sensing that he was troubled, left her chair. She knelt on the floor and resting her arm on his knees bent her head. Jean-Paul stroked her hair and curled one lock through his fingers. He began to speak as if months of pent up thoughts had become crystallised and were now so rehearsed as to be almost delivered by rote.

'The years before the war now seem to have been years of amazing and unattainable plenty. There was at the same time great social discontent and waste. There was an extravagant search for personal indulgence. We saw it, both of us, and were part of it. I saw the other side but tried to ignore it. The war was visibly approaching yet there was neither the will nor the understanding to stop it. In the mood of the time it did not seem to be real, perhaps this was necessary for the human mind to progress.'

Ruth was overwhelmed by Jean-Paul's stark appraisal of what they had lost and his feeling that they had brought the catastrophe upon themselves. Even with her tendency to pessimism she was struck by his dark gloom.

'Is there no hope?' She asked timidly.

Jean-Paul hardly heard her. 'For those ready to look for them, this is the time when we can awake to the fact that there are realities worth seeking. There are also evils that are not to be tolerated. The mental and moral backgrounds of hundreds of minds have been altered by the bleak lessons of the last four years. The feeling of brotherhood through the sadness of common sufferings is spreading across the world. Our lives are spoiled because there is no world wide justice, people are beginning to see a need for this.'

Ruth waited, not knowing whether she was expected to question or to continue listening. Eventually she asked, 'Is this possible?'

'If you look at an Atlas most of the European countries own the rest of the world, so a united Europe could achieve this. A league, so to speak, of European nations. There are a certain number of people who are working towards this end, but set against their ideals of unity are the old traditions and ancient antagonisms. Can there be unity?'

'They say the war will end all wars.'

'That's true. German imperialism with its grip on

education and its alliance with aggressive commercialism is finished. On the other hand, Britain, Italy and France are now feeble and disorganised. No European power will ever get the same proportion of its people into the ranks and into the munitions works again. War fever is over.'

Jean-Paul took Ruth's face in his hands. She lifted her head to scrutinise his face, expecting to see the intense look that she was beginning to become accustomed to which indicated that he was barely aware of his audience, instead he was smiling and had clearly shaken himself free from his reverie.

'In due course I might be able to help with that process. It's late, and we have both had a long day.'

Their lives took on a new rhythm, Jean-Paul was away from Paris less often and Ruth only spent the mornings with Marie since their need of her was diminished.

Although it was a logical result of so many years of disruption, no one had anticipated that the aftermath of the war might be as tough if not tougher than the years of conflict. The sense of anticlimax left people fatigued and drained. Physically the nation was malnourished and mentally many were depressed by the dearth of work and the slow rate of change in their circumstances.

Then came the bitterest blow. An epidemic of influenza, that seized an already debilitated population, claimed countless lives and left a fresh wave of misery. Marie, anxious for Ruth and Bertrand, forbade them from coming to the clinic, and suggested that they meet Ronald in the open air by taking him to the park.

The leaders were, as Jean-Paul explained to Ruth, working to the best of their abilities to bring a treaty to a conclusion so that it could be signed, but the aftermath of war is messy. 'I have to finish my work for the Military. Weapons of every description have to be removed from Germany. Stores have to be identified, transport secured, and then disposal arranged. It's a slow process. Repossessing weapons is only one of the directives. There has to be an exchange prisoners, France and the Allies have to be compensated financially, war criminals have to be tried.

'We have some leads at last.' Ruth understood that Jean-Paul was referring to the concerns he had had for many months that information from the factory was leaked to the enemy. There had been acts of sabotage and uncannily accurate attacks upon railway consignments of munitions to the front. Jean-Paul had, intermittently, kept Ruth abreast of developments. There was to be a tribunal consisting of a representative of each of the Allied countries to investigate the allegations.

Early in July, Jean-Paul broke the news. The tribunal was scheduled for the following week and then he would have discharged his war duties and could concentrate his efforts on rebuilding his firm. Not everyone was impoverished by the events of the last four years, he commented rather cynically, there were always those who profited as the quantity of people shopping in the boulevards and the burgeoning of merchandise proved. He saw no reason why business should not prosper again.

Chapter Twenty-Two

On the evening of the first day of the tribunal Jean-Paul told Ruth that he had been asked to give evidence. He had been struck by how much they knew already and surmised that the tribunal, consisting of an American lawyer, an English major, and a Frenchman from the War Office, had been well prepared.

At the end of the second day Marie and Henri invited the family to share their evening meal. While Ruth and Marie were distracted by Bertrand, supervising his meal and then playing, Jean-Paul recounted to Henri the events of the previous two days.

The extent of the leakage of information and the scale of the sabotage was far greater than Jean-Paul had been led to believe. A greater part of the second day had been spent questioning the main suspect, but several other possible informants who had operated further along the chain, had been uncovered.

'The interviews take place at Army Headquarters. It seems at this stage that they are gathering information. I was called to attend at eleven o'clock. They have a heavy schedule because I glanced at the list held by the soldier at the desk, and the interviews were timed for every half hour.'

'What is the purpose of these interviews?' Henri asked, puzzled. 'You say that they were military men.

You were not in the Army so how are you involved?'

'Probably because my work affected the war effort.'

'So who was conducting the interviews?'

'It was led by an English major, who speaks execrable French.'

'What sort of questions? What did they want to know?'

'It was generalisations. They were interested in deliveries of silk to the Concy district. Who placed the orders. Who despatched them. How many workers were involved in preparing and parcelling the orders. All the men who were working for me.'

'Why the Concy district?' Henri asked.

Jean-Paul looked furtively towards Ruth but she appeared to be engrossed in conversation with Marie. 'That's the district where they store the ammunition.' He saw that Henri did not understand. 'When the ammunition is transported, each batch is wrapped in silk. If there is a risk of explosion silk is fire resistant.'

As Henri absorbed this information he began to see the implications. Even if Jean-Paul's firm was a textile industry, they had links with the military. His firm must have been a front for quite a substantial amount of covert activity.

'But of what interest is this to the Army?'

'At this stage I do not know. I had to give them the names of the key workers at the factory. They will recall me if necessary.' Seeing that Henri looked concerned Jean-Paul leaned back in his chair and reassured him with a smile. 'Probably auditing Army supplies,' he suggested.

The two men became aware that Marie was addressing them. 'You two are so deep in your discussion that you're missing all the fun. Aren't they Ruth?'

The carpeted floor was almost completely covered by Bertrand's bricks and the boy was pushing a wooden engine between them. Ruth knelt down to rearrange the bricks. Jean-Paul registered that Marie also noticed that Henri seemed concerned. He pushed his chair back and rose, intending to join Ruth and Bertrand. Henri remained seated and detained the younger man. 'Why the English Major?' Jean-Paul shrugged and shook his head.

On the Friday night Jean-Paul arrived home, put his hat on the hall table, hung his coat on the hook and started speaking as soon as he entered the living room.

'Ruth, I have to go back to the Tribunal on Monday. We have all these orders to be seen to and I'm meant to go to Nice because we're planning a large investment there. Work is picking up again. I can ill afford the time.'

'Can someone else go in your place?'

'No. It seems that it's me that they want.' Jean-Paul struggled to bury his irritation and walked swiftly across to Ruth. 'On the other hand,' he said as he kissed her, 'I shall be here after all.' He bent down to sweep his small son into his arms. 'And we can spend the whole weekend together. Where shall we go?'

Ruth smiled happily, 'Bertrand likes the park and the ducks are always hungry.'

When she woke the next morning Ruth experienced a strange feeling of relaxed warmth in her limbs, a light emptiness in her head, and the feeling of oppression that had accompanied every waking moment of the previous week had evaporated. Despite the Tribunal and the disruption to Jean-Paul's regular work, Ruth remembered a time of leisure and pleasure and freedom from worry. She looked across at her sleeping husband and listened for sounds from Bertrand's room. It was still dark outside, the thick curtains protected them from the stirrings of activity in the street below, and there was no incentive to leave the warm bed covers. Impulsively, as if to capture the moment, Ruth planned the day ahead. It felt like a pledge of gratitude, love and faith. She would make it a perfect day.

Even Bertrand caught Ruth's feverish excitement. She dressed him in his best blue shorts and a shirt with a sailor collar that Marie had made for him. 'It'll be hot in the Park,' Ruth said gaily to Bertrand as he held out a foot for her to tie his shoelaces.

'Ruth, I think it's time to see if the shops can offer a replacement to that dress you're wearing. This is a good opportunity to find you some new clothes.' Ruth did not protest and each holding Bertrand's hands they headed for the lift.

In the foyer the concierge called, 'Bonjour!'

'Bonjour,' they replied, and Bertrand added, 'We are going to the Park.'

'Ç'est bon, mon petit,' replied the concierge cheerily.

Before they reached the Park, Jean-Paul guided them to a toy shop to indulge his son with the purchase of a wooden sailing boat. It was then imperative that they revive themselves with a cool drink and chocolate croissants. How they had missed chocolate and how rare had been the occasions in their life as a family to treat themselves to such exquisite patisseries. It was not until Ruth had chosen a green and grey cotton frock at Jean-Paul's insistence, that they finally reached the Park.

The air was crisp and still and the sun had not yet reached its midday heat. Bertrand ran ahead and then doubled back, seeming to reflect the happiness that was felt by Ruth and Jean-Paul.

Only now did it seem safe to speak about the war in the past. To remind each other of events that had occurred which were not part of peacetime; troops mustering, soldiers returning, anxiety over food, coal, medicines, passes, inspections, bombs and explosives. Although life was still austere there was a feeling of hope now that their city was no longer under threat.

As they walked, others seemed to demonstrate the same relief. It was almost as if the children were playing with more energy, their laughter richer and their comments cheekier. Jean-Paul teased his son and she watched the confident way in which Bertrand responded. She found herself laughing gaily and saw Jean-Paul look at her in surprise. Ruth linked her arm through his and they walked companionably, speaking only intermittently, in step with one another. The paths had been swept clean and the grass, glistening in the sun, was scattered with daisies and only where footprints had scuffed the ground were there patches of exposed earth.

The vastness of the park was more noticeable in winter when the trees were stripped of their foliage. In summer the explosion of vegetation gave a more intimate atmosphere. Above them arched full leaved trees, beech, oak and elm. The differing shapes of their branches, the oak short and angled, the beech graceful and the elm flowing, soared against a background of pure blue sky. The rugged barks of their trunks surrounded them. The air, the earth, and the trees, in comparison to the blocked drains, piles of steaming manure from the horses and the dust from the streets, smelt clean and clear.

The ornamental ponds were edged with shrubs and areas had been paved where children could reach the water and sail their boats. For a while Bertrand tested out his new toy. He then joined a group of children who were throwing crusts to entice the ducks, their heads bobbing and their tails swaying from side to side, to swim towards them.

Tired at last, Bertrand asked to be carried. Swinging his child onto his shoulder and taking Ruth's hand, Jean-Paul suggested that it was time to turn for home. When they reached the apartment, Bertrand was asleep.

'It really does feel as if the war is finally over, yet it's as if we are having to learn again how to live,' Ruth commented as they entered the hall.

'It has been a splendid day,' Jean-Paul leant across to kiss Ruth and so doing woke up Bertrand. He then hugged his child for so long that eventually Bertrand wriggled free.

'Papa,' he giggled

Late that night Jean-Paul switched off the light and drew Ruth to him. Her sense of foreboding, which she had so successfully extinguished for the whole day, returned. 'There is something about this tribunal that I need to tell you.' Ruth's body stiffened and she took a sharp intake of breath. 'I heard in the Office that they are also interviewing Raoul. Raoul is manager of the factory.'

'Why is that significant?'

Jean-Paul held her close. 'There was a time, in the months before the Armistice when I suspected Raoul of underhand activity. I could never prove it but I kept a close eye. We could ill afford mistakes but I never did discover to whom he could be selling.'

'But that's over now.'

'Ruth, I just can't figure it out. One moment I think that the tribunal is a routine check, and the next I imagine an undercover investigation. Perhaps it will become clearer. I did try to get Raoul transferred, but I had no convincing argument to put forward. In the chaos of the last months no real audit of our accounts was prepared, so I had no proof.'

'But you're worried, aren't you?' They lay listening as the sound of a single horse-drawn carriage drifted up to their window.

'I have no reason to be, and nor have you.' Jean-Paul relaxed his hold on Ruth's shoulder. She was aware that he had been gripping tightly, transmitting his tension to her. He whispered, 'One week and this will be over.'

It was not until they had finished their evening meal on the Monday night, and Bertrand was in bed, that Jean Paul told Ruth about his day. Ruth knew better than to press him for information before he was ready. He went through to the living room and opened the windows to allow the cooler evening air to permeate the room.

'They were interrogating me,' Jean-Paul told Ruth disgustedly. 'I've spent months investigating this problem. I identified it. I set discreet inquiries in motion, and they question me. The American is quite civil and the Frenchman who is in the chair manages to remain focussed, but the English Major...! I tell you Ruth, he is not very bright and he cannot follow an argument. He is incapable of listening. You have to repeat things to him. He has that pompous attitude that infers that he has knowledge that you are not privy to. I don't know where all this will lead.'

Jean-Paul then said, 'They have arrested Raoul. That's how serious they consider this case.'

'Raoul? Your manager? Why? You said that you thought that he was cheating but why would they arrest him? What are the charges?'

Jean-Paul continued as if he was trying to unravel the day's events. 'There were two sets of orders, not every day, but always on the same days, the first and the fifteenth of every month. A double set of orders went out, but only one went through the books. Raoul just arranged for a duplicate order and no-one, until now, has checked.'

'How long has this been happening?'

'For the whole of the last year of the war. The consignment went to Concy on those days. There were no receipts for payment. The tribunal wanted to know who had requested the orders and where they were destined for. They asked me if I knew.'

'How could you know?'

'I could tell them, now that it is no longer secret, that the orders were going to the munitions factory. I gave them the name of the foreman. I met him every month so there was no point withholding his name.' Jean-Paul looked across at Ruth and saw that she was alarmed, 'What is it?'

'I didn't know that your firm dealt with ammunition. I suppose it was naïve of me to think that you would be exempt from going to the front just for supplying parachutes and packing for army explosives. Your work was dangerous and vital to the war effort.'

'That's beside the point. The tribunal are trying to find out to whom Raoul was supplying the materials. It could hardly be our side, what would be the point and where was the gain? If our Army wanted these materials, they would requisition them.'

Ruth was anxious all the next day. The fears that they had experienced in the war all returned. People were not always what they appeared to be. There were the carpet baggers, opportunists, ready to use any chance to augment their income. Bartering and the black market were widespread since food and commodities were scarce and Ruth wondered if silk could have been used as a commodity for profit. It certainly was not used for clothing, no one would be seen to flaunt their wealth in wartime. Silk was used for parachutes but there were not so many airmen that factories would be overstretched. Jean-Paul had never mentioned any involvement with aircraft or pilots. His firm had turned mainly to fabrics for uniforms, tents and camp beds, from manufacturer to procurer Jean-Paul told her, so as to keep the firm afloat. Now she realised that the company was a front, a cover for the main product. Jean-Paul had not been called to fight because he was considered indispensable to the war effort.

'It wasn't a good day, was it?'

Jean-Paul barely looked at her. His face was drawn and throughout their evening meal even Bertrand's antics could not raise him from his silent brooding. When they were finally together in the drawing room, Ruth prodded gently, 'What sort of questions did they ask?'

'Where were you on March twenty-third? Where were you on March twenty-ninth? Why were you near Concy?' Jean-Paul spat out the words, a bitterness in his voice.

'Were you near Concy?' Ruth asked, choosing to sit so that she could see his face.

'One of our depots is near there. Everything to do with the war is as near to the front as possible. Concy is seventy-five kilometres from Paris.'

'So what are they looking for?'

'All I understand is that it's something to do with that shell, the one that landed in the Jardin de Tuileries.' There could be no one in Paris who was not shocked by the explosion. There was something more that troubled Jean-Paul. As he went across to the dresser Ruth caught his look of exhaustion in the mirror. She watched the way he bent to open the cupboard, the way his hair fell forward as he removed a bottle and the change in his expression as he turned towards her. He smiled, but Ruth remained tense. He took two glasses from a shelf beside the mirror, filled each with cognac, and handed one to Ruth. She thought she would have more control if she stayed seated, her knees felt unreliable.

Jean-Paul remained standing. 'There were more questions. To put it bluntly they began to speak aggressively. 'Are you proud that two hundred and fifty people were killed when a church roof was shelled on Good Friday?' I had no idea, Ruth, where this was leading. How could I have been involved?' He lifted his glass hardly aware of the action.

'The English major has very poor French, but the officer speaks fluent English. At one point the Major was becoming very animated, firing questions in English at the Frenchman. The Major was asking about a large gun, top secret Paris or William gun, wanting to know about the placements and whether there had been communication with the army artillery surrounding it. They had quite an argument, and then the Frenchman asked me if we delivered ammunition that could have found its way to Concy? I said that I did not know. Then the Major said that I used this as a conduit for messages.'

'Could it have been?' Ruth said heavily. 'By someone else?'

'It must have been or they would not have asked. The last question was 'Was I aware that Raoul travelled to Concy every Monday.''

'And were you?'

'Of course. That's what we do. Raoul and I every week, sometimes more.'

'So why does it interest them?'

Jean-Paul turned the glass around in his hand,

watching the golden liquid rotate and then running his finger around the rim. 'Knowing what we do now, about the shells that were shot from the Paris gun, I can only think that the Germans were disseminating misinformation.'

'And Raoul was involved?' Ruth said in a shocked voice.

'That seems to be their suspicion. The secretary brought through a file and passed it to the French officer. It was a log book. The man pointed at dates and times which the officer then explained in English. On every occasion that Raoul went to Concy, my name was alongside. On the two dates that they mentioned, in August, we had both gone to the factory in Nice. Raoul insisted quite early on, that, with deliveries as vulnerable and sensitive to the military as were our goods, he would not take responsibility. I then offered to go alone but Raoul had the technical ability and knowledge of all the consignments. My role was to oversee all the operations, so we went together to both Nice and Concy.'

When a war is in progress it is hard to imagine a life without conflict. There was no certainty that the Germans would be defeated and it was natural that some people might feel it was prudent to make overtures to the potential winning side. Ruth tried not to judge Raoul too harshly. The gamble might have paid off but now his actions would be judged harshly. Ruth felt no emotion over Raoul, but was upset and angry that Jean-Paul had been implicated because of their working association. Jean-Paul worked with Raoul throughout the war. He trusted him and his dedication to the war on the side of the allies. How must Jean-Paul feel when he had possibly harboured and unwittingly protected a traitor?

Perhaps it would prove unfounded. So far no mention had been made of who Raoul passed the information to or how he had been recruited. Until this was evident the Military could not justify their allegations. It was unlikely that the tribunal would proceed with a prosecution and when Jean-Paul said that there was little concrete evidence, and that he thought the whole episode would be wound up after the following day's hearing, Ruth was eager to believe him. Jean-Paul took Ruth's empty glass and placed it beside his own on the dresser. Then he gestured to Ruth with outstretched hands and she moved towards him.

'Never have I regretted marrying you,' he said holding her close, 'but this is disturbing me more than it warrants.' He kissed her gently and then still holding her hands said, 'Let's go and say goodnight to our sleeping son.'

The moment was so solemn that Ruth felt light-headed, her feelings indecipherable. She drifted willingly, disconnected from reality, glad for this simple act that they could perform together.

Ruth was perturbed that Jean-Paul said so little the next day about how the tribunal was proceeding. He seemed determined that they should have as relaxed a family evening as they could, untroubled by outside events. He did not, for some reason want to discuss it and Ruth refrained from asking.

Bertrand was bathed and put into his pyjamas, Jean-Paul hung around and helped ineffectually. He was entranced by his small son who in turn responded to the unusual attention by entertaining his parents with endless chatter.

'Is there time for a game before bed?' Jean-Paul asked Ruth.

She smiled indulgently. 'A quiet one.'

Father and son constructed a large fort with bricks and then carefully placed soldiers in rows for battle. 'Which are the baddies?' Bertrand asked. Jean-Paul looked across at Ruth and shrugged his shoulders sardonically.

'It's up to you. You choose.' Jean-Paul instructed him. Bertrand stared hard at each set of soldiers and then choosing those in green uniforms, and ignoring the red, lifted his arm and swept them off their feet so that they fell to the ground.

'There,' he said proudly, 'will you read me a story?'

Ruth followed them to the bedroom. Bertrand wriggled under the cover and Jean-Paul rested his head against the headboard. He wrapped one arm around the boy and with his other he held the book. Ruth perched on the end of the bed to listen.

Nothing was said during the evening in reference to the Tribunal. Jean-Paul seemed weary and they retired early. Ruth thought that she heard him walking around the apartment in the night, but she could not be sure, perhaps he had only fetched a glass of water or opened another window to try and catch some breeze in the hot night air.

The next day Jean-Paul had not returned when Ruth bathed Bertrand, nor during his playtime, and eventually she read a story and tucked him up for the night. Their evening meal was prepared but still he had not appeared. She stood at the window and looked down. On the other side of the street she identified their car. Jean-Paul was sitting in the driver's seat. She stared more attentively. He had his hands on the wheel and his head on his hands. While she watched, he lifted his head and dragged the palms of his hands over his eyes. She leaned against the balustrade and shaded her face with her hand. Jean-Paul turned his head and saw her. He then opened the door and, as if his body was too heavy to move, slowly stood up.

Ruth turned from the balcony, left the door to the apartment open and ran down the stairs. At the door onto the street she stopped. Jean-Paul crossed the road lifting each leg as if urging them to walk. Ruth opened the gates to the lift and he stumbled in. His eyes were red and puffy, his hair damp and stuck to his forehead. He tried to stand upright but it was as if his stomach ached and he pressed his arms one on top of the other over his abdomen.

In the drawing room Jean-Paul sat in an armchair and stared ahead of him. Ruth fetched a glass of water.

'On m'accuse! They think it was me,' said Jean-Paul.

'What do you mean?'

'Because the information appears to have leaked from a man who is under me, who I direct, they say that it was me or that I am in collusion.'

'But you initiated the investigation. You told them about it.'

'And now the suspicion has fallen on me. It was our

visit to Strasbourg. They said, 'Wouldn't I have sympathies with the Germans because I came from Alsace?' and 'Didn't I have a German name?' and 'What better job could I have had if I wanted to help the enemy?"

'They can't hold that against you.'

'But they have done. They are. That Major is cocksure of himself. It was only thanks to the American that they are delaying their deliberation until tomorrow.'

'Make a decision?'

'Raoul has been released,' Jean-Paul stated flatly.

'So he's saved his own skin,' Ruth said quietly. A deep despair flooded her as she realised that Jean-Paul was trapped.

He looked up at her. 'You know how I said that the Major always acted smugly, as if he had trump card?' Ruth nodded. 'He played it.'

Ruth waited.

'Madder Red. That's all he said.'

'Madder Red?'

'It's a dye. It's only made in Germany.'

Jean-Paul spoke as if reciting a well learned poem. 'The major said, 'We have evidence of collaboration between you and a German under the pretext of commissioning stocks of madder red.'

'I told him that my communication with the Germans regarding the dye was made before the outbreak of war. We could have no conception that war would be declared and therefore this cannot be construed as collaboration, but he answered, 'My understanding is that this supply route continued well into the first year of the war.' I explained that we continued to use the dye but they were suspicious because the supply chain came through Switzerland.'

Ruth tried to understand.

'If there had been a direct line of communication, I cannot see how this would make any difference. However the major was blunt and said that it depended on the point of view of those examining the facts. It appears that I had a method of communicating with the enemy and that I used it conveniently for my own nefarious ends.' He paused. 'I am defeated. When facts are interpreted like this I can see no way of trying to convince the interrogators otherwise, without giving them the chance to further incriminate me.'

'What happens now?' Ruth asked, bewildered.

'The case goes to court. Whoever they suspect will be arrested until the court case.'

'You're innocent. The court has to prove you, or whoever it is, guilty. They won't be able to do that because it is not true.'

'That is not how the system works. Not here. Not in France. In France you are guilty until you can prove you're innocent.'

Ruth was aghast. Immediately she could see the impossibility of proving innocence in this case. People would lie to save their own skins. What was this system where you were not considered innocent until proven guilty? Jean-Paul knew he was trapped, and had had time to consider the consequences.

'I will be labelled a traitor, a spy, an informer, whatever the outcome. But there is only one outcome.'

Ruth could not speak. Her mind spun in a thousand directions and would not settle to a single coherent thought because the implications were unthinkable.

'We have to protect our son. I know that you will stand by me, Ruth. Why else would I have chosen you? I cannot ruin my son's life. He would always be tainted and his father vilified. I'd be better dead.'

They continued to sit, the distance between their chairs seeming to symbolise their already severed marriage.

'My parents are gone. You must survive for Bertrand's sake. I will leave tonight and no one will ever trace me.'

Ruth wanted to protest, to tell him to trust that innocence would be rewarded.

'Change to your maiden name. Go to Marie. She can be relied upon. Others will waver. It's human nature.'

For a long time they sat alone with their thoughts, occasionally finding it imperative to say something, but aware of the futility of everything they now said.

'Will I ever know if you are all right?' said Ruth.

'I came while Bertrand was in bed or I could not have done this.' said Jean-Paul.

'Will you survive?'

'You must survive.'

'And I thought the war had claimed all its victims.'

It grew dark. Jean-Paul stood up. Ruth hesitated and she looked at him fearfully. She was too numb for tears, and frightened because she felt nothing. What was the point in feeling anything? Yet she needed to comfort him and to say goodbye. Ruth stood. Jean-Paul led her to the window and kissed her.

'Keep looking. Look as far as you can into the distance. Don't turn around. Don't look down. I'm going now. Goodbye.' Slowly his hands slipped from her shoulders and Ruth was alone. Ruth obeyed. She never turned round. She strained her ears to hear if she could make out his footsteps on the pavement. She never looked down.

Chapter Twenty-Three

'Why did Uncle Jean-Paul ask me to look after you?' Ronald inquired of Ruth. Ruth looked around quickly to see if Monsieur or Madame Cuanez was within hearing distance. She hurried Ronald out into the courtyard. He was now twelve and had matured into a personable boy with girlish good looks which were not an asset now that he attended secondary school.

'When did he say that?' Ruth demanded.

'The last time he was here.'

Ruth tried to maintain control. 'When was that?'

'When the Tribunal was being held.'

'What else did he say?' Ruth, who had been standing, found a step on which she could sit down.

'He told me that the Tribunal would be finished that week and that things were not always what they seemed. That I must speak the truth whatever the consequences. He said that was what he had done. When is he coming to see me. Is he in his office?'

'No. Yes. Probably.' Ruth waved a hand distractedly as if she was chasing him away. Ronald went in search of Bertrand.

After this Ruth found excuses not to visit Ronald. She could not bring herself to say aloud the words she would have to use when giving him an explanation. What explanation could she give that did not condemn Jean-Paul? How could it be interpreted other than that Jean-Paul was an accused man on the run from the law?

A few days after this incident, the concierge knocked at her door. 'Madame, this is the second month that your husband has not paid me the rent. Could you please remind him? I have not seen him to ask him myself.'

Marie began to detect inaccuracies in her work. When she spoke to Henri of her concerns he observed that Ruth had not looked well recently and that Bertrand had been unusually clinging.

'Ruth, stop your work and look at me,' Marie said, 'I want the truth. To be blunt, your work is worrying me, and if I can't find a reasonable excuse we will have to think again. Has Jean-Paul left you?'

'No,' then she paused. 'Yes.'

'Ruth, what d'you mean? Neither of us has heard a word from Jean-Paul since the Tribunal. What happened?'

'He was innocent! Innocent!' Ruth said furiously. 'They blamed him for allowing it to happen. They said he must have been involved. They accused Jean-Paul.'

'Oh, my poor dear,' Marie gasped. 'I shall have to fetch Henri. He has to be told.'

When Henri entered the room Ruth was still standing, staring into the distance.

'I had such a foreboding about that Tribunal, Ruth. It was as if they had to find a culprit in order to close the case, and the odds were stacked against Jean-Paul. It's outrageous, Jean-Paul of all people. My dear, stay here tonight and tomorrow we'll see what needs to be done.'

Ruth looked blankly at him, 'You can't do this again.'

'What do you mean, again?' Henri looked to Marie for clarification, but she shook her head.

'I mean, you rescued us before, my sister Veeve and me.' This time it was Marie who looked to Henri for an explanation.

'I was seventeen.'

'Hotel Impérial. The lady with the baby. That baby was Ronald, and you were the loyal sister. Marie, I'll explain it all later.'

Within the week Ruth had moved in. Henri investigated her finances which were grave. It seemed that Jean-Paul had almost no savings. His money was tied up in war bonds. The sale of the car and the contents of the apartment covered the arrears and Ruth was able to retain a few items to furnish her room. She boxed up books, photographs and documents and carefully wrapped the clock and vases.

Despite his intention to disappear they expected to hear from Jean-Paul, but as months went by the truth of the situation made itself clear. How could he return when to prevent a verdict it was imperative that he was not found? Only if Ruth knew nothing, was he safe, as she discovered once the Police came to interrogate her.

No one had seen Jean-Paul at the apartment on that final night and Ruth could say with honesty that he had been home on the Wednesday and had appeared disturbed. The Police followed endless trails but neither the concierge, the Bank, his friends or his colleagues could tell them anything that they did not already know.

Ruth, distraught as she was, could only admire the courage and foresight that Jean-Paul had shown. How easy it might have been to have packed a suitcase, to have withdrawn money from the bank, to have taken a memento, or to have contacted them. He had done none of these things. He had abandoned them in every practical way, but essentially, in the sense of being accepted by society and not ostracised, he had saved them.

Despite this Ruth was angry. Angry that he had had to sacrifice himself, that he had to forsake them and that now she was no different from the thousands of other widows bereft by the war. Yet her situation was worse. She had no story of a heroic death to relate, she was not entitled to a widow's pension, she and Bertrand were abandoned to the charity of friends. Strangers questions were like an interrogation. Even Bertrand's happy chatter struck a discord within her.

Marie and Henri watched helplessly. Ruth retreated into herself, and they deliberated anxiously over her fate. The boy was transferring his affection to them. He needed to make friends and he required a Mother who paid attention to him. Henri consulted Marie. 'The girl must not be allowed to pine forever. This necessitates a fresh start. The only course of action is to contact her family.'

'I have mentioned this to Ruth, but she is adamant that we do not. She feels a failure and is ashamed. Moreover she has become a French woman and to return to England is not a welcome proposition'

'The child needs her family. Nothing has to be said. Jean-Paul is missing. Countless men are missing, most of them are dead. How can we find her family?'

A few days later Henri brought up the subject again. 'Why do you think that we can't ask Ruth directly? You don't think we could say that we are worried and that we think that she should go back home?'

'She would not agree. I feel certain. Ruth has made it plain that she intends to stay in France. It is understandable. She has lived here all her adult life and Paris has been her home for six years. Besides, she must hope that Jean-Paul will return one day.'

'I'm sorry Marie, but I fear that if Jean-Paul comes back he will be discovered and arrested. The authorities only need to watch Ruth. She is his magnet, and they know it. Ruth's hopes are unrealistic.'

'What do you suggest?'

Henri leaned back, closed his eyes and sighed. He then rubbed his face with both hands as if to eradicate a headache. Marie went to the door and opened it slightly. She waited until she could hear Ruth talking to Bertram while she bathed him, and, knowing that they would not be disturbed, closed the door and returned to her chair.

'I am trying to think who might know something of Ruth's background. What about Pierre, Jean-Paul's friend who came to see Bertrand when he was born? I believe that he knew Ruth when she first came to France.'

Henri sat forward, his hands on the arms of the chair. 'Sandy haired, married, and had recently had a child himself. Yes, I remember.' Marie waited. Henri seemed to be chasing an idea. 'You know, he was also, when much younger, a friend of Ruth's sister. When I looked after her sister, there was an Aunt.' He turned to Marie triumphantly. 'That's it! She summoned Pierre to escort Ruth and her sister to Nice.'

'So he met Ruth's Aunt?'

'No. He knew her already. That's why he was there. Give me time and I will track down this Pierre.' Henri and Marie sat silently.

'I'll go to Jean-Paul's office tomorrow,' Henri said decidedly. 'I'll go as soon as I have finished my clinic.'

'Pierre,' Marie said happily. 'he is the only person who knew Ruth before she was married. He should be able to help.'

Henri walked. It was a crisp February day. The stark leafless trees allowed the low sun to reach the stone exteriors of the terraced buildings. He walked briskly, glad to have a purpose after the weeks of anxiety. It seemed to him that other pedestrians moved with less urgency. He wondered whether this was merely due to the more relaxed attitude that people exhibited since the war was over, or whether it was influenced by the approach of Spring. The people around him appeared to carry an air of expectancy and hope which was not one that Henri had felt recently. He could envisage no future for Ruth in France, or in England although that would be the one he would wish for her.

He turned into Avenue Wagram, noting as he passed them, the houses where he had tended to the sick. How he wished that he was attending a sick bed now where he could take charge and bring reassurance and relief. He went along the Avenue des Ternes to avoid the chaos at the Place d'Etoile. Then he crossed Place de Neuilly and began to think that he should have taken a motor-taxi or even the metro. He was feeling hot and beginning to sweat. He did not want to arrive flustered. The street skirted the Bois de Boulogne and Henri slowed his pace. He began to rehearse for the forthcoming meeting. How much easier it would be if he could see Pierre at his home. What if Pierre was not at the office?

As Ronald had discovered a few years earlier when he had stood on those wide steps below the front door and ran his finger over the brass plaque, the office looked no different from any of the houses on either side. It hardly resembled the central office of a thriving firm. When he entered, the effect was compounded. A young man opened the door and he was led through a small hall into a drawing room. Henri was invited to wait. When asked, he explained that he was looking for a man named Pierre who worked with their company, and whose surname he believed began with 'Du'. He then added that he was a doctor. This seemed to change the man's attitude. Henri had decided to refrain from mentioning Jean-Paul, and only as a last resort.

The room, like the exterior, had an air of opulence. Few businesses had recovered their pre-war status and Henri was surprised. He surmised that the switch from military supplies to civilian had not resulted in a drop in clients. Perhaps the profits from the war had been considerable and had enabled this conversion. Henri was deep in thought when he heard a commotion on the first floor. The door was ajar and a slightly agitated male voice was saying. 'Pourquoi? Vous ne savez pas?'

The man began to descend the stairs when through the half open door he caught sight of Henri.

'Docteur!' he exclaimed in shock as he recognised Henri. Immediately he turned back and rapidly ascended the stairs. The receptionist continued down the stairs and entered the living room.

'Je suis désolé,' he apologised.

Henri did not move. The receptionist hovered. Henri asked for some paper and ink. He wrote 'Forgive me for disturbing you. I am searching for the family of Ruth Barthold so that she can return to England. You are my sole contact. Please help. Henri Thiel.'

Henri handed the note to the receptionist. 'Please?' he requested. The receptionist took the note and went back up the stairs. After a short while he returned. 'Monsieur Dupont asks you to follow me.'

Henri entered a large but cluttered office. Tall windows overlooked the street filling the room with light. Crates of papers were stacked haphazardly on the wooden floor and shelves of files filled the wall space. Pierre stood uncertainly, away from the windows in the centre of the room, and gestured to Henri to remain near the door. He dismissed the young man.

'We must be brief. We knew that Jean-Paul was missing. The police have been asking questions. I don't know what to think.' Pierre looked uncomfortable. 'Any contact with Jean-Paul for me and my family can be dangerous. We have been interrogated once. I do not wish that to happen again. A second time the outcome could be more serious.'

Henri said, 'I understand.'

'It would be for the best if Ruth went to England. The scandal won't follow her there. I knew Ruth's sister, Veeve. I met her at her Aunt in London, but I can remember the address. We had some good times and I was young and excited at being part of the social whirl in London.' Pierre spoke rapidly, 'Of course, Ronald wouldn't know his grandfather's address?'

'Ronald!' Henri was aghast. They had forgotten Ronald. They had neglected him for months. 'No, I don't suppose he knows anything.' Although it was distressing to imagine Ronald alone with the Cuanez, there was nothing to gained by involving him at present.

'You say that this is about Ruth. If she were to return to England the agents would follow her there. They would be less interested in Paris. This might help. Help us I mean. So I will help you.' Pierre spoke hastily but promised to write to Helen in London.

Henri stepped forward, grateful, but not knowing how to show it. 'I must thank you.'

'That is all I can do. Bonne chance, Docteur.' He said softening, but despite his change in mood he ushered Henri immediately to the door. 'It is best for us all, and Ruth, if she returns to England.' Before Henri could answer, the door was closed. The receptionist stared nervously as Henri slowly made his way down the stairs and let himself out into the street.

A week later Pierre telephoned Marie at the Clinic. His letter had been returned. He was sorry but he could not see how he could help them further. Henri called back to ask for the address. He would travel to London. There might be someone who could provide him with information. He arranged for a replacement doctor and such was Ruth's state of mind that she barely paid attention to the limp excuse for his intended absence. Five days later he was back in Paris.

Henri was elated at having tracked down Ruth's family. 'When I found Aunt Helen's house, it was empty, bombed. I booked into a hotel nearby.' He recounted to Marie. 'I asked many people up and down the street but none could help me. People had been dispossessed and removed to the country, others had no memory of any previous owner. I asked in the local shops. One person thought that she had gone to relatives. I went to the local library where a librarian recalled that she used to come in wearing her WRVS uniform and gave me the address of the secretary. It was about four o'clock, the English tea time, when I knocked at the woman's door. She said that Aunt Helen used to visit her brother in Leicester.'

'Leicester?' Marie echoed.

'Yes. It's not too far from London. I caught the train the next day. Her father's name had to be Hefford. Ruth has been using that name I noticed, so I made a plan.' Henri's eyes twinkled. 'I decided to pretend to be a lawyer. I inferred that I had information regarding a legacy, something like that, and ask for details of a Mr. Hefford.'

'Was it that easy?'

'No. But I knew the Banks would be interested. All I had to go on was that he was an elderly gentleman. There were four Banks in the centre of the town so I wrote four identical letters. The bank managers were happy to accept them. I told them that I was acting on behalf of his daughter Ruth, and had information of interest to him. That made them curious. I feel certain that they will forward them. Now we wait.'

'What did you write?'

'I told the truth. I said that his daughter Ruth was in great distress, and had grave financial difficulties. That her husband was missing due to the war and that she was at present under our care.'

'Did you mention Bertrand?'

'I'm afraid I did. Who can resist the lure of a grandson?'

Marie, who had been so impressed by Henri's resourcefulness, now faced the consequences. The loss of Bertrand would be a bitter blow to her. She had resigned herself to having no children of her own and Bertrand had taken the place of the child she would never have. She began to hope that there would be no answer to Henri's letters. It was a forlorn hope. Within a week a distinguished looking gentleman arrived at their door and in halting French introduced himself as Reginald Hefford. Marie saw a tired and slightly frail man to whom she warmed at once.

Two days earlier, as was his habit, Reginald went into his study after breakfast. He did not receive many letters because all business correspondence went directly to the mill. On his desk were a few bills and their weekly letter from Flo.

It was a dull day and Reginald sat down at his desk and switched on the lamp. He had a partially completed letter open on the pad of blotting paper. He read it over and then reached for the letters that had arrived with the morning post. He sifted through them and, curious that he had a communication from the Bank that he was not expecting, decided to open it first. He took hold of the letter opener, and sliced cleanly along the top of the envelope. Inside was a second envelope which Reginald turned over in his hand. The paper had an unusual feel to it and the style of writing was foreign. He reached into the original envelope and found a covering letter from his bank manager.

He clutched the envelopes for several seconds, a myriad of thoughts prevented him from opening them immediately. France and news of Ruth? What sort of news? How often had Eleanor asked why there had been no news from Ruth when the war had been over for so long. She had taught herself to fear the worst and yet not knowing, she had confessed to Reginald, was less bearable than news of her death.

Reginald opened the letter from the Bank and read it slowly. The letter was short.

'Dear Sir, It has recently come to our attention that a gentleman is attempting to contact you. He has news of the whereabouts of your daughter Ruth Hefford and of her son. I take the liberty of forwarding the enclosed letter to you from Docteur Henri Thiel. If we can be of further assistance please do not hesitate to advise us. Assuring you of our continued service, E. Bell.'

Ruth was alive, but there were no details except that she had a son. Reginald removed the second letter from its envelope. It was dated five days previously;

'115 Rue de Cardinet, 17eme arrondissement.
Cher Monsieur Hefford,
Your daughter Ruth Hefford and her son Bertrand are living with us and are well. Your daughter's circumstances are such that I believe only a Father can help. If you were able to come to Paris it would be a consolation to us.
Dr Henri Thiel.'

There was little space for recrimination, or even exasperation, in a Father's heart when he is begged for help. Reginald had, in the last months, felt the lack of direction in his daily existence, and he experienced a surge of energy such as he had not felt since the Armistice.

'Eleanor,' he said as he rose from his chair, although it was unlikely from that distance that she would hear him. 'Eleanor,' as he entered the drawing room he waved the envelopes in the air with a vague gesture that indicated authorisation of what he was going to tell her.

'It's Ruth. She's in Paris. She needs our help. Eleanor, she has a boy.' He wanted to say grandson but the leap was too great, the concept at this early stage was too ephemeral.

'What has happened?' Eleanor gasped, and moved to sit beside him on the settee.

'This is all I know,' Reginald said as he handed her the letters.

'Reginald, you must go at once. How quickly can we arrange it? And a boy! But why has she not written to us? Why has she hidden in Paris? Do you think that she has no money? What can have happened to her husband? If he had died why did not she tell us?'

Reginald placed a hand on her arm.

'Eleanor dear, I will find out. There's no point in asking all these questions. Don't imagine that I am not thinking the same, but it's idle to speculate.'

'Do you want to go as far as London tonight? You could stay with Lil. Send a telegram.'

'Let me look at the rail time table and ring for the times of the ferries. If you wanted you could start putting a bag together for me.'

'And Elsie, what shall I tell her?'

'Perhaps it would be best to say nothing at present. I can telegraph from Paris. We cannot assume that she is coming home. There may be other reasons for her needing me.'

Reginald remembered the last time that he had been called to France nearly fourteen years earlier. The dismay caused by that visit, the inexplicable behaviour of Veeve's husband, and the loss of both their daughters to exile in France, had left its mark. With seven daughters, Reginald wondered how only two were happily married with children, and one happily married without. There was Bett with her step-daughter Sheila, Veeve with a son who had been lost during the war with no-one seeming to know whether he was dead or alive, least of all Veeve, and then Maisie who showed no sign of marrying. Now here was Ruth, from whom they had heard nothing for years, who had not even written to Flo and about whom Veeve appeared to be extraordinarily vague, appearing in Paris.

'I do not understand why Ruth could not have written to us herself,' Eleanor remarked.

'Perhaps Ruth does not know. It would have been simple for this Henri Thiel to obtain our address from her, yet he has approached us through the Bank.'

'And how does he know where we bank?' Eleanor asked.

'That is one of the many things that I shall find out. I hope that this journey will have a happier result than the last,' Reginald sighed. 'I really am getting too old to still be running around after our daughters.'

'But Reginald, it's Ruth.'

Within a week of Henri's return from England a distinguished looking elderly gentleman arrived at 115 Rue de Cardinet. Reginald had aged considerably in the six years since he had last seen Ruth. His once thick head of hair was now white and receding. His eyes were deeper set in their sockets making his eyebrows more pronounced.

Reginald was welcomed by Marie. 'Follow me,' She said and took him directly to Henri's study.

'Monsieur, how glad we are that you have arrived.

That we have found you. Your poor Ruth. How she has suffered.' Henri took Reginald hands in his and shook them warmly.

Reginald learnt that it was sometime since her husband had gone. Hampered by the barrier of language he was unable to distinguish whether Henri meant that he had died or had disappeared. Ruth had been reluctant to write to her family. Reginald could understand Ruth's wounded pride. She had more than her sisters but was less able to face the world on her own.

When Ruth walked through the door Reginald's heart went out to her. She went towards him like a sleepwalker, almost child-like.

'I've come to take you home,' he said resting his cheek against her hair, his eyes welling with tears. Over the top of Ruth's head he saw a similar emotion reflected in Henri's face. 'Thank you,' he said, so as to include Marie. When he released Ruth, Marie took both his hands in hers.

'It is for the best,' she said ambiguously, 'for her Mother.'

Ruth maintained the detached manner that had become so much more pronounced over the recent months.

'Will you come home with me, Ruth?'

'I don't have much,' Ruth spoke decisively. 'It will not take me long to pack my things, or Bertrand's.'

'Bertrand?' Reginald's face lit up.

Marie said eagerly, 'Monsieur, such a charming boy. So amusing and sensitive. Already he plays with such concentration and is so keen to learn. Have you come to fetch his cousin too, le pauvre Ronald?'

Reginald put a hand to the back of the chair to steady himself.

'Ronald? He's in Paris? I had not dared to hope. His Mother was resigned never to see him again. Madame, where is he?'

'He's in good hands, Father,' Ruth answered. 'A schoolmaster took him in. I haven't been able to tell him... tell him that...' Ruth's voice drifted.

Henri said, 'Tomorrow I will take you to him, Monsieur. We must now have supper and you must rest.'

When she was certain that everyone was asleep Ruth began to gather her clothes, books, and her few valuable possessions. She made her way down to the study with a box of papers. She sorted through them lingering over each one as the refrain 'protect our son' echoed in her head. How could she protect him. Was this what Jean-Paul would want. For her to take Bertrand to England. Would he be safe there. Would the stigma follow them or could they leave it with everything else that had been lost and buried as a result of the war, on the other side of the channel?

Ruth picked up the photograph that Henri had taken of their little family on their return from Strasbourg. She studied it for a long time, then, reaching for a pair of scissors from Henri's desk, she deliberately cut through the photograph to remove Jean-Paul. Then she took a box of matches and struck one, held the flame to the corner of the cut photograph and watched it curl, turn brown, shrink and disappear. For the first time for months the tears fell willingly. In just such a way had her heart curled and shrunk since Jean-Paul had disappeared. Her long hair, loose for the night, was wet and the remaining documents on her knees became damp as they absorbed her tears.

'No one must trace him. I must not leave a single clue.' She told herself feverishly. One by one she set alight the bank accounts, lease agreements, motor licence. All the incriminating evidence of their life together. Finally only two documents remained side by side. They seemed to challenge her. One was Bertrand's birth certificate, the other the record of the registration of their marriage. Clasping both to her she paced the room. It was the ultimate betrayal and yet the ultimate sacrifice. Would Jean-Paul understand. Was this the reality of his final request to her. By denying Bertrand a father would she be able to protect him?

Ruth shivered, but not from cold, laid both documents into the grate and watched them burn.

Henri and Reginald arrived at the house of Monsieur and Madame Cuanez late the next morning. Reginald had met his youngest grandson and now he was to meet his other grandson Ronald who he had seen briefly as a baby over twelve years previously. Both men were silent on the journey except for an occasional polite comment.

Henri knocked at the door. 'Monsieur Cuanez, a thousand apologies,' Henri began, 'May I introduce Ronald's grandfather?'

'Is there bad news?'

They were led into the house and introduced to Ronald.

'You are my grandfather?' Ronald said in schoolboy English. He stood nearly as tall as his grandfather, a strong, handsome, thirteen year old, still with unruly blond hair. Reginald went across and shook the boy's hand, too choked to speak. Ronald waited until he had dropped his hand and, as if he had been preparing the sentence carefully before saying it aloud asked, 'Do you know where my Mother is?'

'In London,' the words tumbled out, 'I've come to take you home.'

'Home?' Ronald repeated, 'Where is home?'

Reginald was confused. 'England.'

Marie searched through the house for Ruth and found her in Bertrand's bedroom, sorting his clothes. Bertrand was collecting his toys but he had found a wooden car that he had not seen for a while and was dragging it by a piece of string along the corridor. Ruth was on her knees in front of an open drawer. When she heard Marie enter she froze, and started to twist her wedding ring, a simple platinum band, around her finger. Marie saw that Ruth was ablaze with anger.

'What have you done?' Ruth said glaring at the open drawer. 'You have called my Father although you know that I never wanted you to. You went behind my back.' Marie had been partially ready for this tirade but when the morning had passed and Ruth had acquiesced with all the arrangements, including that of collecting Ronald, she thought it had been avoided.

'It had to be, Ruth. Don't you realise that it breaks our hearts to lose you and Bertrand? You have become our family but your place is with yours. The boys need your family.'

Ruth's shoulders sank, defeated.

'Ronald needs his mother,' Marie added.

At this Ruth rallied and scoffed, 'You think so?' It was enough to bring Ruth to her feet. 'What have you told my Father?'

'Nothing that you would not have approved of. That Jean-Paul has gone.'

Ruth winced as she heard the name that they had all evaded for so long and knelt down to finish her task. Bertrand ran into the room to claim Marie's attention.

Chapter Twenty-Four

Bertrand sat silently staring at his older cousin while they travelled through the streets towards the Gare du Nord. On the platform Ronald stood beside Reginald but faced away from him towards the crowds of waiting passengers as if to deter him from engaging in conversation. Bertrand circled until he was facing Ronald. There was little else to attract his attention.

'Nous irons au train,' Bertrand ventured. He continued to gaze up at Ronald.

'Have you been on a train before?'

'No,' answered Bertrand. 'Have you been on a train before?'

Ronald crouched down on his heels, 'Not for a long

time. Do you know where we are going?'

The vast station forecourt was largely empty at this time of the morning. The early bustle of people heading for work had thinned and there were mainly family groups, like their own, or the elderly. It was a busy time for porters.

Ruth and her father stood either side of the trolley on which were stacked their trunks. 'What are the lads saying, Ruth? Damn my inadequate French.'

'Just about the train, Papa.' Reginald was startled by his daughter calling him by the French, Papa.

'Ruth, do the boys know no English?'

'Ronald learnt some at school, but he is more proficient in German.'

'And Bertrand?'

'None.'

There was a loud hiss from a train that was drawing into a nearby platform. Bertrand held up his arms to Ronald, alarmed at the explosion of noise. Ronald lifted him clear of the ground. He pointed to the engine, the steam now pouring from beneath its wheels, over its cab and into the space above. Bertrand checked Ronald's face, saw his lack of fear, and pointed. The porter tipped the trolley onto its wheels and turning to Ruth asked the family to follow him. On reaching the carriages he left the trolley by the door and went to secure their seats.

'Ronald. Bertrand. Follow.' Reginald beckoned to the boys and indicated that they should board. 'You go too, Ruth. I can oversee the luggage.'

Reginald was agitated by the burden of responsibility for his three charges and with exaggerated concern he settled his largely unfamiliar relatives around him. He contemplated, however, with a secret sense of triumph, his successful mission to rescue these three waifs from foreign soil.

The journey to Calais took three hours. How vividly Ruth remembered her journey, so many years before, on this train with George and the baby. Would she ever tell Ronald about those events. Would it benefit the lad to be told that he had been abandoned before, when his mother had wilfully travelled to France. Veeve had not thought about Ronald when she went to join George. In fairness to Veeve she had been so ill and had spent so little time with him that she probably forgot that she had a child. However, with the knowledge that Veeve chose to leave France and Ronald, at the first whiff of war, Ruth with hindsight was less forgiving.

It was preferable to think about Ronald and Veeve than to look ahead to her welcome, or otherwise, in England. She knew she was not being fair to her father by withholding an explanation, but she was determined not to lie, and equally determined not to tell the truth. She therefore set herself the task of imagining the reunion between Ronald and his mother. Veeve had fled to Spain. Where was she in England? Veeve must know that Ronald was with her and might be coming home. She probably thought that Ronald had lived with her all these years, and could have no conception of how the war had affected their lives. Ruth wondered what had happened to the legacy that had been left to her nephew. Where was the money and had Veeve had the use of it? These were not questions that she could ask her father.

Ruth hoped that Ronald's future was secure financially because she had no way of supporting him. As for herself, Ruth felt that she had lost all her personality and hoped that, somewhere on the other side of the Channel, she would learn to inhabit a new one.

She was shocked into this sooner than she anticipated. On leaving France there had been a cursory appraisal of their passports by the officials, but on arrival in Dover the process was less perfunctory.

'My grandsons,' Reginald explained proudly as he presented his passport. The official was accompanied by a brash, swarthy officer who stepped forward with a hand outstretched to demand Ruth's passport and, barely looking at him, she placed it into his coarse reddened hand. He appeared to be irritated that a young woman should feign ignorance of his presence.

He opened the passport and held it open, until Ruth looked up at him.

'Miss Hefford,' he leered.

Ruth registered his insinuation and saw him smirk knowingly. 'Mrs. Barthold, if you would show some respect,' she snapped, 'my documents were destroyed in the war.'

The insult had the effect of stimulating her with a dignity that surprised her. She removed the passport from the officer in the moments that he had been halted by her rebuff, and moved on ahead of her family. Her father followed her with one hand on Ronald's shoulder and his other hand in Bertrand's.

Ruth had not consciously distanced herself from her family. In the early months before her marriage she had, perhaps from a false sense of independence and fear of criticism, failed to communicate. Subsequent events had catapulted her, along with the rest of the world, into a situation where survival was paramount. When she did finally think of contacting them she excused her reluctance to do so because she could not hope that they would understand either her silence or her foreign lifestyle. Latterly, with the disappearance of Jean-Paul she was grateful that she had never done so. How could she face their pity and incomprehension? She marvelled at her father's unquestioning support knowing that, now that she had to face the other members of her family, they would be less forbearing.

Ruth found her old home emptier, cold and slightly musty. She discovered that her parents now lived alone in the large house, occupying just three rooms. The exigencies caused by the privations of the war had somehow carried on. Ruth, whose memories were of a house full of children and young people, felt that Bertrand was out of place and that Ronald was too large and too vibrant. Eleanor seemed overwhelmed by their youthful chatter.

Elsie, Mitchell and their two girls came over at the earliest opportunity.

Elsie greeted Ruth warily with a kiss.

'Isn't it wonderful,' Eleanor commented, 'so wonderful. Ronald, here are your long lost cousins.' Ronald could not talk to his two cousins, Joan and Mary aged twelve and ten, instead he found a game to amuse Bertrand. The two girls sat primly beside their mother with their eyes glued on the small boy.

Elsie was subdued. When Ruth greeted Mitchell she understood the reason. He was unrecognisable from those pre-war years. His once athletic body had been exchanged for the round shouldered frame of someone much older than his years. He stood with a stoop and his face was grey from pain. Ruth held back from asking what the war had done to him.

Elsie filled the silence. 'There are still shortages of everything. Work for Mitchell is slow as few people can afford lawyers. Unemployment is a great grievance for everyone.' Ruth was astonished that Elsie was in tune with current problems. She had always been able to skim the surface of affairs and centre her attention on bonnets and shoes, suitable friends for her daughters, and the social circuit.

'Everything has changed,' Ruth commented but she suspected that Elsie failed to appreciate that she was apportioning some of the changes to those within themselves.

Mitchell smiled wearily, 'I expect it has been the same for you.' His kindly remark fell unnoticed except by Ruth, who suddenly found a reason to speak to Bertrand with a flow of French that threw the conversation off its tracks.

'Bertrand?' Eleanor asked rather disapprovingly.

'Bertram, Mother. We'll call him Bertram.' Ruth acquiesced at once, anxious to defuse any potential cause for disagreement.

'The girls are both at Wyggeston School like we were,' Elsie retrieved their conversation. 'The uniforms are the same. Do you remember how we so hated our hats? The girls are the same.'

'Your parents live quite alone now,' Mitchell said. 'Sheilagh has her own place and works at the hospital. She's not married, you see. As for Maisie, she has decided that a hotel on the coast for holiday makers is a shrewd investment and your Father backed her. Ever the optimist, your younger sister.'

Ruth digested this information and felt proud of her little sister, no longer a girl but nearly thirty and proving as independent as ever. The afternoon whirled around Ruth as she swum in and out of the conversation. Now that their dutiful enquiries were over they, her parents, her sister and Mitchell could, without feeling impolite, revert to their comfortable exchanges of local news and mutual acquaintances. The two girls continued to stare at their unconventional cousins and their new aunt whenever they felt that they were unobserved.

'Elsie is so happy to have you home,' Eleanor stated as a matter of form once the family had left. 'Poor Mitchell. To think how he used to be. Elsie does so well.'

The next day Lil breezed in with Henry in tow. 'Hello, Mother,' she gave her mother a quick peck on the cheek and handed her a kilner jar of fruit. 'I've brought you my last jar of plums. Where's Ruth?'

At that moment Ruth entered the room holding Bertram by the hand. 'Oh,' Lil exclaimed with more energy than the household had witnessed for a while, and since Ruth stopped her advance Lil swept across the room and enveloped her sister in a hug. 'I've missed you so much. So has Henry, haven't you?' Henry followed behind Lil and planted a brotherly kiss on Ruth's cheek, smiling benignly.

Lil dropped to her knees. 'Hello Bertram,' Bertram looked up at his mother and they exchanged a few words. 'Bien sûr, silly me. Comment ça va ? Je m'appelle, Lil.'

Henry waited until everyone was settled and then examined the wooden toy that was lying on the hearth. Bertram was drawn to him and was soon playing contentedly.

'What did you do in the war, Ruth?' asked Eleanor by way of an opening. 'Lil joined the Woman's Legion.'

Ruth wanted to avoid divulging her link to the munitions factory because this might lead her to let slip information that she was unwilling to disclose. 'Did you Lil? What was that?'

'The idea was to train women to do work usually done by men because there was such an exodus to the war. I joined the agricultural section. There were so few men working on the land that there was a possibility that we would starve to death.'

Ruth was surprised to see Lil exchange an easy smile with Henry.

'Women doing men's work,' Henry interposed, 'it took a bit of getting used to, for all of us but they had to replace the male workers who had been called to the colours!'

'But you couldn't do that in Leicester?'

'No, I moved to a hostel, some converted kennels, and came back here on my days off.'

'To badger me,' Henry added. 'I had to negotiate with

the Navy who were reluctant to be supplied with fruit and vegetables from the Manor House. Gardens were turned into vegetable plots and everyone had allotments.'

Despite herself Ruth was interested.

'Then I had to raise subscriptions for a motor tractor. The women realised that they were unable to keep up with all the ploughing necessary as more and more acres went to corn, and many of the farms had lost their horses, so they learnt to drive tractors. Goaded by Maisie, Lil too learnt to drive one. She even won a ploughing competition!'

Reginald glowed with pleasure and recited. 'She had to set a ridge and plough half a rood of land no deeper than four and a half inches in less than an hour and a half.' He beamed, proud of his new found agricultural knowledge.

'All thanks to Henry,' Lil placed a hand fondly on his knee. 'He organised donations from America for the tractors.'

'I thought that Lil would have difficulty settling back after the war,' Henry continued to address Ruth, 'but she's continued with the bottling industry. Quite the little farmer.'

'Your Uncle Henry,' Lil began, speaking to Bertram.

'Oncle Henri,' There was a sudden silence in the room. Bertram had copied Lil and his clear little voice arrested their chatter.

'Oncle Henri?' He repeated. There was a murmur of approval of the boy's attempt. Bertram looked to his mother. She smiled at their misunderstanding.

'Uncle Henry,' Ruth corrected, and Bertram looked

beyond her, eyes wide, and searched.

'Oncle Henri?' He asked, his eyes now tearful and his face troubled. Ruth hurried towards him, lifted him onto her hip and carried him quickly from the room.

'You see?' Eleanor turned to Henry and Lil, 'we don't understand anything.'

'Oncle Henri is Doctor Thiel,' Reginald explained, 'it's obvious that Bertram is fond of him, and of his sister Marie.'

Henry asked, 'Would they not be able to tell us what happened? Perhaps they know about Jean-Paul.'

'Reginald did not find out nearly enough,' Eleanor complained.

'Perhaps it was not the right time, Mother.'

'Perhaps, Lil, you could ask?'

Lil and Henry exchanged glances and Henry nodded with a shrug of his shoulders indicating that it might be worth a try.

'If you want, Mother. If you think it might help.'

'It would help me,' Eleanor emphasised.

'But what about Ruth?' Reginald wondered aloud.

They waited for Henry. 'I think,' he said cautiously, 'that we should wait. Ruth has suffered, that is certain, as have many women in the war, and we must tread warily.'

Ruth returned holding a mollified Bertram by the hand.

Henry said, 'We were worried about you in fourteen, when you left here and went back to Paris.' Ruth nodded in agreement. 'Paris was so near to being surrounded,' Henry continued, 'we thought the Allies were at breaking point. Then the Belgians resorted to their age old strategy.'

'They did.' Ruth was surprised that Henry should be informed about what she considered her war. He went on to explain the Belgian response, knowing that Eleanor was ill-informed about the various stages of the war. 'It eventually came through our censorship. They flooded the country nearest the channel killing six thousand Germans. It was more effective than guns and probably saved you.' Henry waited, hoping that Ruth would comment, and receiving no answer he asked directly, 'What was it like in Paris?'

'Very much like it was here to judge from what Elsie was saying,' replied Ruth 'less and less of everything.'

Later, when Lil and Henry left to return to London, Eleanor picked up her shawl which was draped around the back of her chair. Ruth saw her shiver and moved to place a few more coals on the fire. Eleanor thanked Ruth but rose and went out of the room without saying a word, leaving her alone with Bertram. Ruth did not blame her mother. She was aware that her silence was irritating. Eleanor crossed the hall and noiselessly turned the handle of the door to Reginald's study. He turned and waved a letter in the air.

'Flo?' Eleanor asked.

'As usual. There's not much news but you will enjoy hearing about the girls.'

Eleanor, however had other matters on her mind. She did not sit down and this was an indication that she had something to say to which she expected Reginald to pay attention.

'Reginald,' Eleanor's voice contained more urgency than usual. 'Why did you not ask Ruth anything. It really is too bad.'

'All in good time,' Reginald said soothingly, 'when she is ready she will tell us herself. If she does not then nothing can make her and we shall have to accept it. Some events just go too deeply to be spoken of.'

'I've never heard the child say Papa or mention a father when he talks to his mother.' Eleanor observed. She stood behind him and rested her hand on his shoulder. Reginald took her hand and placed it by his cheek.

'There are many children,' he said sadly, 'who will never say the word Papa, I fear.'

'This is different,' Eleanor stated.

It was dark when Henry and Lil left Granby House. It was not far to the station and after the oppressive air in the drawing room it was a relief to stretch their legs and to stride in unison along the pavement. The main street was lit with gas lamps. Lil took a deep breath and sighed expressively. Henry took her arm in his and gave it a squeeze.

'We are the lucky pair, Lil. Flo's Tom had the trenches, Elsie's Mitchell too, but worse. Veeve divorced, through no fault of her own. Maisie, with no hope of a husband because even despite her handicap there are no men. And now Ruth.'

They arrived at the station entrance. There were quite a few passengers heading for the London train. They queued for a ticket and followed the other travellers who were congregating on the platform. Lil found a bench and sat down.

'Do you think,' she began tentatively, 'that Jean-Paul deserted her?'

Henry turned so that he could see Lil's face. It was full of anguish.

'I think it is unlikely. Ruth is not angry. To my mind she is sad and lost.'

'If he'd been killed during the war, Ruth would be a war widow and proud. There would be no need for secrecy. In fact it would be impossible to keep something like that a secret.' Lil declared.

'It's true. There would be records and she would know it. No, it's a mystery.'

'Should we pry?'

'I think we can try and find out, if only to understand. We must be prepared to draw a blank.'

There was a burst of steam as their train drew in. Their compartment was full and they sat in silence, each with their own thoughts until they reached St. Pancras.

Later in the week it was Maisie's turn to visit. She caught the train in the morning and planned to spend the night. 'My guests will survive,' Maisie told Eleanor airily. 'I have excellent staff and the place will run without me for a couple of days.'

Maisie arrived noisily, her sensible shoes resounding on the wooden hall floor. She wore a serviceable suit and an unflattering hat tied carelessly under her chin, with an air of being too preoccupied to be concerned with details. She greeted Ruth in an unsentimental manner which dismissed the intervening years as irrelevant. She launched into her plans for Ruth and then she caught sight of Bertram. She lifted him up and crushed him with a rather inept hug. Bertram looked alarmed and once he had been restored to his feet, ran to the safe haven of his Grandfather's lap where he leant back against his chest until he became habituated to her rasping voice.

Maisie, oblivious of the effect she had created on her nephew, said, 'Ruth, you'll have to do as I did. Having a hotel gives you a home and covers the bills. We have to help ourselves. Why not buy where everyone goes on holiday and is happy, I thought. It's quiet in the winter but my goodness how it makes up for it in the summer months. I have a very good business.'

'And her guests have to be extremely energetic or they have no peace,' Reginald added gently teasing his youngest daughter, although he was proud of her achievement.

'Woe betide them if they don't enjoy themselves,' Maisie said, giving her father a knowing look.

Ruth, obsessed by the conviction that everyone was endeavouring to extract her secret from her, was relieved that for Maisie, her past was of no interest. If asked, Maisie might well have protested that everyone had a heartache from the war and the less people probed the better. Ruth experienced was a imperceptible lightening of her load for which she could not account. Bertram lost his initial reserve and gravitated towards this refreshingly blunt aunt who so obviously wanted to engage with him.

Eleanor very soon became irked by the disruption to

her orderly routine. There had been too many years since a small child with unpredictable demands had lived in her house. She hoped that Ruth would be the companion in the evening that Elsie had been, but it was 'like having a disembodied shell of a daughter' she complained to Reginald. Eleanor resorted, as she had often done in the past when any of her daughter's behaviour had been beyond her limited abilities, to petition Flo. A spell with Flo would sort Ruth out, she told Reginald, who hoped for both their sakes and for Ruth's that she was correct.

While Ruth and Bertram stood on Flo's doorstep, Ruth remembered the day when she had left Flo's house with Jean-Paul's letter tucked into her skirt pocket ready to leave her family. She had never doubted Flo's blessing then, and she did not doubt her acceptance of her and her son that day. The door was wrenched open. Flo had flour on the bib of her apron and wiped her hands on the skirt.

'I have been waiting and hoping for this day,' Flo exclaimed and Ruth felt the warmth of a homecoming for the first time.

Later, when they were sitting at the kitchen table, each cradling a cup of tea in their hands, and with the door to the back garden open so that Bertram could run freely, Flo said. 'No questions?'

'Thank you,' replied Ruth. Flo then began to talk of the war years.

'I did not want to give up my job when the men, when Tom, came back from the front. It seems ungrateful after all that they went through, but I ran a good workshop. The women liked me and in some ways they preferred having a woman in charge. My girls began to enjoy our new lifestyle. They had to share the tasks in the house, see themselves to school and help to plant vegetables for the war effort. We kept hens and they helped in the great egg collecting scheme. Did you have that in France?' Ruth shook her head. 'Perhaps not in Paris. Everyone was doing it here to help feed the troops. Now Nora is about to work at the drapers, she's an able seamstress, and it's a good job for a woman. Sara is a bright girl and perhaps she'll become the teacher I would have liked to be.'

'Tom?' Ruth asked.

'He was one of the lucky ones although he lost many friends and fellow soldiers. He says little, he's quieter than he was, but at least he was able to return to a job. But we're all right. Ruth, you have to think about yourself and Bertram now and how you will live. Have you thought of asking Veeve, you used to be so close.'

'Veeve,' Ruth replied scornfully, 'how could she help?'

Eventually, however, a meeting between Veeve and Ruth was inevitable. The two women appraised each other silently.

'I wondered when you would come and see me,' Veeve said archly. She looked magnificent. She owned one of the most fashionable hotels on the right side of the Thames secure financially due to the legacy of her divorced husband. She entertained a circle of society friends who were drawn by the glittering reputation that

Veeve had acquired. Her plush drawing room was hung with heavy brocade curtains and was amply provided with sedate upholstered furniture. On the walls the embellished frames around the pictures and mirrors were a match for the grandiose chandelier and the deep tasselled lampshades. This superb setting was crowned by Veeve who, with her matronly figure draped with jewellery at her throat, ears and fingers, reigned over her empire with éclat.

Veeve surveyed her sister. Ruth had not attended to her wardrobe or spent any time with her appearance. 'So you're back. Are you going to tell me what happened?'

Ruth's lack of response irritated her.

'So, he left you, did he?' Veeve saw that her remark had struck home and goaded Ruth into a reply, as Veeve had intended that it should.

'It's of no concern of yours,' she snapped.

'It's of extreme interest to me,' Veeve retorted in a measured tone. 'You might as well sit down.' Ruth obeyed. 'Are you going to tell me?'

Ruth stared stubbornly ahead of her.

'If you don't tell me I can find out. There are people I can ask.'

'Why didn't you find out before,' Ruth countered. 'Perhaps you didn't want to discover the truth about Ronald. Your convenient story had everyone's sympathy and allowed you to continue as you've always done.'

'You can hardly say that Jean-Paul looked after my son very creditably. I understand that Ronald was fostered out for the length of the war, and left there even when it ended.' Veeve resorted to sarcasm. 'So, what happened? Where is your Jean-Paul. How is it you are alone?'

Ruth breathed rapidly. 'If,' she said with as much venom as she could muster and desperate to check any move of Veeve's to use her contacts, 'if you ever do anything to jeopardise my position by delving into the past, I assure you, Veeve, that I will make certain that everyone knows that you spent the war with a German.'

Ruth knew that she had hit the mark. One whiff of scandal in the fragile post-war climate and Veeve's small kingdom would topple.

Veeve appeared to change tack.

'How are you going to support yourself since you have been left penniless? Ronald's first trust matures when he is eighteen and he has another at twenty-one. What future has Bertram do you think?'

Ruth had plenty to say but none of it would have gained her any advantage at this point.

'What about Ronald? How are you going to look after him?' Ruth asked, to gain time.

'Ronald?' Veeve said without emotion. 'He'll go to Boarding School.'

'At least he will continue his music.'

Ruth's reply put Veeve on the defensive. 'What music?'

'His piano and his composing. He's very talented.'

'How do you know?' The older sister demanded.

'Well, you will see for yourself, should you care to ask him.'

Antagonism between the siblings simmered. Veeve

broke the impasse. 'This is ridiculous, Ruth, quarrelling like this. I'll call for tea and then we will have a sensible discussion. Father's at his wit's end to know what to do with you. There is only one answer. You will have to run your own Hotel. Father says that you will then have a roof over your head and an income.'

When Ruth had been home for some weeks Elsie and Mitchell arrived for a visit. Reginald was quick to intercept Mitchell. 'Can you spare a moment?'

Mitchell began to take off his overcoat as they entered the study and Reginald saw him wince with pain. He stepped forward, 'Let me help,' he offered. Mitchell allowed him to remove his coat and hang it on the stand and then absent-mindedly rubbed his shoulder.

'I want to discuss Ruth's position privately with you,' Reginald flicked a nod towards the living room. 'Sorry it's a bit chilly in here,' he apologized. The dying embers of the fire gave a faint glow but no warmth. 'You probably should have kept your coat on.' Reginald smiled.

They sat on either side of the desk and Reginald placed his hands, with fingers linked, on the leather blotter. 'We are no further on in discovering what happened to Ruth. This leads me to think that we need to look at how she is to be supported, financially.'

Mitchell's eyes brightened as his attention was directed away from his pain. 'Elsie and I have been wondering,' he admitted, 'I have been looking into war pensions.'

'Yes?' said Reginald expectantly.

'If she were a widow she would receive a government pension of ten shillings a week, and a further small sum for Bertram.'

'That would be a help,' Reginald assented,

'But to apply she would have to have a marriage certificate and a death certificate.'

'I know she has neither. I asked her what papers she had in her possession. She only produced her passport and that was in her maiden name.'

Mitchell nodded thoughtfully. 'She never did come over to England after she was married, hence the passport being under Hefford. There is also a pension for a separated wife of ten shillings but without supporting documents she could not apply for that either. Our only recourse would be to apply on her behalf as an unmarried wife. The pension is only seven shillings a week and that is not enough to live on.'

Reginald looked shocked, 'We could not do that. Ruth would never consent. I shall have to think of an alternative solution. She's a retiring sort of girl but she's bright.' With an imploring look seemed to beg Mitchell to find a solution.

'Is it possible, Sir, that Ruth would respond to having some work? A home and routine of her own. It must be difficult for her now.'

'Of course. Like her sisters? We cannot rely on a pension then. There's no hurry. Eleanor is enjoying the boy and it has added an interest to her life although she might pretend otherwise. Come, before we freeze, let's join the others.'

A few months later Reginald arranged his affairs so

that he had some capital to spare and he bought a hotel in central London, confident that Ruth would have a good head for business.

Everyone agreed that this was the perfect answer except for the undeniable fact that Ruth had neither Veeve's nor Maisie's strength of character and natural ebullience, however, in the circumstances there did not seem to be many alternatives.

To everyone's' surprise the Hotel at 13 Stanley Gardens proved a thriving concern. Ruth's steady business sense and ability to steer her staff from behind, created an efficient if not flamboyant establishment. Its position was ideal because it was within walking distance of Bett's apartment and this gave Ruth the companionship and solace that was missing in her life.

'Ruth, you are managing very well,' Bett greeted her sister warmly. Ruth had been at Stanley Court for six months and Bett had heard nothing but good reports. She was proud of her sister and pleased that she was beginning to look healthy and even pretty again. She was on the verge of asking Ruth what she had done in France that could have given her some relevant experience, but remembered in time that any reference to the war drew a blank.

"I always knew you were capable. The war has produced some welcome changes.' Bett looked around happily at her own snug little apartment. Every wall space was covered in pictures, every shelf was full of nick knacks, cushions were piled onto armchairs, books were stuffed into shelves and pieces of knitting and sewing were strewn around on table tops.

'Brinsley-Smith had what they call a good war,' she said disdainfully, 'and it has enabled me to have a place of my own. Sheilagh visits whenever she's off duty, and now I have you and Bertram.'

Henry called intermittently at his Club and when unable to avoid it had a whisky in the company of Brinsley-Smith. Usually it was an occasion for Brindsley-Smith to enquire after his estranged family, but on this instance it was Henry who volunteered some news.

'Bett's sister has been discovered in Paris and has come home. No husband.' Henry informed Brindsley-Smith. 'Got a small boy with her, about three I'd say. Poor blighter couldn't speak a word of English. Bertrand, they called him, Bertram now, I suppose. Bertram Barthold. Curious name.'

'That's strange! Barthold was the name of the chap that we tried to put away on that case I told you about. You know, sabotaging ammunition and informing the Boche. He did a runner. Funny if it was the same bloke. We never did get a prosecution. But I got my promotion.' He ended smugly.

'Hardly likely to be the same man,' Henry said hastily. 'The name is probably two a penny over there. How could you be sure that man was guilty? I thought you told me that Barthold himself had been investigating the case before you arrived.'

'Whole point, my dear man, wool over our eyes. With a name like that what do you expect? Of course the man was a German sympathiser. Guilty all along.'

Henry was disturbed, but he knew that he would not mention this conversation to Lil, or to anyone.

Chapter Twenty-Five

1929

'Are you not taking your cricket bag this year?' Ruth asked, as Bertram dragged his kit across the hall floor ready to return to school after the Easter holidays.

Ruth had watched Bertram drag his bag down the stairs and felt the familiar nausea and restriction in her chest that was her response to the knowledge that it would be three months before she saw her son again.

It had not been an easy decision, where to send Bertram to school. The assumption by the family had been that when he was seven years old Ruth would send him to board at the preparatory school associated with Ronald's public school. A letter from Marie Thiel had set Ruth on an alternative course.

'I believe that last night, and possibly on other nights, Jean-Paul was standing in the doorway of the house opposite, shielded from the lamplight but looking up at the windows of Henri's study.' Marie wrote. 'Why don't you and Bertrand come for a visit?'

It did not take much to persuade Ruth. She had missed her friends, and leaving Bett to inform the family that she had taken Bertram on a short holiday, they set off for Paris. Bertram was of an age where the journey was an adventure and although he was too young to have any memory of their return to England, it resurrected emotions of a traumatic nature for his mother. She could not have foreseen the consequences of their visit.

During their stay, the affection that Bertram had shown Marie and Henri as a small boy resurfaced and was reciprocated. Eventually Marie could restrain herself no longer.

'Ruth, could Bertram not go to school here, in Paris? Stay with us during the term time?' The French couple, unused to the British custom of sending children to board at school were dismayed at the thought of their young friend facing, as they saw it, such an ordeal. Ruth had grown accustomed to the idea and it held no especial fears in her mind for Bertram, however there was another consideration beyond the welfare of her son.

Ruth had become obsessed with the conviction that Jean-Paul was trying to reach them. What point of contact did he have beyond the Thiels. If Bertram was to board with them, and if he was to spend more than half of every year in Paris, how much more were the chances of communication. She soon persuaded herself that it would be the best solution for her, the Thiels and for Bertram. She would justify it to her family by saying that she could not yet afford the fees of an English private school, and this was in part true as she was anxious to repay her loan to her Father. The boy was half French and it was foolish to deny him his cultural heritage.

Marie's proposal seemed to suit on both counts.

When they left Paris for London, Ruth agreed to return with Bertram a few days before the beginning of the autumn term to settle him in. Bertram, when told the news, accepted it without demur.

Bertram had not been very long at the Lycée, crossing the Channel regularly at the beginning and end of each term, when he told his Mother that he could manage the journey on his own. This presented an unexpected problem. Bertram would need a passport, but without a birth certificate this would not be easy to procure. It was Veeve who devised a solution.

Veeve had originally been faintly amused by Ruth's whim to educate Bertram in France, an attitude that was preferable to Ruth than her Mother and Elsie's cries of appalled dismay, and advised, 'Ask the Rotter.'

She had smiled at Ruth's look of incomprehension. 'Do you not remember the Rotter? Brinsley-Smith? Bett never sees him but he sidles in here occasionally on the coat-tails of one or other of my more welcome guests. He can be useful, though. He seems to have contacts that one doesn't enquire about. He sorted Ronald's papers for me.' Ruth appeared to consent. 'I'll arrange it for you. There's no reason for you or Bertram to meet him.'

Ruth found herself grateful to her sister who had refrained from censorship and even shown unspoken approval of her decision. From then onwards Bertram travelled the Newhaven-Dieppe route to Paris alone, and only in rare instances did Ruth travel herself across the Channel. As the months went by, and there was no further mention of Jean-Paul by Marie, Ruth discovered that her commitment to her Hotel predominated over her quest for an elusive sighting of her beloved husband.

In the Easter holidays Bertram spent long hours in the nearest park with others from the local cricket team practising his bowling and batting. For his tenth birthday he had been given his own cricket bat, and, convinced that his school friends would enjoy this English game, had set out to teach them.

The game had attracted much attention and a collection of passers-by began to stop on their walks beside the school playing fields to watch. Bertram gathered enough interest to create two teams. At the beginning of the following summer he added to his equipment some pads, stumps and leather cricket balls to replace the tennis balls that they had used the previous year.

'Some grown-ups are really curious and ask about the rules, and even retrieve the ball.' Bertram related to Ruth before setting off for school. 'There's no real wicket or boundary,' he explained, 'so the ball can stray off the playing field if the batsman is going for a six.'

'Yes, I see.' Ruth imagined the incongruous sight of a group of French boys, albeit not dressed in white, standing around the stumps being directed by her over zealous son.

'One man asked me how to throw the ball, so I showed him, bringing my hand up by my ear, pacing out the steps, and stretching out my left arm to line up the throw onto the wicket. I told him some of the rules, which he said had been a mystery to him, and how we scored. He asked me what a French boy was doing playing an English game. I told him that I was only half French. 'Which half?' he asked me.'

'What did you say?' asked his Mother.

'I said I wasn't sure because my Mother was English but cricket was a man's game.'

'Yes,' Ruth paused, 'did he say anything else?'

'He said...' Bertram tipped his head to one side and bit the end of his tongue as he tried to remember, 'he said, he had always wondered how a boy with an English Mother and a French Father would turn out.'

Ruth had mulled over that phrase so many times since then that she had convinced herself that Jean-Paul had spoken to her.

'So why are you not taking your cricket bag this year?' She asked. It seemed a pity since this was his last term at the junior school. Bertram fussed over the strap of his kit bag, his cheeks rather reddened by embarrassment.

'One boy got hit on the head. You know what French mothers are like, their sons are so precious. We were told that the game was too dangerous. Cricket is forbidden.'

Ruth had to accept that this route to Jean-Paul, had it ever existed, would serve her purpose no longer and as she waved Bertram off at the dockside, Veeve's observation seemed to mock her.

'How do you think Bertram can grow up as a Englishman if he keeps going back to Paris. Ruth, what are you doing to the boy? You were scathing enough about Ronald when he returned with you from France.'

Ruth had silenced Veeve with a look which reminded Veeve of their pact. Neither of them, if they were frank, wanted a second estrangement. It irritated Ruth, however, to have to acknowledge that there was some foundation in Veeve's taunt, yet she dealt with the problem by procrastinating. There was a whole term before a senior school for Bertram would have to be chosen. Besides, there had been a welcome distraction. Bett told her a remarkable piece of news.

'It's Maisie, she's going to have a child. Adopt one. It always seemed so hard that she never married, but now at least she can have a baby of her own.'

'Bett, what are you telling me?' Ruth asked.

'It's Maisie's housemaid. She and a cook from another hotel were sweet on each other and had a baby. The maid came to Maisie in tears not knowing what to do because she couldn't afford to keep the baby. Then she said that she and the cook have been offered a very good placement in a large hotel, and what was she to do? So Maisie said that she would adopt the little girl.'

'Maisie really offered to have the baby?'

'Yes, I think it is wonderful.'

'Bett, you always think anything to do with children is wonderful. How do you suppose that Maisie will manage.'

'Maisie is extremely capable,' Bett said robustly and failed to see the slight droop of Ruth's shoulders at the implied inadequacy of her own capabilities.

Ronald offered to drive Ruth and Bertram down to the coast to see Maisie's new baby. Ronald had no particular interest in babies but he had bought a new car and saw this as an excuse for a run. His Aunt Ruth, he suspected, would scold him for his extravagance, but if a chap has been left a handsome legacy he would be a fool not to enjoy it. He had great respect for his Aunt and he preferred her company to his mother's. This knowledge softened any rebuke. Ronald was assured of Ruth's affection if not her approval and he enjoyed the hero worship that he saw in young Bertram's eyes.

Maisie took Ruth, Ronald and Bertram through to the rear of the the Hotel where she had her private apartment and into the nursery.

'She's called Catherine, but I like to call her Catkin. It's a pretty name for a spring baby.'

Although both Ronald and Bertram were used to hotels and the restrictions on their movements in consideration of the guests, they were soon bored by the sisters' conversation, which revolved around a silent and motionless child.

Before long Bertram was fidgeting and Maisie suggested that Ronald take him down to the beach. 'I keep an old cricket bat in the hall, and you'll find a ball somewhere in the umbrella stand,' she called after them.

'Does Catkin have a father?' Bertram asked Ronald as they crossed the street.

'No. Aunt Maisie has adopted her because her parents couldn't look after her.' Ronald explained.

'That means that none of us have fathers. What happened to yours? Did he die?'

'Mother divorced Father soon after I was born. He's not dead, at least I don't think he is, but I've never seen him. What about your Father?' Ronald parried.

'I don't know. Mother has never told me so I have never asked. I think he must be dead.'

Ronald hesitated and then he said, I met your Father.'

Bertram appeared less interested than Ronald had expected, but he asked politely. 'What was he like?'

'He was exactly how a father ought to be,' Ronald replied.

The end of the academic year drew to a close and Ruth made arrangements for Bertram to be enrolled the following September at Ronald's old boarding school. She told Bett that she had decided that if Bertram was going to grow up in England he had better become an Englishman.

She was in her office listening with half an ear for her son who was to return from Paris at the end of his last term, when she heard the door of a taxi slam. Bertram run up the steps, through the lobby, and burst through her door. He looked particularly long and lanky in his short trousers, with arms too long for the sleeves of his jacket and wool socks that barely reached his knees. His hair had been cut neatly exposing his rather prominent ears and accentuating his thin neck. Ruth looked up and saw only his brilliant blue eyes and his wide generous smile.

'Mother I'm home! Shall I ask the porter to leave my trunk in the hall or would you like it taken upstairs?' Bertram kissed the top of his Mother's head and hurried on. 'I need to change out of my school uniform. Goodbye to short trousers. Do you know what my uniform will be like at my new school? When is the next cricket match? Is Ronald going to come and see us? And here's a letter from Marie.' Without waiting for a reply to any of his questions Bertram dashed out of the office. Ruth smiled fondly. If she waited patiently she would hear all his news. In the meantime she opened the letter.

Marie wrote that she understood Ruth's decision. Bertrand's years at the lycée were over as it was time for him to move to the senior school. He had to become either fully French or fully English but she and Henri were saddened at his departure because Bertrand had added such lustre to their lives.

Without Bertram and the excuse that she needed to accompany him, or to see his school, there was no longer a valid reason for Ruth to return to France, and besides it was too painful for her when all she had was hope. Reluctantly she closed all doors in that direction to enable Bertram, with a public school education, to become a young English boy. The die was cast. There was no longer any pretence that Bertrand's presence in France might provide the answer to the enigma of Jean-Paul.

On the first evening of every school holiday Ruth arranged to have supper alone with Bertram. The end of term had involved several leaving rituals, the climax had been Speech Day when the staff, the parents, and all the pupils, assembled in the school Hall.

'This year the speaker and prize giver was General Pétain, you know, the war hero? Last year do you remember I got a certificate for History? They still don't have too many cups because they were lost in the war.

There was a new one this summer given by an anonymous donor.'

'Yes,' said Ruth, happy to listen to her son for as long as he wanted, 'what cup was that?'

'It was quite different from all the others, not like a cup but more like a vase. Like the one on your mantelpiece. They called it the Saint Cloud Cup. It's a place near Paris, did you know?'

Ruth became very still. Bertram chattered on oblivious of the effect on his mother.

'What subject was the Saint Cloud cup awarded for?'

'For the pupil who comes top in English.'

Bertram seemed to remember something and sat with his fork poised.

'An embarrassing thing happened just before they were going to give out the St Cloud cup. The base came away and a piece of paper fell to the ground. So I picked it up. They reassembled the cup and then presented it.'

'Can I see it?' Ruth asked in an unsteady voice.

'I didn't get that cup,' Bertram saw that his mother was disappointed, 'I got another one. I came top in French.'

Ruth looked at her son, registered his innocence and knew that his future was now determined, and with this knowledge she experienced a heavy sensation which spread through her body and concentrated on her heart, sealing it and encapsulating it forever.

She managed, despite feeling choked, to ask, 'That piece of paper you picked up, did it have any writing on it?'

'Yes. Just two words.'

Ruth felt a thud in the pit of her stomach and barely able to breathe she asked, 'What were they?'

'Madder Red.'

Book Three

Prussian Blue

1919-1939

Chapter Twenty-Six

The only sound audible to Jean-Paul were his footsteps as they struck the pavement. The sound was confused with that of the thumping in his chest. He walked with no particular direction in mind, the turmoil of his emotions blocked out coherent thought. After some time the rhythm of his feet settled the rate of his heart and he was more able to focus on his situation. He had, he decided, no more than twelve hours in which to make a start on his pursuers. This urgency erased any retrospective regrets or overwhelming misery and forced him to concentrate on his immediate plans.

There was, in effect, only one place to go. He ran his fingers through the coins in his pocket calculating how many francs he possessed. He resisted the urge to increase the pace of his walking for fear of drawing attention to himself. Within an hour he had turned into the forecourt of the Gare du Nord and bought a ticket for the last train to Strasbourg. He could afford to travel as far as Metz, leaving him a few coins for food, arriving there early in the morning and from that point onwards he would have to rely on lifts.

Jean-Paul picked up a discarded newspaper from a bench and, adopting the air of someone who travelled regularly, climbed into the carriage that drew up directly opposite to where he was standing. He chose a seat by the window, sat down and when two men entered became engrossed in the centre pages. The first, wearing a suit of reasonable quality, lifted his briefcase onto the overhead rack and took a book out of his pocket. The other, an older man from the artisan class, took a somewhat battered baguette from out of a crumpled brown bag and began to eat. Neither showed any intention of communicating which was a relief, and once the train was underway and the conductor had passed down the corridor, Jean-Paul folded his paper onto his lap and closed his eyes. He never expected to sleep, certain that he would spend the night turning possible options over in his mind, but after the briefest of speculation as to what Ruth might be thinking, and closing his mind to imagining his small son in his bed, he woke with a start and realised that he had indeed slept, and that the train was stationary. The dimly lit platform clock showed him that it was two o' clock, and that his fellow travellers had nodded off.

How vigorously would they chase him, he wondered. Was the tribunal empowered to issue warrants and to alert a network of police in order to pursue one war criminal? Now that hostilities had been over for nine months would his escape be considered a high priority? He had to assume that some effort would be authorised to trace him, and he needed to anticipate which avenues they would use. A few telephone calls could alert police officers and station masters. An immediate investigation would soon ascertain that he had not used his own vehicle and that he had no luggage and discreet calls to the main banks would inform them that he had not accessed his account.

Despite his anxiety to put distance between himself and Paris, he decided to alight a stop before reaching Metz where there was less chance of an official being on the look-out for him. Once he was on country roads he was unlikely to be identified since many people relied on lifts in these post war days, and those with transport tended to be sympathetic.

Jean-Paul was concocting a story to explain himself to whoever he might encounter once he left the train, when he dozed again. This time he was roused by the opening of the carriage door. The newcomer had the eager, bustling manner of one accustomed to rising early, and his efforts at conversation were targeted towards the man with the briefcase. They exchanged a few words while Jean-Paul shifted his position so that his face was averted and his gaze directed out of the window. In this way he could keep an eye on the names of the passing stations and avoid being drawn into the conversation. Later he left the carriage to wait in the corridor until his destination. He did not want to find himself caught unawares. To those habituated to the journey, as he had attempted to portray himself, a hurried departure would be an occasion for comment, and might later, should any of them be questioned, set the law on his tail.

Jean-Paul hoped that by heading towards his homeland as the obvious route of escape, this might by some peculiar machination of reasoning, be the last place that they would look. Perhaps a perfunctory search, resulting in the knowledge that his family and their land were both destroyed during the war, would persuade them to abandon Alsace, and look elsewhere. Such was his hope, but, in reality he had no other option. Only by finding Max, who he had so fortunately encountered earlier in the year, had he any chance of gaining assistance in his effort to escape.

He was overtaken by a farmer heading for market and then handed to another who was delivering livestock further along the route. His story seemed to be accepted. Instead of devising a tale whereby he was leaving Paris, he made out that he had been on a trip in search of work and had underestimated the time needed to catch the return train. A night on the platform explained his dishevelled appearance. He had received only gruff acknowledgements, reticence being acceptable in a country where people were accustomed to keep themselves to themselves. The experiences of the previous years under occupation had taught everyone that knowledge could be dangerous, and it was not a habit that would easily be discarded.

Jean-Paul sat on the parapet of the bridge over the river and ate a section of the loaf that he had purchased on arrival in Strasbourg. It was high summer and the city dwellers were enjoying their opportunity to promenade, a freedom that they had been unable to indulge under German occupation. No-one glanced at Jean-Paul, which gave him some temporary peace of mind, and he decided that he could safely go in search of Max without delay.

Max was overjoyed at seeing him and did not question him. Later, however, when Jean-Paul suggested that they walk by the canal so that they could speak alone, he became aware of how extraordinary his sudden appearance must seem. However, it was Jean-Paul who took the initiative and who began to probe Max with regard to his war experience.

'How was it that you were not called up?' Jean-Paul asked.

'Here in Alsace we were in no man's land and yet were in the thick of it,' Max explained. 'We were occupied immediately at the beginning of the war, and so we were unable to respond to France's call, yet it was unthinkable that we should fight for Germany. Many were sent to Germany to work, but I stayed on the farm and waited to see what would happen. I reasoned that if they sent us all away there would be no-one to provide food, either for them or for ourselves. The problem was a large one because more and more troops were arriving and the Commandant was having to rely on supplies from inland Germany. I took matters into my own hands and requested an interview with the senior officer responsible. The junior officers were undecided how to treat someone who spoke their language and yet was the enemy, and were reluctant to let me pass, but I persisted and eventually one of the guards, irritated I expect, thought that it was the only way to deal with me. I suggested that I might be useful by staying on the farm and, with the co-operation of neighbouring farmers, ensure food supplies. Once the system was in place subsequent officers accepted it. This then allowed me to start running the organisation as I wanted, and as the war progressed and I could see that our people were receiving less and less, I found ways around it.'

'How did you do that?' Jean-Paul asked, impressed at his friend's initiative.

'There are farms, like your own, that are relatively remote and inaccessible except by footpaths, and situated within vast areas of forested land. These create natural barriers and the paths to them are known to us but not to the enemy, nor were they interested, so long as we provided their supplies. We made sure that there were flocks of sheep in these remote areas, and that cattle were allocated to different locations so as to make accountability difficult. We ploughed up fields forpotatoes and turnips that the villagers would be responsible for cultivating. We managed. No one ate well but we staved off starvation.'

'What about now? Why do you live in Strasbourg?'

Max, his parents and his married sister were all living together in the town.

'They burnt our house before leaving,' Max spoke in a flat tone devoid of emotion. 'Without the extra labour provided by the army to work the farms it is impossible to tend the land.' He trailed off. 'You know how quickly the land reverts.' Max looked, and sounded, as if he was beaten by the events of those years. He and his family now survived on what they could grow on a small part of the land that they had tilled earlier in the year. 'We plan to buy a cow, or pig and some sheep, but we are uncertain how to husband them in the winter. We'll have to construct a shed, but there is little hope that there will be enough fodder for the animals to survive over the winter.'

Jean-Paul judged that Max's situation was sufficiently dire for him to seek work elsewhere and might be ready to listen to his plan. However, he ran the grave risk of alienating his friend if he confessed his circumstances. If for any reason Max disbelieved him, then his route from the authorities was effectively barred and that was if he did not immediately hand him over. He expected Max was waiting with only barely concealed curiosity for him to reveal his history. He had evaluated Max's situation, and now he was to be evaluated in turn, but inevitably with suspicion.

'Are you in trouble?' Max asked.

Recent years had taught people to observe before speaking or committing themselves to confidences. Where no suspicions were harboured, it was a measure of respect for whatever personal ordeals had been endured, to be reticent. Yet even where there were doubts, silence was often the best policy.

Jean-Paul looked furtively around him.

'Walk this way, we'll go beyond the bridge, it's quieter there.' Max took him by the elbow and guided him down a side street towards the water. They passed a boulangerie where they bought some bread and, once they had found the place that Max considered safe, ate hungrily while propped against the canal wall.

Eventually Jean-Paul spoke. 'Nothing is ever what it seems in war. There is no obvious right or wrong. I was caught up in a web of deceit and it looks to all the world as if I betrayed my country. I pray that there are a few people who know me who will believe that I am incapable of doing so.' The facts seemed so stark when put into words. Starting with his work in the silk trade and how it led to links with munitions, he told Max how his work went mainly undercover so as to reduce the chances of information leaking to the enemy.

'But information of our operations did become disclosed to the Germans. Someone was passing and receiving information. I suspected this towards the end of the war but we were working such long hours that I did not have the opportunity to investigate thoroughly. The authorities held a tribunal. I had to flee here.'

'You mean that they accused you?' Max gasped incredulously.

'To save his own skin my subordinate turned the heat on me. They found other so-called evidence that they said corroborated it, they even used our visit here in January against me.'

Max asked, 'And Ruth? And your boy?'

'I have deserted them. What else could I do? Drag them down with me?' Jean-Paul tugged at his bread but ate none. He did not have to wait for Max's verdict.

'You can stay with us, but it is better that our neighbours do not see you. You must pretend to be delivering something. I'll work it out. Come to us at nightfall.'

Jean-Paul was barely able to absorb what he was being told except to register that Max did not question the veracity of his story. Suddenly overcome with tiredness he allowed his friend to take control. After a short discussion Max arranged that they would meet later that day at the market square. There, Max would hand over a parcel which, once it was dark, he would bring with him to the house. Max instructed him to take a circuitous route and to try and arrive at the house unnoticed. Should he be observed Max hoped this would provide a legitimate reason for calling.

Late that evening Max opened the door and Jean-Paul slipped into the house. Max's concern was then to prevent his sister's two children from knowing of his presence and he asked Jean-Paul to leave at first light. He gave him a rug and showed him an armchair.

'Sleep here tonight. I'll leave you a parcel of food for the morning. Tomorrow we will meet again in the square.'

Jean-Paul had barely relaxed his guard since leaving Paris. It was as if the whole episode had a timeless quality. Feeling safe for the first time he fell into a deep sleep.

At around midday the next morning Jean-Paul sat on the steps of the Church and ran his hand over his chin. He had woken while the house was still in darkness and had washed and shaved before leaving, because a man with two days of stubble would be conspicuous. He had spent the hours reacquainting himself with the town, curious to see which businesses were flourishing, and what produce the market had on sale. He ambled with the rhythm of the townsfolk, milling amongst the workers as they followed their morning routes. He passed children as they dawdled on their way to school, he merged with office workers and smartly dressed women, until finally he slowed his pace and found his way to the central square. Here he watched mothers with their baskets gathering together at the market stalls to greet one another or passing the time of day with the vendors. From his vantage spot he idled away the time observing the tables in the cafés beginning to fill with elderly men taking their coffee and brandy, lighting pipes and reading newspapers. Others, with no work to go to, sat around him on the steps and he merged into anonymity.

There was a noticeable absence of young men and, in Jean-Paul's opinion, a lack of attractive girls. The young people, who had been ill fed and deprived for so long would be unlikely to regain their health and vitality for some time yet, and he felt a surge of anger at all the unnecessary suffering as a result of the war. When he spotted Max, his friend was remarkable only in so far as he blended in.

Max guided him to a café and chose a table against a

wall some distance from the pavement so that they could not be overheard. Neither man was willing to break the silence and begin their discussion. Jean-Paul eventually started by apologising. 'This is a great imposition, Max. I can't even pay for my coffee.'

Max shook his head and dismissed the need for an apology. 'You could say that perhaps your arrival is timely. I was not sure that I could go on much longer as things are, and there was no one to talk to.'

Jean-Paul felt encouraged and the schemes over which he had ruminated the previous day tumbled out. 'It was instinct that drove me here but my greatest need is to work, and to work where no questions will be asked. France is closed to me. Besides, work is hard to come by.' Max grunted in agreement. 'I thought about all our ideals, of how it would be after the war, how we would build a better country, but then I realised that there are no jobs for us, and moreover, I begin to understand the reason.'

'And they are?' Max prompted.

'When they made the arrangements for peace and reparation they little thought that by squeezing Germany dry we would deprive ourselves of vital employment. We insist that Germany pays in kind and what happens? She pays in coal and other commodities, borrowing money so as to reopen her collieries and factories, and then our market is flooded. They can sell their products because they can undercut ours.' He gave Max a few moments, nervous about the impact of the plan that he was ready to propose. 'The work, Max, is to be found in Germany. No-one is going to look for me there.'

Jean-Paul looked at Max for his reaction, would he be repulsed by the idea of working for the enemy.

Max nodded slowly, 'I understand your thinking. It's one way of getting our own back. Take their pay, the coal is going to France anyway so we aren't depriving our lads of work. You've quite a point there.' He stirred his coffee and a slight colour appeared in the yellow-tinged skin of his cheeks. He seemed excited by some thought. 'Would you mind if I tried my luck with you?'

Jean-Paul guessed that they would be recruiting labour and that Germany, like France, would have a shortage of able bodied young men but he had doubts about whether Max would be physically strong enough. Max sensed his hesitation.

'I'm fitter than you think. I could manage. We might not even have to go down the mines, there may be other jobs we could do.'

'Not if I don't want to be noticed,' Jean-Paul observed wryly. However the lift to his spirits at the thought of having Max's company prevented him from raising too many objections.

'What about your family?' There was another long silence.

'The only way that I can leave them is with a promise that I will find work. There is no need to say where I am heading. They will assume that I will travel to Lille or Paris. I can transfer money regularly to them and they would be better off than they are now.' Max did not elaborate but Jean-Paul suspected that it was not only financially that his family would benefit. The speed with which he had decided to throw in his lot indicated that he was disenchanted with his peace-time role, and that perhaps his family was too. 'I can organise some papers for us. You'll be Johannes?'

Jean-Paul had not thought that far ahead and appreciated Max's practical mind. 'Can you fix me some clothes?'

Max gave a wry smile before he answered, 'They're not up to much but if you are to revert to being, like myself, an agricultural worker, they'll do. Some dirt under your nails would help. Once I've sorted out our papers I'll find you a bicycle and we'll go to the farm together. I usually spend a night or two in the bothy. You can hide there until we are ready to leave.'

They arranged to meet later in the day and Jean-Paul was once again left alone with his thoughts to walk the streets of Strasbourg. He tried to discipline his mind to concentrate on the present and to allow no analysis of his recent decision. He would not allow himself to imagine Ruth's predicament. There was nothing to be gained by reviewing the past and instead he contemplated the lives of the people he passed. How does a man or woman recover from years of fear. How does the habit of suspicion of the motives of all with whom you come in contact, enforced by the ultimate penalty of losing one's life, disappear. When does a mind that has been beset with anxiety, whose sleep has been disturbed and which anticipates little hope of change, recover. Jean-Paul wondered whether it was because he felt old, although thirty-five was not such an age, that he meditated over subjects that a younger man might not consider.

There was plenty to watch as he forced his tired legs to keep moving. Once, in that life which was now denied him, he would have been content in such a place. Freshly cut flowers in buckets of water were placed on the pavements, clean glass-fronted shops displayed tailored clothes and hats, and the cafés were elegant and recently painted. The war had benefited some, Jean-Paul observed, as it had done in Paris. Children played outside in the blazing summer sun. Their clothes were shabby and their shoes mostly discarded, but their vitality was evident. Singly or in small groups, the elderly sat to supervise their grandchildren. If they were too old to walk or too weary they passed the time in idle conversation. He moved on from the canal to the park, and from the side streets to the square.

The stalls were more or less deserted by late afternoon. He perched on low balustrades or leaned against a wall, but never rested for long. He felt ill clad in his crumpled clothes accentuated by the air of affluence portrayed by the main street which he needed to cross to reach his rendez-vous, and realised with a pang of anguish all that he had lost.

Instinctively he felt in his jacket for his book. He had a habit of carrying one with him, and, finding his pocket empty, was reminded sharply of his present circumstances. He made a mental note to ask Max to bring him one, something in German, he would need to become more familiar with the language. As he walked he recited some poems that he had learnt years before, and in this way he arrived at his meeting place.

Chapter Twenty-Seven

Veeve's return from the continent, after Armistice, was a flamboyant affair. She had telegraphed her parents in advance and the family rallied to welcome her. Somehow it was necessary for the family to spring clean the house, pool coupons to buy and bake, and to seek out old clothes to refashion them. All commodities were in short supply but Veeve's return provided the impetus that the family needed to adapt to post war life, and start exploring opportunities to ameliorate their erstwhile restrictive lifestyle.

There was a certain glamour to be gained among their immediate acquaintances in being associated with a relative who had endured the war on the continent. Eleanor and Elsie dwelt on the possible terrors that Veeve experienced in Spain, so as to gloss over the years of disgrace due to her divorce and the opprobrium surrounding her dissolute life on the Mediterranean shores. Those events had occurred in a time which was remembered only with nostalgia, and because so many women were now left without husbands, they could safely reabsorb her into their social circle.

Although Veeve had exasperated them during her

childhood, until her fortuitous early marriage, her strong personality and infectious vitality had been missed. Her irritating traits had been minimised with the passage of time and her murky past, combined with her irresponsible lifestyle, added an extra frisson to their curiosity.

Veeve orchestrated her arrival with maximum effect. She sent her trunks ahead and after an overnight stay in London she proposed to arrive at midday but indicated that she would require a rest in the afternoon before seeing all her sisters. Eleanor had no choice but to direct that the dust sheets be removed from the dining room, arrange for the silver to be cleaned, and to prepare a menu. This involved organising for food and flowers to be purchased, or at the very least ensure that someone, probably Elsie, was detailed to do so, in order not to disappoint the expectations of her sophisticated daughter.

Elsie, who supported her on all occasions, saw no reason why she should be burdened with all the preparations, and called upon Flo. Flo, her long suffering and devoted older sister, came to stay with her two daughters Nora and Sara who were of an age to be useful. Elsie was not so keen to include her own daughters, Joan and Mary, in the allocation of tasks, but she decided that they could stay up for the family dinner. They were eleven and nine years old and the family thought privately that a little hard work would do them no harm.

Elsie despaired of gaining any help from Lil because she insisted on continuing to work, encouraged by

Henry and consequently was of no use to her. Moreover, she anticipated that Lil and Henry would arrive when all the preparations were completed and then steal Veeve's attention because their City lives were so much more interesting than her own. She felt aggrieved that her war-traumatised husband was now overshadowed by her two brothers-in-law. Neither Flo's husband Tom, who had fought in the war but returned unscathed, nor Henry, who had been spared the fighting due to a defect of his heart, felt anything but affection and respect for Mitchell, but Elsie persisted in maintaining a sense of grievance.

Bett and Maisie could not be excluded. Bett, the quiet, sickly sister had recently had the good fortune to acquire a flat of her own, due to an unexpected increase in her settlement. Except for the short time in Quebec when she was married to Brindsley-Smith, Bett had lived with her parents. She would join them for the evening. She had travelled to Leicester the previous day so as not to be fatigued.

Maisie, their forthright, awkward, but loved youngest sister, on the other hand, could be guaranteed to breeze in at the last moment, determined not to waste a second of her time, while informing them of her recent work with some good cause, and would depart as briskly as she arrived. No one mentioned Ruth whose disappearance in France had been the cause of many months of speculation.

While Veeve was resting, Eleanor and Elsie repaired to the drawing room to restore their equilibrium prior to the influx of their family. Reginald was already ensconced in his armchair engrossed in the newspaper. This would be the largest gathering of the Hefford family since before the war.

'Well, what did you think?' Elsie asked, speaking to neither parent in particular.

Eleanor looked anxiously at Reginald, 'Isn't it lovely to have her home?'

Reginald grunted non-committally, and then seeing his wife's anxious face added, 'Of course it's grand to have Veeve home. I can't think why she stayed away so long.'

Elsie and her father had been the only ones to witness her arrival. 'To be candid,' Elsie observed, 'I am a little disappointed. Veeve is beautifully dressed and chic but I somehow she is a little matronly.'

'Remember, dear, it is fully ten years or more since we saw her.' Eleanor replied.

'Twelve years,' Elsie corrected. 'What can she have in all those trunks?'

'Never ask a woman, Elsie. What I have been asking myself is where is Veeve going to live, and what is she going to do?'

Eleanor interrupted, 'Don't let anything spoil the evening, Reginald. It will all become clearer in time. Have we ever been able to guide Veeve? It is unlikely to change now.'

Veeve delayed her entry to the drawing room until everyone had arrived. Reginald and Eleanor wore relatively formal attire, her sisters, as reflected the new trend, wore tailored frocks while the men were in lounge suits. Elsie's two girls, in their best dresses looked especially pretty while Flo's imitated their mother in a simpler style.

The men gravitated to Reginald where Henry held forth on the evils of the city, a subject that always gratified his relatives. Bett sat in a chair beside her mother, while Lil and Maisie tried to draw the girls into conversation. Elsie flitted around overseeing the final details with the cook, lighting the candles in the dining room, and giving a last touch to the flower arrangements. Their staff were now much reduced and most of the work fell to her.

Veeve swept into the room, her small figure encased in a dress of rich greenized green taffeta, and advanced with outstretched arms towards her Mother. Her sisters moved towards her to receive their kisses and then she delighted the men by greeting them each with the continental custom of a kiss on both cheeks. Finally she descended on her nieces, calling them each by name.

'Now don't all ask me questions at the same time,' Veeve began, speaking to the silenced room. 'Let me get to know you all again. Firstly, Bett.'

The small groups reassembled with relief, suddenly shy and in awe of this self-confident newcomer, until Elsie summoned them to the dining room. She arranged the seating so that Reginald headed the table at one end with Mitchell at the other. She could then ensure that her husband would have his fair share of attention. It was an unbalanced table, due to the preponderance of females, and so she placed Henry and Tom in the centre opposite each other. If Eleanor disliked being displaced by her son-in-law she said nothing, as she was very fond of Mitchell and she knew that it made Elsie happy.

Veeve, sitting on Reginald's right, with Elsie opposite her, sparkled and entertained her father. She gently teased him and softly flattered him, and Eleanor, from a distance watched her husband become more animated than she had seen him for months. Veeve, a master at her art, who had learnt that it was more satisfying to embrace female friends than to antagonise them, used the same magic on Elsie and enmeshed her into her web.

Elsie's eldest daughter Joan listened to her new aunt, entranced, and was finally rewarded for her patience when Veeve turned to her and said, 'I've brought a few presents with me and I am going to need your help.'

Once the ladies had retired Veeve held court as one by one she handed over her gifts. The brightly wrapped parcels in themselves created a festive atmosphere. Her sisters and nieces paraded fans and shawls, purses and slippers and Eleanor exclaimed over everything, but especially over her vanity case, which was made from contrasting colours of silk embroidery.

Nor were the men denied presents. Veeve presented them each with a silk tie. Although she disguised it well she had been considerably shocked by the change in Mitchell. As a child, along with Ruth and Maisie, Mitchell had been the perfect older brother figure, and to see how the war had left him stooped and grey-faced affected her. He sat in one corner of the room and was the last to receive his tie. He half rose to accept it, but Veeve perched on the arm of his chair to single him out for her especial attention.

Maisie was the first to leave and the rest soon

followed until only Bett and her parents remained. Bett was tired. 'I'll walk with you up the stairs,' Veeve said linking arms with her sister.

When they reached her room Bett asked, 'What happened to Ronald?' Veeve was caught off her guard and had no ready reply.

'I don't know,' she answered and paused to give herself time. Whatever she said now she would have to live with. She had anticipated the need for an explanation regarding her abandonment of Ronald, delivering a story that set her in a good light, but she was unable to fabricate where Bett was concerned.

'When war broke out Ronald was with Ruth in France and I had gone briefly to Spain. It was not possible to cross the frontier.' Veeve warmed to her tragedy yet avoided a direct lie. 'Ruth, it seems, could not make her way to join me. I never heard from her again.'

Bett gave her sister a hug and Veeve used that moment to leave for her own room before Bett probed further.

Downstairs Eleanor and Reginald were finally alone.

'What did you discover, Reginald?'

Reginald looked surprised, 'Discover? What about? We had a most entertaining evening.'

'About Ronald. About Spain or where ever it was Veeve was living for five years. Reginald you are exasperating. Surely she said something?'

Reginald was bemused. 'Oh. No. Nothing like that, we just had a charming evening. Elsie is never as amusing. She's like a tonic, our Veeve.'

'We certainly have missed her,' she conceded, but

could not resist adding, 'but I wonder what dance she is going to lead us now.'

'Clever little minx,' said Henry to Lil as they discussed the evening. Henry had not had much opportunity to know Veeve prior to his marriage. He had, early on, sensed that Veeve was both attractive and manipulative, but that had not prevented him from being intrigued and he had been as eager as Lil to travel to Leicester.

'What makes you say that?' Lil said and grinned as she slipped her hand into the crook of his elbow.

'Did you notice that none of us are any the wiser as to where she has been, nor why she decided to return now?'

'How right you are,' agreed Lil, 'unless she has told Father.'

'That's not likely. Did you notice how she flirted with him? There were no secrets divulged at that end of the table I guarantee. She has class, I give her that.'

'And I have none?' teased Lil.

'I wouldn't want you to have that kind of class.'

No similar conversation took place between Elsie and Mitchell, and Elsie was unaware that she had been hoodwinked. Her only comment was in regard to her father. 'Isn't it a shame that Father only has granddaughters, as if it wasn't enough that his infant son died. What do you think happened to Ronald? And what about Ruth?'

'Perhaps Ruth feels that Veeve's ban from England also applied to her. I must talk to Henry, between us we might hear more from Veeve.'

'Would you do that, Mitchell,' Elsie said happily, 'now that Veeve has returned, Father seems to have relented and is pleased to have her home.'

Tom and Flo had their chance to discuss the evening once the girls had gone to bed. Nora and Sara had talked about their gifts for almost the entire journey home. Never had they seen such exotic craftwork. Flo felt sad that for most of their young lives her daughters had been deprived of the chance to wear party dresses, cheerful coloured jumpers or have small extravagances such as sweets or toys. She smiled to herself as she remembered Veeve at the same age, needing to be the centre of attention, wanting to shock, and enlivening every occasion.

'That was good of Veeve, wasn't it Tom, to find presents for Nora and Sara as well,' Flo said.

'It was nice of her to include us men too, but when do you think I'll be sporting a silk tie? What do you think she will do? I mean, it is not so bad being divorced now that there are so many women on their own. People will probably assume she's a widow.'

'She won't be working in a shop, not Veeve. She is used to the high life. I wonder if she realises that everything has changed in Britain.'

'I expect she'll go to London,' pronounced Tom.

Veeve had no intention of upsetting her family and had, in fact, a definite plan for her future. 'Father you do not need to fuss about me. I have decided that I shall buy a hotel. You and Mitchell can help me but I have lots of money. You can't really spend money during a war so I have saved, enough for a hotel in a smart area of London. Prices are still low and I need a home and to be in the swim of things.'

'Have you any idea about running an establishment like that, how to engage staff for example,' asked her mother.

'I have lived in enough hotels in my life,' Veeve declared, 'I should be able to run one.'

'Well my dear, we will help you in every way we can, if you are certain that you can afford it.' After a lengthy pause Reginald added, 'I am sure it will be a great success.'

'Who will come to your hotel? You won't know who they are or where they've come from.'

'Don't worry Mother. I have plenty of friends who flit from capital to capital, following the races or regattas or the London season. Top class types, you know, and there is always someone with money, whatever the general impression of hardship. They will come once they hear.'

'Really?' exclaimed Eleanor, 'then I hope you know what you are doing and keep a good business head on your shoulders.'

'I'll tell you what I'll do, Mother, to reassure you, I'll ask Henry to do my accounts, and he will keep me right. Does that satisfy you?'

Not many weeks later Veeve, Mitchell and her father, signed the papers for the new property. Mitchell cautioned her not to launch into extravagant alterations too soon. People in London, he advised, were still accustomed to faded wall paper and thinning upholstery, and were tolerant towards minor defects in the bathrooms. If Veeve created the right atmosphere and ensured her food was palatable, she could progress in due course. With some regret Veeve acquiesced since it was her natural instinct to be ostentatious.

What her hotel lacked in that respect Veeve amply made up with her presence. She handed over the management of her hotel and set about attracting the set of people she had socialised with for most of her life. She saw no difficulty with being the hostess where her guests were expected to pay. She made no secret of the fact that she was a divorcee, since no one would be enticed by the picture of a meek and sorrowing widow, and she maintained that the mystery of her past and her brazen stance added to her appeal.

Chapter Twenty-Eight

When Ruth arrived in Leicester with Ronald and Bertram none of Veeve's sisters was anxious to be the one to inform her. Veeve was regarded with more than a little awe and her quick tongue was a weapon that they attempted to avoid. Besides, they felt some restraint when they tried to envisage how they themselves would react to the sudden appearance of a child who had for a long time been presumed lost.

Veeve's sisters were, in varying degrees, critical of

her lack of demonstrative emotion regarding her son, and the reluctance she had shown to ascertain how Ronald had disappeared. They understood that France had undergone upheavals which were inconceivable to the inhabitants of England, and assumed that it would be possible for someone to be buried, if not physically, then figuratively, but now that Ronald was alive and well their sense of indignation on his behalf was roused.

Mitchell was detailed to convey the news. The choice had been tacitly agreed once Elsie suggested that her husband had always been entrusted with family affairs. This was one such occasion, and Mitchell himself felt that he alone could contain the feelings that were threatening to surge against Veeve. Although as a lawyer the family respected him, it was because they had witnessed the gentleness of touch with which Veeve habitually interacted with her battle-scarred brother-in-law that they delegated the task to him. Histrionics made no impact on Mitchell and ensured that when he imparted the news to Veeve there would be none.

Veeve was visibly shaken as the impact of the imminent arrival of this lost child caused her to betray a rare emotion.

'What shall I do?' she asked.

'Aren't you pleased?' he asked patiently.

'Of course I am pleased, what do you take me for, Mitchell? But I have a hotel. This is an adult environment. It is no place for a thirteen year old.'

Mitchell nodded, but Veeve suspected that her upstanding brother-in-law had only a bare conception of the late nights, eccentricities, and noisy parties conducted by her guests. He did, however, have some experience of children and mentioned that many of their contemporaries sent their sons to board at school. Some even sent them to the Navy.

'It seems a bit extreme to send a boy away to the Services now that he has arrived home, but boarding at school is a possibility. Besides, he can always spend time with Ruth in the holidays.'

Veeve was undergoing some turmoil and disliked herself for it. She was prepared for most situations, but this was one she had not reckoned with. She was ambivalent towards her son although she recognised that her attitude was only experienced by a minority of women. She felt that it was too simplistic to attribute it to his association with George, but suspected that if she and George had not parted under such agonising circumstances, Ronald might have featured more highly on her agenda. As it was she was not naturally maternal and she had grown into the picture that she had painted of herself as a society hostess. To create a new portrait as a sorrowful mother would have been counterproductive in the early days, but how was she to react now?

When Veeve finally saw Ronald she was more than delighted. He stood beside Mitchell in the doorway of the drawing room, and she gave a satisfied sigh at his appearance. How could she have doubted that he would be handsome.

'Ronald, here is your Mama,' Mitchell introduced them somewhat formally. Ronald came forward to shake hands, but Veeve adopted the French fashion and kissed him on both cheeks.

'Hello, Mother,' Veeve noticed his heavy French accent.

'Don't go, Mitchell, we'll need your help. Where is the boy staying?' She checked herself. 'Où habites-tu?' She addressed Ronald.

'Chez grand-mère.'

'Bien sûr,' said Veeve. She turned to Mitchell. 'I'll need time to find a room for Ronald. Can Mother keep him a bit longer?' She continued in French. 'Would you like to see round my hotel, and perhaps choose a room?'

Veeve started on a tour of her premises, and introduced Ronald to the members of her staff. On each occasion the news was greeted with some emotion, but Ronald seemed strangely quiet and she attributed it to his obvious admiration of her establishment.

On his first day in the care of his mother some guests volunteered to take him with them on an excursion. Soon all Veeve's guests were vying with each other to entertain him, and she decided that her fears were unfounded. Ronald was easy to please and his enthusiasm for places of interest around London, the variety of activities and his burgeoning obsession with motor cars, made the task gratifying. His progress in English was rapid and he was keen to learn.

'We had better make an appointment to fit you for your school uniform,' Veeve announced towards the end of August.

'What will I wear at my school?'

Veeve described the blazer, tie, cap, and long trousers. She then went on to recite, sportswear, towels, pyjamas and a trunk.

'Why do I need a trunk?'

'To put your clothes in. Each boy has a trunk, and a tuck box. The tuck box is filled with sweets and biscuits. I'll get cook to bake you some.'

'Do boys sleep at school in England?'

Veeve looked at her son and saw a foreigner. She had expected Mitchell to explain about boarding school.

'Yes,' she said smoothly, 'you'll enjoy it. You will make lots of friends of your own age. The school is not far away. You will come home in the middle of the term.'

Ronald was not unhappy at his new school. Initially he was bewildered by the quantity of rules, and the inexorable pace of the school time table which dictated his lessons, preparations, sports, meals and bedtimes in a way that made him think nostalgically of the Cuanez. In many ways it was easier to fit to this new environment, than into the fickle world of his mother's, however much he had enjoyed being spoilt by well-meaning adults. He was passably good at games which he soon realised was an advantage as those with less ability were disparaged by the dominant set. He was accepted into a group of boys and although the others in his year soon uncovered his aptitude for music, this was accepted as an allowable eccentricity. None of the boys talked about their homes so the absence of a father, although a relatively common affliction among his contemporaries, was no handicap. Most boys were more interested in the make and model of their family's car and here Ronald could hold his own, since Veeve always insisted in having the latest model.

Hugh, one of Ronald's friends, asked him to stay during the summer holidays. Ronald was introduced to a style of living that he only guessed at from his observations of the guests at the hotel. The household had all the same services but they were delivered by the family's servants. Hugh's mother was free to entertain, or to go out, or to play tennis or golf with her son whenever she wished.

'It's too bad that we can't shoot,' Hugh said to Ronald on the first morning of his visit. 'It's the wrong time of year, but we might be able to go fishing if you want.'

On the lawn in front of the house a collection of people were playing croquet.

'They are all Mother's friends,' Hugh explained. 'I usually go this way,' and he led Ronald along a gravel path towards a yew hedge which hid a formal rose garden. From there they exited by a iron gate towards an orchard where the grass was unkempt, the fences were more utilitarian and clambering over a style, they landed in a field. Ronald could not remember ever having seen such space, such an expanse of fields and woods and sky.

'Come on,' Hugh called, 'I'll show you where we swim.' He ran ahead and then disappeared down the side of the wood. Trees were overhanging a bend in the river and when Ronald caught up with him Hugh had already stripped to his underwear.

'It is only deep in the middle. You can feel the rocks under your feet.' Ronald entered gingerly until he stood waist deep in the cold water. At that moment Hugh launched himself to swim to the further bank, and Ronald followed suit without giving himself time to think. Gasping, he scrambled to find his footing, stumbled and laughed. It was the most exhilarating feeling he had experienced. Hugh looked surprised, but finding Ronald's elation infectious, challenged him. 'I'll race you back.'

'Where have you two been?' Hugh's mother asked affectionately when the boys reappeared. 'There's almost no tea left,' she teased, and she handed each boy a plate with a generous slice of Madeira cake. 'Drink? Orange, or lemon?' She smiled at Ronald. 'Hugh never takes tea. Do you?' Ronald was content to do whatever Hugh did and unused to being in a large family began to enjoy his visit.

The boys were left to their own devices for a large part of the time and joined the adults for meals. Occasionally they were included in excursions, or, when it rained, schooled in the rules of billiards.

'We aren't allowed to play on our own. Father says that we would scuff the baize and then the table would be ruined.' Ronald understood, from the awe in Hugh's voice, that this would be a serious offence, though he was unsure how the crime could be committed. It was also the first time that Hugh had mentioned his father. Ronald's world had had such a singular lack of fathers that he was surprised at the nonchalance with which Hugh talked of his. He did not like to inquire further, but a few days later the even temper of the household changed and Ronald discovered that this disruption was due to the imminent arrival of Hugh's father.

The hours between five and seven o'clock were designated for the young as a time to amuse themselves, while the adults changed. Ronald had discovered the library and after much deliberation chose a book from the history section. Taking it up to his room he continued to read until Hugh came in to fetch him for dinner.

'Why aren't you ready?'

Ronald looked up blearily from his comfortable position. 'Is there a hurry?'

'When Father's here we cannot just drift downstairs at the gong like we do with Mother, and we have to be dressed and wear a tie. Do come on, Ronald.'

The boys arrived as his father was escorting his wife from the drawing room, and the other guests were pairing up.

'There you are, you scallywags. Introduce me to your friend.'

Towards the end of the meal he seemed to remember Ronald's presence.

'Well, my boy,' he addressed Ronald, 'So you are at school with Hugh? What do you make of it? Are you sporty?' His tone was jovial, but Ronald, seeing all eyes turn in his direction, felt embarrassed.

'Ronald is musical, Father. He even composes.' Ronald gave his friend a grateful look.

'Capital, more sense than running around a playing field. What does your Father do?'

'Ronald does not have a Father.'

'Silly of me, my apologies. The war has a lot to answer for. So, what are your hobbies?'

'Cars,' Ronald blurted out, safe on a topic with which he was conversant.

'Wonderful,' said his host, 'I drive a Lagonda. What about your family?' He turned to the guest on his right. 'We purchase ours from Mintors. And you?' Attention was deflected from Ronald and general conversation continued until the end of the meal, when the young were able to escape.

'Dashed clever of you to talk about cars,' Hugh commented appreciatively once they had left the room, 'the old man is besotted with them.'

'I know nearly all the makes. You learn them from the Players cards. I have eighty-five of them at the moment.'

'Can I see them?'

'They are at my home in London. If you come and stay I could show you.'

At the end of Ronald's visit, Hugh asked his Father for permission to go to London.

'Excellent idea. And where do you live?'

'Mansion Court in Hammersmith.'

'Ah,' Hugh's father's eyes twinkled and he gave a knowing nod, 'you'll enjoy yourself in the metropolis, Hugh. It'll be quite an experience for you.'

Hugh stayed for a week. There had been nothing remarkable about the visit. Veeve had given Ronald permission to go into town, to take his friend for meals or to the cinema. For the most part they had amused themselves, playing cricket on the lawn or cards when it rained. It was when Ronald returned to school that he sensed a subtle change. He saw no sign of it in his friend, but there had been a few snide comments when the boys had discussed their holidays. Gradually Ronald became aware that living in a hotel was not considered quite 'comme il faut.' To have a working Mother was also a topic for scrutiny. Slowly he withdrew into himself in an effort to deflect unwanted attention. There were those who enjoyed inflicting discomfort and Ronald spent increasing amounts of time in the music room.

'Are you spending the day with Ruth again?' Veeve asked Ronald rather tetchily when he'd been home for several weeks of his holiday. 'Why not invite one of your school friends over, like you did last year? You seem to be moping around the whole time. Is it a wonder that you have not been invited anywhere to stay.'

His interest in motorcars enabled Ronald to, once again, interact with the hotel guests. On the fringe of Veeve's most valued, because they were the most moneyed, guests was a slightly older man who claimed to be a relative. When this claim came to Veeve's ears she was at first curious. Later, as his appearances became more frequent and she noticed that he attached himself to her wealthier guests, she became irritated enough to seek him out. This relative proved to be Brindsley-Smith, the estranged husband of her sister Bett, who the family had labelled 'the rotter'. Veeve was too polished a hostess to allow Brindsley-Smith either to be conscious that she was aware of the family connection, or to discourage his visits. She had no choice if she were not to be seen to be discriminating. She was not so sure of her ground when she saw a growing friendship between her son and this distant relative. It started when Brindsley-Smith introduced himself to Ronald.

'I'm an uncle of yours, of a sort.' The remark was covered with a kind of guffaw. 'Take a friendly interest, what? Have some friends with some very fast cars. Like to see them?'

Ronald was enthralled and before long was spending his spare time tinkering with splendid machines, or attending race meetings. Although she could not justify her misgivings, and while admitting that the paternal influence was probably beneficial for her fatherless son, Veeve could not completely bury an unease about this relationship.

Chapter Twenty-Nine

Max procured papers and carrying two small haversacks containing some spare clothes and a supply of food, told Jean-Paul that he was ready for them to set off the following day. All this had taken time and Jean-Paul was glad that the inertia he had been experiencing disappeared with the prospect of work.

Max discovered where the borders were most likely to be porous. Although he was not expecting trouble, he decided that they would board the train at the nearby town of Buhl. They had to walk several miles because they were wary of asking for lifts.

'Why do you want to leave your family and come

with me? I might even be a liability.' Jean-Paul asked.

Max laughed roughly. 'I might be one myself. The Germans tried to make life as uncomfortable for us as they could. They made petty rules, restricted food, but the worst was having soldiers billeted in our homes.'

Jean-Paul tried to imagine the awkwardness, the restraints on conversations, the effect of permanent surveillance and the often uncouth youths with their ill-bred habits.

'They were homesick, you see, and lonely but some were decent. They were hurt that we did not like them. It was difficult to isolate them, especially for my wife who did not spend all her days in the fields as I did. At the end of the war I told her that she better go. To Germany. She could not stay. Everything is known here. People gossip and accusations fly. The Germans ruined every part of our lives.'

Jean-Paul began to see that his tragedy was just one among a multitude.

'I could have borne it all, the strategies to deprive us of food, forcing us to queue for hours, the constant rules governing our lives, if they had left our women alone.'

Once they boarded the train that was creaking through lack of maintenance, both men were preoccupied by their thoughts. They passed many sections of line that were needing or were under construction, and the stations that they passed had no shelter for passengers who stood wearily enduring the cold. Enterprising vendors had set up stalls selling unappetising food, or walked the length of the platform carrying trays of tea around their necks. It was dark when they arrived at a station a few stops after Köln. Here they alighted and spent an uncomfortable night, not visible from the ebb and flow of fellow travellers, in a carriage in a siding. They decided to seek work before finding lodgings.

Max had chosen for their starting point a mining colony around which houses were built by the owners to accommodate their workers. From here they would be within walking distance of the office where recruitment took place and they tagged along behind the morning shift workers to see what developed. They fell into step behind a young lad who was hurrying to join the body of workmen, and engaged him in conversation. Few of the older men looked up, most appeared bent and surly in the half light, but the lad was flushed from exercise and not bowed from years of toil.

'My friend is ill,' the lad informed them, 'I went to wake him because we always walk together, but he called to me that he is sick. The foreman will take it out on me if I tell him and my friend could lose his job.'

'How does the foreman identify you?'

'Are you new around here? We are all recent recruits. He just makes a mark against our name. Like school.' He looked at Max with a grin.

'One of us could take your friend's place. Can you show us what to do? Is it difficult to learn?'

The lad laughed, and then lowered his voice as he attracted the attention of the men around them. 'An imbecile could do my job. Stick with me.' He addressed Max. 'You can wear my friend's overalls and boots. What about you?'

Jean-Paul nodded encouragingly. 'Do it Max. I'll try and take a look at the list. There might be a name that is not marked. I could risk it, if I drop to the end of the queue.'

With the experience of their first day as their credentials Max and Jean-Paul presented themselves to the office on the following day and, as Max Edler and Johannes Barthold, were placed on the pay roll. They did not see their friend again and so were unable to seek his advice regarding accommodation and, after a few days of sleeping rough, took matters into their own hands. Their first week's pay secured lodgings with a middle-aged widow.

Their landlady was morose and grumbled as she showed them to their room, that there was no other option for a woman who had lost her husband and son, and she had no fear of strange men in her house. She later expressed the opinion that the extra income would enable her to live less frugally, and she hoped that they would behave with more consideration than the last good-for-nothing miners she had housed.

After a while, when her lodgers gave her no trouble, she began to show some pleasure as they returned each evening. However neither man communicated with more than a few passing comments, so that whatever interest she might have shown them, soon died.

'Do you hate the Germans?' Jean-Paul asked Max. They were walking through an area that was relatively uninhabited, with no particular direction in mind, but responding to the urge to exercise their bodies in the open air after the week's work in the cramped confines below the ground.

'Do you hate the English?' Max replied.

Jean-Paul nodded in understanding, with the detestable English major in his thoughts. 'You can intensely dislike individuals but as soon as war is over you cannot sustain hate for a whole race. Even in war it is not until you are touched by it personally that hate is added to your reason for fighting. Patriotism is the original motive. It is an outrage that our freedom was assaulted. I cannot hate a whole race. It does not make me anxious to make friends with them however.' Max was not certain whether John-Paul was referring to the English or the Germans. 'Knowing what we have done to each other, it is awkward. At present I do not feel I can trust anyone.'

'I wonder how long we will remain here.'

This gave Jean-Paul a jolt. He had not thought about the future. For him there was only the need to keep living, the why and the where were of no consequence. For Max it was different. He could go home. He had family and friends waiting for him.

'I'm not leaving,' Max reassured Jean-Paul, 'not for a while. The money that I send home is more than I had hoped for. It will set the farm to rights if I stick this out. I'll go back sometime.'

After several months Max did return home but it was only for a visit, he promised Jean-Paul.

'You are on your own, you say, for a few nights.' The landlady attempted to engage Jean-Paul in conversation. So as not to encourage their landlady to pry into their affairs their habit had been to eat in silence. Jean-Paul was taken by surprise.

'You are not from around here, are you?' She asked.

Jean-Paul answered tersely. 'We are from Lübeck.' He focussed his attention on his knife and fork and cut into his meat. The flicker of animation that he had seen was quickly extinguished.

Once the landlady had left the room he found more than his meal to focus on. Why had he said Lübeck? What strange quirk of his brain had remembered that town? A town he had never seen, yet the name conjured up a familiarity. He climbed the stairs to his room and took up his book. Then it came to him. The Count. The south of France. Ruth's sister Veeve and her entourage. Veeve had gone with the German Count to Spain at the outbreak of the war and had left Ronald with Ruth. What would happen to Ronald now? Who would support the kind musician and his wife who had taken him in? Jean-Paul brought himself sharply under control. Speculation was pointless when he was helpless. He took up a book and tried to read.

Max was back and working within the week. Jean-Paul was glad to see him. The hours alone were a trial as he battled to prevent himself dwelling on the past. His eyes were strained with reading, and lack of sleep.

'I have brought you some new books.' Max announced, knowing how pleased his friend would be.

The routine that Max and Jean-Paul established continued for many months. Jean-Paul discovered that the physical exhaustion generated each day and the relentless rhythm of their work helped him to forget. Occasionally Max would return home, coming back with news that they were unlikely to read in the daily papers. Jean-Paul took a day off work here and there to break the monotony and went walking in the nearby forests. When they had been there for around three years Max came back bearing extraordinary news.

'There's a rumour that we are planning to occupy this area, part of the Ruhr anyway. Germany is defaulting on her reparation payments. We thought that our efforts here were helping to pay France back, but instead they have been withholding the money.'

Soon the rumour became a reality but while the northern Ruhr at Essen was occupied, their colliery and its neighbours were not affected. For a while the tenor of their lives was unchanged, however Jean-Paul predicted that if the action extended, occupation might expose his hiding place. Once they were among their countrymen speaking French and with familiar customs they might inadvertently betray themselves.

Jean-Paul was not only worried for himself. He and Max had isolated themselves as far as had been practical from communicating with the men around them, however the close proximity with which they worked meant that they were aware of the mood which had been generated. He saw the bitterness and anger as a consequence of a war which was none of their making. If he and Max were discovered for who they were, they would not be spared from violence.

Jean-Paul disclosed his disquiet to Max. 'Why are we taking this action?' It took Max a moment to realise that Jean-Paul was speaking as a Frenchman. 'We have taken a unilateral stance without either England or

America. This campaign to make an independent Rhineland under our control, where will it lead? France fears Germany, that we know, but how can they fear these miserable creatures?'

Max appeared elated. 'Now we will let them know what they put us through. Now they will feel what it is like to have your country taken over, to be told what to do, to have curfews, and fines, and suffer like we did.'

Jean-Paul was divided in his sentiments. He had not, like Max, endured day to day tyranny.

'Max,' he said wearily, 'is their life so very different from ours? Do you think they wanted the war any more than we did? They are pawns in all this.'

'They are German pawns. They are the enemy. They will always threaten us. Give them an inch and they will take the whole mile. It has always been like this. We should have been allowed to extend our border to the Rhine and then none of this would have happened.'

'If you feel like this, Max, then you will give yourself away. What would happen if you were discovered to be working for the Germans?'

'What would happen to you?' Max retorted.

'I no longer have anything to fear. I belong nowhere and no one belongs to me.'

'Well I do belong. I cannot and will not stay here. I could not contain myself, you are right. I would give myself away. I will take my chances back in France. I cannot understand your tolerance, if I didn't know you better, I would suspect you of German sympathies.'

Max calmed slightly, 'I am going, Jean-Paul.'

'I know.'

'What will you do?'

'I haven't thought. In any case it is probably better that you do not know. Association with me is not to your advantage and someone may yet be searching. There has to be a file on me somewhere.'

'Where is your friend?' Jean-Paul was addressed by one of the miners. He had little interaction with anyone since Max had left and for someone to approach him was unusual. Men at the colliery tended to form small groups with whom they worked and messed together. Max and Jean-Paul had isolated themselves and therefore had not fraternised with other miners.

'You had a friend with you. Is he sick?' Jean-Paul recognised the young lad who had enabled them to find work on their first day. Dusk was falling as they walked away from the mine. The lad began to walk beside Jean-Paul, who did not shrug off his new companion.

'He was called by his family.' Something in Jean-Paul must have touched the boy, perhaps he sensed his loneliness, or recognised a kindred spirit.

'My name is Gustav,' he said, 'I'll look out for you at the break tomorrow.'

It soon became a regular feature of their day that when Jean-Paul sat down at the long wooden trestle table, Gustav would join him. At first, all he was required to do was to listen. Gustav, he discovered, had a young person's energy and his enthusiasm was infectious. Gustav had been unable to go to University due to his family's straightened circumstances, had been too young to be conscripted, and now began to regard

Jean-Paul as his tutor.

'I notice that you always have a book with you. You are reading Goethe's poems. I too enjoy reading.'

Sometime later Gustav asked about French literature. Did Jean-Paul read that too? On discovering that he was, coming from Alsace, a fluent French speaker, Gustav begged to be taught the language. 'I have read Mérimée in translation. We can discuss it tomorrow. And you can start me on my language course.'

The lunch break discussions began to spill over into their walks to and from the colliery, but never as far as Jean-Paul's lodgings. He kept a jealous guard on his anonymity. At no time did Gustav inquire into his tutor's background, treating him with the deference due to a professor by his student. One day, however, when they were out of earshot of the other miners, Gustav introduced a new topic.

'Is there going to be another war?'

'War between whom, and for what reason?' Jean-Paul asked cautiously.

'Well, France against us.' It seemed logical when Gustav stated it. 'I have heard it from the others.' He indicated with a jerk of his head the miners who they had left in the distance.

'You need to look at this from France's perspective. Frenchmen feel that since Germany initiated the war they should pay the price. A sort of forfeit for all the destruction caused. It seems fair enough on paper.'

'But how can we pay? Our infrastructure is in a bad state.' Gustav looked distressed. 'We never wanted the war. I don't know who wanted it. We were all right before. We had work. Our life was peaceful. But, we did start it.' He conceded

'War never benefits anyone except perhaps the money lenders.' Jean-Paul commented.

Not long after this conversation when their colliery was occupied, it was not war that it provoked, however, but dumb insolence.

'Jean-Paul,' Gustav called breathlessly as he hurried after him the day after the occupation. 'We are going on strike! Our leaders are refusing to obey instructions. They say that the government will print money so that we can pay our debts. We'll sort them now.'

'Not so fast, Gustav,' Jean-Paul warned. 'Flooding a country with notes cripples everyone, Germany's economy as well. Money becomes worthless. I'm not sure what to advise you to do, but I shall be seeking work elsewhere. There's no future here and it could take months to resolve. You do not need to be mixed up in it.'

Jean-Paul had not decided that his time in the Ruhr was over until he found himself explaining the stark facts of the present crisis to Gustav. From now onwards he would have to rely on his instincts. He felt an intense homesickness, and whether his course of action was sensible played no part in his decision to seek out Max, and then proceed to Paris.

He gave notice to his landlady and intimated to both her and Gustav that he had opportunities for less arduous employment in Lübeck. He then set off for the station and headed south for Strasbourg.

Jean-Paul clasped his friend by the shoulders, 'Max,

you've changed.' The grey tinge to his skin, exacerbated by their work in the mines where the grime never completely cleared, had gone. His gaunt face had filled out and his eyes seemed to glisten.

Max smiled shyly, 'I am married, Jean-Paul.'

On the site where a shed had once stood there was now a house. Around it the land was well cultivated. Crops had been harvested, grain stored and cattle were grazing on the stubble. Behind the house hay was stacked, there was a cow tethered in the paddock, and a pig in a makeshift pigsty. Jean-Paul and Max crossed the fields until they came to a viewpoint from where he was able to see other developments. Max and his neighbours shared a tractor, helped each other at hay time, and cultivated their joint acreage for greater efficiency.

'I am able to provide for both families. We struggle, but in time I will repay my debts and enlarge the farm.'

'What about your wife, Max?' Jean-Paul was rewarded with a grin.

'She should be home shortly. I have so much wanted you to meet her. You'll like her.' Jean-Paul was glad he was leaving and ignored the stab of misery that shot through him. 'What have you decided to do? Strasbourg? Live here?' Max sounded mildly incredulous.

'I have not taken leave of my senses. Alsace is the least safe place for me to be. I am going back to Paris, but not for long. I will return to Germany. I have a perverse interest in that country now and I can live there without looking over my shoulder.'

Jean-Paul had left the city he loved in a cloud of

confusion but having lived through four years of wartime he wanted the chance to see it how it had recovered. How was his city now. Would his fellow countrymen be striding along their boulevards with pride. Would they have regained the self-esteem that they had lost since their humiliation at the enemy's hands forty years before, so recently that many could still remember it. France had the confidence to advance onto German soil and reclaim what was theirs from their erstwhile oppressors. Would that be reflected in the Paris he was soon to see. Even as he thought along these lines Jean-Paul felt that he walked with longer strides and with renewed energy.

On arrival he walked instinctively in the direction of the apartment that he shared with Ruth. He shrank away from any memories of Bertrand that strayed into his consciousness, and disciplined himself by rationalising that he would no longer recognise his son even were he to see him. Bertrand was no longer a toddler but a boy. Weary with travelling and speculation, he checked into a hotel.

He spent the next day drinking coffee in pavement cafés, indulging in a familiar patisserie, reading the daily papers in his own language, and delaying the moment of reckoning. As dusk fell he approached the street where, in one of the terraced houses, was his apartment People would be returning from work, from a walk in the cooler air, or with purchases for dinner. He might catch a glimpse of his family. He watched for a while from a distance and then, seeing no one around, he walked up the steps to the main entrance and scanned the names beside the doorbells. None were known to him. He turned away abruptly, his heart thumping as it had done before when he had scurried away from this building on that fateful day. He would not visit it again.

Almost without thinking he took the once well-trodden route towards Marie and Henri Thiel. It was to them that he had turned when Ruth needed a place to have her baby, and it was to them that he had instructed Ruth to go if she needed help. They, at least, were unlikely to have moved. Many businesses would have foundered but, Jean-Paul smiled wryly, babies continued to be born and Marie's skill would still be in demand.

It was dark and the weak light from the street lamps enabled him to remain in shadow as he made his way along the pavements until he faced the house. He did not know how long he stood there. The grey building, part of a long impressive terrace with classical windows, each with a set of shutters and wide welcoming doorways, enticed him to draw closer. He saw light through the curtains in the rooms on the first floor. He recognised the position of the study and the drawing room. He waited until they had all been extinguished, and with an empty feeling at having no more insight into Ruth's whereabouts from his day's activities than he had at the beginning of the day, forced his exhausted legs to walk back to his hotel.

Night after night Jean-Paul watched the windows of the house. Once he walked by during the day and ascertained that the house was still a thriving clinic. Marie was indeed working there and taking women for their lying in. Then came the night when Marie, instead of sweeping the curtain across the window as she usually did, stood looking out, holding the drape in one hand. He became aware that the moonlight had caught his face. Marie turned as if to speak to someone in the room. Jean-Paul felt an inexplicable terror. He frightened himself with the realisation of how much he wanted Marie to come to her door and open it. Why was he torturing himself like this? Marie suddenly drew the curtain across and that action, which he interpreted as confirmation that he had been seen, catapulted him into the street. He walked away rapidly with his head down, desolate with the certain knowledge that Ruth was not there.

He cast his mind back over his early months with Ruth, their arrival in Paris as war broke out, Ruth's efforts to arrange for their wedding in England, and her courageous decision to return to war torn France to marry him. His thoughts drifted to the moment that he saw her for the first time pedalling her bicycle, when she returned to Paris and put herself under the friendly wing of Hortense. Hortense, who had, at his request, befriended Ruth, found work for her and attended their wedding. What had become of Hortense? Was it possible that she had heard nothing of his disgrace, he wondered. Could there be one friend that would not reject him? He determined that the very next day he would call on her and risk her condemnation.

Rue de Lappe was a narrow, gloomy street. The buildings on either side tended to occlude the sun, except on the upper stories and only during certain parts of the day. The shutters were bleached of their paint, and the unadorned balconies gave an air of neglect. There was no washing hanging from those balconies, as could be seen in the poorer districts, but neither were there cheerful curtains in the windows or pots of flowers on the sills. This street housed working people whose lives were concerned with surviving on a modest income. Proximity to the busy stations of Gare de Vincennes and Gare de Lyon meant that it was not an area sought after by wealthy Parisians. There was a singular lack of shops or street cafés, the area was purely utilitarian.

Jean-Paul had called at Hortense's previous apartment, the one she had shared with Ruth, and had been fortunate to meet a neighbour who knew of her whereabouts. It had not been a great distance to walk but Jean-Paul was conscious that Hortense must have suffered a down turn in her situation. He spent the afternoon pacing between the Place de la Bastille and the Place Voltaire and at intervals walking the length of the rue de Lappe. He had no wish to startle Hortense by calling at her home, but he hoped to catch her, either leaving or entering the building.

Then he spotted her. He recognised her crisp purposeful walk and, since she was heading away from him, he followed unobserved. Her demeanour would give him some idea whether to risk accosting her. Hortense wore a neat but not stylish suit and carried a small bag which probably contained her evening meal. She looked as if she was returning from a workplace. He confirmed where she was living and then disappeared down a side street. The next day he would wait on the corner and intercept her.

He rose early and stationed himself in good time. Once he was certain that she was retracing her steps from the previous evening, he stepped out. He caught up with her and, taking her arm gently so that there was no reduction in her pace, he said urgently.

'It's Jean-Paul. Don't be alarmed. If you are prepared to speak to me walk straight on. If not, then cross the road and you will never hear from me again.'

He felt her react with a change in her stride. Almost instantaneously she regained her pace and Jean-Paul released her arm. She continued along the pavement and Jean-Paul followed close behind.

'I don't know what you have heard. Whatever it was I assure you it is untrue.'

Hortense did not turn around. 'I heard. It's difficult to suppress such rumours. I was glad you got away. I never understood what happened.'

Jean-Paul was concerned. 'You might not want to be seen with me.'

She dropped back beside him and laughed. 'There is no one around who would know me. We'll meet this evening.'

Hortense was sitting drinking a coffee when Jean-Paul slipped quietly into the seat opposite her. He caught the waiter's eye, gave his order and only when his coffee was on the table did he say, 'Tell me about yourself.'

'I was adrift for several months after the war. I was no longer needed in the factory. I stayed with my family in La Vendée, but I missed the city. Then I made friends with two injured soldiers. I wanted work but I also wanted to find work for them and the only way was to start up my own business. One of the soldiers had worked previously as a cobbler's apprentice, and that decided me. I rented out my flat and with the money could afford to move here, and rent a small site. To begin with we mended boots and shoes, but in time we started to make new shoes. People might not be able to afford much in the way of clothes but they all need shoes.'

'Now you,' Hortense looked up expectantly, and when he had finished she said, 'Why Germany?'

'Because I thought that it would be the last place that they would look.'

'But if they had found you, it would have been difficult to convince them that you were not working on their behalf.'

'I know,' Jean-Paul smiled, 'but I was already condemned.'

'So why have you come back?'

Jean-Paul sighed, 'I am not entirely sure. I will be leaving again soon.'

'For Germany?'

'I can't stay here,' he answered bluntly. 'Ruth's not at Marie's. I hoped that you might have had some communication.'

Hortense shook her head.

'If you hear anything and if you are agreeable, would you contact me? I can't believe that Ruth would cut off all links with France. Ruth was French, she lived here for so long that she would not know how to be English.' Jean-Paul's voice, which had been unsteady, was suddenly infused with conviction.

Hortense took his hand. For some time Jean-Paul

allowed his to rest in hers, and then he gave her hand a squeeze. 'Can you invent a reason for me to visit Count Von Kuder?' He was amused to see her grin with the recollection. 'You remember the Count? What possible mission could I have that would involve me going to Lübeck?

Hortense answered at once. 'I need a buyer. Leather is hard to find, but I understand that already shoe shops in Paris are selling German made shoes. Often they arrive through an intermediary so they appear not to be imported, but that is where they're made. There must be some reasonable tanners in Prussia.' Hortense used the old name for northern Germany. 'Would that work?'

'Apart from the fact that I know nothing about leather or the tanning industry.'

'You could learn.'

'I'll head for the library, the idea has promise.'

Jean-Paul set about reading up on tannin and how to treat skins and hides to produce leather.

'There's only one problem,' Hortense said.

'And that is?' Jean-Paul could envisage a number of problems and was amused. 'How about the extremely distasteful process by which leather is cured?' He teased her.

'Urine! That's not something that I have to deal with,' Hortense conceded, 'my problem is that I have no money to pay you.'

'In which case there is no problem. I have enough money put by in Germany to enable me to live for several months, providing the mark does not devalue again. We will put this on a commercial footing. I feel enthusiastic about this already.'

'I've given you the excuse to travel, but I'll be glad to see you again. We could talk about old times.' She stopped. 'Perhaps we shouldn't, but I can keep you informed on Parisian gossip and current affairs.'

'That's more to my thinking,' Jean-Paul eased the awkwardness and then without warning stood up, gave Hortense a kiss on each cheek, and left.

A few days later he descended from the train in Lübeck, and once more calling himself Johannes, went in search of an opening in German industry.

Chapter Thirty

'Why do I need a chaperone?' Ronald demanded of his mother when she heard her plan. 'I am quite capable of travelling by myself. The Count said in his letter that he had everything in hand.'

'It is perfectly proper to be accompanied, Ronald. It is good of Brindsley-Smith to offer and churlish of us to refuse.'

'He is a stuffy old codger,' Ronald declared but he knew how to deal with his mother. He would go along with her arrangements and once out of her reach he would manipulate the situation so that Brindsley-Smith was cast away as early as possible.

'As you say, Mother. There is no point in arguing with you.' Ronald threw Veeve one of his beguiling smiles.

There were a few months until money would be released from the trust that was held for Ronald until he reached the age of eighteen, but Veeve, seeing his school days drawing to a close, planned ahead. Ronald's obsession with cars was a harmless diversion, especially since he had shown no particular direction regarding his future, except to say that he was a musician. This aspiration satisfied all who heard it, except for Veeve who had no time for art as a career, and who silently thanked providence for the vast trust which would allow him to live the life of a gentleman without the necessity of earning a living.

She decided that Ronald should tour the continent, although not, on account of the unfortunate events that took place there, to France. To this end she sent a tentative letter to her old flame, Count Von Kuder, partially curious about him on her own behalf. A trip to Germany no longer caused gossip since public opinion had become much less aggressive. She was aided from an unexpected quarter when Brindsley-Smith offered to accompany him.

Brindsley-Smith's fortunes had been greatly helped by the war, he was instrumental in introducing new practices to the firm and he had learnt that the Germans were pioneering new ways of producing dyes for materials. As suspicion of their former enemy receded, Brindsley-Smith saw the potential of these new methods. Natural dyes were cumbersome, costly and slow. The firm were persuaded by him to invest in some innovative colour ranges by adopting the German methods. An introduction to their laboratories using Ronald's contact could only be to his advantage.

Ronald and his uncle were met on their arrival by the Count, a small man with a portly figure and a cheery, rubicund face. He walked towards them with fast small steps, and greeted them with ebullient good humour.

Count Von Kuder proposed that they spend two days in Lübeck before proceeding to his estate. He had some business to see to, and he wanted Ronald and his companion to see the sights. Lübeck was an ancient town and Ronald liked it at once. He had a preconceived picture of German towns as utilitarian and dour, but the lofty spires of the churches, cobbled squares and the fine brick houses with their gabled fronts, decided him immediately that he was wrong.

'Lübeck is situated on an oval shaped island,' the Count told them enthusiastically, 'and the large building which towers over the town is the Holstentor.' This was a castle in the true sense with squat twin towers and a drawbridge. The Count took them to the shipmen's guild house, the main hall of which was filled with local burghers crowding the room for lunch. It was furnished with heavy wooden tables and chairs, and the walls were lined with wood panelling. The Count found a corner table and secured chairs for his guests, and while they waited to order, Ronald felt the thrill of being treated as an adult accompanied by a delicious sense of freedom.

He started to work immediately towards effecting the departure of his chaperone. 'There is so much to see in this city. Do not you wish that we were staying here longer?' His uncle looked surprised while the Count responded with delight.

'I can arrange that for you if you like,' he said to Brindsley-Smith. When he turned to the waiter to order some wine, Ronald stole a look at his uncle. There he saw a dogged determination not to be drawn into any such plan.

'Perhaps my uncle is keen to see your estate.'

'I have a house party arriving almost as soon as you have settled in,' The Count told them. 'We have a regular arrangement to go hunting, not on horses like you English, we are the country type, rough and tough,' he joked, 'but we are not all philistines. I have artists and musicians amongst my friends.' Ronald was pleased with this information. He knew that Brindsley-Smith would be out of his depth and unlikely to impress this group with his usual store of self-congratulatory stories. He took the opportunity to press home his discomfiture.

'Are we expected to shoot too?' Ronald asked eagerly.

'If you want, I shall teach you. It's a knack that comes with practice. There is also a code, an unwritten code, which we abide by, to prevent anyone getting hurt. The difficulty with a gun, until you are used to it, is the ricochet, it is not very comfortable to absorb the recoil.' Ronald increasingly enjoyed himself as he observed Brindsley-Smith's dismay.

Brindsley-Smith's eyes glassed over and he stuttered his apologies at being unable to see himself entering the fun. However Ronald had not bargained with his uncle's tenacity.

Brindsley-Smith broached the subject of business

contacts that he could make, starting with the Count's own factory laboratories and suggested that their common interest in dyes could prove advantageous.

The Count waved a hand airily. 'Some other day, my friend. That is just one of my many enterprises. There is no hurry. We can speak of business in due course, but for now we are tourists and I am your guide.'

The Count's estate was several miles north of the town. Each day followed a similar pattern with various outdoor activities arranged for the amusement of his guests. In the evenings, after the day's strenuous exercise which often started before dawn, the company sat down to dinner amidst a glow of goodwill and easy fraternity. Ronald remembered with what apprehension he had viewed the evenings when he had stayed with his friend Hugh, and marvelled at how people sought him out, eager to learn how the English regarded Germany. Isolated as he had been at school, he would have had no insight into these matters had he not been on the fringe of his mother's circle of acquaintances where he had garnered some views, albeit representative of a small section of society.

Ronald became less irritated with Brindsley-Smith because he rarely encountered him. The last night before travelling onwards he felt more generous towards him and sought him out to say farewell. He came across him in the Count's study where he found his uncle in earnest conversation with a younger bearded German of stocky build. This man was gesticulating with his hands as he delivered an animated monologue in heavily accented English. The two men were so engrossed that they did not notice Ronald who waited by the doorway. It was unusual to see his uncle other than amidst a collection of men and women in a social setting, and for a moment he grudgingly admitted that there might be more substance to him. It appeared that they were having a technical discussion about chemicals for dyes.

'The basic dyestuffs have the disadvantage of losing their colour, or they rub off onto other paler material,' said his uncle, 'and we are especially interested, as I told the Count, in 'Prussian Blue'.'

'You need to use the sulphides, they are especially useful for cotton. The only drawback is a shortage of colours, there is no bright red, for example.'

'What about toluene, do you not use a nitration process there?'

'Yes, when we don't produce TNT, the explosive, you understand,' the German laughed morbidly, 'if you continue the nitration process you get trinitrotoluene or TNT. Seriously, though, it is an excellent intermediary for acid and base dyes.' He turned to indicate the material covering the chair behind him and then he saw Ronald.

'How impolite of me, come in. Your uncle is interested in my work and the Count invited me over. It has been a pleasure to meet such a knowledgeable man. We hope to do business together.'

'I have come to say goodbye. I am going to Hamburg. The Count says it is a city I ought to visit.'

'Indeed it is,' agreed the scientist, 'Germany has many cities that you should see. She is a very cultured country.'

Ronald shook hands with Brindsley-Smith, 'Give my regards to Mother.'

'I am not leaving immediately, but I shall give her a good report when I return.'

Ronald bristled and his decision to unfetter himself from his unwelcome chaperone was confirmed.

Brindsley-Smith lingered for several days during which he awaited an opportunity to speak to the Count alone. He opened the conversation by thanking the Count profusely for his hospitality, which the Count brushed aside aware that neither of them was being completely honest. Brindsley-Smith was following social formalities and the Count knew that he had not gone out of his way to accommodate his guest, apart from inviting the scientist from the laboratory. To make amends he invited Brindsley-Smith to stop for a drink with him.

Brindsley-Smith walked to the fireplace which was flanked by gun cases and stag's antlers. Beneath each set of antlers was a brass plate giving the date that the stag had been shot. In the cases the guns were in pairs.

'I use that pair. We stalk deer and also hunt wild boar,' the Count said but received no reply. Brindsley-Smith crossed to a cabinet with a glass inset in the lid. Inside the rectangular case was a pair of heavy guns with short barrels.

'And what do you shoot with those?' he asked.

'Those are a pair of duelling pistols.' The Count waited a moment before adding, 'They have not been used for many years.'

Brindsley-Smith sat down in one of the armchairs as if his legs had failed him.

'Don't be alarmed,' said the Count, 'we only shoot for sport.' Brindsley-Smith was looking distractedly around the room and appeared to be focussed on a box of cigars on the table beside him.

'A cigar?' The Count offered, 'they have a delicate aroma.'

'Oh, no,' said Brindsley-Smith confused, 'but I believe that is a particularly fine brand.'

'Indeed,' said the Count companionably, 'direct from Havana. Tell me, what news from England? It's been delightful having Ronald here, and quite a surprise to hear from his mother.'

'You are a friend of Veeve's, I understand?'

'From before the war,' the Count answered shortly.

'Her hotel is very popular and she is surrounded by all the best type of people. Quite the thing. If you knew Veeve from before the war then you probably know that she has a way with people.'

'It was certainly one of her main assets. Does she run the hotel alone?'

'She has a manager if that's what you mean.'

'She's happy then, I take it?'

'Never better. Although no-one knows where Veeve was in the war, one of those neutral countries like Switzerland or Spain more likely, no sooner does she reappeared than she is ensconced in this hotel with anybody who is anybody at her feet.'

The Count laughed, 'It does not sound as if she has changed.'

'Do you know where she went once war broke out?' Brindsley-Smith asked, and then muttered, 'How could you?'

The Count was determined not to furnish any information. 'And you. What did you do in the war?'

Brindsley-Smith's attitude changed at once. 'I ended up working with the Army. Intelligence and the like.'

'You weren't required to fight?'

'Varicose veins,' Brindsley-Smith explained. 'I was exempt from active service.' He hurried on, 'I had quite important work flushing out informers. They gave me the rank of Major so that I was in uniform and protected from insolent questions. We had a fair amount of success except for a Frenchman spying for your side. He slipped through the net.'

The Count could see that this fact still bothered Brindsley-Smith, 'It's all over now. Water under the bridge. Need to move on.'

They made their farewells and the Count went along to his study and closed the door. It was his sanctuary. Gregarious and generous hearted, his whole house was available to his guests, but most respected the privacy of his study. The day to day running of his house was in the more than efficient hands of his housekeeper. The Count had a steady temperament but if his servants avoided him it was not to escape his displeasure, rather that his energetic programmes rarely gave them a chance to slacken and they did not want to stimulate him further. Their sporadic moments of peace were welcome.

He went across to his desk and lifting the flap opened one of the side drawers. It contained his personal letters and from the open drawer he took out a letter from Veeve. He then delved into the opposite drawer of keepsakes and found one with Veeve's writing from several years before. Then he sat down to read the earlier one. He remembered the emotions which accompanied it. Veeve had written it a few weeks after she had left him at the end of the war and returned to London to start afresh. Although at the time, and again now, he scoured it for signs of regret, he saw none. When no further letters followed he began to doubt.

Then she had written. Veeve asked if he remembered her son. The letter said that Ronald had recently left school and was reasonably presentable. The crux of the letter was a request to have him to stay because the lad needed to broaden his horizons. His Uncle had offered to accompany him as had some business affairs to attend to in the area. At no point in the letter did Veeve make any reference to their previous relationship, and nowhere was there any indication that she wanted to renew their friendship. Nevertheless, the Count dared to hope that this was an overture and once Ronald's visit came to an end he could reciprocate by visiting England. Perhaps Veeve was testing the ground. He hoped so.

But now this blow, dealt by that insufferable uncle of Ronald's, that Veeve was 'quite the thing'. The Count placed both letters back in their respective drawers. He took a glass from his cabinet and filled it from the decanter. A morose feeling overcame him and a sombre thought emerged from his cogitations. Perhaps Veeve had followed him to flee from the war, and not primarily because she wanted to be with him.

Only by visiting London would he find out. He would wait until Ronald returned from his tour. After such a long time a few more weeks would not make any difference, and they might help him to clear his thoughts.

Unfortunately, during the intervening weeks, the opposite occurred. Far from resolving any of his emotions, the Count was more perturbed than at any time since parting from her and more than ever, wished to have Veeve by his side. If she did not consent to leave her hotel, which surely she would since he was unable to imagine that any woman would willingly work in such a milieu, then he would have to find a way to spend time in England. Attitudes had changed and he knew several of his acquaintances who worked or lived across the North Sea.

Chapter Thirty-One

'I am certain that I've seen Jean-Paul,' Marie said as she drew the curtain across the window. Henri looked at her sharply. She knew that he thought that she was deluding herself. 'He was standing there, across the street. I could see his face. Who else would be standing watching us?'

'What good could it do for any of us?' Henri answered sadly, 'Ruth has gone, resigned that she will never see him. It's true we have little to fear by speaking to him, not after all this time, but who would it benefit?'

'If it was us that he wanted to see he would manage

it somehow. He knows he can trust us. It's Ruth he's looking for. Ruth and Bertrand. It's understandable that he would want to see them.'

'Where's the lad been all these years?' Henri mused.

'If he's started to look for her he will not give up. He'll never find her unless we help.'

'What's the use?' Henri objected. 'Better to do nothing.'

'If it was me,' Marie said, 'I would want to know. I could bear his desertion more easily if I just knew.'

'Knew what?'

'There's nothing worse than not knowing,' Marie persisted perversely. 'I think I shall tell Ruth. Not to tell her would be wrong. Then she can make up her own mind.'

'Is that wise?' Henri said gently. 'Should we not leave her undisturbed? She seems to have fashioned a reasonable life for herself and Bertrand.'

Despite her resolve, Marie woke in the night troubled by doubts. She rose, put a wrap around her shoulders, her feet into her worn fleece slippers, and walked along the corridor to the study. Her conflicting thoughts spun between a picture of Ruth reunited with Jean-Paul, to another of Ruth alone and desolate. If Ruth had created a tolerable life for herself, as her letters were beginning to suggest, would telling her about Jean-Paul upset her tenuous hold on a future where she seemed to have accepted her loss? Jean-Paul had made Ruth swear never to acknowledge him, yet she pitied him and his present state of mind.

Eventually she opened her brother's desk, took some

writing paper, and wrote her letter. Almost as if she had tossed a coin, she sealed it and, until she received Ruth's reply, would not know which way her coin had landed.

Marie could never have anticipated how heavily the coin fell. Within the year Bertrand had been enrolled into the lycée and she was walking her beloved boy to his new school. Bertrand was to spend the school terms with her and return to London for the holidays.

Ruth told her family that she could not afford to send Bertram, now aged eight, to boarding school, and that this decision of hers was a compromise. Two weeks before the beginning of the term she set off with Bertram from Newhaven to settle him in with Marie.

'Eh bien, Maman, qu'est-ce que..' Bertram relapsed into French whenever his mother addressed him in that language, and he took his move to France in his stride. Ruth continued to speak to him regularly in French, a language that had almost become easier to her than her own, and she was now grateful that she had done so. His transition to his new school would be less troublesome.

The lycée had been remarkably accommodating when Marie asked if she could enrol Bertrand. They assured her, with the air of educationalists who believe that it can only be to a child's advantage to enrol in their system, one which relied on years of wisdom and did not pander to modern trends, that Bertrand would thrive.

Bertrand did thrive. Marie was free at weekends to indulge him in trips to museums, meals with families where there were children of his own age, and sports with local teams. His school did not set much store by physical activity, but Marie's enthusiasm for exercise counter-balanced the lack of provision. Bertrand also gained an uncle. Henri spent hours with the young boy constructing models, discussing the working of gadgets and making a third party to any outing.

Although she would not admit it, Ruth adapted well to her role as owner of a hotel. The nature of the business, its constant demands and its inexorable routine suited someone for whom leisure time meant time to brood. She found that the days passed without her giving thought to anything other than the next demand, and when Bertram was at home, to his supervision. Her boy was not a difficult child and, having him constantly with her in the hotel, eased her shyness with her guests who tended to direct their attention to him.

Now, after five years, she had many guests who came regularly and who had become friends, as far as any hotel owner can have friends when the reciprocal arrangements of friendships are mostly barred.

Ruth had steeled herself to be prepared for her feeling of loss. She reassured herself that he was much better staying with tante marie than undergoing the rigours of boarding school. A hotel is not an ideal milieu in which to nurture a child. Ruth was satisfied with her decision, which she had made influenced only in part by her own private agenda which she hoped might include a glimpse of Jean-Paul, was disappointed.

Relief from loneliness came in the form of her nephew. Ronald had returned from his tour of the continent, as his mother described it, and was not insensitive to his aunt's feelings.

'I had to come to show you my new car,' Ronald began, giving Ruth a kiss. 'It's parked outside in the street.'

Ruth smiled indulgently, 'I'll come, but I don't approve of this extravagance. What does Veeve think she's doing allowing you a brand new motor car.'

'Mother doesn't mind at all, in fact she's rather proud of me and keeps telling her guests what a swell guy I am,' Ronald teased. Ruth could imagine that Veeve would revel in having such a dashing son.

Ronald led her down the steps and there, parked at the kerbside, was a shiny, cream and black Rover 8. Its steel wheels, the spare resting above the running board, were gleaming. The hood was folded back showing the soft leather twin seats. 'It's powered by two cylinders and has an air cooled engine,' Ronald said proudly. 'It can go up to forty-five miles an hour. Such a pity that I can't take Bertram for a spin. Would you come with me?' Ronald's generous spirit melted the puritan in Ruth and she agreed to go with him.

Ronald drove her towards the centre of town and then treated her to lunch. Thereafter he became a frequent visitor and Ruth suspected that he was considerably more at ease with her than he was with his mother, where he always had to play a part. Ronald's conversation was intelligent and he could share with Ruth ideas which would have been disparaged by Veeve. Ruth looked forward to his visits and would miss him when he went up to University. Fortunately the terms were short.

'Count! How good to see you again. How long is your visit ?' Veeve engulfed the Count in a generous embrace and he fell once again under her spell.

'I've come to entice you away,' he said as he returned her welcome somewhat formally. 'Can I persuade you? My house, my estate, and I await you.' Half-believing his words, Veeve invited the Count to join her after dinner in her private sitting room.

'Close the door. Let it be just the two of us.' Veeve patted the seat beside her. 'It's so comfortable with you here,' She said happily. 'We are such old friends, aren't we?'

Travelling with more trunks than seemed necessary for a bachelor on a short trip, the reason soon became apparent. Determined to spoil Veeve one trunk was filled entirely with clothes from which she could choose, and another with trinkets, embroidered cushions, wood cut figures and ceramic bowls.

Veeve could be generous but she appreciated it when she was the recipient, and when the Count, laden with gifts, presented them to her she was excited. Tearing away the tissue paper she delved into the trunks while the Count sat back complacently as she tried on the clothes and arranged the ornaments. When she had finished he brought out a velvet box containing a necklace.

'I always wanted to find you a beautiful necklace, and now I have.' Deftly he fastened it behind her neck. It was crafted from garnets and tiny diamonds, colours that he knew suited her.

For a while Veeve recounted anecdotes from the

recent weeks and entertained the Count with stories of those who had stayed, but when she noticed that his attention was straying and she could think up no more in that vein, she turned on him the full intensity of her affection. Placing a hand on his arm she leant forward and with eyes twinkling, she said, 'Now tell me about Brindsley-Smith.'

The Count responded with alacrity, 'What an odd fish. I can't make him out at all.'

'He seems to have become a favourite uncle to Ronald.'

'Not in the boy's opinion, I think,' answered the Count, 'but it may be that it offends him to have a chaperone.'

Veeve was quickly on the defensive. 'I hardly had any choice, the man was quite insistent and besides he seemed to have a genuine reason for visiting Lübeck.'

'He had some business to attend to,' he said to placate her, 'but he also knows how to enjoy another's hospitality.'

Happily agreeing on their views of Brindsley-Smith, Veeve returned to the subject of Paris.

'Will you be long in Paris? Are you going to look up old friends? Pierre?' She queried.

'Why would I want to see Pierre? It's years since we were all together and he and his wife probably have a brood of children and are steeped in domesticity.'

'For old times' sake. You might find out what happened to Jean-Paul.'

'Why?' he asked, and Veeve was aware that he was on his guard.

'Because no one has heard from him, or Pierre, since the war. They were our good friends.' She said sweetly.

'I could,' he answered studiedly.

'You could find Pierre through his firm, if it still exists. Here, I'll write the address for you.'

Veeve was triumphant that her ruse had succeeded and was oblivious to the effect on her faithful friend. She handed him a piece of paper. 'You can let me know next time you come,' she said nonchalantly.

'I'll be coming straight back here,' he told her.

As the Count descended from the train and emerged onto the railway station in Paris he thought, 'Twelve years.' He walked onto the Boulevard Haussmann. 'Has it really been that long since we were all friends here in Paris.' He walked, dazed with the feeling of release that permeated his whole body. Somehow, being here in France where people were going about their lives in peacetime, brought home to him more forcefully than when he was at home, the realisation that the war was over. No-one, as he made his way to the Place d'Etiole would know that he was a German, and he wondered how much that would matter. Could the French continue to hate now that peace reigned. Could the French and the Germans return to their former relationship. His impending meeting with Pierre would enlighten him.

Stopping to rest in the gardens of Les Invalides he imagined his meeting with Pierre and wondered how he should approach him. He also wondered why he had agreed to Veeve's request when the outcome might be to his disadvantage.

'Mon ami, my old friend, what a surprise. Je suis enchanté. How many years is it since we were together?' Pierre clasped both of the Count's hands beaming with pleasure.

Pierre had not changed except that his hair was thinning and his face was more chiselled. He showed no sign of war wounds or deprivation or shell shock.

'Come, there is a café around the corner, we often lunch there.' Hardly able to release the Count's hands, Pierre called to the receptionist that he would be out of the office and led the way into the street.

The intoxicating smell of ground coffee beans welcomed them. Inside, the hum of conversation, the dimly seen figures through the screen of tobacco smoke, and the clink of glasses as cognac was poured at the bar, revived in the Count a nostalgia for a time long past.

'It is wonderful to be back in Paris,' he said.

Pierre responded, 'It is wonderful that you can be here.' The Count realised that he was referring to the slow entente between their two countries.

'You have chosen a good time to come. Memories are short and people do not want to be reminded of the war years. Paris is full of tourists again from all over the world, so why not welcome our old friends and neighbours as well?'

'I am surprised, is this a universal attitude or am I just lucky to have a loyal friend?'

'Not universal but increasingly so, and the young have no memories to prejudice their views. There is nothing to be gained by perpetuating an enmity, particularly since it is not personal but between governments and ideologies. I suspect that on the latter we agree. All we want is a peaceful life for our wives and children. Do you have either?'

'No. As you know my wife and I were estranged long ago and we had no children. You and Armelle?'

Pierre was flattered that the Count remembered his wife's name. 'Two children. They are all absorbing.'

'Any motorcars?'

'Not any more. How about you?'

'Aeroplanes are more my line now. There's the added thrill of being in the air.'

'And the increase in the danger element,'

'Of course,' he grinned boyishly.

'You and Veeve?' Pierre began.

'No and yes. I have come from London and hope to see her regularly.' He was not sure why he withheld the information about her hotel.

'She was quite some lady,' Pierre said reflectively. They sipped their coffee, each content to pause before embarking on a new subject. The Count looked around apprehensively at the faces at the nearby tables to see if he could detect any aggression triggered by his German accent. There seemed to be none. He wondered whether to introduce the topic of their mutual interest in the silk trade, but instead he said, 'From the moment we were introduced at Aunt Helen's house we were all captivated by Veeve. Those were carefree times. Do you remember the American, Sam Blair?'

Pierre nodded, 'He's not been seen since the beginning of the war.'

'And Jean-Paul?' said the Count, musing.

'Oh, he died,' said Pierre abruptly.

The Count showed a polite interest. 'He did? In the war?'

'Sometime afterward. We were never sure of the facts.'

It suited the Count to ask no more questions and he suspected that this was Pierre's intention.

When he walked back to his hotel he was puzzled by Pierre's response. He appeared to show no regret for the loss of a friend, nor did he appear to have tried to discover any details of his death. The Count admitted to himself that it was curious, but for his purposes, the fact of Jean-Paul's death was sufficient.

On the day that the Count returned from Paris Veeve was mildly vexed on seeing him in the residents' lounge, and not appearing as he usually did in the quiet hour before dinner when they had the chance to talk privately. It was the lunch hour, a time that she emerged resplendent, to greet her guests. She habitually made a grand entrance and everyone was happy to indulge her.

'And you, dear Count. How unexpected. Are you lunching here?' She asked with a slight edge to her voice.

'With friends, dear Veeve. I shall be without engagements later today and will hope to speak with you perhaps?'

Veeve knew that she had no option. She listened distractedly to her guests, gave unnecessary instructions to her staff, and changed her clothes at least twice, all the while wondering at her agitation. When later in the day he walked with a group of friends towards the reception desk, she intercepted him.

'I believe we have an assignation,' she smiled brilliantly as she took his arm and detached him from his party. Ever the perfect host she called over her shoulder to the Count's bewildered friends, 'And I shall see you all for dinner. A toute a l'heure.' Veeve found that a little French added a mildly exotic flavour to her image, and, as she had used English in France to excuse any faut pas or awkwardness, so she now used the same tactic in reverse.

Once he had closed the door of her drawing room Veeve released his arm, and drifted over to the sideboard. She picked up two glasses and held them in her hand as an enquiry. The Count shook his head. 'A good trip?' Veeve asked graciously.

'Paris is magnificent. I am surprised that you have not been back.'

'There's nothing there for me any more,' Veeve replied airily, 'but for you, to whom to visit Paris is a form of reparation, it is different.'

'Making our peace? Veeve, You forget that you won the war.'

'But you made it and made it very uncomfortable for the French. But enough. Paris hasn't changed?'

'Hardly at all.'

'And Pierre?'

'A little older, a family man, no racing cars.'

Veeve waited. The Count inspected his cuffs, slowly, and then looked Veeve squarely in the face. 'I asked him about Jean-Paul.' The solemn tone caused Veeve to feel a chill. 'He's dead, Veeve, I am sorry.'

Veeve swallowed, looked distractedly passed the Count, and then collected herself quickly.

'Do you know when or how?'

'Pierre did not know. A short while after the war.'

Veeve was determined to show as little emotion as possible under the Count's scrutiny. 'The toll of war,' she remarked. Then she said quietly, 'I think after all I won't join your friends. Would you dine with me tonight?'

Chapter Thirty-Two

Bertrand was eleven and a gangly youth. Never a child to waste time, he always had a project or a subject to discuss, and was a daily joy to his 'Tante' and 'Oncle'.

'What is it this time?' Marie asked indulgently as Bertram breezed in from school throwing his satchel onto the table dumping his canvas bag onto the floor.

'You can give that bag away,' Bertrand answered grumpily. 'What is there for goutez?' Marie cut a slice from a baguette, spread some jam and passed it to him. Perhaps he would be more jovial with some food.

Bertrand sat down at the table and Marie took this as an invitation for her to join him. 'Do we need Henri to join us?'

'There's nothing he can do. They won't change their minds. I'm not allowed to take my cricket stuff any more'

'Why's that?' Marie had always wondered whether the English game would upset some of the teachers.

'It's too dangerous.'

Marie laughed.

'It's true! Antoine was hit on the head and passed out. That's it. No more cricket.'

Marie was alarmed when she realised that Bertrand was serious, and saddened. The game had not only entertained Bertrand's friends but had attracted quite a group of curious bystanders.

Bertrand added, reflectively, 'He'll be upset too.'

'Who will?'

'The man who always comes to watch whenever he's in Paris. He fields the ball for us. My friends and I have explained the game to him.' Marie felt shaky, but not wanting to dwell on the subject distracted him by calling Henri.

'Henri, we need a new game for this lad, how about taking him to the park and teaching him petanque?'

'It's not quite the same, is it Tante?'

'No, but it's a good game and a useful skill. Now off you go!'

Later, Marie divulged her suspicions to Henri. 'I think that the lad has seen Jean-Paul. Or rather the other way around. Bertrand has no notion who the stranger is, why should he?'

'I hope it gives him pleasure,' said Henri wearily, 'it must be hard to see your son, as a person watches an animal in a cage, and not be able to do more than look.'

'So long as no harm comes to Bertrand,' Marie said.

'That would never happen. Jean-Paul would not allow that. It's eight years now and he could have revealed himself at any time. Bertrand is safe.'

Bertrand threw his energies into another sport, there were no more complaints from the school and Marie was content. By the end of the following year Bertrand gathered up certificates for excellent work.

'They'll be presented at prize giving, you will come, won't you?' Bertrand urged.

They needed no persuading. Since Ruth had decided that Bertrand was to continue his senior education in England, every moment spent with Bertrand was precious. Their last duty was to accompany him to the end of term Speech Day and they would attend even if it meant, for Marie at least, that her tears would be visible for all to see.

The ceremony was endless in the tradition of school prize-giving, although, because of the war, the collection of glittering cups had reduced and certificates of excellence had proliferated. Marie, unused to being among children en masse was impressed. It was inspiring to see so many children on their best behaviour.

Henri rejoiced in the sight of so many healthy boys. With the terrible massacre of their young men France's hopes rested on this new generation. He hoped fervently that they would be worthy of the legacy that their fathers, and the many men who never had a chance to become fathers, had bequeathed them. Perhaps he was being unreasonable and it was unfair to expect them to comprehend their sacrifice since many of the children had not been born, and even Bertrand was only a baby.

These children would grow up as selfish or as altruistic as any previous generation, and that was their prerogative. 'Bertrand, now,' he mused, 'can be relied on, with the parents he was blessed with.'

At that moment Marie nudged him and indicated that he should look to the dais. The Headmaster was announcing the presentation of a new cup. 'It's for English,' Marie whispered. Both Marie and Henri confidently expected that, as the only English child in the leaving class, Bertrand would win it.

'We now come to the Saint Cloud cup for English.' Marie felt a frisson. She remembered Ruth telling her, 'I could never part with these vases, they were Jean-Paul's wedding present. They were from Saint Cloud, because my nickname was miserable or under a cloud.'

'The anonymous donor asked that we respect his request for this name which has a particular significance for him.' A boy's name was read out and Marie watched with dismay as the cup was handed over and received by someone other than Bertrand. There was a moment of confusion as the base of the vase-shaped cup fell to the ground, but this was soon rectified, and she followed the journey of the cup as the boy, brimming with pride, made his way to his seat a few rows behind them. She was so distracted that she did not pay attention to the further announcements, until she was conscious of Henri clapping enthusiastically.

'Bertrand's won the French Cup,' Henri said gleefully. 'What an irony. We've turned him into a proper Frenchman.' He then noticed that Marie had tears in her eyes and misinterpreting the reason, said to her kindly. 'He will not be gone forever, Marie.'

She let Henri think that she was upset due to Bertrand's departure because she could not put herself in the position of being, however gently, mocked for her fanciful notion that the Saint Cloud cup held a clue to the mystery of Jean-Paul's whereabouts. She was probably being a romantic spinster, but she could not rid herself of the conviction that Jean-Paul had donated the cup with the intention of conveying a message to Ruth. If she had divulged her fantastic idea to Henri, he might have been able to comfort her with the thought that the cup itself was sufficient proof that he had not forsaken them.

Jean-Paul, when in Paris, stayed with Hortense. On these occasions she would return from work to find him ensconced with a glass of wine, a book, and with a meal ready. He calculated his visits to coincide with the school terms, particularly in the summer when the children were out of doors.

Over the years Hortense's Spartan accommodation had been transformed with her deft artistic touch into one which was increasingly attractive. Jean-Paul felt the lack of a home and riled against the rootlessness of his existence. He speculated on Ruth's situation and the reasons behind her choice of Marie and Henri as a term-time home for their son. He feared that she must be struggling to fend for the two of them, and to ward off the ever-hovering grief that threatened to engulf him when he thought of the hardship he had imposed on her, he concentrated on making life for Hortense as pleasant as possible.

Hortense had no conception of the strength of his determination to keep the taint of disgrace from his son. She was increasingly enjoying Jean-Paul's company and wondered if he was prepared to relinquish his hold on Ruth's memory. As his interest in the boy had grown so had he reverted to the light-hearted, passionate character that she had known in the past. She wondered how long a man could continue to watch his son from a distance and not succumb to the temptation of befriending the child, and she was almost grateful when she heard Jean-Paul say despondently, 'Bertrand can no longer be in France. Ruth must have given up on me.'

She had no understanding of the thought processes behind his comment but feared that their relationship might revert to a business-like footing, with Jean-Paul once more withdrawn and focused solely on their joint enterprise.

It was fortunate that their business was thriving and that she would continue to see him. The contacts in Germany which he had established were now reaping profits. The demand for the competitively priced German goods had expanded and not only was her workshop flourishing but her shop too, as demand for imported goods increased. She could not help his despair but she hoped to rally his spirits.

'I know an art student who has been designing handbags. By using surplus leather from our shoes, we can increase our profit. I have some of her drawings here. They are unlikely to take up an excessive amount of time, they are relatively simple, and in fact an

apprentice could soon manage the marking and cutting.'
Hortense went to the cupboard and brought out a folder.

'Pass it to me and I'll have a look,'Jean-Paul said, 'I take it that you would like me to sell them? I am happier marketing our own goods, and France has a reputation for taking the lead in fashion.' He nodded approvingly at the designs. 'We should remember that our future depends on our flair and innovation.'

Hortense was pleased that an idea that had germinated as much to help Jean-Paul as to diversify the goods that they sold, had the possibility of fulfilling both aspirations. She never asked about his contacts in Germany, or with Count Von Kuder, relationships with Germans, although more common, were still looked upon with a certain amount of suspicion. Hortense was aware of the collective national antagonism that was directed in many quarters towards all Germans. Influenced by Jean-Paul, however, she was intrigued by the advance in the technological expertise developed by their erstwhile enemy, and was eager to profit by it.

Jean-Paul introduced bright and unusual colours to the leather with which they were working. At the same time he had not been able to resist investigating some of the new processes in his previous trade in silks, and they began to include scarves in novel designs amongst their products. One of these new dyes, Prussian blue, was a midnight blue not seen out of Germany, and this had attracted both existing and new customers. Jean-Paul expressed his opinion that her shop was on the brink of becoming popular to a new set of clients. 'You are going to have to think about relocating your shop to a more fashionable area and name it a boutique,' Jean-Paul told Hortense, only half in jest.

'I am not convinced,' she answered him. 'The hardship years are still real and not a memory to be erased quite yet.' The drive and energy that Jean-Paul injected from his dealings in Germany was seductive and she hoped to realise that dream one day. However she was aware that this success was due to deals with the enemy that she could not have brought herself to undertake, and that it would also depend on her future relationship with Jean-Paul.

Chapter Thirty-Three

The young seem to have an endless capacity to enjoy themselves.' Veeve observed, but Ruth wondered how, now that Ronald had graduated, he would fill the long summer months. She need not have worried. It appeared that some of the young guests at her hotel attracted Ronald, and she began to notice that one particularly pretty girl, who was staying for a month with her parents, had caught his attention. Her name was Olivia and she was seventeen.

Olivia was petite and lively and conformed to the new image currently in vogue. The streamlined, figure-encasing clothes seemed made for such an entrancing girl. Ronald appeared to think so and Olivia's parents, somewhat at a loss as to how to amuse their daughter during their London visit, were delighted to have an affluent and respectable graduate to take her off their hands.

Olivia had no knowledge of, or interest in, the various specialised attributes of a Rover 8-hp, but she did appreciate the image that she portrayed when travelling in one, as well as enjoying the advantage of having her own chauffeur.

Each time he called for her he had a new expedition organised and on her last day he planned a longer trip than usual. 'Where are we going?' Olivia asked.

'I am taking you to Oxford. I've told my Aunt that we may be late, and she can inform your parents.'

'Why Oxford?'

'It's where I was at University. I think you'll like it.' Olivia was disappointed. Who wanted to go to a rum old University? It was only a school for older brothers who no-one knew what to do with. Olivia was polite and did not demure, because the alternative was another day traipsing around with her parents.

Despite her privileged upbringing, Olivia had only a rudimentary knowledge of her native land. She was familiar with her local town and to some extent the metropolis of London, but apart from the homes of friends in similar circumstances to her own, the rich variety of the English countryside was alien to her. She saw that Ronald was exhilarated by the open road once it left London, and she was surprised at the effect on her of the old University town. As its solid ancient architecture and its skyline of towers and spires came into view, she found herself infected by Ronald's enthusiasm. He told her he was disappointed that the river was not awash with undergraduates, or that the streets and alleyways were not thronged with students in flannels, boaters and flowing gowns. Olivia was amused how, with boyish excitement, the day was not long enough for all the places that he wanted to show her.

He reserved the river until the end. It was less crowded as people departed to take children home, or return to their lodgings for tea, and the early evening was a peaceful time to convey the magic of punting.

She was dressed for the part in a pale cotton frock with puffed sleeves and a leather belt and she wore a straw hat with flowers around the linen band. She trailed her fingers in the water as Ronald propelled the punt lazily through the slowly flowing river. She felt the ripples as the river dragged against the sides of the punt. She smiled happily, and looked up from watching the small waves caused by the rhythmical movements of the pole, to watch Ronald as he effortlessly swung it forward and release it behind him. She realised that he was engrossed and detached and she wanted to recall him from his reverie. She had become used to being the centre of his attention and this retreat disturbed her. She wanted his former companionship and called his name.

Immediately the fleeting glimpse she had of a remote and isolated individual disappeared. She saw a handsome man, devoted to her, at one with his surroundings wearing white flannels and a straw boater, who was looking down on her with undisguised appreciation. Ronald complimented her on her stamina, and suggested that they tie up at the next landing stage and seek some dinner before returning to town.

Olivia had never felt so contented. She, who looked for ever-changing entertainment, desired nothing more than for this day to continue unending. The response that she had elicited in Ronald when she called his name suggested an ownership that was novel. She did not feel owned by him yet she felt the stirrings of her will over his. She was definitely in love with him. It was a novel sensation and when Ronald brushed his hand across hers as he handed her a glass, she understood that it might be reciprocated.

'It will be dull when I go home,' Olivia said.

'Do you have to? Can you not find a way to extend your stay in London?'

'My parents would think it most peculiar. Unless we were engaged.' Olivia was not sure if she was stating a fact or presenting a possibility.

'We could be,' Ronald looked at her earnestly. 'Would you marry me, Olivia? Could you marry me?'

Olivia thought it was the most likely event in the world. Before they reached London she had scanned the requirements for marriage and it appeared to her to be simple. They needed a home. Her father's house was too large for their family. Ronald presented as a young man with plenty of money and Olivia could see no hindrance to securing her parents' blessing. She had rarely been denied anything that did not inconvenience them, and she anticipated no objections. Her mother might even enjoy preparing a wedding.

Olivia was correct in all her assumptions and only Ruth had misgivings. These she kept to herself not even raising them when she had an unexpected visit from Veeve.

The two sisters had little opportunity to compare each other's hotels and both knew that they would disapprove of the other's establishment.

'You must have seen what was happening,' Veeve accused her sister. Ruth did not deign to answer. How could anyone have foreseen such a rapid development from friendship to marriage? Ruth was not unduly worried by Veeve's outburst since she was holding the ace in the pack. She waited for Veeve to continue her tirade.

'So what have they been up to, and how are they so certain that a holiday affair will translate into marriage?'

'Ronald has been showing Olivia the sights and entertaining her while her parents followed their own agenda. Who can tell which friendships will endure and which are a passing phase? Age appears to have nothing to do with it.'

'But Ronald is no age at all,' Veeve countered. 'And the girl's only seventeen.'

'Much the same age as you were when you married George.'

'Who is she? What do you know about her?'

'Quite a lot,' Ruth answered, 'her father is a Marquis and owns Harwood Castle.'

Ruth was gratified with the reaction that she elicited from Veeve, who found an excuse to gather up her handbag.

'Well Ronald won't find too many calls on his inheritance, if that is the case,' Veeve said with satisfaction.

Veeve and her family enjoyed a lavish Wedding ceremony and Ronald, who had never known a family life, exchanged the restrictions of a hotel for the novelty of a home. It had been remarkably easy, he told Ruth, and he now had a companion, a home, and could pursue his new obsession.

'What does Olivia think about your preoccupation with racing cars?' Ruth asked Ronald tartly. 'It's hardly an occupation for a girl.'

'She's a good sport. I'm teaching her to drive. She goes on the circuit when there are no trials on.'

'Isn't it rather a man's world?'

'I suppose it is but Olivia spends most of her time playing tennis and going into town with her friends. Her father has put me in touch with a first rate mechanic. We are redesigning the carburettor.'

Ruth quickly changed the subject. Her nephew could be exasperating once he began explaining the intricacies of engines. As a child it had been mathematics, then music, and now engines. She was sure that he had a fine brain that needed challenges but she was not sure how Olivia would view it.

'How do you find it at Harwood Castle?'

'Splendid,' Ronald answered abstractedly. 'Aunt Ruth, do you think you could give Olivia tea when she returns, there's a workshop I need to pop down to.'

Ruth enjoyed Olivia's company and it was a change to have a girl around. It gave her an insight into how the young conducted their lives. She compared Olivia's emancipation to her own young adulthood. Olivia's status as a married woman gave her extended freedom. She envied Olivia her poise, yet she did wonder how resilient she would be should events turn against her. It forced her to think over her own situation. Her father had on several occasions commented on her more than adequate ability to manage a business. She found the practicalities of the hotel business tedious and her interaction with the staff was an uneasy one but, although she may not have a flare for this life of service, after more than seven years she derived some comfort from her success. However, she never would be satisfied that this was the best use of her intellect, and when she was able to, she engaged in discussions on books and plays and enjoyed the look of surprise as her guests acknowledged her knowledge and judgement.

As she prepared for Olivia's arrival, she was aware that this young girl was unlikely to engage in conversations on art or literature, but she could certainly enlighten Ruth on the sort of activities in which a young girl of her class indulged. Knowing that, fundamentally, Ronald was intelligent and had an inquiring mind, their two characters seemed so disparate, yet she still hoped that the relationship between Olivia and Ronald would endure.

Chapter Thirty-Four

1931

Tom stood in the porch of the church ready to show the mourners to their pews. He and Flo had been married in this church and here, too, he had been an usher at the wedding of her sister Elsie. Henry and Mitchell waited with him in the porch but as the oldest of the brothers-in-law, and the closest to Reginald whom he had worked for all his life, Tom naturally took the lead.

The church at which the Heffords worshipped was only a few streets away from Granby House. It was a solid Victorian building, straddling two streets, and with its entrance bordered by railings. Uneven flagstones created an area where people could congregate, but there was no space for a flower bed or even a shrub. The austere entrance was only a precursor to the unenlightened architecture within. Above the altar and in the lady chapel were stained glass windows depicting biblical themes but the effect, except in brilliant sunshine, was to increase the gloomy atmosphere. The pews were carved with a simple scroll design but their dark wood did nothing to lighten the overall impression that this was a church attuned to funerals.

Yet Tom remembered the church adorned with flower displays on the window ledges, at the altar and lectern, and ivy tumbling down the pulpit steps. The array of colourful hats which filled the pews that day added to the joyful atmosphere, and Flo, in her white dress and veil, with her sisters in attendance had filled the aisle where lay the coffin with one wreath of lilies.

On that day all eight bells had pealed to proclaim the happy news but today there was tolling of a single bell and it was fitting that for Eleanor the mood was sombre. As her family dwindled, as her seven daughters left home one by one, and as her grandchildren grew older even with the addition of Bertram and Catkin, Eleanor felt that her life lost meaning. Eleanor was tired. She had appeared to be slipping away for so long that when she died it was as if she had already departed. Although she had not been a vital part of their lives for some years, for all of them she had been there at the beginning. She was the centre to which they all had turned, even those of them, like Tom, Mitchell and Henry, who had joined the family through their marriages.

In a ragged file, dark suited men arrived at the church and passed through the porch. They nodded to Tom, or his brothers-in-law as they removed their hats with a sympathetic look, or if they were better acquainted, with a few words or clasp of their hand. Reginald had earned, in the years that he had lived and worked in Leicester, the respect of many, and the pews were soon filled with friends, fellow townsmen and work colleagues.

Reginald was driven to the church, despite the short distance because he became breathless on exertion. The car door was opened for him and he and his oldest daughter alighted. Reginald held himself upright but his clothes hung from his slight frame. Flo, in a black coat trimmed with fur and a narrow brimmed black hat with a velvet trim, took his arm and accompanied him towards the church. Tom came forward to take his other arm and, although he could walk unaided, Reginald was grateful for their support as they made their way, watched by sympathetic mourners, up the aisle to the pew which had been reserved for them.

Within touching distance, the coffin rested on its stand between the choir stalls. The organ was silent, unlike the day when Flo and her father had walked up the aisle on her wedding day. As they took their places the hum of voices dimmed. The Vicar emerged from the vestry towards the centre of the church and proceeded to conduct the funeral service in the ancient words with which Reginald, at his age, was familiar.

A short distance from the church was the graveyard where Eleanor's coffin was to be laid. Surrounded by a low wall and yew trees there was little to distract from the sight of the many headstones due to the war, which were starkly prominent and still relatively untouched by weathering. The committal of the coffin into the ground was a solemn, poignant ceremony. Reginald, who had held up well during the service, was unable to restrain his tears, and Flo was only able to do so because her father needed comforting. He rallied when the men shook his hand on parting and finally he was left with his three faithful sons-in law and Flo.

'Thank you, boys,' Reginald managed a smile. They were accompanying him back to Granby House. 'The girls will be waiting for us. I hope that some of these kind people who came to say goodbye to my dear Eleanor, will come back for refreshments. You did invite them, didn't you?'

Tom reassured his father-in-law and then, leaving the others to go ahead, he held back. He had seen Ronald in the distance, hovering shyly, clearly hesitating whether to join the older men, and hurried to speak to him. 'It's quite an ordeal, one's first funeral. The old man did very well. Shall we walk to the house?'

They watched the car carrying Reginald and the family members draw away. Ronald had little contact with Tom but instinctively liked him. Flo's husband had no airs and it was impossible not to admire someone who had fought in the war, and who had worked all his life. If anything, he wondered if Tom had any time for him.

'Grandmother didn't suffer did she?'

'No. I think she was just tired. Flo saw her regularly and Eleanor never complained of pain.'

'That's good. Grandfather will be lonely now.'

'I never regretted one day that I worked for your grandfather, and wish I thank him for trusting me when he permitted me to marry Flo. Many would not have done. He moved the family to Leicester to give the girls a better chance in the marriage stakes, but he was soft on Flo, and could not have refused her anything, even marrying his foreman.'

They slowed their pace, delaying entering the house.

'Your grandparents were closest to Elsie, and Mitchell has advised them at every stage. My hunch is that Reginald will go and live with them.'

'Was Mitchell badly wounded in the war? I mean, he

wasn't always like this?'

'No. He was as fine, athletic and handsome man as you could find when I first knew him. He introduced Henry to Lil, you know, but he was once engaged to Lil himself. There's some history for you.'

When they reached the house they were the last to arrive. At a funeral family members reconnect but generations reshuffle. Tom, in his new role, introduced Ronald to his little-known relatives.

'Now you have a chance to meet the whole family, it's not often that we gather together. Your cousins, my daughters, are here. We'll find them later.'

'I can hardly remember my cousins. Nora and Sara?'

'You're right. Go on in.'

Lil was greeting the guests and Elsie was organising the refreshments, and both looked up as they entered.

'Tom, you'll know many more of Reginald's associates than we do, be a dear and help Flo look after them. You'll find everyone in the drawing room. Ronald, just make yourself useful and look out for anyone who looks lost.'

Ronald felt that, as a graduate with a hectic social life, this should be a task that he could undertake with ease, but he was far from comfortable, knowing that at some point in the proceedings, his own life would be under discussion.

The guests were dispersed through the reception rooms. Ronald made his way to the centre of the dining room where Sheilagh had positioned Bett in her wheelchair and where a succession of relatives were eager to speak to her. Her face lit up as she spied Ronald.

'Ronald, I so rarely see you. Tell me what you are doing, not still fast cars?'

'I am afraid so, Aunt. One day they will adapt them for wheelchairs and then you can feel the thrill for yourself.'

'Not for me, thank you. I don't think speed and I go together, but you are not forgetting your music, I hope.'

Ronald made a rueful face, 'For the moment.'

'Well not for ever. Now, go and talk to your cousins and leave your old aunt to her generation.'

'What has happened to Olivia?' Elsie asked Bett under cover of the many conversations that reverberated around the room.

'It did not last. They were too young. I think the divorce cited desertion. It had to be that because neither adultery or cruelty was appropriate.'

'Ronald seems unstable, somehow, unsettled,' Elsie commented.

Bett did not want to be drawn into a discussion. 'Possibly. How are your girls?' Elsie could be relied upon to talk at length about her daughters.

Ronald, looking around, was disappointed not to see his young cousin, the only other male, when Tom called him over to meet Nora and Sara.

Nora, the oldest, had a country complexion, a sturdy compact body, unruly brown hair tied behind her neck in a bow, in a style that would have suited a much younger girl. She did, however, have an expression that made an onlooker forget her figure when they noticed the joy that radiated from her face as she expressed her pleasure at everything and everyone. Sara, perhaps because she was able to, remained in her sister's shadow. Slight, with pale skin and somewhat lank hair which she cheered up with clips, she had a thoughtful expression and a shy smile, which melted the heart of any viewer who might at first have thought her insipid.

Ronald absorbed all this while Tom introduced them, and was captivated by Sara as her father moved away. Nora said a polite, 'Nice to meet you,' before leaving them together.

'Nora is practising,' she informed Ronald. 'She has her heart set on the new doctor and has gone to find Catkin to play with. She dotes on children.'

'And will she capture her doctor, do you think?' Ronald asked, amused.

'Without a doubt. He's set his heart on her.'

'That is very satisfactory.'

'Isn't it,' Sara grinned up at her cousin. 'We don't really know you, do we?'

'I suppose not. There haven't been any occasions like this for the family to meet.'

'The only one I can remember is when you came back from France, and could only speak French.'

'That was rather a long time ago. I am quite good at English now, you know.'

Sara giggled.

Each member of the family, afterwards, was certain that they remembered the moment that Ronald set eyes on Sara. The attraction was mutual and instantaneous, and probably only Sara's parents were surprised when, two months later, Ronald asked her to marry him.

Tom and Flo were more than surprised, they were dismayed at the prospect of their daughter marrying Ronald. His reputation was anything but ideal for a future husband since he was so recently divorced, moreover the situation was awkward because they were loath to create a family rift. Inevitably they accepted the relationship when nothing they could say would change Sara's mind. Tom hoped that the character that he had glimpsed on the day of Eleanor's funeral, was one that Sara had discovered under the surface of her pleasant but outwardly aimless cousin.

Sara and Ronald celebrated their wedding, which took place in a registry office, with a small reception attended by the family. The unusual circumstances of the bride and bridegroom sharing relatives avoided the disapproval of others outside the family that might have been caused due to Sara marrying a divorcee. No one could fail, however, to be touched by the adoration in Ronald's eyes, and the happiness of his bride. Nor could they fail to be amused by the discomfiture of Veeve when they recalled the lavish wedding with Olivia's family little more than two years previously.

This event was soon overshadowed when, within a few months, news circulated that Sara was expecting a baby. Veeve, who for so long had been on the fringe of the family, mostly from choice, found herself once again, although with Flo this time, the centre of attention. She was mildly disturbed at becoming a grandmother, since this was not compatible with the image she portrayed of herself, and besides, all discussions of baby affairs bored her.

She was pleased, however, how Ronald's marriage with Sara had matured her son, and she did enjoy her renewed relationship with Flo. She would have understood if Flo had borne some sort of grudge towards her, because she understood that from her point of view, Ronald was not an ideal match. Fortunately Flo's happiness on behalf of the couple seemed genuine, and Veeve was relieved not to have been the cause of another scandal in the family.

Ronald began to call in on Veeve more often than he had done for many years, and that alone predisposed her to be fond of Sara. Soon after the announcement that Sara was to have a baby, he sought her out showing an anxiety that was uncharacteristic.

'Mother!' Veeve immediately stopped what she was doing and paid attention. It was rare that Ronald was anything other than flippant or in a hurry and the tone of his voice worried her. 'Sara is ill. It's more than the usual morning sickness. The doctor says it will pass and to give her broth and warm drinks, but even these she is unable to retain. Can you find a good doctor? You know I can pay.' Ronald touched a raw spot inside Veeve's outwardly steely exterior. A flashback to her own miserable pregnancy, although she was not excessively sick, meant that she responded with sympathy.

'I know exactly who to call. What about Flo? Will she mind?'

'She was with Sara when I said that I was coming to you for help. She is anxious but did not want to go against the doctor's advice.'

Ronald's plight and his concern for Sara over the following weeks found his aunts united in their distress, and their affection for him grew. 'He was always sound at the core,' Ruth said to Betts as they discussed Sara's pregnancy and Ronald's care of her.

'He's a loving lad,' Bett agreed.

'You love everybody, but it is true that this has brought out the best in him, and when Sara recovers they will be able to enjoy life together.'

'And there'll be a new baby in the family,' Bett said joyfully.

But it was not to be. Sara became weaker and her sickness did not abate until, despite the best doctors and constant nursing, she slipped into a coma and died.

Within a year of Eleanor's death the family reassembled at the church to lay Sara to rest. On this occasion as on many others, when someone was needed to conduct Hefford family affairs, it was Mitchell who took control of proceedings, Tom and Flo supported each other as chief mourners, and only Bett remembered to comfort Sara's sister, Nora.

In the months leading up to Sara's death, Ronald and Veeve communicated as at no other time, and it was Veeve who accompanied her son as he walked up the aisle to the front pew. There were fewer in the congregation than on that previous occasion, and all were family members. There was no one who was not affected by the loss of a young girl and the promise of the new life within her. Some worried, and Ruth most especially, how Ronald would react now that his short-lived spell of stability and happiness had been abruptly curtailed. Ruth feared for him because, despite Veeve being on a more amicable footing with her son, it was she who had a longer and more intimate knowledge of her vulnerable nephew and it would be to her that he would turn. She did not know how to help with another's misfortune.

Henry and Mitchell stayed in the churchyard until the undertakers had left and then ensured that, when the sidesman closed up the church, they were there to collect the wreaths. By the time they reached Granby house the family had been assembled for some time. Everyone had congregated in the drawing room. The two men placed the flowers in the hall and then stood on the threshold unsure how to conduct themselves on this tragic occasion.

Henry turned to Mitchell. 'Elsie needs you, your girls are upset. It's a shock for them to lose a cousin.'

'Joan and Sara were the same age. It's hard to know what to say.'

Henry's eyes focussed on Lil. He wondered how she felt, having never had a child. However, he watched her encircle Nora's shoulders while at the same time handing her a handkerchief, and knew the strength she could impart just by her presence. He saw Bett's look of relief that, because she was confined to her wheel chair and was unable to help, another of her sisters was comforting their niece.

Henry slipped his hand into Lil's, and then looked around the room. 'I'll join you presently, I need to find Ruth.'

Henry intercepted her in the hall where she was preparing to leave. She seemed close to tears. 'Do you need your coat?' He asked, selecting it from the coat rack.

He walked her to the door and called a taxi. 'This revives so many memories,' he said, closing the door of the cab and marvelling at Ruth's stoical exterior.

The journey through the streets and the subsequent train ride to London helped Ruth to gain control of her emotions. By the time she arrived at her hotel she hoped she would be in a relatively calm frame of mind.

Returning to the drawing room he gravitated towards Lil seeking some solace. 'Ruth's gone home.' He explained. Lil looked crestfallen, as if she had failed Ruth, but then she remembered that Veeve also had no one to turn to.

'This is heart breaking for all of us,' Veeve said, 'Sara was a thoroughly decent girl. Ronald was lucky. Even to have a glimpse of happiness is better than never to have experienced it.' Henry wondered if she was commenting on her own brief marriage, of which he knew so little. 'It's strange how history has a habit of repeating itself, but I am glad that there is no child, at least that is one less person to suffer.'

Henry had not seen Veeve as vulnerable, nor heard her have regrets about Ronald's childhood. She always gave the impression of being mistress of her affairs.

'There is something you can do for me.' Veeve spoke confidentially, the background murmur of the various groups around the room gave the impression of privacy, which Henry felt was her intention. 'Bett's husband,

Brindsley-Smith.'

Henry felt a moment's apprehension, unable to contemplate Brindsley-Smith without some inexplicable aversion.

'He was good to Ronald when he left school, and took and interest in him, whatever you might think of the man. Would you tell him for me, about Ronald, being on his own, I believe that you are members of the same club?'

Brindsley-Smith was with a couple of men at his usual corner of the club, laughing a little more loudly than was necessary, and lounging back in his chair with more than usual exaggeration. Henry sat at an empty table and within a few minutes Brindsley-Smith made his way across. 'You're looking very sober. Have you been to a funeral?' His tone was jovial.

'Yes, I have I'm sorry to say. It's one that I need to tell you about. Veeve asked me to see you.' He managed to extinguish Brindsley-Smith's forced good humour.

'Veeve?'

'Her daughter-in law, Ronald's wife, we have just buried her.'

'Ronald. Her son. That's right. Is Veeve very shaken?'

'They all are,' Henry answered brusquely. Brindsley-Smith did not seem to understand the tragedy that had befallen Ronald.

'I'll go and see Veeve and give her my condolences.'

'It's not Veeve we are worried about,' Henry started to say, when he realised that for some reason Brindsley-Smith did not want to acknowledge the extent to which he had once known Ronald, possibly he had lost interest over the years.

'The girl was Olivia, wasn't it?'

Henry was speechless.

'I really must go and see Veeve.'

Henry was angry and decided not to disabuse him of his misinformation. 'That would be kind.' Then he stood up and said, 'It's been a fraught day. I'll bid you good evening.'

'I don't understand it,' Henry remarked to Lil when he returned home. 'The man pretended not to know Ronald, or not very well.'

Lil was upset by the day's events and did not listen, but instead she said, 'I can't imagine what it must be like to be Flo tonight.'

'What can have been his motive?' Henry was puzzled and a past conversation came to him. Brindsley-Smith seemed obsessed by the French informer who he had failed to apprehend, and which in some way reflected badly on him. He was unable to relinquish his vendetta and Henry felt certain that, despite his attempt to defuse his fixation with the fact that Ruth's husband had the same name, he may have decided that the informer, and Ruth's husband, were one and the same person. Was it because the informer would therefore be Ronald's uncle? Was it because Ronald could have knowledge that might be useful to him that Brindsley-Smith was trying to cultivated that friendship? He was unable to confide his suspicions to Lil because this was information that, once again, was best kept kept hidden.

Chapter Thirty-Five

1938

Ruth was handed the receiver by her receptionist. 'Your sister'. Before she could ask which one, she recognised the voice as Veeve's.

Ruth noticed that the entrance hall rug was set askew at the same moment that she heard that there had been a motorcar accident, and while simultaneously realising that Veeve was speaking about Ronald, that a letter had failed to be posted.

'Are you still there?' Veeve asked. 'You have not said anything.'

'Is Ronald alive? You said he was badly injured.'

'That's what I mean. He was unconscious, but both his legs are broken.' Ruth picked up a pen and found a pad of notepaper. 'Where is he? What hospital is he in?'

'You can't visit him. They are operating today. Why don't you come over and I can tell you everything properly.'

Ruth laid down the receiver. Veeve had only once before invited her to her hotel, and that was when she had returned from France. She had a suspicion that this was Veeve's way of requesting her company and that she was needed.

'Now I can tell you what happened.'

Ruth understood her sister too well to expect her gratitude but it was not necessary because she had been worried about her nephew. She had not seen Ronald for several years, not since Sara's death. She assumed that he must have immersed himself in the world of racing. The annual schedule took him around Britain as well as on the continent, and he would be surrounded by like-minded drivers with no mention of Sara.

Veeve led Ruth from the foyer and through the main reception rooms. Long windows looked out onto a town garden laid out with symmetrical rose beds which were bordered with low clipped box hedges. Ruth's hotel did not boast a garden, but she did feel that her décor was more tasteful and that it attracted the kind of clientèle that she wanted. She knew she would feel ill at ease with the nouveaux riches, the young and racy, and the recent influx of foreigners that Veeve told her made up the greater proportion of her guests.

'I have redecorated the dining room. I'll show you later. My little snug room is still the same.' Veeve opened the door to her private room but Ruth did not recognise it. With Veeve's love of nick-knacks the room was unlikely to have remained unchanged.

'From what I was told it happened in the first lap of the race. The steward who came to tell me about the accident said that it was not Ronald's fault. Ronald is an old hand and too experienced to have made a mistake. The other driver was new to the track. He made an almost fatal error. Ronald was lucky, and the steward said that if he had not had such quick reactions, he would have lost his life.'

Ruth asked. 'Did you say that he broke both his legs?'

'Both, below the knees. Both ankles are badly broken. I think it means that his racing days are over. Part of me is glad about that.'

'I would be extremely glad if he were my son,' Ruth exclaimed indignantly, 'he's fortunate to be alive.'

'Yes,' Veeve said slowly, 'but what is he going to do now? I think he used racing as an antidote to losing Sara.'

'He couldn't do that for ever.' Ruth realised that it was not a helpful remark. 'What I mean is, at some point he would have to live like everyone else. Besides, if war comes, which seems likely from all this talk about Yugoslavia and that man Hitler, Ronald would have to join up to fight.'

'If he is fit to fight. Your Bertram will have to fight too, he's twenty-one.'

'Bertram's already in the Royal Air Force,' Ruth responded 'but this is not about him. When would you like me to visit?'

'He'll be in hospital for at least another week but I've a problem. This hotel is not conducive to an invalid in a wheelchair. We need to be practical. Could he come to you? Bertram's room is on the ground floor and you have just told me that he is in the Forces. I can organise a nurse. Both legs will be in plaster of Paris.'

Ronald was in plaster for three months, and only then could he begin to move around using crutches. When the initial crisis was over and his other injuries healing, Ronald began to behave, as Ruth described it, as a real convalescent. He fell into a depression, was quick to complain and even managed to upset those friends who made an effort to visit him. All this Ruth could understand and she was struggling to find a solution, when a letter arrived from Marie which reminded her about his youthful passion for music. That day she went out and bought a set of pencils and a block of manuscript paper.

'The piano in the lounge is free until late afternoon.' She said, in a tone that suggested that argument was useless. 'Your nurse can wheel you there. You are going to have to accept that it will be weeks before you can walk, and you need to occupy yourself.' Ruth handed him her purchases and walked away before Ronald had a chance to reply.

Another three months passed and Ronald had turned the corner from misery and despair to a man with a sense of purpose. One morning Ruth, on a whim, decided to enter the lounge while he was working. There was manuscript paper strewn all over the surface of the piano, Ronald's fair hair hung across his face as, with pencil on one hand and with the other searching out chords, he sat on the music stool composing with fierce concentration.

'Am I disturbing you?' Ruth said.

'Not really. I am a bit stuck over the development of the second movement. Listen to the theme.' Ruth liked what she heard although the intricacies of composing were beyond her realm of knowledge. Ronald finished the section and then turned to her.

'I am very grateful Ruth. You've seen me through a

black period. Not only Sara dying.' He looked directly into her face, his eyes filled with tears and Ruth feared that she might also succumb. 'I know I can't race any more My ankles are wrecked.'

Ruth hoped that he had some plan in mind because she had none for him.

'I can keep composing but if I am on my own, I am frightened that I'll sink back into self-pity.'

'Do you have any plans?'.

'I don't need good ankles to fly an aeroplane. This was Mother's idea. She told me that the Count has been flying for years.'

Ruth was alarmed that Ronald was exchanging one dangerous sport for another, but knew better than to raise objections.

'There's another reason. If there is a war I will have to do something and I keep thinking of Bertram. I would not be accepted into the Army, but if I could fly already...' He left the sentence unfinished. Then he added, 'The Count could teach me.'

'So you want to go to Germany?' Ruth stated. 'Have you thought that one day you might have to fight the Germans?'

'That did occur to me, but I can't face seeing my old mates while I am so crippled, nor memories of Sara wherever I go.'

The recent news had alarmed everyone and was the only topic of conversation. The chancellor of Germany, Adolf Hitler, was angling for war and demanding that, where ever there was a greater proportion of Germans than the indigenous population, those territories should become part of Germany.

No country that had been involved in the previous war could believe that Hitler would use force and propel Europe into another, even deadlier, conflict. In fact, so fearful were the major countries, Britain and France, that they were prepared to concede to almost any of Hitler's demands in order to maintain peace.

Within Germany, especially among the elite, namely the Prussian military, there were groups of men who were equally fearful but not for the same reason. They believed that Hitler was leading them into a war that they were in no position to win, and that such a war would ruin Germany. It was with this conviction that the group made overtures to Britain. Only if Britain stood firmly and resisted Hitler's moves to annexe parts of Yugoslavia could they halt his expansionist ambitions.

Veeve and the Count had repaired to her private room. Politics and world affairs were an abiding diversion for Veeve and the recent developments, fuelled by the discussions and the varied opinions from some of her guests who were actively contributing at cabinet level, meant that she was anxious to ascertain the Count's views.

'Will Hitler stop at nothing to achieve his demands?' Veeve asked. 'There are some who say that he is bent on making war whatever we or the French agree to.'

'I am of that opinion, but to read your papers or to listen to your Ministers, they do not seem to be alert to the extreme danger. They are fair and decent men and they believe their reasonable approach will be reciprocated. Those of us who have seen the rise of Hitler and his party know that they are ruthless in pursuit of their aims. Hitler talks of living space and needing more territory, but Germany lacks many of the minerals and other resources that countries adjacent to us have in abundance, and which he also needs if he is to expand.'

'Does he see it as a way of redressing the balance? Of winning a war to make up for losing the last one?'

'Without a doubt. It is a useful emotion to stir within our nation, so many of whom are already brainwashed.'

'Why are you telling me this?' Veeve said. She knew that the Count would not have initiated the discussion, or revealed his sentiments, without a reason.

'I, along with others, plan to do away with Hitler if he invades Czechoslovakia, but we need assurances from Britain that they would retaliate and be prepared to fight if he did so. I have been asked to put out feelers to influential people in your government. I thought you might know a useful contact.'

'Isn't this dangerous for you and for those of you who think like this?' Veeve was both shocked and thrilled at the proximity of such an action. 'Would killing him solve the problem?' She asked, genuinely curious.

'It is more complicated than that. The Nazi party would have to be dismantled by removing the leaders. There would have to be alternative leaders ready to install in their place. I am not sure that the instigators of this plan are determined or organised enough, but if there is a chance of toppling Hitler before disaster strikes, I am prepared to help them achieve it.'

Veeve was excited at the prospect of aiding such a preposterously outrageous plot. She knew the Count moved in influential circles but had no inkling that he was as closely linked to the corridors of power as he appeared to be.

'It will have to be someone I know well and who I can trust' Veeve awaited his reaction. 'Although he is a slippery eel I think I can safely say that he is loyal to his country.'

'Who?'

'You know him too, or did some years ago. Brindsley-Smith.' Veeve looked for the Count's approval. 'He's weak, but he likes to feel important and it would flatter him to be asked who you should contact.'

The Count thought for a while. 'I think that I can lean on him, and scare him into keeping his counsel.'

'You mean, stop him blabbing?'

'That's my concern. That he might boast that he was instrumental in enabling the dialogue. Any careless talk could cost us our lives.'

'You could tell him that it would cost his. He's impressionable and would believe you. It would make him feel even more important.'

'That would be no bad thing. He might try harder to help me reach the right people.'

A week later, as Henry entered the smoking room of his club, his heart sank. He was not able to avoid speaking to Brindsley-Smith. The man was already advancing towards him. Since the encounter following Sara's funeral several years before, he had managed to limit their intercourse to a few polite platitudes. Henry recognised Brindsley-Smith in this mood, it was invariably when he had something to impart, and this was usually in an attempt to enhance his standing. If it was not so irritating it would be pitiable and he prepared his face for a cordial greeting.

'A Scotch?' Brindsley-Smith asked in a tone that implied that this was a regular habit between them.

'A Martini.' Henry found himself asking for a drink he rarely took, but which repelled the assumption by Brindsley-Smith, and those within earshot, that they were intimate friends.

Brindsley-Smith seemed impervious. 'I'll have one too.' As soon as they were settled he said, 'I've been involved in some very hush-hush affairs.'

'Should you be telling me?' Henry asked intrigued, but disturbed that Brindsley-Smith seemed so quick to impart what he assumed was confidential information.

'I can trust you, old fellow. A brother-in-law and all that.' Henry flinched, unwilling to acknowledge their relationship. 'I've been doing some useful work for the Count.'

'The Count?'

'You know, Veeve's friend. The German that Ronald visits, well, used to visit.' Henry decided not to tell Brindsley-Smith that he did not know the Count, but he was interested to hear that Brindsley-Smith had contact with a German.

'And how do you know him?'

'I escorted Ronald to the Count's estate when Ronald left school. I see him on occasions at Veeve's hotel.' It was news to Henry that Veeve had a German as a close friend.

Henry tried to disguise his curiosity. It pained him to let Brindsley-Smith think that anything he said impressed him.

'There is a plot afoot. The Count needed influential contacts at the highest decision-making level in our Government. I have a few. Through the Army.'

Henry realised that he was just the sort of person to cultivate usefully placed people. 'So you averted a war!'

'Possibly.' Brindsley-Smith answered seriously.

Henry was disturbed. He had previously dismissed Brindsley-Smith as a man with delusions of his own importance, but it appeared to be otherwise. Despite the passage of time it seemed that he was actively nurturing those contacts. Henry wondered what could be driving him and decided that he had better maintain some contact, especially if war became a reality because Brindsley-Smith might use its resurgence to further his own unfinished business.

Chapter Thirty-Six

A European crisis had been averted and everyone, except a few sceptics, slipped into a false sense of security. War, which few believed would happen again on European soil, was a sinister shadow that they could ignore, and the prosperity that was evident in all aspects of life could continue on its steady path.

In Paris, Hortense had expanded her business by opening a shop off the Boulevard Haussmann. She attributed part of her success to the fact that she not only maintained control of purchasing and distribution, but kept in touch with her customers by periodically serving at the counter. She kept a tight rein on her finances and treated her employees fairly.

Within a few years of arriving back in Paris and working with Hortense, Jean-Paul was able to secure his own accommodation. As time passed he feared exposure less and less and, although he was careful not to attract undue attention, or to frequent the area of his old firm and business associates, he created a tolerable existence. Although he was not a partner in the business, Jean-Paul's relationship with Hortense was that of an equal and she valued his advice.

Hortense felt it was time for her to consider her future. Soon she would want to sell her shop and decide whether to stay in Paris, which would mean a move to the outskirts due to her reduced income, or return to her home town in La Vendée.

'Jean-Paul, have you thought what you will do when you stop working?' They met regularly at a Brasserie that came to expect them and kept them a table.

'I never look ahead,' Jean-Paul answered. 'I just presume I'll keep working. Why do you ask? Are you planning to sell?'

Hortense tried to avoid reminding him that they were reaching the age when people started to make these decisions.

'I think about it. Possibly in the next year or two. It's a good business. I could manage, if I stop working, I mean.'

Jean-Paul nodded in agreement. 'Thinking about the crisis, I wonder whether it is just a delaying tactic and war is inevitable anyway. If this is the case, you should sell now.'

Hortense was taken unawares. 'I hadn't expected that response.'

'I've been watching what's happening in Germany. The massive build-up of all the necessities for war. The flying clubs that have proliferated under the guise of glider clubs. The recruitment to the armed forces. The militarisation. Hortense, you should see the Hitler youth and the manner in which they are brainwashed.'

'I've read some of the speeches. They seem so radical it is hard to believe that ordinary people can be swayed by them.'

'The power of the masses. It's a curious phenomenon. You gather the crowds and it's like hysteria, everyone becomes infected, and then not to agree isolates a person and they become suspect. It's easy for us to remain critical, but in German society, especially in the south, the influence of Nazism is all pervasive.'

'Will we be dragged into another war? Surely none of our countrymen have the stomach for it.' Hortense asked, willing Jean-Paul to reassure her.

'We may have no choice.'

Once their meal was over Hortense suggested that

they walk back to her apartment. Jean-Paul accepted. The nature of their conversation was unusual and Hortense was disturbed.

'A glass of wine or a coffee, or both?' Hortense called as she made her way to the kitchen. Jean-Paul stopped to look at one of her pictures.

'Both,' answered Jean-Paul without appearing to have his mind on the subject. After a few moments he commented, 'I think you have a gem here.'

'He's an artist that I've seen on the Quai d'Orsay. After a few days of stopping to look at it each time I passed, he offered it to me at a reasonable price. It's good isn't it? What do you think of my other pictures?' She disappeared leaving Jean-Paul to study the rest of her collection.

She emerged from the kitchen carrying two glasses of wine and handed one to Jean-Paul. He pointed to a small water colour. 'There's a landscape here that's familiar but I can't place it.'

She hesitated, while he looked expectantly. 'It's La Vendée. That's how it looked when I lived there.'

'Where Ruth and Bertrand stayed?' Hortense was relieved that he had said the words she dared not.

'It's so beautiful there but you hardly saw it.' She walked from the hall to the living room, uncomfortable with the subject yet feeling mildly liberated that Ruth's name had been spoken. 'Choose a seat and I'll fetch the coffee.'

When Hortense returned with the tray Jean-Paul was still standing. He turned to her and indicated another picture, a photograph in a black frame above her desk.

'Is this him?' he asked.

Hortense nodded. 'We were together for so short a time that sometimes I wonder if it was real. I tend to pigeon-hole those years because we were so happy, and I can't see that it can ever be repeated. Yet, would it, or could it, have lasted at such an intensity?'

'I think what we had in intensity, other people gain in longevity despite their inevitable high and low points. Whenever you lose a loved one the trauma in one's body and in one's soul must be the same, because they have gone. I don't think that length of time necessarily makes any difference. You find someone, which in itself is a miracle, who wants to be with you, and then they are taken away. We have just got to keep living.' He smiled. 'Tell me about him.'

Jean-Paul sat in Hortense's capacious armchair and leaned back. Occasionally he would put down his glass and take up his coffee cup, but all the time he silently encouraged her to talk. In her narrative she came to the years that they had spent together with Veeve. 'I was happy again then, even if it was a different sort of happiness. There, finally, I had a group of friends, and we had some good times together without worrying about forming relationships. There was always something to look forward to. That was what I had missed. And then the war ruined it all.'

After a while Hortense broke the silence by fetching the bottle of wine and refilling their glasses. When she sat down she saw tears in Jean-Paul's eyes. Hortense went around the back of his chair and placed her hands on his shoulders.

'I think it is worse for you because there has not been an ending. Do you think that you could ever accept that it is over?' He reached up to take one of her hands. 'Do you think there might be a future for you and me, one day? It would be second best, I know, but neither of us would be lonely, and we've known each other for a long time now.'

He held her hand more firmly and seemed to be struggling within himself. Hortense laid her head on his. 'What is it? What is the stumbling block?'

'Bertrand.'

Hortense released his hand. She walked back from behind his chair and knelt down on the rug. She took one of his hands in hers, and then the other. He stared through her.

'I need to know. I need to see him. Just once. What if there is a war?'

Neither spoke for a while, and then releasing his hands, Hortense stood and faced him.

'It could be done.' She announced. She stepped back to lean against her desk. 'How old will he be?'

'Twenty-One'

'The age of a soldier. If we find him, would you tell him who you are?' Hortense asked brutally.

'No, that would not be fair. I am a stranger.'

'Would he not guess?'

'There's no reason why he should. I don't know what he has been told but I presume he thinks I am dead, so why should he suspect?'

'It's a risk we could take. Could you ask Marie?'

Jean-Paul thought for a moment. 'The only way she could find out is to contact Ruth. That is not a route I could use.'

'Pierre?'

'I can't communicate with my old firm. It would be too easy for the authorities to trace me.'

'Why would they bother, now?'

'If there's another war, files will come out. I wouldn't trust the English major not to re-open the case.'

'His ego is at stake?'

'Exactly.' Jean-Paul answered bitterly.

'Then we are left with the Count. Can you ask him? Could you tell him why? Does he know what happened?'

'I've never spoken to him.'

Hortense stopped her pacing. 'You never contacted him?' She asked incredulously. 'With whom have you been securing all the contracts?'

'Directly with the company.'

'But why not? Did you not contact the Count?'

'Because he was my contact, before the war. It was my communication with him that was the final piece of evidence, as they called it, in the tribunal.'

Hortense was stunned. The Count was their only hope if Jean-Paul seriously wanted to find his son.

'I did intend to,' Jean-Paul said, 'but I recognised Ronald, he was with him. I feel certain it was him, and then I understood how complicated it could all become. It was easier not to involve the Count.'

'Then I'll write to him. It's a risk we will have to take. It's unlikely that they will trace you through me.

The Count is hardly going to betray you when I tell him that you were accused of working for Germany.' She waited for Jean-Paul to object. 'So that's what I'm going to do.'

She sat down defiantly, sad that the gentle atmosphere of their evening had developed from one of renewed closeness into a combined effort to solve a practical problem. It would benefit neither of them if Jean-Paul yearned to pursue his quest and she was reluctant to help him.

'And one day, you and I can talk again about possibly growing old together.' She said gaily and was heartened to see an answering smile.

'One day we will talk about it,' he promised.

The Count was intrigued by a renewed overture from those years in Nice. Hortense wrote wondering if he remembered her, and said that she had a request on behalf of a friend. Did he ever visit Paris?

He felt certain that her letter was in some way concerned with Jean-Paul. He had never been convinced that Pierre had told him the truth, and with the mystery of his disappearance in no way resolved, he was eager to meet up. He remembered her with her dark hair swept up into a chignon, and with a pleasing, lively personality. He looked forward to meeting her and to hear how she had managed during and since the war.

The Count was aware that he had grown a little more portly and was slowing with age, but his brain was a sharp as ever and his love of company as compelling. He speculated whether Hortense had remarried, but her contacting him like this and her withholding a reason for their meeting, suggested that she had not settled into the sedentary life of a hausfrau. His social circle had not changed for several years and the Count enjoyed the prospect of a trip to Paris with the revival of an old acquaintance, all the more so since his rendezvous was with a member of the fairer sex.

In order to impress Hortense, the Count arranged for them to meet at the Hôtel Georges Cinq, which had one of the most luxurious lounges in Paris, and where everyone, from the commissaire to the bellboy was in uniform, and where the waiters wore white gloves. He dressed carefully in an immaculately tailored pale grey three piece suit with a grey and magenta cravat and a carnation in his buttonhole. Across his chest was a thick gold chain attached to his pocket watch, and a gold tie pin completed his outfit. He had not felt as tense or excited for some while.

When Hortense stood in the doorway of the lounge he knew at once that it was her. She had retained an elegance and carried herself with confidence. Her trim figure was striking for a woman no longer young. She was dressed in a waisted jacket of green velvet and a light wool skirt which fell in pleats. Her shoes had a small heel, perhaps because she remembered that she was taller than the Count, and wore a close fitting cloche hat over her neat bobbed hair. The Count was impressed and rose to greet her, effusive in his welcome.

'This calls for a celebration. So many years and you look marvellous. Time has been good to you.' Hortense was flattered and she smiled her appreciation. A waiter hovered in the background.

'Some champagne,' the Count instructed, 'I have found a long lost friend.' He led her to a quiet corner of the lounge to protect her from curious stares, and to give them some privacy.

'Count, this is splendid,' Hortense said, as the waiter filled their glasses. 'I am not often lost for words.'

'Santé!' said the Count. Hortense replied, and each waited for the other to speak. The Count was first. 'Shall I tell you a little about myself? There is not so much. After the war I settled into a comfortable bachelor existence with many friends. Really there is no excitement.'

Hortense raised her glass. 'That I cannot imagine,' she said challenging him.

'Unless you include my visits to England, to see Veeve. Have you seen her? Or Pierre?' Hortense shook her head. 'Then I have plenty to tell you, but first, what about you?' The Count listened and commented enthusiastically as Hortense described her venture into the shoe business and its success.

'I can see before me a determined woman, and I commend her achievement. And did you ever marry?' Hortense shook her head again. 'Neither did I but not for want of trying.' The Count excused himself. When he returned he said, 'I have reserved a table for us for dinner. Do tell me that you can stay. I have not had the company of such a enchanting friend for many years and I can't bear to part with you yet.'

'Of course, I would be delighted,' Hortense assured him. There stretched ahead of them the whole evening and they could converse and reminisce, and it would allow Hortense to choose her moment to deliver her request.

'I saw Pierre many years ago,' The Count said. 'It was at the request of Veeve.' Hortense looked surprised. 'She wanted to find out what had happened to Jean-Paul.' Hortense was non-committal.

'Pierre knew nothing. If he did, he didn't say. He told me Jean-Paul was dead. He seemed to be alarmed at my questions and reluctant to renew our friendship.'

'And Veeve?'

'I thought it was easier to report what Jean-Paul said.'

'Did she accept that?'

'She had no option as she had no other way of finding out. I doubt Ronald knew anything, he was only a boy. She certainly did not ask again.'

'But you seem doubtful?'

'Pierre was very guarded. He seemed to have his answer ready and no credible explanation.' The Count then regaled Hortense with accounts of his visits to Veeve's hotel, and how it was much like the old days with Veeve at the centre, except that now they were paying guests. 'Except me,' The Count said cheerfully, 'she has never been able to completely give me up, yet I have never been able to persuade her to leave London. She was always one to hedge her bets and come out on top. If there is another war, she will once again choose the winning side.'

'Do you think we're heading for more conflict.'

'I fear so, but a war would ruin Germany.'

'And it would ruin France too?'

'Certainly, my dear, we are both doomed. But it is time for dinner. Shall we meet here in, say, ten minutes?'

Hortense had not tasted a meal to match the one that she had that night, nor enjoyed the attention of such silent and efficient waiters. 'I feel that we are back in Nice.' Hortense thanked the Count effusively.

He raised his glass. 'It is my pleasure. But I think that it is now time for you to tell me why we are here.' He paused. 'I notice that you have not mentioned Jean-Paul, although I have. Is this about him?'

Hortense chose her words carefully. 'He is alive, but he is, in a sense, in hiding.'

'So this request. Is it from him or on his behalf?'

She weighed up how much to tell him. 'Jean-Paul wants to see his son.' Hortense finally spelt it out.

'So Jean-Paul did not die. I wondered. But it suited me. Why now?'

'His son is twenty-one and if there is another war... You are the only person who I know who may be able to arrange it.'

'I need to think about this and I need to know what happened all these years ago. It might be that I cannot help you, unless I know.'

'I can't tell you here,' Hortense indicated the crowded dining-room.

'Let us take coffee in the lounge.' He led Hortense through the dining room. They were too preoccupied to notice the appreciative glances from their fellow dinner guests. They made a striking couple, particularly since they appeared aloof and unaware of their impact. In the lounge a pianist was playing and they found a table in an alcove behind it. 'The music will give us privacy.'

Their coffee was served and Hortense had no choice but to tell her story.

'So the English major decided that Jean-Paul was an informer, and from what Jean-Paul understood, the other two men on the tribunal needed more information. I take it that the discussion was in English and that Jean-Paul did not mistake their conclusions? Well, it's of no consequence now.'

For a while they listened to the music, neither of them speaking.

'I can understand a man wanting to see his son,' The Count concluded finally and Hortense sighed with relief. 'I am curious about this English Major. I have met one who complained about a French spy slipping through his fingers.'

Hortense wondered whether she had been able to convince him of Jean-Paul's innocence.

'Am I to be given the name of his son?'

'Bertrand Barthold. When I wrote to you there was the imminent threat of war. However, now that the Czechoslovakian crisis has been averted, there is no urgency.'

'So what do we do now? Do you want me to keep in contact with you?'

'To protect Jean-Paul, and any trail leading via me to him, there should be no record of our meeting,' Hortense said. 'At the risk of sounding as if I am overdramatising, only contact me if war seems inevitable. Send a telegram.'

'It may be that Jean-Paul will have to move fast. Once I have found his son, if I do, I will just say the time, day and place. I will send a message in which I will include the words Prussian Blue.'

'Prussian Blue?' Hortense remembered that Jean-Paul's intention was to search for that dye.

He gave her an enigmatic look. 'It amuses me.'

She tipped her head with a shrug of her shoulders.

'I am sorry that you and I are prohibited, due to these uncertain times, from renewing our acquaintance and putting our friendship on a firmer footing.' The Count looked wistful and Hortense too felt a pang of loneliness. 'It seems that I choose my ladies from the wrong countries. My dear, this evening has given me enormous pleasure.'

'As it has to me too, dear Count.'

He kissed her hand, and when Hortense looked up at him, a twinkle lit his eyes.

Chapter Thirty-Seven

It took the Count most of the summer to come to a decision. He listened to the various guests who came, as they did annually, to hunt and spend their evenings discussing the political situation, and he pressed his colleagues on the different committees on which he served, for their views. He moved in circles where there were men who were close to the corridors of power, and he tried to gauge from them their forecast for the future of Germany. All the time he attempted to assess the mood of the English.

The messages were mixed. There were those who blatantly admired the Führer, and it had to be admitted that Germany had been galvanised, over the past decade, to put its finances on a firm footing and to regain national pride. This was to his country's advantage but the majority of the English public did not witness the methods by which this had been achieved.

There were those who wanted peace to continue indefinitely, whatever the cost. France and England were ancient antagonists. France had lost too many of their countrymen and were only now seeing a generation of virile young men which they would be unwilling to sacrifice. From what he had gleaned, it seemed unlikely that England would fight on behalf of France. However, even with the realities of Germany's re-armament, war did not look as if it would erupt at any time soon.

In the light of this the Count felt it was time to find a solution to his relationship with Veeve. They were in their mid-fifties and the prospect of an easier life beckoned. In his view, it would be preferable if they could spend the time that they had left, together.

He packed carefully, the weather even in summer could be changeable and it was best to be prepared with clothes suitable for both town and country. He decided not to announce his impending visit, and booked under an assumed one hoping that the element of surprise might work in his favour.

He did, however, make a reservation in a hotel near Windsor for a week prior to his arrival in London. He had only a hazy idea about cottages in rural villages, and he had a romanticised picture, mainly drawn from paintings and books written for the discerning tourist. He had heard that Windsor was a suitable retreat from London, yet within easy reach. The latter was important if he was to convince Veeve to go along with his proposal.

He called in at the nearest garage where he leased a two-seater and spent the week touring the county, in ever widening circles. He became increasingly enchanted by the quaint villages, ancient woodlands and picturesque houses. How could anyone not want to spend time in such idyllic surroundings. Fired with enthusiasm, and rested and healthy from a week enjoying his own company, sleeping soundly and eating as well as English food allowed, the Count packed his luggage into the boot of the car, paid his hotel bill, leaving a generous tip which reflected his sanguine mood rather than the quality of the service, and headed for London.

Veeve's hotel guests were scattered around the lounge sipping cocktails, sophisticated and smart, having changed for dinner. Veeve entered, as she did most evenings, with precise timing. She may have lost her figure, her hair may be grey and her fingers gnarled with arthritis, but she had not lost her vibrancy and her ability to enliven a room. She was careful to dress well and enjoyed her daily ritual, changing her jewellery to match her dress and keeping up with whatever was in fashion. Modern dress did not flatter her ageing body, but a skilled couturier could do wonders with pleats and folds of material, and a well managed shawl could mask the loss of a waistline.

She had no sooner entered the room than the Count stepped forward from where he had been entertaining friends. 'Veeve,' he extended both hands.

A momentary irritation flickered across her face. 'Well, Count, back again, I see.' She held his hands briefly then searched with a sweep all the faces turned in her direction. She was quick to manipulated the situation. 'May I introduce you to a new guest of ours. You will have much in common, but I'll leave you to find out the connection.'

'Delighted, my dear Veeve, and later we must catch up on old times.'

Veeve moved away, more agitated than her smooth demeanour indicated. She had seen the name of a German Baron in the register who was due to arrive that day, and had been excited at the prospect of a new conquest. Every guest had to be made to feel unique and Veeve had perfected this art. She was more annoyed than pleased, therefore, to discover that the Count had surprised her. She circled the room with her gentle banter gratifying each set of guests, all the while puzzling over the fact that her old friend had not used this subterfuge before.

By the time the guests had left the dining room, and Veeve had retreated to her drawing room, she was ready for the discreet tap on her door.

'I won't disturb you for more than a few minutes,'

The Count announced, as if his visit was of little consequence and that he had equally important matters to attend to.

'Don't be foolish,' Veeve retorted, riled, 'it's months since I saw you and I want to know to what I owe this unexpected pleasure.'

'Now you're being foolish, Veeve. You don't have to switch on your charm for me.'

Veeve grinned, acknowledging that a truce had been established. 'You're looking good.'

The Count poured each of them a glass from the decanter on the sideboard, and leant back against it. 'You, on the other hand, dear girl, look done in and in need of a change of scene. It's been a long season and we are, none of us, getting any younger.'

'What are you suggesting?' Veeve gave a coquettish smile as she accepted her glass. 'But perhaps you're right, I probably am looking jaded. It's not the guests, it's managing the staff, and keeping them happy, that is the greater headache.'

'I've arranged a small jaunt for you, if you'll accept. Take a couple of days away from here. I've found a delightful place only a short drive away.'

She was tempted, but moved onto other subjects. His glass empty, the Count stood up, 'Well, Veeve? What's the answer?'

'Thursday and Friday. You don't need to tell me more until then. Are you leaving?'

'I'll wish you good night.' And he gave her a light kiss on the cheek.

A few days later, Veeve stood and watched while her

bags were carried to the door, and for the Count to escort her. 'My ebony stick,' she called to the porter. 'It's an affectation,' she explained. However, as she descended the steps she winced with pain, but he did not comment.

There were autumn tints on all the leaves and along the hedgerows. Veeve had not thought that being back in the countryside would affect her as strongly. The flashes of sunlight as they drove through woodland, the smell of meadows and crops, the feeling of unlimited space after so long in the city, was exhilarating. The Count was correct, she did need a change of scenery.

It was not only the scenery she realised, she had missed, but the the variety of people and places. She had forgotten that there was another life outside her hotel containing intimate eating houses and busy workshops, blacksmiths and carpenters, butchers, ironmongers, and drays with milk churns. She watched with unusual interest working men and women, children running, mothers with prams, old men seated, women gossiping, real existences playing out as they drove by. .

'It's a far cry from hotel life,' The Count caught her mood, 'One is artificial and the other essential.'

'What I do for people is essential,' Veeve retorted huffily.

'Everyone can do with an escape, in their own way, and yours is one way.'

'What other ways are there?'

The Count described how, on his estate and in the nearby village there were Saint's days and fetes, weddings and christenings, excuses for camaraderie, eating and drinking. There were sporting events, festivals and impromptu parties. All these were escapes from the drudgery of earning a living. 'It's not only in high society establishments that an escape to the country is sought after.'

Two days were not enough and Veeve regretted having to head back to London.

'I have a surprise,' The Count was driving effortlessly, navigating the narrow lanes with obvious enjoyment, 'it's not far from here.'

The road led through a village, over a bridge by a squat-towered church, and at a bifurcation beneath a copper beech, he slowed the car and drew up beside a stretch of woodland. He walked around the car, opened the door for Veeve, and taking her elbow escorted her to the wooden gate. A cottage was tucked down behind a thick hedge, sheltered on three sides by trees, with a path leading up to the front door bordered with chrysanthemums, sweet William and late flowering roses.

Involuntarily Veeve gasped. 'It's hardly real, it looks like a painting. Why are you showing me this?'

'Because I thought I would buy it.'

Veeve gazed at the scene before her. Every part of the property was in miniature, from the stocky chimneys to the leaded windows and from the weathered wooden door to the neatly manicured garden. 'Why would you do that?' She asked, She understood that it was perfect in the manner of a collectable item.

'For us.'

Veeve needed to be clear in her own mind how she

interpreted the Count's proposal, and to buy herself time. 'Let's not talk about that now. We'll discuss it later, this evening.'

If the cottage was to be an occasional retreat, that was a fanciful idea since neither of them had the least idea how to run a house. Alternatively it seemed unlikely that the Count was planning to live there by himself, and she had to consider how this would reflect not only on her business but her social position. Although there were those, with whom she sympathised, who openly admitted connections with Germans she did not think that the appeasement policy would be long lasting. Finally, it did occur to her that he might, once again, be offering marriage.

'Which is it?' Veeve came straight to the point when they were alone. She laid out her three scenarios, watching her friend's reaction to each, but he was inscrutable.

'I said it was for us, by which I meant we could discuss the future. Our future. Owning a hotel in war time, I assure you, is a daunting prospect. Many have to take on long term occupants who, being homeless, are irritable and bored. The better, younger staff are drawn to more lucrative work in factories or are called up. It is fair to add that you are hardly strong enough to continue much longer.'

'So what are you offering me?'

'Companionship, or even marriage. You have never visited my estate but I can provide every luxury. Should there be a war, it is not in a militarily strategic position. You would be safe.'

'So the cottage?'

'As an alternative, should events go against us.'

'You mean, depending on which country wins. I thought you were working to bring down Hitler, to prevent war.'

'That is not so certain now.'

For the first time that she could remember, Veeve felt fear. Fear of disability. Her pain and loss of movement were increasing but she had been able to ignore their implications. Fear that her life would feel meaningless without the constant variety provided by her hotel. Finally, fear of being left in her old age without an income. The Count was offering a solution to all her fears if she stepped into the unknown.

'If your attempt against Hitler has failed does that mean war? Perhaps we won't be involved this time. His plans for expansion can hardly extend across here.'

'His lebensraum. If he became too ambitious it's possible that war could extend to England.'

Veeve had avoided one war, waiting it out to be sure to pitch in on the winning side. Once again she had to weigh her options, and keep them open. She moved away to give herself time to think. She stiffened her back, fighting against the pain in her hips and clasping her damaged hands together at her waist. She only ever allowed the Count to see her vulnerability.

'If England collapses, if we are beaten, then come to me with a ring.' She sighed, and added sadly, 'but something tells me that we won't be seeing each other for a very long time.'

Chapter Thirty-Eight

1939

Henry placed his hat and coat in the arms of the doorman. He handed Henry an envelope. 'This arrived for you, Sir, about an hour ago.'

The gentleman's club to which Henry belonged was discreetly placed in a side street off one of the main thoroughfares through the city. It was convenient for his office, whose site had not changed since he joined the firm, a few years before his marriage to Lil. His step was not so sprightly as it had been, all those years ago, and his heart condition did bother him on occasions. It was useful to be able rest at the club after work before heading home. Besides, the exchange of views that he enjoyed with his old acquaintances added interest to his conversation over dinner.

On this occasion, however, Henry was waiting at his club to meet Lil before heading in to town.

The old building was needing some attention. The entrance on the street looked neglected, and the décor shabby. The arms of the leather armchairs were scuffed and worn and the seats sagged. The wallpaper was tanned from the smoke of pipes and cigars, and the pictures dated back to the earliest years of be-whiskered chairmen.

If only Lil could transfer her skills from costumes to

interiors, what a difference she could make, but no-one in the present uncertain climate was prepared to invest in refurbishment.

Henry looked at the envelope which was addressed in ungainly handwriting that he did not recognise. He gave his order, a sherry at this time of day, before picking up the letter and asking for a knife and slicing it open.

'Would you believe it,' He told Lil as they walked to the theatre, 'Brindsley-Smith wants to meet with me, urgently. That's how it comes across. I know things are hotting up but for the life of me I can't see what is so pressing. If you don't mind, I sent him a note to say to meet me after the performance. Can I send you home in a cab?'

'I'm all agog,' Lil said.

The pleasant lift to his spirits that he felt when they were out together never left him. 'Will you wait up?'

In the club Brindsley-Smith was standing by a bay window looking out. No one had drawn the curtains. It was raining and by the light of the street lamps the raindrops fell as if the viewer was in the centre of a fountain. Brindsley-Smith was silhouetted, his back to the room. Henry had only a few moments to appreciate a scene that was an archetypal snapshot of the London he loved, in black, grey and silver. Then Brindsley-Smith spun round and his nostalgic picture was replaced with another, more immediate reminder, that all was not well with the world.

Brindsley-Smith, his grey hair slicked back over his scalp, with bushy eyebrows and craggy face, was in good shape for a man who had just turned sixty. Perhaps because he was agitated, his movements were those of younger man. He strode towards Henry and shook his hand energetically. 'Good of you to come. Been to the theatre?'

Henry, unlike his reaction on most previous encounters, felt more kindly disposed to this distant relative. Time had softened him. 'What's up, old boy? Do you need a drink?'

Brindsley-Smith waved a hand dismissively. 'No need. Do I have your confidence?'

'My dear man, what could have happened?' Henry avoided a direct answer.

They sat down, one on each side of the window. Leaning forward, his elbows on his knees, Brindsley-Smith began speaking rapidly.

'You remember that I was dealing with some hush-hush stuff a while ago. Well, there have been developments recently that I have been made aware of. It's time for me to make a move.'

'What do you mean?'

'We're on the brink, you know. I've not cleared it with my department, it's a bit premature for that because hostilities are not declared, but once they are, movement on the continent will be restricted. Ronald's heading for Germany. This is my chance.'

Henry's light-hearted mood changed abruptly and with it his previously softened attitude.

'You are going after the informer?' He asked, intent on disguising his dismay.

'Before he can do any more damage, and I intend to bring him to justice.'

Henry tried to imagine the depth of commitment to this case that the man sitting opposite him must feel. It appeared that over the years his original mission had become an obsession. Was he, also, unconsciously striking a blow against a family that had rejected him. Henry stalled. 'You need to act now?'

Brindsley-Smith began to give him details of his department, who he answered to, and how if he achieved his aim, there would be no questions asked as to why he had proceeded on his own initiative. Henry listened as the other man made plans to resurrect the case after all these years. He was almost certain, now, that the man Brindsley-Smith was pursuing was Bertram's father. Henry, meanwhile, envisaged the implications of an arrest. The most innocent, gentle, retiring member of the Hefford family would be dealt a most grievous blow, one from which she would never recover. Ruth, reserved and unapproachable, was to have her secret exposed, and his nephew Bertram to have his life shattered.

He tried one more time to dissuade him. 'So you think that by confronting Ronald with the facts, he will help you find an Uncle whom he last saw when he was thirteen?'

'Why not, if he was a traitor?'

'Why should Ronald know where he is? Ronald, along with the rest of the family, thinks that he is dead.'

Henry hoped, from Brindsley-Smith's reaction, that he had finally scored a winning shot. Brindsley-Smith started to pace around the room and Henry felt a minor sense of victory. He also began to feel annoyed that he was being used to justify the man's vendetta, and uncharacteristically said sarcastically. 'I suppose that you'll go after Bertram instead, since you can't use Ronald.'

Brindsley-Smith looked at him, surprised. 'That's exactly what I'll do. Ronald can tell me where Bertram is, and I have great hopes that the Count might also be of some use, if I play my cards right.'

'The Count?'

'Ronald's pal. Count Von Kuder. Lübeck. Schloss Wildenrath, ' He could not resist the boast.

They parted soon afterwards. Brindsley-Smith called after him on the steps to the street. 'If I don't come back, you'll be the only person who will know where to find me!' But he said it triumphantly, like a warrior heading for battle.

Henry, head down, his heart beating arythmically, turned the corner and, once out of sight of his odious companion, slowed to a stop and hailed a taxi.

Lil was waiting, as she had promised.

'Henry, you look terrible. Can I call someone?'

'There's something I have to do. Lil, a telegram.'

They had not moved from the hall, and Lil guided him to a seat that was usually the recipient of coats and shawls. She handed him the pad from beside the telephone. Henry, his hand shaking, fumbled inside his jacket pocket. Lil deftly found his pen and half knelt beside his chair. He gave her the pad.

'Count Von Kuder. Schloss Wildenrath. Lübeck.' He dictated. 'Request your help. B-S knows all. Imperative stop him.'

Ronald took off his flying goggles, removed his helmet and ran his fingers through his sweat soaked hair. Although not unduly concerned about his looks, he was unwilling to walk in to the hanger with his hair flattened against his head, in case it gave the mechanics the impression that he was a nervous pilot. Ronald then unwound the cravat from around his neck and, using one corner of it, wiped his face. He now had many flying hours in his logbook but the crossing was his first and it had not been easy. He had experienced several anxious moments. He pushed back the overhead sliding section of the cockpit and clambered out, pulling himself up and then stepping onto the wing. The plane had answered well to the controls and at no point in the journey had he mistrusted his machine, it was his navigation that had been tested, and he was exhilarated that he had risen to the challenge.

With a slightly ungainly walk, encumbered as he was by the straps of his bulky flying suit, and with his stiff ankles shod in padded flying boots, Ronald made his way to the hanger to meet the ground crew. They knew him well. He had learnt to fly on their airstrip and, it being a small operation, everyone was involved in either training the pilots or servicing their aircraft. They took pride in their novices. His particular team would be eager to hear about his round trip to England.

The Count was already in the hanger to meet him. Ronald remembered a similar feeling of unexpected contentment whenever Monsieur Cuanez collected him from school.

'Well done, my boy. Gut gemacht.' The Count

slapped Ronald on the back and then led him to his team. 'They'll want to hear all about your trip. I'll leave you with them while I deal with the paperwork.'

Ronald watched the mechanics put his aeroplane to bed, and then joined the Count.

'I've brought my new car, it's a Mercedes Benz.'

'A two thirty?'

'Come and see.'

However, excited by his adventure, Ronald spent less time than he might have done asking about the new model, and for the duration of their journey, recounted the details of his flight.

'That's quite an achievement,' The Count said appreciatively.

The Count felt a paternal attitude towards Ronald. Although no longer a young man, in many ways Ronald was still vulnerable and despite the distance in years, had not appeared to have recovered from the death of his young wife. With his recent knowledge about Jean-Paul he wanted to ask Ronald questions about events in his past, especially those days in Paris at the end of the last war. On the other hand if he kept Ronald in ignorance of his suspicions regarding Brindsley-Smith, he might achieve his own goals more effectively. He was therefore disconcerted when Ronald appeared to read his thoughts.

'My uncle is planning a visit.'

The Count took his hands off the wheel and made a despairing gesture.

'We all find him rather a bore but he seemed to infer that he had something important to say to you.

Something he could not send with me. I offered him a lift. He was not to know that the plane is a single seater.' Ronald gave the Count a knowing look and both men chortled with laughter. They were driving along narrow roads which signalled the approach to the estate. The woods became denser, the tall trees occluded much of the light, and it was possible to imagine the hidden haunts of wild boar that were the quarry for the frequent hunting trips, before the wall surrounding the estate began to come into view.

'Next time I fly, I'll try out my two-seater, but I'll pay more attention to the weather reports. What's the longest flight you have done?' The conversation turned to flight paths and fuelling distances and the Count decided, after all, not to burden Ronald with questions.

Chapter Thirty-Nine

'What are you doing here?' Ruth asked sharply. It was unusual for her to be positioned behind the reception desk as it was her habit to remain in her own office and leave the initial procedures to her staff.

'I am your brother-in-law,' he announced.

'I know exactly who you are.'

If Brindsley-Smith was discomforted by Ruth's greeting he gave no sign of it. He was confident that Ruth would be unaware that he had discovered the secret of her past, and assumed that her hostility was due to the disintegration of his marriage. Since this had occurred many years ago, and since he had made a good settlement for Betts, his conscience was clear and he felt that her attitude was unwarranted.

'I have come to render you a service, Ruth.' Brindsley-Smith leant one elbow on the surface of the wooden desk.

'Why ever would you want to do that?' Ruth said, 'Why do I need your service?'

This antagonism was more than Brindsley-Smith had bargained for. He laughed, rather too loudly. 'You are probably aware that a war is brewing.'

Ruth gave him with a scornful look.

'Ruth,' he said, as if delivering information the source of which was confidential and to which only he was privy. 'I have it on good authority that it is a matter of days and not weeks. I have business in Germany. I could arrange to meet Bertram, should you have a letter or special message for him. This may be your last chance for a long while.' In saying this he was taking a gamble.

He saw that she hesitated. 'I can warn him to seek a safer country to travel through.' The change in her expression convinced him that he had hit his mark.

The picture that rose in Ruth's imagination was of Bertram stranded in Germany and possibly interned. It was true, it could be weeks before Bertram was settled in whatever area of India his squadron was posted, his letters were arriving regularly but she was unable to reply because he was constantly on the move.

Ruth relented, allowing that perhaps his gesture was one of concern, offered him a chair and disappeared into her office. She was disconcerted, however, by his manner. Bett's former husband carried the supercilious air of one who expected rejection, and was therefore overly obsequious and pleasant. His smile was too wide and his gestures too expansive. However, she prided herself in being abreast of the news, and hoped that she could distinguish possible rumours from printed facts.

She had been vociferous in her rejection of Bertram's intention to travel back to India, across the continent. She had been unable to dissuade him, even although he had seen how aghast she had been when his proposed itinerary meant that he would be passing through Germany. She could not understand his reason for doing so, but he told her that he needed to see for himself the resurgence of industry and culture in the country of their former enemy.

Once on her own she became flustered, her thoughts a whirl. She instinctively mistrusted Brindsley-Smith but could see no reason to do so. She had only his treatment of Bett to go on. Taking up her pen she began to write. The concentration that writing required and the ease with which she performed this task, calmed her. As she wrote her letter to Bertram she succumbed to the argument that her son would want to hear from her, and she needed the link with him. For now that was her sole motivation. Her deepest fear being that she might never see him again.

Later she would try and unravel her tangled thoughts and understand why this distant relative felt the need to carry a letter to her son.

Brindsley-Smith rose from his chair and, with

impeccable courtesy took the letter which Ruth handed to him and said, 'And is Bertram planning to go to Munich to hear Herr Hitler?'

'It's possible.'

'The event is well publicised and I am planning to be in that area. At times like this families have to help each other,' he said unctuously.

Ruth interrupted him, making it clear that such sentiments meant little to her. 'I thank you for your kindness. I expect you will be seeing Ronald, please give him my warmest regards.' She offered her hand and they exchanged the briefest of handshakes. Brindsley-Smith knew better than to prolong his visit, and with studied formality turned towards the door. He walked with the slightly stiff gait of an ageing man, aware of Ruth's critical stare, through the hall and into the street.

He walked a short way along the pavement, and then called a taxi. He expected to feel elated at the ease with which he had accomplished his mission, but Ruth's demeanour reinforced his sense of her family's disapproval and once again he felt aggrieved. A little way into the taxi ride this emotion developed into defiance. Who was Ruth to treat him with such disdain, a merchant's daughter who had married a foreigner and a traitor? His indignation gave him justification for his deceit. He calculated the times of the ferries including time to pack up his luggage. If he was in luck he would be in Le Havre before nightfall. He then started planning for the climax, as he predicted it, of his years of patience, and anticipated his journey across the channel with smug confidence.

Chapter Forty

Many hours later, and following a restful night en route, Brindsley-Smith strode with proprietorial familiarity into the hall of the house of Count Von Kuder. In his limited German and with his embarrassingly atrocious accent, which never improved despite the numerous occasions that he visited the country, he called to a manservant to ask if the master was in residence. Brindsley-Smith made up for the paucity of his vocabulary by using complex English words and adding a German accent. Surprisingly this stratagem often worked. This was probably due to the passable English acquired by the staff who discreetly allowed him to be duped.

On being directed outside to where the Count was entertaining his guests, Brindsley-Smith discovered to his relief that the afternoon's tennis was drawing to a close. His lack of proficiency in this essential social skill had been a regular source of agitation, fortunately, now that he had reached the revered age of sixty years, he had a reasonable excuse not to play.

The Count flung out an arm in greeting and introduced him to the assembled company. Due to the sweltering summer heat a marquee had been erected beside the veranda under which were laid out drinks and English style tea. Brindsley-Smith was presented with a china cup and saucer, and since no one had yet taken possession of the wicker chairs, sought one in the shade to wait for the last of the tennis players whose exuberant shouts and athletic antics could be heard on the other side of a yew hedge. Brindsley-Smith was exceedingly relieved to see, when they emerged, that Ronald was among the animated, muscular young men.

Brindsley-Smith was accepted as one of the Count's old cronies and everyone spoke to him in English. Since their command of the language was in most cases proficient, he had no incentive to improve his German. The conversation consisted of easy banter between the, almost exclusively, male company. Women tended to ignore him. Today he was glad that he was marginalised because he was looking for an opportunity to speak to Ronald alone, without appearing to single him out. It was not until the other guests began to disperse that he had his chance.

He heaved himself out of his chair to intercept Ronald, and then fell in step with him. 'I came across your Aunt Ruth a few days ago.'

'You did?' Ronald's interest was gained at once. 'How was that? I did not think you had much contact with that branch of the family.'

Brindsley-Smith indicated that they should continue along the path towards the tennis court. 'I've not seen her for years,' he admitted frankly. 'It was your idea.'

'Mine?' said Ronald astonished.

'You were saying that your cousin is travelling on the continent. With a war brewing, you know, your Aunt may not see him again for a long time to come.'

'Oh, I had not thought of that. If it happens, which is only conjecture, I shall head back for Blighty in the hope of there being something suitable for me to do.'

'Good,' encouraged Brindsley-Smith, 'plenty of opportunities for a young man like yourself. A flyer too. No push over in the mathematics department either.'

'Could be useful with navigation.' Ronald pursued the topic, but his uncle was perturbed at the direction of the conversation.

'It will be for the long haul. Everything indicates that this will be a prolonged war. You have only got to see how serious preparations are over here.' With Ronald's attention focussed on the chasm that was set to rent England and Germany apart, he proceeded. 'So I thought I would be of service to your Aunt. I've a letter here for Bertram. Possibly the last he'll receive for a while from his mother. Do you happen to know where he's heading?'

'He seemed pretty keen to hear Herr Hitler. There's a big rally in Munich where the Führer is expected to speak.'

'Where will he stay?'

'With friends of mine in Willemstrasse. Useful contact wouldn't you say?' Ronald was pleased to have been able to help his cousin.

'You couldn't give me their address could you? Easy enough to post the letter in time to reach him.'

They completed the circuit of the tennis court, ascended the steps of the veranda and entered the library. 'Any chance that you could give it to me now? No time like the present.'

Ronald's tolerance of his uncle was always limited. He went across to a bureau, lifted the lid, and took out some stationery. He tore off the top sheet and scribbled rapidly on the handsome headed notepaper. 'This is it, Uncle. Got to rush and change.'

Brindsley-Smith was glad that Ronald had taken off in a hurry because he could not conceal his look of triumph. He settled into a leather armchair by the marble-fronted fireplace. This oak panelled room with its generously proportioned windows, expensive drapes and furnishings, hunting pictures and souvenirs, was where Brindsley-Smith felt that this was the destiny that he deserved. These were the surroundings he would have liked to belong to and here, amongst a different race, his shortfalls were minimised or taken as an English eccentricity. Here, his opinions held worth because, although they were often copied editions of those he heard in his club, they were regarded as his own.

On this occasion, however, he hoped that information from the Count and his close friends, some of whom were military leaders, might furnish him with material to carry back to London. Not only to his club, where he would gain some prestige for the exclusivity of his knowledge, but also to his former superiors in the intelligence service. He wondered if he was too old to be used again by his department, but he was certain that by concluding unfinished business, he might receive recognition and possibly even be awarded some sort of a medal.

Interrupting his cogitations the Count, resplendent in a military style green jacket and trousers, with brass buckle and belt, entered the room and placed a hand on

Brindsley-Smith's shoulder.

'Well old man,' he said jocularly, 'I fear that we may not have your company for much longer.' Brindsley-Smith reacted sharply under the Count's palm. 'This talk of war,' he explained, 'it could spark off at any time.'

Several guests filed into the library to join them, and the Count moved to the sideboard. 'What will you have, Ladies? Gentlemen? Some whisky for our English guest.'

Once his friends were all served the Count spoke in a confidential manner to his visitor. 'What news from England? Is she really preparing for hostilities?'

'If the allocation of masks and blankets in London is anything to go by, I think she is. Shelters are being prepared and information circulated. As for the military, I am afraid I am not in a position to say, except that the talk in the club is that we would have been better able to face you a year ago. Not that we were better prepared, but that at that time we were stronger than you.'

'It was a year ago that your leader came here to smooth things over, you have had ample time.'

'You have increased your manpower by over ten million, that is if you count the Germans in the Sudetenland and Austria.'

'And there will be more, mark my words.'

Brindsley-Smith felt a frisson of excitement. This was the sort of information that he was hoping to hear.

'Hitler will soon be annexing a lot more.' The Count gave a jerk of his head. 'Poland.'

Brindsley-Smith ventured to ask when this might happen.

'Watch Munich! That is why I say that we may not see you for much longer.'

The next morning Brindsley-Smith came across the Count and Ronald in earnest conversation. They were standing on the landing at the turn of the stairs, and the Count had obviously waylaid Ronald as he was heading out, attired for flying.

'Oh, it's you, Uncle.'

As he could see that his Uncle was not planning to pass but had stopped beside them, he said, by way of explanation, 'The Count is telling me that I should sell my aeroplanes. The Luftwaffe is buying all civilian planes. What do you say?'

'You can hardly fly them both back to England. It seems a shame to scupper the one you leave. Why not mothball the second one over here? You may need it one day.'

The Count shook his head. 'I would never get away with it. Ronald, you need to fly them back to England somehow.'

'I could take you with me,' Ronald suggested to his uncle. 'You'll be wanting to return. One of the planes is an old Comet Racer, a two seater.'

The Count looked for his reaction. With the full glare of the light from the window he could see that Ronald's uncle was unhappy with the suggestion. Ronald, however, energised by the crisis, hurried away. 'See you this evening, Sir.' And he clattered down the last flight of stairs, his equipment trailing, crossed the hall and the side door slammed behind him.

'What's holding you back?' The Count asked, 'not

that you are not welcome here for as long as you want.'

'I have to reach my nephew, Bertram. He is in Munich.'

'Have you any connections there? You do realise that with the knowledge that you've gained, if you are trapped within our boundaries once war is declared, you could be in serious danger?'

Brindsley-Smith reckoned that he could counteract any possibilities of such an accusation, if he were to deliver an informer into the hands of either the French or the British. He could see that it might be awkward if this arrest took place on German soil, but this was where he hoped to enlist the help of the Count. He had resisted seeking permission from higher authority for his actions when he was so near his goal, because he did not intend to be thwarted at this late stage.

The Count put an arm around his guest's shoulders. 'I admire your courage. We must all do what we can to avert disaster. Call in on my study later, I have a proposal to make to you. It might furnish you with transport and facilitate a safe exit should you require it.'

Brindsley-Smith felt an unaccustomed sense of importance as he left the Count, and anticipated their interview. He had never been credited with courage. In his nefarious dealings his own safety had not been jeopardised. He thought he could reach Bertram and then accept an offer of a flight home. He began to see that this would suit him very well. If the traitor was let loose again, as his country teetered on the brink of another war, he would not be able to forgive himself. He felt a righteous indignation on behalf of his country, but an even more strongly, he felt a final vindication for himself.

Brindsley-Smith became uncharacteristically sentimental as he walked through the magnificent grounds which encircled the Count's schloss. To the original castle had been added two wings, and extensive stables formed a fourth boundary to a vast gravelled courtyard. Formal gardens were set out below the veranda, rose beds divided by neatly clipped hedges, avenues dedicated to herbaceous borders, arches of laburnums and pools for water features. This would be the last time he would walk along the gravelled path or make a circuit around the tennis court. He was flattered by the status that he had been given in this alien environment due to his knowledge of his trade. It was in marked contrast to his standing in England, and only served to emphasise the loss that he would feel on his return.

Everything depended on whether the Count knew the whereabouts of Bertram's father. It was fortuitous that Bertram had chosen this time to travel on the continent, and it was a chance not to be missed. A few more days, and Bertram would be on his way to India and out of his reach. All that remained was to throw Bertram as bait and draw in his father. He trusted that the secret information that he was party to in England, might give him some leverage.

'But all our chances were lost the minute your Chancellor gave in,' the Count said. The two men were discussing the information that Brindsley-Smith had brought with him from London.

Brindsley-Smith seemed unconvinced. 'Surely there's no reason not to continue with the plan. The plan by the Military who, you gave us to understand, were opposed to Hitler.'

'They were opposed to Hitler making war. When he appeared no longer to be going to war, because your Chamberlain gave him everything he wanted, there was no compelling motive to unite people to remove him. Can't you see? Only a crisis, and firm backing from England, could have furthered our plans. You cannot motivate people with the threat of war, only the reality. No. What you are telling me is now useless.' The Count showed his irritation by walking around his desk, lifting and replacing the receiver of the telephone and sweeping papers into piles destined for the fire. 'I can't think why you saw the need to come here.'

'Perhaps I have another reason,' Brindsley-Smith sat stolidly and did not appear to be at all embarrassed by the Count's tirade.

This further frustrated the Count, but rather than give Brindsley-Smith the satisfaction of seeing his anger, he turned his back on him and looked out of the window. 'What can that be?' He asked contemptuously.

'You haven't got a cigar, have you?'

The Count was aware of the shift in their relationship, however by fetching the cigar box and offering one, he was able to move from the window without appearing to acquiesce with Brindsley-Smith's demand for attention.

Brindsley-Smith said, 'You were a friend of Jean-Paul Barthold?'

The Count was determined not to show how his guest had shocked him, and turned away abruptly, walking over to one of the bookcases. 'Johannes? Ah, Jean-Paul. Same difference. Before the war. It is of no consequence now.'

'You have probably observed that I have taken a keen interest in the boy Ronald for several years. Veeve's son is the only person who knew the Frenchman, the one who slipped through the net. His uncle was a suspected spy. Johannes, as you call him, was married to Ronald's Aunt Ruth.'

It was only since his meeting with Hortense that the Count had known that Jean-Paul was alive, that he had married Ruth. Only Henry's telegram had alerted him that Brindsley-Smith was the major who had been on the tribunal.

Suddenly the Count understood everything. Veeve's unexpected decision to spend the war with him in Spain, and the sibling rivalry. Later the request to him to ascertain Jean-Paul's whereabouts, reinforcing his knowledge that she preferred Jean-Paul over all her admirers, even including himself. Jean-Paul must have proposed to Ruth at the outbreak of the war. This revelation added a new dimension to the drama at the outbreak of the war, when he had taken Veeve under his protection, and she had so precipitately left the south of France, her sister and her son.

'Why Ronald? What would he know?'

'Because Ronald stayed with Ruth. When she returned from Paris two years after the war, she had Ronald in tow.'

The Count remembered wondering who had looked after Ronald during the war, and Veeve's unconvincing story about arranging for him to follow her, and this completed yet another piece of the jigsaw.

All the while Brindsley-Smith held his cigar so that the tobacco smouldered, he did not seem overly enthusiastic about smoking it. The Count had no intention of communicating his thoughts to the man opposite him.

'So,' the Count said softly, careful only to elicit information and to give away none, 'you are still pursuing Johannes Barthold, and planning to use Ronald as bait?'

'I was, until I learnt that Ronald believes that Jean-Paul is dead.'

The Count realised that his trip to Paris on Veeve's behalf had paid dividends. 'How did you discover that?'

'In the club. Another Uncle of his let it slip.'

'So what are your plans now?'

'Somehow to lure the man to meet his son.'

The Count held his breath as he remembered Hortense's request. 'You mean because of the war.'

Brindsley-Smith gave him a knowing look and the Count had the impression that he was not beyond telling Ronald the reason for trying to find Bertram. With Hortense's plea in his ear, to protect Bertram, he knew he had to probe further.

'And his son? He is English?'

'Half English, obviously. The other half, well, who knows?'

'And you are convinced that the man you want to

apprehend, who has an English wife and a half English son, was betraying secrets to us?'

'He's as good a German as yourself.'

'How do you explain that?'

'His surname, his country of origin, his links with a German, camouflaged by using an intermediary in Switzerland'

The Count was gratified that Brindsley-Smith had not identified him as the German contact, and that he was not as sure of his ground as he made out.

Brindsely-Smith pressed his point,' And then there's his facility with the language.'

'And English.'

'I never knew that.'

'Did it ever occur to you that he might be a double agent?'

The Count saw that he had wrong-footed Brindsley-Smith who looked disconcerted, but he recovered quickly, 'In that case you should be as keen as I am to see him arrested.'

'Did it ever occur to you that he might have been framed?'

Brindsley-Smith seemed unimpressed.

The Count reverted to his original question. 'And if he was a double agent, how do you intend to find out where this Bertram is?'

Brindsley-Smith seemed sure of his ground. 'And if Johannes was a double agent, you would want to know too.'

Unexpectedly the Count felt a surge of rage against this man who was so determined to ruin another man's life, a man who might, or might not, have behaved incorrectly in war, but of how many thousands of people could the same not be said? Peace time was for forgiveness and the chance to live beside one another, and opposite him sat a man who for his own aggrandisement was pursuing another. 'I think I can manage to lure him, to use your expression, to meet his son. Leave it to me.'

He picked up a telegram that had recently arrived and opening a drawer, placed it carefully out of sight.

'You must do as you think best.' He said curtly as he stood up and expected Brindsley-Smith to do the same. 'We'll meet in the morning. I need to go into town to hear the latest news and find out exactly what is likely to happen in the next few days.'

'I can count on your help? You'll keep me informed?' Brindsley-Smith finally stood and offered a handshake.

'Of course.' The Count made certain that his expression was inscrutable.

Striding along the passages of his large mansion, ignoring the guests that he passed, the Count's mind was in confusion. With a knowledge of the current situation and of Brindsley-Smith's intentions he needed to come a decision. The next day, as he drove back from the town, barely concentrating on the road, his hands alone guiding the motorcar, he worked through his plan of action. Poland, so his sources among the Military told him, was under threat of imminent invasion. The consequences would in all probability be an all-out war, which would include England.

If that was the case, the Count rationalised, he would

not see Veeve again, or not for a very long time. The Count was not certain whether this was not, in fact, a welcome solution. How could he visit Veeve with the knowledge he now had of Jean-Paul's rejection of her in favour of Ruth. How could he resist questioning her about her abandonment of Ronald. He felt a profound sadness at the loss of her as a friend, combined with a sense of betrayal.

He then wondered what use he should make of the information he had of the impending invasion. In his paternal role towards Ronald he was outraged that the perfidious Brindsley-Smith had been using him for his own ends. He wracked his brains to find a method to remove his influence from Ronald's life.

The second telegram that he had received from England only increased his determination to prevent Brindsley-Smith from whatever plan he was forming. His inclination was to dispatch him back to England, but for the time being he decided to keep him on his estate, until it was convenient to see him go, or, unless it suited his purposes. Meanwhile it also suited him to withhold the fact that their two countries could be on the brink of war.

Finally he made up his mind to protect Jean-Paul. Ruth he had known for many years as the sister of Veeve. He had admired her quiet loyalty and genuine affection towards Veeve and Ronald. Ruth's love for Ronald had continued through all of his young life. As a person, when allowed to, she had shown an intelligence which he wished he had cultivated. During those halcyon days before the first war he had liked and respected Jean-Paul and he thought that Ruth must have lowered her guard for her emotions to be touched by him. He felt that they would have made a good match and as a consequence, the fate of their son Bertram was also his concern. It was obvious that Ruth had never breathed a word about Jean-Paul's disappearance, and he admired her courage. Yet he could not see, now, how he could deny a father's desire to see his son.

As the gates of the drive to his estate came into view, the Count formulated his plan, the first part of which was to contact Hortense.

Chapter Forty-One

It was late into the night when the Count, who had been in his study for some hours, finally decided on the wording of his telegram to Hortense. He had to convey to her and Jean-Paul that he knew the whereabouts of his son and also that Jean-Paul would have to be prepared to travel at a moment's notice. The evening was airless and the temperature had not dropped in any noticeable manner. All his windows were open but there was no breeze to be captured. In the stifling heat he dropped off to sleep in his chair, and only when he heard the crunch of wheels on the gravel did he wake to see that it was already dawn. A glance at his mantle clock told him that it was a little before five o'clock.

Rising hastily he sped through the ground floor of the house and unlocked the rear door, wanting to intercept the rider before anyone awoke. A young courier on his bicycle, with a canvas bag slung across his shoulders, was searching inside the flap. The Count waited for the telegram to be handed to him.

'Wait here for a few minutes, please.' The Count was fully awake and, because of the unexpectedly early hour that the boy had arrived, felt certain that the telegram held news that he had been expecting. The message did not take long to read. He folded it and tucked it into his jacket pocket. 'I'll fetch you a drink.'

When the Count returned he held a mug in one hand and an envelope in the other. He handed the mug to the boy with the bicycle. Taking a note out of his pocket he read it one last time. 'Consignment of Prussian Blue imminent. Await instructions.' He folded the paper, placed it into the envelope and sealed it. As he handed it to the courier he pressed some coins into the young man's hands. 'Please arrange for this to be sent as soon as possible.'

Once back in his study the Count removed the telegram, spread it out on the blotter and re-read it. 'Troops mobilised. Invasion of Poland commenced.' It was unsigned, but the Count had a fair idea who had sent it. He now had a great deal to accomplish.

When Brindsley-Smith came down to breakfast several hours later, at the hour when guests were usually to be found in the dining room, their time being their own and their pursuits being purely for leisure, he discovered the room deserted and the table laid for one.

It was eerily quiet and he wondered if perhaps there was an early hunting party or excursion that he had failed to be told was planned for that morning.

A servant came into the room with a silver dish of piping hot eggs and meats, but when Brindsley-Smith asked why he was alone, the man appeared not to speak English. He was finishing his coffee when he was relieved to hear footsteps outside in the hall, and then the door was flung open and the Count entered.

'What's happening, Count? The place is deserted.'

'There was a telegram in the early hours. I had to arrange for my guests to return home by any method that I could. The Germany Army have crossed into Poland. We are in a state of war.'

Brindsley-Smith was flustered, 'You didn't think to wake me?'

'First things first,' said the Count with a placatory gesture, 'there's no word of Britain being involved, or France for that matter, yet. Besides, you and I have business to complete. Please sit down again.'

The Count, with slow deliberation, helped himself to coffee from the jug on the hotplate and then took his place at the head of the table. 'Move to sit here if you wish.' He indicated a chair on his right and then, looking down the length of the table and holding one hand in the other, he rested his elbows on the table.

'It's like this. I've been thinking. This is your chance to catch your French spy.'

Brindsley-Smith took a sharp intake of breath. 'You believe he was a double agent?'

'We won't know unless he's arrested. As you know I

was once friendly with Johannes. I was his contact, through an agent in Switzerland, and I know what I'm talking about. I know where he is and I can contact him. It is possible that your idea of using his son as bait will bring him in. But we must move fast.'

Brindsley-Smith tried to cover his excitement, 'We must find Ronald. Where is he? He can tell us where Bertram will be.'

The Count spoke with authority, 'Ronald has already taken off for Munich. He will accompany him to a train tomorrow afternoon. He knows where he is staying and I believe you do too, do you not have a letter for him from his mother?'

'I sent it,' he admitted bitterly, 'there is no reason that Bertram would respond to me if I gave it to him. That was my plan originally, but my standing in the family is not very high, and there is every chance that he would not see me.'

The Count reacted with a nod, as if he could understand, but that it was not important. 'Here are the arrangements that I've already put in place and the plan that I propose that we set in motion. You will go by train to Munich. It is essential that you take two of my men. Not only will they interpret for you and guide you to the correct place, but they will in some measure protect you.'

The Count was not specific about why Brindsley-Smith needed protection, but now that the crisis had arrived, Brindsley-Smith was ill-prepared and was grateful to be able to put himself into the capable hands of the Count, especially since they had the same objective. He would have been unable to organise an arrest, and that part of the plan could be safely entrusted to his new ally.

The Count continued with his instructions. 'By my calculations we have just over twenty-four hours to get you and your men to Munich. This can be done with ease in normal circumstances, but with troop movements it will mean leaving as soon as possible, and if necessary taking a circuitous route. You have no need to worry. My men are well trained and will ensure that you are there on time. They will also help you to apprehend Johannes.'

Brindsley-Smith was having difficulty in keeping up with the pace of events. 'Will you not be there? Where do you suggest we take Johannes once arrested?' Brindsley-Smith was prepared to accept all of the Count's decisions.

'I shall send word to the Superintendent of the Police in Munich. He can be held there and the authorities can liaise with each other.'

Suddenly the Count changed tempo. 'Now hurry. You leave in thirty minutes. Only pack the minimum for your journey. I will forward your trunk.'

Half an hour later Brindsley-Smith was in the hall where the Count was talking urgently to two men. Reassuringly well built, with close cropped hair similar to the style worn by those who serve in the Army, the two men wore suits which sat awkwardly on them. It passed through his mind that these men were usually in uniform and heavy boots. One carried a canvas bag which bulged ominously, suggesting a weapon.

'Here are Claus and Hans. They are fully informed. The very best, my friend. You are in good hands.'

A few minutes later the three men were driving at speed towards Lübeck.

As the Count walked back to the house, he thought of the other car that he had watched drive away earlier that morning. He could not have felt more bereft if Ronald had been his own son. Perhaps he would not have another chance to speak with him, and now realised that all that he wanted to say, would go unsaid. How long would it be before their two countries were at peace with one another, and even once peace was declared, how much longer before people would forget. It had been years until he had been able to reconnect with Veeve, and through her meet Ronald. He might not be alive to see them again, or, even more worrying, Ronald might not survive a war.

He had done all he could to enable Ronald to leave Germany should the borders close. Not only had he supplied papers for Bertram, which could prove that he was legitimately in the country, but he had done the same for Ronald. He tried to anticipate the obstacles that could be put in their way by diligent officials.

He returned to his study to collect the papers that remained on his desk and lock them in the safe. He smiled ruefully at the irony of the situation. The papers that would ensure Bertram's exit from Germany, were those that had been used to authorise the courier to pass through the frontier post to their agent in Switzerland, with the madder red dye that the Count despatched regularly at the beginning of the last war. As for Ronald, he had named him as his son.

By midday the house was deserted. At intervals during the morning, post-boys on bicycles conveyed news from Lübeck. It seemed that no other countries were reacting yet to Germany's aggressive move. The Count found this curious and formed his plans on the assumption that this lull was only temporary. Early in the afternoon he wrote a second telegram to Hortense and decided to deliver it himself to the Post Office, only then could he be certain that, in the chaos of increased activity, it would be sent.

The second telegram was as brief as the first. 'Prussian blue. Munich. Basel train. Tomorrow 3pm.' It would have the day's date and there would be no ambiguity. Jean-Paul would have to travel all night if necessary. The Count could envisage no reason for him not to act immediately. Meanwhile he would have the mechanics prepare his own plane in readiness.

Chapter Forty-Two

Hortense heard a hammering on the door to the street and when she looked out of the window she saw a boy gazing up as if searching for someone. She raised the sash. 'Who do you want?'

'Madame Hortense.' Calling to him to wait, she closed the window and made for the stairs.

'I've tried twice already,' the boy said resentfully, but

his only recompense was a quick smile of thanks as she took the telegram, before the door was firmly shut.

She was both nervous and excited. Not much interrupted her daily routine, nor that of her neighbours, and there was sure to be gossip. She opened the envelope leaning back against the door. There were the words. 'Prussian Blue. Imminent.'

Hortense was hungry but speed was imperative, the Count had said. She cut a length of baguette, split it with a knife and cutting some slices of cheese and salami inserted them between the two halves. Wrapping her lunch in a cloth she packed it and an apple, in her bag. She found a notepad and pencil and stuffed them alongside. Throwing the strap over her shoulder she tucked the telegram deep into one of the compartments and, once in the corridor, locked the door and placed the key securely in her purse. Bicycles were kept in the communal hall at street level, Hortense's bicycle was easily accessible and Jean-Paul's apartment was a ten minute ride. The streets were usually quiet at this hour because every family assembled for lunch, while office workers emptied into nearby cafés.

The door onto the street below Jean-Paul's apartment was always unlocked. This suited him because he did not want a concierge watching his movements, nor notice taken of those who visited him. Although Hortense knocked on his door several times, there was no answer and there was no knowing how long he would be. She dared not go back to her shop, because in the circumstances he should not meet her there, so she left a note, slipped it under his door, and resigned herself to returning home. She would have to think up a story to tell them at work, and one that would also satisfy the curiosity of her neighbours.

She felt deflated as she cycled back, she had hoped to speak to Jean-Paul and make plans at once. As she climbed the stairs she was caught unprepared.

'A telegram, Hortense? I hope that it's not bad news.'

'An old acquaintance, Madame, who is very sick, very dear to me.'

'I am sorry. Does that mean travelling?'

'Very possibly. Thank you for asking.'

This would be the story she would stick with. It struck her that travelling might be involved.

Eating her baguette she began to plan. Jean-Paul would need tickets, money, food and even an overnight bag. Some of this she could supply and some she had ready since her meeting with the Count. The telegram said 'imminent' and she began to assemble provisions.

Hortense tried to imagine what was driving her friend. It had been so long since Jean-Paul had last seen his son, but there were few parents who did not long for just one meeting. There had been those snatched moments when Bertrand was a school boy, playing cricket. He had related their few conversations to her. The boy was innocent but engaging, lively and enterprising and a father's pride was visible as he described their interaction. But that was ten years ago. How would you recognise a grown man from the boy in short trousers, who had looked so French and who would now look so English? This time there would be no exchange, the most he might achieve was a glimpse of the adult that he had become. Would that resolve anything? Even if he met Bertrand, what would he feel except that he had been unable to be part of his life, guiding, playing, loving. This might increase his sense of loss. Alternatively, to see your son, even fleetingly, emerge into manhood and able to strike out on his own, that might allay some regrets.

Finally, at the end of the day, there was a rap on the door and Jean-Paul entered. As could be expected in a man who lived on nervous energy, he was thin, his collar bones visible through his cotton jacket, and his trousers held up around his waist with a leather belt. His hair, worn slightly longer than was fashionable was edged with grey. His eyes, a pale but clear blue, had not changed. They drew a person to him, as they did Hortense, with their ability to pierce through any interaction and connect. It was his gift, and his weakness. He expected others to accept him as generously as he welcomed them.

'Have you heard? From the Count?'

Hortense handed him the telegram, 'He kept his promise.'

'It's you I have to thank. What do we do now?'

Hortense handed him a glass of water, 'We wait.'

'And you?'

'I've been getting ready. Money for tickets, food, maps.'

'But you don't know where or when.'

'In which case we'd better eat.'

Jean-Paul took two plates from the dresser and some cutlery from a drawer.

'Sit,' Hortense commanded and proceeded to ladle out spaghetti and toss a salad. Jean-Paul seemed to struggle to eat. 'It's understandable,' she said.

She made some coffee and when she returned to the table Jean-Paul was staring ahead as if stunned. All the while Hortense was repressing her sense of urgency, her mind racing, envisaging a possible rendez-vous and the moment when he would see his son.

'I can't do it, Hortense.'

She did not immediately understand his meaning.

'What if it's a trap.'

Hortense stared at him. 'Why would you think that?'

He shrugged his shoulders. 'It's been on my mind for a while. Why would the Count want to help me? There is nothing in it for him. Unless, that is, he doesn't believe me and thinks that I was double-dealing. You can't control people's thoughts once a suspicion has been planted.' He smiled wistfully at Hortense. 'I know he did it for you. Anyone would want to grant a request to you, who ask so little.'

Hortense was giving him the opportunity to heal a wound that had been raw since Bertrand left France all those years ago. Could he let her down now? Why was he drawing back at the brink of possibly his last chance to resolve his greatest wish. She urged him. 'I trust the Count, and you may have to accept the risk. This is almost certainly the last and only time in your life to see Bertrand, and I don't need to remind you of all the reasons why.'

Jean-Paul sighed, 'My age, the war, my son's whereabouts.'

'When else are we going to be able to find out where he is?'

'How is the Count certain?'

'He must be or he would not have sent me that message. We can only find out if we follow his lead.'

At that moment there was another hammering at the door. 'Already? So soon?' Jean-Paul gasped.

Hortense hurried to the window and looking out recognised the same post boy. This time she waved, hastily opened the door and went down the stairs.

When she returned Jean-Paul was sitting with his head in his hands, his hair ruffled.

'Do you want to open it?'

'No, you,' he grunted, his face hidden.

Hortense opened the envelope, read the message, and passed it to Jean-Paul. He took it reluctantly.

'It says Munich,' he said, his voice desperate. 'I can't go, it's too dangerous with the political situation so volatile.'

'Yes we can, we can use the chaos as cover,' she replied quietly, 'we have passports.'

'Why do you say 'we'?' He raised his head.

'I have a passport, the Count thought this all out and sent one weeks ago, only it's not in my name. If I am to go with you, we need to go as a couple.'

She gained his attention and felt a change in his mood. 'It is less conspicuous. Besides, my neighbours are expecting me to travel. They asked about the telegram.'

Suddenly, there was a need to hurry. Unless they started immediately they had no chance of reaching

Munich by the following afternoon. Action spurred Jean-Paul out of his negative mood. There was no time to weigh up options, if they did not leave now, there would be no choices to make.

From her bedroom Hortense called, 'I'll be ready in five minutes. Pile the food into that bag. Add anything you think we might need. I'm packing for a funeral. You can do the same. We'll cycle to your apartment and go to the station from there.'

'We'll be going through Strasbourg,' Jean-Paul commented, 'we could reach there tonight. Stay at the station hotel.'

It was late when they booked into the hotel, and it was early the next morning that they caught the train to Munich. By then they were dressed in mourning black and passed through border control without comment.

Sitting beside each other in the compartment on the last leg of their journey, Hortense squeezed her friend's hand. An hour to go and they would steam into the station.

Jean-Paul said, 'It's better that I don't speak to him, to Bertrand. I have a feeling that an absent father can only be a disappointment. It would be so easy for a child to project their ideals onto a mythical parent.'

Hortense did not reply that the opposite might also be true. That Jean-Paul could not imagine that any son of his could be anything but all that he had hoped for. How much could he discover from seeing Bertrand from a distance? Was he on a fool's errand? Perhaps he would only know once he had completed this journey.

An hour later and they were to expect Bertrand.

How had the Count organised this, she wondered. She did not dwell on whether this was a sensible pilgrimage for Jean-Paul, reason was not relevant because emotions were instinctive. However, she did anticipate that, once they were on their homeward journey, he would need her. Both of them knew that it was unlikely that Jean-Paul would ever see his son again.

Chapter Forty-Three

The skies were blue, the clouds high and wispy, and Ronald was able to navigate with clear visibility. Strapped to his knee was the map given to him by one of the ground crew, with his first airfield marked with a pencilled circle. His itinerary, with regular fuelling stops, had been traced out for him on a series of maps, one tucked beneath the other. He checked his instruments when he reached cruising height, and then checked that the ground below matched his position. All seemed in order and Ronald was finally able to sift through the events that had been triggered by an early call from the Count.

Ronald was a deep sleeper, and the Count had to shake his shoulder to wake him, but he was immediately alert. It could only be something to do with the German mobilisation, but that did not seem to be a reason for the Count to wake him so urgently.

'Ronald, get dressed, you need to be away as soon as

possible.'

'To England? Is it war?'

'Listen. German troops have mobilised but England is not involved, yet. You need to reach your cousin and warn him.'

'Bertram? Of course, he will have to be told. He must be in Munich at the moment.'

'You must take your plane. You might need to leave Germany in haste. I'll give you a set of papers if you encounter any difficulty. You must tell Bertram to go to Basel by train and cross into Switzerland. When you see him, tell him to take an afternoon train, the Army tends to commandeer the earlier trains. Can you do that?'

Ronald was caught up in the urgency of the moment and thrilled at the idea of flying over Germany on routes he had never explored.

'Take my car. Our ground crew live beside the airstrip, you know their houses. Give one of them this note, it explains your route. I've asked them to map out your onward journey from Munich. One of them can return the car. I'll need it to get my guests to Lübeck as they will be anxious to return home.'

While the Count related all that he had recently learnt from his contacts, Ronald dressed, picked up his haversack and selected a few clothes, his shaving soap, stick and comb. He collected his wallet and personal papers from the dressing table and declared that he was ready. 'What about my Uncle?' He asked as an afterthought.

'I'll sort him out. He'd best return to England immediately. You need to reach Bertram.'

They descended the stairs, the house silent with sleeping guests and the servants not yet at their appointed tasks. They made their way towards the study where the Count beckoned Ronald to follow him. From out of a drawer in the desk he pulled a brown envelope and tipped the contents onto the blotter. Quickly he selected some papers and a passport. Then he took some headed notepaper and wrote a short message, signed it, shook the paper to dry the ink and placed it and the documents into the envelope before sealing it.

Once they were in the garage and were able to speak without the risk of waking anyone, the Count gave the package to Ronald. 'This should cover any eventuality you might meet. If Bertram has difficulty leaving the country these papers should secure his passage. Keep them safe.' Ronald unbuttoned his jacket and placed the documents in an inner pocket. 'Here are the keys. Safe flight.'

Ronald was too bemused to say anything. He opened the car door and started the engine. The Count unlocked the garage and then, leaning through the window, gave Ronald a brief handshake. Ronald thought that he looked suddenly like a much older man.

Now that he was airborne he wished that he had shown his gratitude to the Count more fully, but he could not dwell on his regret and besides, he was embarked on an adventure.

The cockpit was as compact a space for a pilot as the driver's seat and console were to a racing driver. The dials were only slightly more numerous. Ronald compared the two and came to the conclusion that he infinitely preferred flying. When he was motor racing he was competing against others, but in the air his skill was pitted against the elements. The level of expertise needed to fly an aeroplane and navigate at the same time was considerably more demanding than driving a motor car, even at speed. When he compared the intricacies of manipulating each of the two machines and weighed up the challenges of the one against the other, nothing could compare to the exhilaration of being in the sky.

Ronald adjusted the joystick a fraction and the aeroplane responded smoothly, a touch in the other direction and he was back on course. At no time in his life before he had learnt to fly, had he experienced such affinity with a machine. His mind ran ahead to the impending war. If Britain was propelled into the conflict he was determined to join the Air Force. Single combat in the air was preferable to fighting on sea or land. In both the Navy and the Army men had to rely on each other, and it was human nature to want to have your comrades around you, but to have their lives in your hands was a great burden. He knew about death, and had already lost his soul mate. If he was to be involved in the war he wanted control of his destiny and the air was the answer for him. If he had to die he would rather be master of his own fate. Death did not seem so terrible since Sara had gone, but the excitement at this, his first mission, whetted his appetite for further challenges.

Ronald's schedule meant that he would be in Munich by nightfall with time to find Bertram and to spend the evening with him. He did wonder why the Count seemed so keen for him to meet with Bertram in person, when it could have been possible, he suspected, to send a telegram. However, the Count had experienced war, and knowing that nothing in the future was certain, he must have empathised with the young airman and wanted someone to ensure that he was safe. It was too risky to hope that a telegram alone was sufficient. Pleased to be able to look after his cousin and warn him to leave Germany, he patted the documents in his pocket. His own documents, along with those given to him by his German friend, were safely in a separate pocket.

Munich was an imposing city and Ronald was, if not enamoured, impressed. The young man who walked beside him was lean and fit, a result of institutionalised training he surmised, but there was more than mere physical energy, he seemed to bound along with a fierce intellectual curiosity that Ronald envied. Although not classically handsome, Bertram's regulation haircut and his almost gaunt aquiline features did not lend themselves to that trite description, Ronald was captivated by the intensity of purpose that he saw in his cousin's deep-set eyes.

The railway station was in the centre of the city and Bertram insisted on taking Ronald on foot past the National Museum, which was constructed like a wedding cake in layers, and the Gothic-style Town Hall.

'We don't have buildings on this scale in Britain. I wish we had longer here and I could show you around. Their Art collections are magnificent and their library is vast.'

Their route took them past the Theatre. 'It's designed on Roman lines,' Bertram told Ronald, 'the whole city feels so grand, so orderly, but I find it intimidating. It's interesting to visit but I shall be glad to leave.'

Central station was enormous with lines serving the entire south of Bavaria. Everywhere people were congregating with piles of luggage, or moving with a deliberate purpose. There were no family holiday groups but many relatives lingering to say farewell. Ronald was infected by the subdued atmosphere as they joined the throngs of people, mainly civilians, on one of the long queues at the ticket kiosks. He was relived that his cousin would soon be safely in Switzerland.

Eventually, with Bertram holding his ticket like a trophy, they searched for the platform for his train to Basel

'I wonder if they all came to hear the Führer and now realise there will be no rally,' Bertram commented.

'Or wanting to join up, or just wanting to get home,' Ronald answered.

'Like us.'

'You have the papers?'

'I'll only use them if I have to. Hopefully the border guards will be so overworked I'll slip through.'

'Don't risk it, Bertram. I'm flying out as soon as I see you off. I can spend the night near Saint Gallen.'

'Tell Mother I'm safe!'

Ronald was anxious for his young cousin to move towards the edge of the platform, so that he could board ahead of the throngs of passengers now gathering around them.

'I'll help you board, be ready. When I open the door,

don't hesitate.'

There seemed no more to say. They had talked well into the night; excited yet overawed by the momentous events that were about to dictate their lives. They hoped that one day they might be stationed together. As they heard the train approach, the moment that they would be parted, perhaps for years, became a reality. Ronald consoled himself that India was a very long way from any battles on the continent.

Chapter Forty-Four

Brindsley-Smith and his two protectors had a relatively uneventful journey from Lübeck to Munich, with only one detour, although they travelled all day. Brindsley-Smith gleaned very little because neither Claus nor Hans were willing to speak any more than was necessary, and his fellow travellers seemed to be of the same mind. Amongst the cataclysmic upheaval that rocked the lives of every German citizen, people were preoccupied with their own affairs. As the journey progressed he worried increasingly that he was acting without the authority of his seniors in attempting to arrest Johannes, but the wheels were now in motion and he had no choice. He was not sure whether he was grateful that the Count had arranged for the arrest, but there was no turning back, and if the mission was successful the means would not be an issue. His concern was whether Claus and Hans were ready to follow his instructions following the arrest, but again he had no control. In some respects he felt that he was a spectator in an event that he had initiated, and had been anticipating for years.

As the Count had advised, he arrived at the station soon after midday to watch the trains that were departing for Basel. It was more confusing than he had visualised, because the platform was crowded with a seething mass of people every time a train drew in. Brindsley-Smith wondered if they would ever identify Johannes or Bertram, the one he had seen nearly twenty years ago, and the other he knew only from photographs. Something told him that he would recognise them. Partly because, while every other passenger would be boarding the train, Johannes would be distinctive in that he would be searching for Bertram. If he was fortunate Ronald would accompany Bertram and his task would be easier.

The three men made their way to the small building on the platform which sold drinks and food. Due to the heat there were seats outside on the platform and they were able to find a table. From his position between Claus and Hans, Brindsley-Smith had a good view in both directions. Along the length of the platform tall arches reached up to support the predominantly glass ceiling, and almost directly to his right was the thoroughfare to and from the main hall.

Each time a train arrived there would be a surge of passengers frantically trying to board, until the carriages were so full that it was not possible to add any more. Railway officials would close the doors and direct the remaining passengers away to where the next train would arrive. Within a few minutes the platform would clear and the officials would march up and down the side of the train ensuring that the doors remained closed until the train was due to leave. Sometimes more than ten minutes would elapse with the whole area empty and the train waiting to depart.

Brindsley-Smith watched six or seven trains arrive and leave and began to wonder if he had missed his quarry. His consoling thought was that, since his superiors were unaware of his mission, if it failed they would be none the wiser, and his reputation would be unscathed.

Once again the platform cleared, railway officials were parading up and down checking doors and repelling newcomers with copious use of their whistles, when Brindsley-Smith recognised Ronald.

Ronald was alone approaching the train which was crammed, soldiers and civilians leaning out of windows for a last glimpse of a loved one, or frantically waving into the distance. He was running hurriedly towards a carriage in Brindsley-Smith's line of sight, to where a young man was standing leaning out of a window which had been pushed down so that it was completely open.

'Bertram!' Ronald called breathlessly. He approached the carriage, and Ronald passed a rolled up newspaper through the window. 'I've just heard that Britain declared war about three hours ago. Use the papers I gave you.' Bertram was barely able to reply before a guard, blowing his whistle, hounded Ronald away from the train and gesticulated for him to leave the area.

The platform was deserted but the train, after shunting a few yards, came to a halt.

Simultaneously two events happened. Brindsley-Smith watched Bertram's cousin retreat to the main hall while at the same time he saw Bertram's gaze fix on a part of the platform where, under one of the pillars, stood a figure. Brindsley-Smith knew at that moment for certain that Bertram had seen Johannes. He started to his feet, but immediately Claus's hand bore down on his shoulder restraining him. 'Our orders are to wait here.'

Jean-Paul appeared from the shadow of the pillar and could be seen about to take strides towards the train, when another familiar figure emerged from the main hall and hastened to reach him.

'Jean-Paul!' The Count shouted. Jean-Paul hesitated and turned towards the voice. This gave the Count time to reach his side, take hold of his arm and drag him back to the relative protection of the pillars. While Jean-Paul struggled the Count led him away.

'Jean-Paul, think, don't do it.' The expression on Jean-Paul's face was one of misery. Near to tears he clung onto the Count and looked back over his shoulder. For one short second Bertram and Jean-Paul looked each other in the eyes, and then Bertram withdrew into the carriage and was gone.

Brindsley-Smith from his sedentary position watched as the Count restrained Johannes.

'That's our man.' He turned from Claus to Hans who were unmoved. 'He is resisting arrest.' He spoke louder. 'The Count is trying to hold him, are you not going to help him?'

Brindsley-Smith's felt his face flush and become red. Angry at their deliberate refusal to do as he asked. He knew very well that they understood him, but was powerless to insist on them obeying him. They were under orders only from the Count.

Brindsley-Smith pushed back his chair and stood up. Immediately Claus and Hans were beside him. He felt his arms pinned to his sides and was intimidated by their physical presence. 'Our orders are to wait here.' repeated Claus, and Hans said, 'Please sit.'

'I will not sit and watch that man escape again,' Brindsley-Smith spluttered. With the two Germans on either side of him he was unable to do anything but watch.

Ronald had disappeared and Brindsley-Smith only momentarily speculated why. The train moved off and only two men could be seen. They were side by side with their heads bowed as if in conversation and Brindsley-Smith began to be irritated that the Count was delaying the arrest of Johannes.

As they drew near to the barrier he could hear the men speaking.

Jean-Paul said earnestly to the Count, 'I saw him. That was Bertrand, wasn't it?'

'It had to be. None of us would have recognised him, but I arranged for Ronald to meet him, and by suggesting that he accompany Bertram to the station, we could be sure.'

'But Count. How are you here? How can I thank you?'

The Count raised one hand. No reply was needed.

Jean-Paul then said anxiously, 'But war is declared. How will the lads leave Germany?'

'Ronald will be flying out in less than an hour. As for Bertram I have given him safe passage, he has papers that will see him through the border. He is on his way to India.'

'India,' Jean-Paul gave a sigh of relief. 'He'll be safe then,' Jean-Paul said, almost to himself.

'We must go now,' said the Count, 'We have unfinished business.'

'I'll never know the answers. Not until this war is over. And we are growing older.'

The Count was guiding Jean-Paul.

'Unfinished business?' Jean-Paul asked. He looked up. He was now facing the group seated on the platform. 'Who is that man? The one in the middle.'

'That is your English major,' said the Count and Brindsley-Smith heard him clearly. He felt a moment of triumph. The Count continued, 'He also happens to be your brother-in-law. Ronald is his nephew also.' The Count paused while Jean-Paul's breath came in rapid gasps.

'Why is he here?' Jean-Paul said, panic-stricken. 'Are you about to hand me over to him? You know what happened. How could you do this?'

The Count took him by the shoulders. 'Jean-Paul, you are my friend. I arranged for you to see your son but I also took a gamble. You are safe with me, and now we can confront Brindsley-Smith.' He gave Jean-Paul an encouraging squeeze before releasing his hold. 'Trust me.'

There seemed to be no-one else on the platform as the Count and Jean-Paul approached Brindsley-Smith. Railway officials had moved to control another area of the station and the occupants of the other tables had left for their various destinations. Trains could be heard arriving or leaving, their explosive emissions of steam continued on distant platforms, interspersed with the sound of vigorously blown whistles.

'Is this Johannes, the man you are searching for?' The Count asked. 'The man who you accuse of treachery, but for which there is no conclusive evidence?'

Brindsley-Smith felt insulted. He stood up. 'Who do you take me for? There is no question but that he is Barthold, a wanted man.'

The Count raised his hand, 'Calm down.'

Brindsley-Smith suddenly felt enraged and stepped forward intending to face up to the Count, but as he did so Claus and Hans held him by his elbows.

'Why are they not going to arrest him? Why are these men holding me?' Brindsley-Smith fixed his eyes on Johannes. 'This man has been evading justice.'

The Count addressed Brindsley-Smith, 'Nearly twenty years ago Jean-Paul sacrificed his wife and son to protect them from rejection, and the stigma attached to anyone labelled a traitor. If that is not enough, you want to cause more distress and reopen his file, because we have entered another war. I firmly believe that Jean-Paul is innocent.'

Brindsley-Smith was stunned. His conviction that

Johannes was guilty had never been challenged, and it had been his *raison d'être* for so long. He rallied briefly. 'So what are you going to do?'

'Jean-Paul can go free. But you, I am afraid, are on enemy territory. Our countries have been at war since eleven o' clock this morning. You will now be handed over to the authorities to be interned.'

'Interned? How long for?'

'For the duration of the war. This will ensure that your vendetta, which is what this is, this blow to your pride, this pursuit of an innocent man, can no longer continue. You ask how long? The last war took four years. Who knows how long this one will last.'

'But Johannes. He too will be interned,' Brindsley-Smith said, gloating.

'Jean-Paul is a French citizen. As yet there is no state of war between our countries.'

At this Brindsley-Smith crumpled. The Count jerked his head in the direction of Claus and Hans and said, 'You know what to do.'

Brindsley-Smith did not struggle. No spectator would have known, as he walked between the two Germans away from the platform, that he was being delivered into the hands of the police.

'They say that France has not declared, but they may do so at any time.' The Count admitted to Jean-Paul. 'Leave quickly. You are free. No one will open your case now, and we are both too old to be involved in the conflict.' The Count in his extreme emotion became almost formal. 'I am glad I was able to render a friend a service. Now go.'

The Count watched, as Jean-Paul walked briskly in the same direction as his tormentor but to a different destination and one no longer burdened by fear. In the distance, beyond the barrier, the Count saw a figure, in funereal black, standing motionless while all around her was movement and bustle. Hortense raised one gloved hand and the Count responded. Although he knew that Hortense was waiting for Jean-Paul on the other side, he was saddened by all that the Frenchman had lost. He looked around. A train was drawing in, its noisy wheels clanking and steam hissing. Around him passengers were converging and dispersing, weaving their way through fellow passengers, while more were arriving and pressing forward to secure a place in a carriage. While he stood he became aware that he was surrounded by people who all had a purpose, all of whom were tense and anxious, unsettled and frightened.

The Count felt no fear. He was calm. What had he done? He had lost for ever two women that he loved. He had saved a good man. Jean-Paul's secret, if Ruth decided that it should be so, would go with her to her grave. Life as he had known it would never return and he was too old to invent another. The Count smiled and felt the slightest glow of what he interpreted as happiness. You can't change the past. 'When you are old,' he told himself, 'you have to be content with the life you have lived.'

THE END